THE
BLACKWING WAR

The Deep Witches Books

Stoneskin

Also by K.B. Spangler

A Girl and Her Fed
Rise Up Swearing
The Hope Blackwell Books
The Rachel Peng Chronicles
The Josh Glassman Adventures

THE
BLACKWING WAR

K.B. SPANGLER

A GIRL AND HER FED BOOKS

The Blackwing War is a work of fiction. Names, characters, and events are the creations of the author. Any resemblance to actual persons, living or dead, is entirely coincidental. All characters, places, and events are products of the author's imagination.

Printed by CreateSpace, an Amazon.com Company
Available from Amazon.com and other retail outlets.

For those who have loved and lost during the Pandemic

The Deep enjoys animals. The degree to which it cares for them is heartwarming, but I believe it has no pets of its own, unless you count us Witches.

—Williamson, "Notes from the Deep," 16 July 4406 CE

In The Beginning

There was a shining planet, hanging in space, inhabited by ten billion souls. The grand sum of their reach was one pale moon and a small colony on a nearby red planet.

But they had *potential.*

Chapter One

Except for an old white cat that would never die, Tembi Stoneskin's bed was empty. Cooling, but empty, as its usual human occupant was blearily shrugging into her uniform and muttering impolite words about explosions. A splash of water on her face, a scarf to hold back her mutiny of black hair, and Tembi wrapped herself in the Deep and vanished. Five minutes later, she was two solar systems away from her bed and staring at the latest bomb.

She was so very tired of bombs.

Tembi wasn't prone to the dramatic. She was from Adhama, after all, a dry-baked world with windstorms fierce enough to tear itself apart at least five times a season. Her people had a reputation for being quietly practical: as long as you never pushed them to their breaking point, they could micromanage the galaxy. Adhamantians dealt with the latest crisis, prepared for the next, and rested in the moments in between. But this relentless, perpetual, eternal chore of bouncing from one solar system to the next to disarm one bomb after another made her want to scream.

Be fair, she reminded herself. *Better to get here before they've gone off instead of after.*

She had seen more than anyone should of that, too.

Killing was easy. Death was easy. Bombs were *so easy*, a couple of parts banged together and left in a strategic location, and then? Either the Blackwings or the Sabenta took credit for the chaos, and promised next time things would be much worse. That this was said while Tembi was still on-site with the cleanup crew, trying to make sense of the bits and pieces of what had once been people, also made her want to scream. She was so very tired of soldiers who insisted the use of bombs was the ethical choice, or the tactical one, or that circumstances necessitated turning other human beings into distorted flecks of carbon.

But! More than anything else—anything in the entire galaxy!—she was tired of disarming the twice-cursed things in front of panicked onlookers.

This particular bomb had been left in a shopping plaza aboard an orbiting shipping hub. A bit of a misnomer, as the station hung in empty space, with not even a nearby planet to provide a sense of scale. Ships jumped in, ships jumped out, and their crews used the hub to switch cargo or grab a meal in those hurried minutes in between. The station's security team had shooed the travelers back to their ships, but others had been left behind, hundreds of them, those poor souls whose only purpose was to maintain small shares of this groaning chunk of plass and metal.

They stared at her, silent, their worry a palpable force.

Tembi was already sure this was a Blackwing bomb. This station was home to those who lived on the edges, people and companies crushed by the weight of those more powerful than themselves. This far out from the central Earth-normal systems, the definition of what it meant to be human got complicated. Out here, bodies were shaped for survival. Cheaper to modify a genome than a planet, after all, and heavy-duty genetic modding made a tasty target for the Blackwings.

She hated Blackwing bombs, with powerful explosives sealed inside tiny, well-designed packages. The Sagittarius Armed Forces had money and resources and, worst of all, trained engineers. Their bombs were disgustingly clever. They were only slightly easier to defuse than the Sabenta's bombs, which were slapped together from whatever materials the rebels had on hand and were thus the essence of unpredictable.

The security team grumbled and paced, saying the usual things about Witches and the war. Behind them, the crowd was beginning to stir, their worry turning to anger as they muttered about how a Witch had been called instead of any form of law. How this particular Witch didn't look old enough to know what a bomb was, let alone how to take one apart. How Lancaster could stop all of this in a heartbeat if they wanted to.

Well, they're not wrong.

She did her best to ignore them, her eyes shut tight and ears half-curled so her other senses could trace the hard plass shell of the bomb. Except her dear departed ancestors had gone and upgraded their sense of hearing when they sossed around with the shape of their ears, and she couldn't help but overhear when someone mused aloud about how this young woman with her filthy uniform and her bare feet couldn't possibly be a real Witch.

About how they should stop her before she made matters worse.

Tembi turned and stared at the speaker, willing her face to be utterly still, to be devoid of all emotion. It was easy: practice, practice, practice. For Adhamantians and Witches alike, emotions could be more dangerous than bombs. She was doubly damned to bind herself in false serenity for the rest of her life.

The crowd was chastened into silence. Good enough. She turned away from them and back to the device. Its shape told her a large part of what she needed to know about how it was connected to the utility conduits of the shipping hub, how it had been shaped into sleek, perfect tubes and concealed within all of the other sleek, perfect tubes, completely unnoticed except by one sharp-eyed security guard with a keen appreciation for atmospheric maintenance systems.

The scent of cold metal brushed against her senses, followed by birdsong. Tembi didn't bother to open her eyes as she formed the mental question: *"What?"*

An emotion not of her own making rose within her, and she paused to pick it apart. Tension, anxiety, shame, and a dreadful sense of loss: the Deep didn't like this particular bomb at all.

"Can we do this?" she asked her friend. *"Or should we evacuate and let it go off?"*

Two questions stacked against each other was too much for the Deep. The sensation of uncertainty strengthened, anxiety swelling to fill the cracks.

Tembi shoved this new surge of anxiety down into the boiling cauldron of ulcers that served as her stomach. "We've got this," she assured the Deep, molding her thoughts into certainty. The two of them had done this a hundred times, a thousand times, countless times before. Maybe this bomb would be different, but they wouldn't know unless they tried. And they were a team, right? The two of them were unstoppable.

The feelings of anxiety and stress eased as she comforted her friend. The smell of metal rose again, a fresh brassy scent. Tembi grinned to herself as the Deep's confidence swept through her.

"Are you sure you should be doing this?" A new voice, and angry: the station's captain, standing a meter away from her left shoulder. As the captain snapped Tembi's own question at her, this newfound confidence trembled. She crushed her insecurity into a tiny mental ball before the Deep could notice.

Focus, Tembi. Concentrate on the bomb before it detonates and things go from bad to worse.

A calming breath, a moment of stolen silence. The explosive device beneath her fingers was—

"Pardon me, young woman, but are you sure you should be doing this?" The same question again, delivered in a much sharper tone. The captain was losing his patience.

"Yes," Tembi replied without bothering to open her eyes.

"How old are you?"

"I am a Witch," she replied automatically, as she tried to follow the twists and turns of one slick black conduit which hummed a quiet song of murder. "We are timeless."

That usually worked. Except this captain knew Witches, did the endless political meet-and-greets as they jumped into and out of the busy shipping port. He was familiar with their ageless faces and their self-possessed demeanors. Only an experienced Witch could look at another human being and see a problem they merely had to outlive. At twenty-three, Tembi couldn't shake the habit of looking at other human beings as human beings. She was sure she'd grow out of it in a century or so, but for the moment it was an enormous inconvenience.

Be honest, Tembi reminded herself. *Pretty much everything is an enormous inconvenience. Your life is nothing but bombs, bombs, and more bombs, and he's right, you shouldn't be the one responsible—*

Somewhere in the back of her mind, she realized the captain was reaching for her hand to snatch her away from the bomb.

"Deep?" Tembi said aloud. "Bobcat."

The captain—*I should have learned his name. They're never as angry when I call them by name.*—squalled and fell to the ground in a ball, trying to protect himself from the snarling bobcat that the Deep had dropped on his head.

"It's not real," she said to the security team, some of whom had gone for their weapons and found them missing. Behind them, the crowd murmured in restless shock. "It's a synth, programmed to keep him occupied so he doesn't touch me.

"He won't be hurt," she assured the sharp-eyed guard who had discovered the bomb and started this whole mess. "I need to focus, or…" she pointed at the bomb, and flicked her fingers in a semblance of an explosion as she whispered, "…boom."

The guard nodded and went to remove the synthetic bobcat from his captain's face.

"Please evacuate the area," she told the others, who were suddenly more than happy to listen to a girl willing and able to hurl strange animals willy-nilly. Better than any motivational speech, that bobcat. One of the best purchases she'd ever made.

Tembi shut her eyes and ears, and reoriented her attention on the bomb. *Again. By all the small and wriggly gods, this bomb should be dead by now. I should have led with the bobcat.* A calming breath…another…another. She needed to silence her mind so she could let the Deep fill her senses. Her friend spoke in layers upon layers, a sediment of meaning that pressed itself into the fluid fabric of space and time, emotion and memory twisted into dense knots of intent. If she was extremely lucky, the Deep would articulate a word or two, to accompany its true meaning, minuscule decorative sprinkles atop a scoop of ice cream the size of a planet. She didn't grab at those words, oh no, not any more, not since she was first able to speak with the Deep and learn that its opinion of words was the same as her opinion of rocks on a beach, where one was very much like the other and were, for all practical purposes, wholly interchangeable.

(And don't get the Deep started on homonyms, not unless you had an entire week free and were willing to explain the nature of how two things could be both the same and different to a galactic intelligence who knew very well that this was a frequent happenstance but at least it had the good sense to attach a few musical notes and the scent of an extinct animal for the sake of clarity, thank you very much.)

The Deep was good with specifics. Shipping schedules, bills of lading? It understood those, no problem at all, and any confusion was easily resolved by changing problematic line items. "We need to take apart this bomb" was a good directive, too, as failure to pay attention meant messy consequences. The Deep had all of the concentration problems of a small child hopped up on sweets, but it could focus when the stakes were high. So when she shut her eyes and closed her ears, the silence gave the Deep what it needed to fill her with information.

The environment came first: she stood within the mechanical hold of a shipping port stationed a million klicks from anywhere of consequence. A shipping port like hundreds of others, a waystation between a nebulous *here* and an ambiguous *there*.

The shipping port was a fact, a thing, a sterile creation of humanity glittering away against the black. It shouldn't be a thing at all: the Deep made shipping ports irrelevant. Except nothing that humankind touched could exist as the sum of itself alone. This shipping port existed because of three-thousand-year-old laws which declared that, no, the Deep didn't need ports, but we should build them anyway because what if the Deep vanishes as quickly as it first appeared? If that happens, we've got an entire civilization spread throughout the galaxy and no infrastructure to get around.

The next level was commerce: after a couple hundred years of using the Deep to jump from here to there, the Deep had become as much a simple fact as the shipping ports themselves. Nobody thought the Deep would disappear, not any more. But there were industries which made their money from shipping ports, along with all of those employees who depended on the jobs that went along with those shipping ports, and the invisible hand of the market continued to masturbate itself into relevancy. Humans suffered from a dire failure of imagination. This glorious alien entity appears and offers up its services, and all they can think to do is remake what they already had? Shameful, really.

And then came war.

Focus, Tembi.

She grinned. It had been her voice, the kind of thing she said to herself a million times a day. But she never added the petal-soft brush of flowers against her cheeks. By all the invented hells, she couldn't even remember the last time she could feel something as delicate as a—

Focus, Tembi!

Right. Eyes closed, ears sealed. Get this done.

The shipping port. A speck of mechanical brightness within the void. Now fully evacuated of all human life except for the captain and his crew standing around her, standing around the bomb seated deep within its guts.

The shape of the bomb appeared in her mind again, quite quickly this time. Plass, copper and aluminum alloys—*They used metal in the build? For the Blackwings, that's practically prehistoric.*—a dozen different kinds of conductive gels. A fist-sized chunk of atmosphere sealed in stasis field. No 'bots in this one, which was good, as nanotech was single-minded about accomplishing its mission. In this case, the mission would have been to populate the space formerly occupied by the shipping port with brand-new flecks of carbon. 'Bots in bombs were oh so much fun.

"Deep?" she said quietly.

A flutter of musical notes lined the edges of her mental image of the bomb.

"What happens if we were to remove this part here?" As she spoke, she concentrated on one of the parts of the bomb, that particularly nasty-looking black conduit which fed into one of the near-infinite number of tubes. She imagined the conduit as pulsing red.

There was a pause. Then, her mental version of the bomb disappeared into a menace of ugly brown-and-yellow paisley.

"Great," she muttered. Whoever had built the bomb had left a few decoy triggers, just in case it was found and someone tried to disarm it.

Well, they hadn't planned on her and the Deep. Right?

Right.

Back to work. Focus, Tembi, and all that. She let her fingers do the walking. Not by her sense of touch, as she could barely feel anything through her skin of late. But movement was its own form of communication. As her fingers moved, they helped solidify the image of the bomb in her mind, giving it shape and depth, transforming it into a complete object. The Deep kept filling in its invisible guts, those internal pieces she couldn't see or feel. After a few minutes, she finally knew the bomb well enough to take it apart.

"Captain," she said.

"Ma'am?" It was the sharp-eyed guard.

"Tell the crew to do a last sweep and make sure you've moved all residents and irreplaceable equipment to safety," she said, as two short lengths of tubing, identical to some of those supporting the bomb, appeared in the air beside her.

"It's just me," the guard replied.

Tembi looked around; they were alone except for the synth bobcat sprawled across his shoulders, purring.

"The captain thought it would be better to give you some space."

"You mean he's sure I'm about to blow his station apart and he doesn't want to get caught up in it." She had to chuckle at that. "You better clear out, too. Find a ship and get a few klicks away. Just in case."

"Can I stay?" She snuck a glance at his face. He seemed… eager. Not at all the kind of expression that she'd expect to find on the face of someone whose career choices might be about to go up in flecks of carbon.

Watch him, Tembi told the Deep.

Three crystal bubbles appeared in front of the guard. These popped—one, two, three!—each bubble releasing the sound of a cat's meow.

"Um…"

"The Deep likes cats," she said. It wasn't much of an explanation, but she didn't owe him one, especially if he wasn't just a sharp-eyed guard, especially-especially if he was waiting for her full attention to be on the bomb so he could slip something sharp and deadly between her shoulder blades. "It doesn't like assassins," she added. "It hates it when we try to kill each other. I don't know what it does with the people who try to kill me. They don't end up in any prison we know of."

"I…what?" His eyes went wide. "I'm not here to kill you!"

"Sometimes I wonder if there's an island out there," she said, as she reached for the two tubes floating in the air beside her. "A pleasant tropical island, on some planet we haven't explored, and it's full of all the people who've tried to poison me or shoot me or blow me up or shiv me in the back.

"By now, they've probably got a good-sized colony started." Tembi positioned herself in front of the utility conduits. She hated this part. It took her days to recover the little feeling she had left in her fingers. "Wonder if they've named it after me, or the Deep, or if they call it Assassins' Paradise or something equally 'gregious."

She shoved both the tubes and her own hands straight into the central mass of the bomb.

The guard gasped.

Tembi didn't. A gasp was near-kin to pain, and she was already on the verge of crying. Abusing a law of physics was painful as all raw hells. Two objects should never occupy the same space at the same time, even if the Deep assisted by moving molecules around.

"We walked through a wall once, me and the Deep," Tembi said, her eyes closed as she let the Deep paint the alignment of the tubes along her mental image of the bomb. Her hands burned, burned at the cellular level, burned so much she had to keep talking to keep herself from screaming. "I wanted to see if we could do it. Yes, it can be done. No, it's not an experience I want to repeat."

The image of the tubes aligned with reality, and she pulled her hands away, leaving the new tubes in place while sections of the old ones fell to the ship's deck. "Oxygen bomb," she explained, as she pointed to the scraps. "Whole place would have gone up if we had exposed its core to an Earth-normal atmosphere. Safer if I swap out some of the trigger pieces instead of having the Deep try and move them. It's a terrible plumber."

The bobcat wrinkled its nose at Tembi, growling.

"You are," she reminded the cat. "When you tried to fix the bathroom sink, you shot it straight into orbit."

"Um—" The guard jerked in place, as if recent events had given him a sudden twitch. "Is the Deep inside the cat?"

The nervous energy that ran alongside bomb defusal disappeared in a puff of spent adrenaline, leaving Tembi exhausted and shaking. She waved at the pile of scraps on the ground, and the hunks of plass still embedded within the ship's atmospheric input tubes. "Don't touch that," she said. "It's safe now. Mostly. Lancaster has a disposal team to take care of the rest."

"I can't believe you did that." He was staring at her hands. "How did you do that?"

She didn't reply. Exhaustion had grabbed her by the throat. All she wanted to do was sleep, and sleep, and sleep…

Tembi pulled back her shoulders and put some iron into her voice. "Thank you for calling upon Lancaster. We're glad to be of service."

As the guard started to reply, his face froze, motionless.

No! Tembi thought.

Her silent protest was caught out of context. What was wrong? Nothing? No, the Deep never slowed time, never stopped it, not unless—

—the station shredded itself around them. Fire, shrapnel, a roar of pressure and a twist of oxygen, as the bomb she thought she had disarmed exploded. But the guard? Instead of dissolving into tiny flecks of carbon that had once been a human, he *shattered!* Shards of flesh, of bone and brain, fractured into slivers, as if he was made of crystal and thrown at the floor with great force—

"Hey? Hey, um…Witch?"

Tembi blinked. The guard was staring at her, his body whole and unfixed in time. His face was a moving portrait of concern. Around them, the station stood firm. "Are you feeling all right?"

There was a twist in the air, and other people began to arrive through the Deep. They had hard faces beneath their translucent body shields, and carried large, heavy boxes with suspiciously sooty marks along their seams. They stepped over to the bomb and began to prod it with various objects; some nodded to Tembi in professional friendship.

Life had returned to normal.

"Bye," Tembi told the guard, and she wrapped herself within the Deep and disappeared.

The Deep swept her across the galaxy. The space it occupied was made from colors and liquid edges, a swirl of light, a breath of moments.

Tembi couldn't be bothered with its beauty. Not now. "What was that?" she asked. "The vision of the explosion you showed me?"

Plants appeared around her, a grove of slender trees with smooth bark and long, pointed leaves. They began to sing in an unfamiliar language.

She resisted the urge to press her fists against her eyes and scream. Instead, she thought of a calm sea, ever waiting. "I don't understand," she said.

The plants threw up their leaves in frustration and vanished.

"I know," Tembi said. "I wish it was easier, too."

Seashells appeared within her mind, pearlescent traced with gold, followed by the smell of the open ocean cast up by a great green lawn. That was the first layer of sensation: beneath that lay a knot of emotions in all their twisted complexity—love, anger, frustration, and above all else, a sense of belonging.

She could recognize that particular knot anywhere. "No," she said. "Let's not go home. Not yet."

A querulous noise shook the space around them, and then the Deep asked, ::WHY?::

Tembi sighed. It was a musical sound. When she was inside the Deep, everything sounded pure. She usually sang as they crossed the galaxy together: extra-dimensional entities had the perfect acoustics of empty bathrooms.

The Deep was not to be put off. ::WHY?::

A logical question. She needed to go back to Lancaster and be debriefed on the bomb, on the captain, on that sharp-eyed guard. Maybe another bomb had been discovered and they'd need her to disarm it. That would fit her mood quite nicely, as she felt that careening from one potential disaster to another had become the sum of her life.

But…no. Not Lancaster. Not now.

"I'm tired, buddy," she replied.

The Deep solidified around her, faceless, feather-soft, larger than the entire universe and small enough to fit in her pocket, all at once. A thousand downy white wings spread wide on either side, its broad back a welcoming bed. Tembi shook her head, but laid down anyhow.

::GOOD?::

She pressed her cheek against the Deep's back, listening to the quiet-loud sound of its heart. Everything about the Deep was a sweet contradiction. "Yes," she whispered, thinking the word as hard as she could to cover up the silent "No" which clamored around her head like a sparrow in a bell. It was easier to lie, to pretend that she was merely physically tired instead of finding the right combination of words and emotions to convince the Deep that she was wrung dry.

Oh, well. She needed to get some sleep anyhow, and the usual nightmares about things exploding never came when she was safe inside the Deep.

She woke in orbit above a moon.

Now she gasped, a deep heaving breath which proved there was an atmosphere around her, a breath hard enough to shock her awake so she could take stock of the situation.

She was in space. Okay. She'd been here before, zipping around with the Deep functioning as both her suit and her jet-pack. For a Witch, space was manageable.

She wasn't in freefall. That was good. No, that was *great!* Freefall was the absolute worst. And the air wasn't burning her lungs, so she wasn't freezing to death. The planet, small and ominously red, was on the far side of its moon, and its gravity was ignoring her. Everything else could wait until she figured out what the Deep wanted her to learn.

"Deep?" she asked. "Is this real, or is it another vision?"

A tiny meteorite appeared beside her and shot straight towards the moon.

Tembi nodded, and watched, and waited.

And the moon cracked in half.

Chapter Two

Three thousand years ago, there had been Earth. One crowd-ed planet, drowning within a sea of humanity. They were begin-ning to expand into space, but it was too late for them. Their ships were too slow, the space between habitable worlds too vast. They would have died, crushed beneath the hubris of their own greedy selves, were it not for the sudden appearance of the Deep.

It took time for the humans to realize they were no longer alone in the galaxy. The Deep didn't have a body, after all, and humans are prone to ignore that which they can't measure. Ex-cept the shipping lines between Earth and Mars kept reporting packages disappearing, reappearing, disappearing, reappear-ing…utter chaos at the docks. For some time after that, humans still believed they were alone, testing those who worked in the supply lines for latent psionic abilities.

Myopic species, humans.

Then, finally, the Deep found people who were able to trans-late for it.

The first Witches thought…well, there were no good records of what they thought. Everyone was obsessed with the Deep. Extra-terrestrial life—sapient life!—which seemed to enjoy teleporting objects between planets. Hmm. How…useful. And what did the Deep want in exchange? Nothing? Are we sure? We are?

…hmm.

First came the Deep. Then came its Witches. After that came Lancaster, and a great wave of humanity crashed across the Milky Way.

Then, three thousand years later, came Tembi Stoneskin.

She had no illusions about her significance in this long and complicated mess. If the Deep wanted to show her a broken moon? She would listen to her friend, and do her best to understand.

Down to the moon.

Tembi chose to take the long way, to fly instead of teleport. Down, swooping and dodging to avoid chunks of displaced rock, down to where the moon's thin, shattered gravity managed to catch hold of her bare feet. She landed as lightly as she could within the middle of a dusty maelstrom, a sphere of cleansed air surrounding her. Beyond the invisible edge of the sphere was dust, dust everywhere, gray dust, black dust, blue dust, a whole dull rainbow of the stuff, all of it trying to settle into new homes.

It was also reflective, which was unnerving. She saw a dozen fragmented versions of herself keeping pace beside her, their heads and gracefully tapered ears held high, their dark brown skin and the silhouettes of golden birds painted on their cheeks the only source of living color for hundreds of kilometers in any direction.

"Deep?" Tembi asked, more to cut the eerie silence than in hope of an answer. "Why did you bring me here?"

"Let me know what it tells you."

The voice came from the reflective dust cloud. For a moment—one heart-stopping moment—Tembi wondered if she had finally snapped under the strain, if all of this jumping about the galaxy with her near-omniscient invisible telepathic alien friend had finally broken her understanding of what it meant to be real. Maybe, instead of standing on this strange half-a-moon, she was, oh, say, crumpled on the floor of a restaurant where she had been enjoying a nice bowl of soup before she had become mentally and spiritually unmoored, and maybe the faint tingling sensation in her fingertips was the result of the local law hitting her with several thousand volts of well-placed popstick.

Then she recognized the voice, and wondered if it would have been better to lose touch with her sanity after all.

"War Witch," she said, nodding politely.

Her on-again, off-again, currently *extremely*-off-again boy-friend emerged from the dust, wincing at the nickname. "Tembi, don't."

She relented. "Kalais."

They stared at each other. She hadn't seen Kalais for the better part of a year. He was living on Earth these days, trying to convince the Earth Assembly to do this and that and the other on behalf of Lancaster. Life on Earth seemed to suit him. He wore a blue uniform with silver bands along the sleeves, colors which matched the swirling silver-blue patterns the Deep had painted on his cheek to mark him as one of its own. His brown skin was a few shades lighter than her own, and he appeared to be Earth-normal except for his nearly white eyes.

(Her traitor brain reminded her that she was ten different exotic varieties of scruffy in her bomb disposal uniform, which she hadn't washed in weeks, not even after that scene with all of those skittering creatures that weren't *quite* spiders. She mercilessly crushed that thought down and shoved it aside so the Deep wouldn't pick it out of her head and slap a fancy set of dress robes on her. Today didn't need to turn into the most embarrassing day of her life on top of everything else.)

He smiled at her. The small frown lines at the edges at his mouth disappeared. "You look good," he said. "New earrings?"

She held up a hand before he could finish. "Stop," she told him. "Let's figure out why the Deep brought us here, and then we can leave."

Kalais hesitated, his smile fading, and then nodded.

They fell into step beside each other, the sounds of their footsteps muffled by whatever the Deep had done to create a portable atmosphere. The dust had finally been caught up in the low gravity, and was settling around them in dense drifts. The only visual sign that they were still surrounded by a sphere of breathable air was the path it cut in the dust as they walked, the small hillocks falling in on themselves once the edge of it passed them by.

"How long have you been here?" Tembi asked.

"Arrived in time to see the moon split open. You?"

"Same. Do you know what happened?"

"No." He knelt to scoop some of the moon's foamy dust into his hands, and swirled it around as if searching for clues before letting it fall. "Is this one of the Deep's hallucinations?"

"Visions," Tembi corrected him. "Not hallucinations." She paused and shut her eyes, her hands extended, her toes set deep in the dust. The Deep's visions were almost indistinguishable from reality, but if you paused, if you allowed yourself to be still and be present within the moment, you could always find your way. The skin on her feet was as hard as the rest of her, but she was sure she could still feel the shape of the moon. Not sorrow, not pain…no emotions at all. A moon was a rock. A chunk of mass, floating in space. It still shook with the residual energy of an event not of its own making, but it didn't care. It could be crushed down until nothing remained but the dust, and it wouldn't *care*.

"Real," she said, certain that the Deep couldn't invent anything that wasn't grounded in emotion.

Kalais took a deep breath, as if expecting the small sphere of air around them to vanish.

"Relax," Tembi said. "The Deep isn't going to yank it away."

"Maybe for you! You're its favorite. If I soss it off, it might decide to let me die in space."

"Don't." She shook her head. "The Deep wouldn't do that."

He glared at her. "We've heard the same stories, Tembs."

"I'm not having this fight with you again."

He opened his mouth, their old argument ready and waiting, but chose to nod instead.

They resumed walking. With the dust finally clearing from the sky, Tembi could make out the small planet, strange in its colors. A storm appeared to be roaring across its surface, clouds as crimson as blood moving quickly towards the horizon.

Kalais stopped to watch, his pale eyes fixed on the storm.

"See anything?" Tembi asked. He came from a low-light planet, and his nearly white eyes were designed to function in

settings like this. *Similar to this,* she reminded herself. Kalais
had described his homeworld as slow, peaceful. A drowsy place
which basked in the glow of an old red sun. Not this broken
moon hanging next to a bloody planet.

"No," he replied, shaking his head. "Do you know where we
are?"

"Deep?" Tembi asked.

Eight small rocks shot up from the surface and began to orbit
a large central rock. A pebble circled around this, with a long
tail of dust trailing behind it. The comet was the detail needed
for Kalais to put a name to the planetary system: "Stross cluster."

"That's next door to Vega." Tembi glanced towards the black
sky around them, as if she could see the enormous shipping
hubs which dominated her home system.

"Stross is uninhabited," Kalais said. "No native life forms, not
enough water on a Goldilocks planet to make terraforming
worth the cost."

"Seems like a good place to set off new a weapon…" Tembi
replied, the words coming out slowly as she considered each
one. "…uninhabited, but close enough to Vega be discovered by
smugglers using FTL ships."

"Rumors start to spread, word gets back to Earth that someone's blowing up moons," Kalais agreed. "But if that's what happened, why are we the only two people around?"

"FTL ships leave traces," Tembi guessed. "If it were me, I'd
plant the weapon, abandon it for as long as I could, and then
wait to hear what happened."

"No," Kalais said. "If you're testing a weapon for the first time,
you need to gather data. This place should be swarming with
people and 'bots."

"I didn't say they were *testing* the weapon," Tembi replied,
her face pointed towards the bloody planet so Kalais couldn't
see the edges of her mouth twist. This wasn't the time to count
points.

"Small gods," he said quietly. "You think this is a message?"

"You're the War Witch," she replied. "You tell me."

The nickname didn't reach him: Kalais had already leapt into the sky.

Tembi followed.

The two of them moved across the broken moon in great bounds, not quite flying but leaping up, *up,* and then arcing down to land in a cloud of dust. They kept pushing forward, eating up the ground, each step covered the better part of a kilometer. The moon wasn't that large; Tembi thought they'd be able to circle it within an hour or two. As they traveled, they searched, looking for anything different, anything strange, anything that wasn't part of the moon itself.

"There!" Tembi shouted.

Despite the distance and the lack of air, Kalais heard her. He turned and raced towards where she was pointing, quick as lightning. The two of them landed beside a large piece of plass that had been twisted beyond recognition, presumably by the same force that had split the moon.

"I've seen this before," he said, kneeling beside the plass.

"Me, too," Tembi said. "This is what's left from larger pressure bombs." Kalais glanced up at her, surprised. "I disarm bombs, remember? Sometimes they go off."

"I'd forgotten," he muttered. "I only remember how you said you'd never join the war."

"People were dying." She hated how those three words summed up everything. Or how he smiled at them, just a little, just enough so she knew that smile was for her and her alone, and not for the waste of human lives that had finally dragged her into horror. She did her best to move the moment along. "Disarming bombs is the only thing I'm allowed to do, and only if they're found in a location where Lancaster does business."

Kalais nodded, frustrated, and turned away from her to yank on the plass hard enough to lift it from the dust. It was twice his size, but the low gravity let him pull it up like an unwanted weed. "Help me find more pieces."

Into the sky again, looking for anything that might be connected to the bomb. Now that they had found the first piece, they were able to locate more. In a matter of minutes, they had sketched out a space and covered it in shrapnel. When there was nothing left to find, they retreated to the sky to get a bird's-eye view of the mechanism.

"Less of it than there should be," Kalais mused aloud, as they puzzled over the scraps. "Or maybe there's more...I don't know what this thing was. What do you think?"

"I think I've spent the last two years keeping these things from going off," she said. "I don't like being around one that's completed its job. Hey, Deep? Did we miss any of the pieces?"

In reply, the surface of the moon began to jerk as more scraps of the bomb shook themselves loose.

Kalais wrinkled his nose. "Why didn't I think of that?"

"Because you only think about the Deep when you want to jump across the galaxy," she replied, as the Deep maneuvered countless pieces of plass and all kinds of unrecognizable materials into a hastily sketched impression of order. "Deep? Do you know what this looked like before the explosion?"

The pieces paused in midair, and then began to move again, pushing and pulling themselves into a rough device.

"I can't tell what it was supposed to be. There're too many missing parts," Kalais said.

Tembi was about to say something nasty about how it *had* been a *bomb*, after all! but stopped herself. There was something odd about the debris, how the bottom of the structure had suffered more damage than the top. She drifted over to a piece where there was a melted edge along the plass, whole on one side and ruined on the other, as if the strength of the bomb hadn't been quite enough to wipe itself out.

"Doesn't make sense," she said under her breath, her fingers prodding that bubbly line between right and wrong. "This bomb could break something as large as a moon, but..."

"Come on," she said, as she leapt into the sky again. "I want to see something."

They didn't have far to go. The fracture in the moon appeared, clean as the edge of a knife. Tembi paused to wait for Kalais, and the two of them went over the side together.

This side of the moon was in shadow. The half-moon's orbit was still adjusting to the force of the explosion, but was no doubt stabilized to some degree by the Deep. The movement, coupled with the light reflected from the planet below, painted everything in an eerie wiggling red.

The face of the rock was clean of dust, clean of all possible damage. Unnaturally clean.

Unnervingly clean.

She reached out and brushed her fingers along the flat surface. The sound of stone grating across stone caused Kalais to wince. "Oh, Tembs."

"It's been a hard year," she muttered, putting a little more distance between them so he couldn't touch her. Sympathy would get them nowhere. She returned her attention to the rock face. "This reminds me of a shear bomb, but those cut buildings in half. Not slice chunks out of whole moons!"

"I'd swear someone took a plasma cutter to this," Kalais said. "The size of it, though!"

Tembi shook her head, unable to grapple with the implications. She had seen shear bombs do their work too many times. Those hellish devices were good for a single burst of energy strong enough to slice through most materials. Then, their job done, they would be buried within the rubble of the building, or the ship, or that mineral mine…

That mine had been bad. A shear bomb, hidden in an unused tunnel, left dormant until its sentinel 'bots reported that the mine had reached critical capacity, full of workers and machines and various creatures of business who had deigned to go beneath the surface of the asteroid to see how their credits were ground out of the walls. When the bomb went off, it had sent out a single pulse of energy. This pulse formed a single horizontal beam, disk-shaped and all-encompassing, which sliced neatly through everything it encountered along its way until it lost its mojo and trickled out, dispersing into the walls of the asteroid a quarter-kilometer away.

That pulse hadn't been all that wide, starting out with the thickness of a hair and diffusing out to two centimeters at its most lethal point. But in an underground world crafted from careful engineering, two centimeters was more than enough. More than enough to take out walls, to cut through machines, to rip through flesh and bone while still allowing a couple of panicked heartbeats to wonder how you got all of that blood on your trousers—

"Focus, Tembi," she whispered to herself.

She pressed the palms of her hands against the wall, and pushed herself off to float up beside Kalais. "I'm out of my depth," she admitted. "The wreckage we found looks like what's left over from a cheap pressure bomb. This, though? It's beyond anything I've seen. I'll call Cooper. He's the expert." Cooper was the demolitions specialist who had trained her, and she knew he'd be overjoyed to see this moon. He treated bombs as art forms which demanded respect, and he rarely got to see such a dramatic new variant of the theme. He wasn't a Witch himself, but he had the authority to drag a Witch away from their own duties at Lancaster, and she could imagine him setting up camp on the sliced edge of the moon to study it.

Kalais pushed himself away from the shadowed edge, and hung in the air. The red light tugged at the edges of his clothing, his hair, his face, and he blinked to lower the embedded black lenses which allowed him to see in bright sunlight. "I'm going back to Earth," he said. "Come with me. They'll want to hear what you have to say."

She shook her head. "You go to Earth. I'll go to Lancaster. I need to be debriefed anyway."

"I don't know how to explain this," he said.

"Don't bother. Just bring them here."

"It's not going to be that easy," he said. "The Deep brought us here before the bomb went off, remember? How do we explain that?"

"Simple." Tembi shrugged. "The Deep moves through time."

He rolled his eyes. "Tembi—"

"The Deep moves through *time*," she insisted. "It saw the explosion, and brought us back so we could watch it happen."

"That's impossible."

Tembi pointed at the broken moon, at the depths of space around them, at the two of them hanging in an airless sky, and then turned the movement into an especially rude gesture.

"Point taken," he said. "But you're still wrong—they've studied the Deep forever, Tembs! All it can do is manipulate space and matter. We know this. Time travel isn't one of its abilities."

"I'm not saying it moves Witches through time often. Or that it's easy for it to do. But yes, Kalais, the Deep can move us through time as well as space."

"No, it can't." He shook his head in disgust. "Stop. You're giving this...*thing* too much power."

The old argument was bubbling up between them again. It wasn't the place for it, and there was never a right time for it. Except here they were, voices rising while they stood on the edge of impossibility.

"Be realistic, Tembi," he said hotly, arms knotted across his chest. "How often do those bombs go off? Wouldn't the Deep be able to stop that if it could see through time?"

She kept her mouth shut, a thin line tight from anger. If she opened it, she'd say something about what happened when she made a mistake, when those little tubes didn't align properly, when the Deep wrapped her in itself so fast that she couldn't process what was happening, when she was suddenly halfway across a planet and she knew there was now nothing she could do except wait a few minutes, hands clenched, so those flecks of carbon which had been people and buildings could burn out or settle in place before she jumped back to the scene.

"We know nothing about this creature," he said. "The faith you put in it...I'll never understand it. Just because it likes you—"

She finally had enough. "Love," she snapped. "It loves me. And you."

"It lets us *die!*" he roared. "If we soss it off, it punts us into space and we're gone forever! Better to ignore it than convince ourselves it's capable of something like love!"

"Don't be cruel," Tembi replied. "It doesn't let us die."

"Then where do those Witches go? The ones who've disappeared? Or what about the ones who start aging again?" He was pacing, furious. "We're nothing but its toys, Tembs! When it gets bored with us, it kills us off and replaces us with someone new."

He was right. There were Witches who had gone missing, and some Witches who had stopped aging suddenly grew old and then died. The doubts that swarmed Tembi's peace when she was on the verge of sleep swelled and—

No. He's not wrong, but that doesn't mean he's right.

"Stop," she told him. "Just stop. The Deep isn't omniscient. You know that!"

"I don't know anything," he said. "I thought you finally understood that this creature has limits. If it could move through time, it could make sure none of *this*—" and he spread his arms wide. "—would happen! If it could prevent this, why wouldn't it?"

"Because people don't make sense! The Deep is the first intelligent alien we've encountered, and we treat it like a tool! It's a *person*, Kalais! You know that as well as I do! It's got a sense of humor!" She was shouting now, her hands firm on her hips. "It likes cats, for gods' sake! You're a Witch, Kalais, the Deep talks to you! Even if you can't understand most of what it says, you can't deny what you know!"

"I'm the War Witch, remember?" Kalais stared at her with dark eyes. "War's what I know!"

"It doesn't want us to be at war!" she snarled.

"Then why did it choose me?" Kalais pounded himself on the chest with a closed fist. "I'm the first soldier it's chosen. *Ever!* Three thousand years, and I'm the first! If the Deep is a person, then you should respect its choice and listen to me for once!"

That was new: that struck Tembi straight through her heart. Oh, he had been thinking about that one! Well, she had spent many a trip across the galaxy reliving their old fights, too.

"The Deep is an innocent person. Matindi thinks it might even be a child," Tembi said harshly. "It isn't omniscient, and its choices aren't infallible." She stopped before she added: *And it made a mistake when it chose you.*

He knew her too well. Her omission shouted louder than the words themselves.

He took a deep breath. "We don't know what the Deep is," he said, very slowly, very calmly, each word as cutting as if he had sharpened them like razors. "It's told us that it's older than our entire galaxy."

"If you ask a six-year-old how old they are, they'll proudly tell you they're all grown up now." The calmer he got, the more she wanted to throw things at his head, or maybe kick him hard enough to spin him in a wobbly arc towards the planet. Maybe there was enough atmosphere to give him some minor burns before the Deep jumped him to safety—No. Better to try and talk sense into him, this one last time.

Calm. Yes. She was Adhamantian: he could do calm, she could do calm, they would be two adults having a calm adult discussion. While floating in space. In little bubbles of air...oh, she had *such* a stomach ache! "Think, Kalais, please. Lancaster has told the galaxy that the Deep is an unlimited energy field. We can't keep spreading that lie. Not when the Deep is someone we have to protect."

"So what if it is?" Kalais rounded on her, all calm gone, suddenly furious. "*I* was a child soldier. Eight years old, yanked off my homeworld, a weapon shoved into my hands! I didn't have a choice!"

"No, you didn't," Tembi said, her own sense of calm held tight between her clenched teeth. She hadn't meant to push this particular button. "Someone should have defended you. If I had been there, I would have stood between you and those who wanted to use you."

"How?! We're the same age, Tembs. When you were eight, you were eating out of the trash and picking pockets to survive!" Kalais roared. "If the Deep hadn't chosen you to become a Witch, you'd still be on your dead-end planet, selling yourself on the street to get enough credit to buy a meal!"

Too far.

The anger vanished from Kalais as quickly as it had kindled, all of the heat snuffed out by the cruelty of what he had just said. "Gods, Tembi, I'm sorry—"

"Get out of here," she said, as cold and as lifeless as the broken moon. "You've got a duty, War Witch."

Kalais blinked again. The artificial lenses retracted, and he looked at her with his pale defenseless eyes.

"Don't you dare," she warned him.

He turned, wrapped himself in the Deep, and disappeared.

"Someone should have been there for you," Tembi said quietly.

She took one last look at the moon, and stepped into the Deep.

Chapter Three

Not all Witches were equal. Tembi had learned this at a very early age: tradition held that the Deep called each Witch to its service when they were adults, and yet it had yanked Tembi from her home planet of Adhama when she was barely eight.

She knew she should have gone straight to Lancaster to check in, to tell them about the bomb and the moon, about everything except the childish shouting match. Kalais knew his duty; she knew hers. Except procedure stated that Tembi needed to report in with a senior Witch, and nothing about going to Lancaster itself, which she did not want to do until she was sure she wouldn't unload on those useless old walnuts and shout them into oblivion. Besides, of the two senior Witches she'd trust with her life, only one of them lived at Lancaster.

The other...

Well, after a bad day at work and a nasty fight with your ex, sometimes you needed your mother.

Halfway across the galaxy from the Stross system was a planet that would eat you alive if you stood in the same place for too long. Terraforming gone wrong (or poorly planned and executed) had resulted in fast-growing plants that were slightly too eager to break a body down into their component molecules. Woe to the fool who chose to stand in one place while they were still using theirs.

Tembi's second mother loved it. She said it reminded her of home.

Matindi was a short woman who carried herself with the no-nonsense grace of a busy queen. She had the ageless face and body of a mature Witch, and the painted markings the Deep had chosen for her were the branch of a tree, fresh in springtime, its leaves only a few shades darker than the pale green of her own skin.

She was quite possibly the most pragmatic creature in the known galaxy.

"You're sure he went straight to Earth to warn them?"

"Giant gods, yes. Yes, Matindi, I'm sure," snarled Tembi. "Let's be sure to focus on my ex-boyfriend and his overinflated sense of duty, and not on how the war has moved to the sector beside my home planet!"

Matindi smiled and went back to potting a rosebush. As roses went, it wasn't much to look at, with pink petals and green leaves that resembled old leather, and thorns wicked enough to sever a finger. It was one of those rare Earth varieties bred to be vicious enough to survive on Matindi's homeworld, and she had brought it with her to this backwards planet when she had retired.

Her house was in the center of a clearing, at the edge of a village filled with people as tenacious as she was. They were homesteaders and farmers, bound to live as far away from civilization as possible. They had claimed this abandoned disaster of a planet as their own, cloaked their buildings in stasis fields, and kept the native vegetation from their own crops with salted and stoned earth, followed by hearty applications of good old-fashioned fire. Matindi's cottage was small and clean, with vines from her homeworld staking claim to its white-painted walls. The structure itself was heavy-duty plass, and had probably rolled off a production line a thousand at a time, but she had nailed enough handmade pieces to its walls to give it character. Matindi had even made the doors herself from wood taken from trees which grew on a dozen different planets. She wasn't much of a carpenter: the doors shut fairly well, but could only be opened with a good, solid kicking.

"Help me with the chores, and then we'll go inside and talk," Matindi said, as she forgot herself and dusted her hands off on her blue robes. She wrinkled her nose at the dark handprints. "Ah, mildest hells."

The stains vanished.

She frowned. "Leave them, dear. Gardening is all about consequences, and it does me good to remember that."

The handprints reappeared.

::SORRY::

The Deep only spoke aloud when it felt safe, and it often spoke in whole sentences around Matindi. The voice came from everywhere and nowhere; the earth shook, and some of the less tenacious plants stopped their forward advance on Tembi's ankles.

Matindi reached out, as if giving a reassuring hug to a young child. "There's no need to apologize. Want to help us feed the animals?"

At that, a bevy of round birds plucked up their heads from the nearby garden. Tembi and the Deep busied themselves scattering handfuls of seeds. Chickens were strange, alien creatures, somewhat reminiscent of ducks but with misplaced self-confidence. As the plants seemed to leave them alone, Tembi assumed they had come from Matindi's home planet, too.

The goat? There was no doubt that the goat came from old Earth stock. The creature was pure stubbornness from its curly horns to its stubby tail. Whenever a green tendril snaked its way across the rocks which separated the nearby forest from Matindi's gardens, the goat would snap it up.

"Aren't you worried it'll eat the plants you want to keep?" Tembi called to Matindi.

Across the yard, Matindi laughed. "Mine don't move as much," she said. "She's learned to appreciate a challenge."

After half an hour of chores, Tembi felt much better. Work for work's sake had little appeal, but completing it lifted the spirits. She looked at the compost bucket full of native weeds that had, somehow, found their way into the garden, and told herself they weren't squirming towards her in revenge. She went to the dehydration bin on the far side of the yard, chucked the wriggling things inside, and pressed the button to suck all traces of water from the tiny monsters.

"Done?" Matindi was holding the front of her robes to form a small pocket, a handful of eggs nestled within its folds.

"I think so," Tembi said. "Deep?"

A pile of weeds appeared inside the dehydration bin, squashed themselves down, and crumbled into dust.

"Good job, Deep," Matindi said. "I'm thinking about making cookies. Would you like that?"

::*YES!*:: The disembodied voice was eager.

Tembi grinned. As best as she could tell, the Deep didn't eat. Cookies might as well have had hooves or claws for all it cared. Its eagerness came from the happy ritual of baking, with Matindi sifting and measuring and mixing and complaining in her peaceful way, and Tembi watching from her usual chair at the kitchen table.

Into the house (with one well-placed hip against the door to force it open), where the floors looked like stone and the walls looked like old plaster, and were neither. There was more greenery inside, with hanging plants looped around the windows and bundles of herbs drying from the rafters. It smelled of tamed living things, and very slightly of cinnamon.

Tembi took her usual seat at the table. Across from her, one of the other chairs pulled itself out, then shuffled forward, as if an invisible human was making themselves comfortable.

"Matindi—"

"If I had to guess, I'd say the Deep brought you to that moon as a warning," Matindi said, as she began to bustle around the tiny kitchen, pulling pans and plates out of their cupboards, and ingredients from the stasis box. "It didn't know about the bomb until it went off, and it brought you there to learn about this new threat.

"Where's the threat coming from?" she added. "Who knows? But it's obvious why it chose to drag Kalais into this."

"Really." Tembi's tone put her arid homeworld to shame. "How?"

"You have no idea what to do about that boy. He has no idea what to do about you. In a situation where the Deep doesn't know what to do, it's going to try to match up a Witch's skills with their emotions." Matindi began cracking eggs with a little more force than necessary. "It chose correctly, by the way. When it comes to its Witches, you and Kalais are as close as it can come to demolition experts. Except you couldn't put your problems aside and stop shouting about how the Deep is a person."

"But it *is* a—"

"Yes, honey, I know. I've known since before your grandmother's grandmother's grandmother was born." The eggs were set aside in their own separate bowl, a generous scoop of butter on a small dish beside it. "The Deep is a vulnerable person, one we've been exploiting for the better part of three thousand years. You can't say that because nobody wants to hear it."

The empty chair across the table began to wiggle, as if a small child was swinging its legs back and forth.

"Anything to add, dear?" Matindi asked the Deep.

A hesitant ::NO:: rattled the crockery.

"Are you sure?" asked Tembi.

::YES:: This was said with equal hesitation.

Matindi set the mixing bowl on the counter and slowly asked, "Do you want to say something but you're not sure how to say it?"

::YES::

Two questions asked back-to-back, but there was no hesitation this time. *Poor Deep*, Tembi thought. *Smarter than all of us put together, and unable to tell us what we need to hear.*

"Would you like to speak through me?" Matindi asked. "It might help you organize your thoughts."

When Tembi was younger, she had been unable to hear the Deep. It had spoken to her through Matindi, using her second mother's voice as its own. When the Deep spoke through a Witch, it spoke more clearly, as if the process of filtering its thoughts through a human mind distilled them down to a point where it could communicate them to others. Matindi had warned her that it was not a pleasant experience. "Aggressively sobering" was the phrase she had used, and if you weren't used to it, you blacked out and awoke with your mind almost offensively clear. She also said the Deep didn't enjoy it much, either, except at parties when its Witches were too drunk for their own thoughts to get in its way.

There was a long pause where Matindi appeared to brace herself for whatever was to come. Finally, the Deep answered. ::NO::

"It's all right, honey," Matindi said, as she picked up the bowl. "When you can think of a way to tell us, we're ready to listen."

The empty chair stopped moving. The air in the kitchen shifted, as if the weight of a great and binding thunderstorm had passed.

"Poor Deep," Tembi said, mostly to herself.

"Poor you," Matindi replied, as she scraped the wet mix into the dry, and told the bowl to stir them together. "I've never been able to figure out if it has the same sense of ethics as humans. Maybe it comprehends that the human race treats it as an all-purpose slave, and it doesn't care one whit."

"That doesn't matter to me," Tembi said. "I can't live with that." She paused…considering. If she was going to tell Matindi, it should be here, now, in the safety of this little house a million klicks from nowhere. Matindi kept saying she wanted to be kept out of Lancaster's politics, but—

In that pause, Matindi said, "I know."

"Really?" Tembi looked up, startled, wondering what she had done to give her small rebellion away. "How?"

"I struggle with it, too," Matindi sighed. She set the bowl down, took six quick steps across her small house, and kicked the front door open. "Oy! Hooligans!" she shouted. "Cookies!

"Set those to baking," she said to Tembi, as she disappeared into a back room.

Tembi ladled out the dough onto the bakepans as small children began to flood into the kitchen, racing inside almost as fast as if they had been dropped off by the Deep. Almost all of them were Earth-normal, but they had been around Matindi long enough to be used to strange people who came and went, and they didn't give Tembi's ears more than a glance. Some had met Tembi before, and begged her to do the trick with the knife, the one where she stabbed it into the meat of her own arm and the knife's blade *bent!*

"Shhh," Tembi said, as she picked up a knife.

"Don't you dare!" came Matindi's voice from the back room.

The kids groaned in despair as Tembi went to set down the knife, and then, as she whipped it around and thrust the blade at her arm with all of her might, they cheered!

"Tembi!"

"Dropped it!" Tembi called out, as she held up the bent knife and her unmarked arm, and winked at children.

"How did you do that?!" one of them whispered.

"My skin is different than yours," Tembi said, as she rubbed her fingertips together. The sound was that of two small, rough-faced stones grating against each other. "My home planet has violent storms, and they blow around a lot of sand," she explained. "If you're caught outside in those storms, they can strip your skin right off your body. My ancestors chose to mod themselves up for protection." She showed them her second eyelids, the semi-transparent ones which let in enough light and details to allow for a careful stumble towards shelter, and how she could fold back her high-pointed ears to keep out airborne detritus. "We did it to keep ourselves safe."

"My da says people get modded to look *pretty,*" one of the kids said, with an emphasis on "pretty" which made it sound more like a curse than a compliment.

"That does happen," Tembi admitted. "There are a lot of planets out there, and some of them are safe for humans without genetic mods. If you buy a planet, you can decide to live on it however you want." A bit of a dire lie, but she wasn't about to get into intergalactic policymaking with a pack of kids. "If you choose to mod yourself and your own children, what's the harm?"

"My da says it's wrong," said the same child.

Tembi looked at him, at his Earth-normal hair and eyes and skin and everything, his head-to-toes bog-standard Earth-normal body, and her heart twisted a little. *Even here,* she thought. *Here, where we're half a galaxy away from everything.* "I know that when I was your age, I was caught outside in a couple of storms," she said. "I wouldn't have survived if it wasn't for the decisions my ancestors made. I'm grateful for my mods."

The child ignored her, his attention firmly transferred to the cookies slowly turning golden brown on the bakepans.

Matindi emerged from her bedroom. She had changed into white robes with silver trim, a matching scarf to cover her head. The painted leaves on her cheek had taken on a slight silver cast, as if they were filtering moonlight. Tembi thought she should have a sword in one hand and a shield in the other.

"Gather 'round, children," Matindi said, as she pulled one of the bakepans to her. "I'm going to tell you a story."

General protests followed, entwined with specific complaints about the promise versus the availability of cookies.

"They're not ready yet," Matindi said, as she poked a doughy cookie with a green fingernail. "So while we wait, let me tell you about how I was called to become a Witch."

Oh, well, this was exciting! The children knocked about the kitchen like small rolling balls until they found places to rest.

"Once upon a time, there was a little green girl with big feet," Matindi began, as she stood on one leg to wiggle the toes on her oversized foot at the children. There was an appropriate amount of giggling. "She lived on an entire planet of green people with big feet, as they were all born before the bioengineers had figured out some critical gene alignments. But it was fine, because she didn't know there were other places where the people looked different."

"Didn't you watch the channels?" shouted one of the children.

Matindi raised an authoritative eyebrow, and the dissident fell silent. "No, the little girl didn't watch any of the channels," she continued. "The channels that you know of weren't invented yet. People on different planets couldn't talk to each other at all."

Gasps all around.

"She listened to songs her parents approved of, and met people her parents approved of, and had very little knowledge of the great big galaxy out there, because she was a very spoiled little girl with very wealthy parents who gave her everything she wanted, and the idea that there was more to life than what existed in front of her own face never occurred to her." Matindi paused to check the bakepans, and then continued. "One day, when she was twenty, she was going to marry a man her parents approved of, and have children they approved of, and nobody would ever be a terrible disappointment to anybody.

"But on the day of her wedding, the man didn't show up."

"Was he dead?!"

Matindi shut her eyes; Tembi had the sneaking suspicion she was slowly counting backwards, *Five, four, three, two, one...* When she opened her eyes again, Matindi said, "No, Kyle. It would have been easier for the girl if he had died. He decided he didn't want to marry a spoiled, selfish woman, and he chose to run away instead.

"The girl was very sad. No one had ever hurt her like that. She thought her heart was breaking. And then she heard a voice in her head, a voice as big as the world. It didn't speak in words but nevertheless she understood it, and it promised the girl that if she came with it and became a Witch, she would never be hurt again.

"The girl agreed." The first bakepan chimed, and converted itself into racks so the cookies could cool. Matindi swatted greedy hands away as she continued: "She became one of the first true Witches, people to whom the Deep gave the choice to leave their past lives and join with a singular power that was remaking the shape of the galaxy."

Matindi paused, turning to look through a small windows. "Nobody knows why the Deep started choosing Witches to serve as its representatives. Nobody knows why it comes to people who have suffered heartache. Nobody knows why it came to our galaxy in the first place! But it was the best thing that ever happened to that spoiled little girl, because once she saw what was truly out there, she finally started to grow up." She turned back to the baketrays. A spatula was found, and the first cookies were removed from the cooling racks and shuffled into greedy, grasping hands. As she passed them around, Matindi asked the children, "Could you imagine what life would be like without the Deep?"

Most of the children shook their heads, along with a small chorus of, "No!"

"Neither could that girl. But as time went on, the girl saw that things weren't fair. Not for the Deep, and not for the people who used the Deep to get around the galaxy. It made her very sad, and she tried to stop being a Witch."

Tembi, who had been watching the cookies cool on the second bakepan, looked up in surprise. This part of the story was new to her. Matindi noticed, and nodded. "Yes," she told the children, and Tembi, too. "The girl tried to stop being a Witch altogether. But that made the Deep sad. The girl didn't want to hurt her wonderful friend, so she spent many, many years trying to find a way that would make things fair, and then everybody would be happy. She never could." There was a single long pause, and then: "So, here we are. Nothing is fair and nobody is happy, but at least we have cookies, and we can take minor comfort from that." She loaded the remaining cookies onto the second rack, and placed them in the arms of the oldest child. "Hanif, dear, give these pans to your mother, and tell your father he's to look after my goat. I'm taking the chickens with me."

The children were herded to the door. There was some kicking, followed by some complaining, and then they were gone, with only Tembi and Matindi standing in the suddenly quiet house.

"I didn't know," Tembi said.

"That I tried to quit, instead of taking a sabbatical? Oh, yes, many times. I've honestly lost count." Matindi closed the door and made sure it was firmly shut. "Now, Deep." Beyond the windows, the colors of the bright day shifted from the usual green to a rainbow hue, and then settled on blue and gold. "One day, I'll finally stop being a spoiled little girl who keeps trying to run from her responsibilities. Until then, the two of you will just have to keep dragging me out of retirement," Matindi said, as she kicked open the door again.

In front of them stood a gleaming white-and-gold spire, its tallest floors punching up against a cloudless blue sky, rising high beyond the rooftops of the ancient village which lay at its feet.

The Deep had brought them home to Lancaster.

Chapter Four

Lancaster. A golden monument to itself.

The center of the Witches' campus was a single great tower modeled after a white nautilus shell, one that had been sliced in half and stretched to absurd heights, its curves and angles gilded to show off its impossible beauty. The tower glittered, white and gold, with windows which caught the sun no matter where it hung in the sky. At night, mirrors embedded within the tower's clean, curving lines caught starlight and reflected it back into the galaxy, a shining beacon which had better things to do with fancy radiation than to keep it.

Around the tower stretched kilometer after kilometer of wide green lawns, perfectly manicured, each blade of grass groomed to a precise length, width, and height. Pathways were used sparingly, and were mostly for decoration. Streets were an abomination and shunned altogether, save for a wide stretch of white cobblestones at the base of the tower for visitors arriving via Lancaster's private hopper. The lawns were dotted with formal gardens and entertainment pavilions, a private library, living quarters for young Witches-in-training, an old museum which described the history of the Deep, and a quaint little gift shop which also served as a commissary for those guests staying in Lancaster's overnight suites.

Past the paraphernalia of Lancaster Tower lay the tidy houses of those Witches who chose to live on Lancaster's campus. Not many did, not when the commute to work was a single jump through the Deep. The purposefully small residential bungalows of Lancaster couldn't compete with the option to buy a mansion (or two, or three, or more) on cosmopolitan planets at the center of the galaxy. Tricks of the landscaping made it so no Witch saw another's house, not unless they wanted to. This philosophy had governed the design of the nearby Witches' village, as most of the older Witches did want to see each other, and not just as distant company on the margins. No, for them, proximity was paramount. All the better to socialize and talk and complain, my dears. About how the city on the other side of Lancaster's high walls encroached ever closer, about the young Witches and their many flaws, about how things used to be… *better.* Had it been different? Yes, of course, but the heart of the problem was that life used to be better in ways that couldn't be summed up by tallying differences alone.

These old Witches—these immortal creatures with their unlined faces and their ancient eyes—had set up a small village for themselves, filled with shops and restaurants and countless other small diversions. It was the perfect illusion of a country town. It was how they thought country towns should be, with buildings crafted from rough-cut stone, and windows made from old-fashioned glass. Rooftops had graceful arches leading up to high peaks. Paint was allowed to flake in a controlled, well-mannered fashion. It was best to not speak of the ivy.

It was a lovely place if you appreciated stagecraft.

And the Deep had set down Matindi's house in the dead center of the village square.

"I take it we're not being subtle?" Tembi said, as Matindi strode into the square, clucking for her chickens.

"Oh, you do know the meaning of the word," Matindi said. "Find some nicer clothes, dear. It's time to put on a show."

A set of dress robes appeared in the air beside Tembi, neatly folded in a careful pile. Tembi recognized them as her own; she didn't have as many colorful badges as most of the older Witches, but the few she had earned were unmistakable. As far as she knew, she was the only Witch to have received an honorary knighthood on Camelot for services rendered to the Throne.

"Yes," Tembi said, and the white and gold robes replaced her bomb disposal uniform, her badges neatly running down the midnight blue stripe which covered her left shoulder. She shifted in place; her underwear was still comfortable. That wasn't always the case, as the Deep seemed to think that fancy clothes should be accompanied by equally fancy undergarments, and didn't understand that such undergarments weren't technically meant to be worn under much of anything, and then not worn for very long at all.

She gave her outfit one last tug to make sure it draped in all the proper places, checked to make sure that the Deep had swapped out her filthy headscarf with a clean white one, and followed Matindi into the village square.

Witches began to appear, packing the picturesque miniature town, each of them calling for Matindi in false outrage. Matindi ignored them all, walking straight towards the pathway which opened onto Lancaster's green-and-gold fields. Tembi followed, dodging and weaving as people teleported into the square around her. The Deep would never stick one Witch through another, oh *no!* Never *that!* But it certainly enjoyed dropping a Witch a few centimeters in front of another to check their reflexes. It was rather like a dance, moving between the newcomers, twisting beneath arms, spinning away before they had a chance to realize one of the two Witches in front of them was somebody they had come to see. Tembi took a moment to check if Matindi needed help... No. Her mentor was wearing a predatory smile, a speck of pale leafy green grinning within a sea of polished jewels, each step taking her further into the grass.

Then it was the two of them, alone, walking across the wide rolling fields towards Lancaster Tower.

No. It was the three of them: Matindi on one side, Tembi on the other, and a set of footprints between them. Except whatever was making these footprints wasn't human, as the tracks bent low into the grass showed paws, or claws, or perhaps the light brushings of feathers or a million different wiggly legs.

Tembi thought the Deep was laughing.

The journey to Lancaster Tower should have taken hours. The Tower was a dozen kilometers distant, and Tembi *knew* they were on foot! But each step they took was a jump of a different kind. *Step,* and the village was behind them. *Step,* and they had cleared the fields. *Step,* and the dormitories were in front of them, and with another step, those had fallen far away...

Step, and they were at the foot of the Tower.

Step, and they were inside.

Step, and they were at an old wooden door with Matindi's name painted in small black print, with bare winter branches etched into the door itself. As Matindi reached for the handle, flecks of green appeared within the wood, and fresh spring leaves unspooled themselves from the carvings.

Matindi paused. "Thank you, dear." One of the smaller carved branches waved merrily at her, and she kissed her fingertips and pressed them against the branch. The door opened, and Matindi ushered Tembi inside.

The office was larger than it should have been, a trick of the Deep's to ensure that Lancaster never ran out of premium space for its administrators. Matindi's taste in decorating ran towards heavy slabs of natural materials, dotted with fragile works of art. Humanity, she always said, might do its best to leave its mark but never appreciated how it could be erased with the shiver of an earthquake. Her office was paneled in wood and slices of live green moss cut into cunning shapes, with a large stone desk at its center. It also had a thick layer of five years' worth of dust, as well as the broken glass left over from the fight Matindi had with Lancaster's Earth Assembly representative on the day she had abandoned her duties and gone into retirement.

They stared at the pile of glass.

"I had almost forgotten," Matindi said quietly.

It had been a fight for the ages. Five years ago, Tembi had watched from her usual seat on the couch as Matindi faced off against a woman nearly half again as tall as her, a woman in white robes, her white hair braided with the colors of rainbows. Domino, the other queen of Lancaster. An unsmiling queen unless it suited her, and *oh!* how she had smiled as Matindi lost her temper and hurled a crystal ewer at her, swearing that she would leave and never return!

Domino had gestured, a small crook of her finger, and the

Deep had obeyed her and turned the ewer into shards. That might have been the end of it, except that the shards had continued through the air and *hit Domino.*

Oh, small and precious gods.

If Domino had not also been a child of Adhama and shared Tembi's rock-hard skin, her face would have been sliced to ribbons. As it was, only a single small cut appeared on Domino's left cheek, marring the paint of the rainbow prisms which the Deep used as her Witch's mark.

The significance of what had happened froze the three of them, shattered their anger like the ewer itself. In Lancaster's political hierarchy, Domino outranked Matindi. The only casualty should have been the old glass jug. The Deep had not followed the order imposed by that hierarchy, and had instead decided to obey both Matindi and Domino.

That was how Witches died.

Matindi had pointed Domino out of her office, shoved a young Tembi into the hall, and sealed the door behind the three of them, instructing the Deep to keep it shut. The green leaves within the wood had curled into withered husks, and had then blown away.

Now, staring at the mess, Matindi seemed lost in thought. "I shouldn't have let her get to me," she sighed, as she knelt to clean up the glass. "She was trying to drive me out. I knew it, and I still allowed her to do it."

"Here," Tembi said, as she nudged Matindi out of the way and started to scoop up the pieces into her bare hands. "My people were made for this. Literally."

"But Domino was hurt—"

"Yes, she was," Tembi agreed, as she intentionally jabbed a large shard straight at her own face. Matindi gasped, but Tembi ran her thumb along the unblemished skin of her cheek, and then lifted her eyes to the ceiling. "She was *hurt.*"

Matindi paused, as if she had never considered that the Deep had truly been responsible for bloodshed. "Right," she finally said, and fell upon the rest of her office, wiping up five years' worth of dust with a hungry suckcloth. As Matindi moved in quick, efficient swipes, Tembi noticed the dust missed by the cloth was sweeping itself into small piles.

"*Stop,*" she thought at the Deep. "*You don't have to clean up after us.*"

A small cloud of dust fluttered in a remarkable approximation of a shrug, and then settled back into its thin patina across the sideboard.

A sound like a small crack of thunder made them both jump as a man in an old-fashioned business suit stepped out of the Deep. His skin was brown, with one side of his face painted with the same branches bending under the weight of spring leaves as Matindi's own Witch's mark.

He stared at Matindi, and then at Tembi, and shook his head.

"Hello, Matthew," Matindi said, not bothering to look up from her dusting.

"Oh, love," Matthew sighed. "Could you please call ahead next time?"

"Ruins the surprise." Matindi stretched, her elbows bending in a way that made Tembi's stomach lurch. "Can you summon the others? This is business, and I'd rather not drop this on you alone."

"Might as well," Matthew said tiredly. "It's going to land on me anyhow."

Tembi's heart went out to him. He was Lancaster's head administrator and was very good at his job. She had never held that against him, as he and Matindi loved each other with the kind of slow-burning passion that could survive across millennia.

"Hey there, sweet girl," he said, sparing a smile for Tembi. "How'd you manage to talk her out of retirement?"

"The Deep took me to watch a moon blow up."

Matthew reached behind him, groping aimlessly for a chair. One shuffled its way across the thick woolen carpet and bumped against his legs until he sat. "I need to hear this story," he said, fingers pressed against his temples.

She told him, omitting the minor detail of her fight with Ka-lais, as Matthew tended to get angry on her behalf. He listened carefully, asking questions here and there, and then... "Matindi, love, why have you come back now?"

"Because it's time for Lancaster to get involved in the war," Matindi said, smiling brightly. "It's not enough that we move refugees or disarm weapons. If the Deep is taking Tembi to see new types of bombs at work, I choose to interpret that as evidence that the Witches should stop pretending to be a neutral party."

Tembi shot a quick look at Matthew. He had his eyes shut, his head now pressed into his hands. "Matindi," he said quietly.

"If the Deep has decided to bring children into the fight—" Matindi paused, and added, "—no offense, Tembi dear, but I *am* twenty-five hundred years old—" Tembi nodded. "—it has decided that the older Witches have abdicated their responsibilities. I cannot stand by and let our youngest generation carry the weight of our failures."

The room fell quiet. Tembi fixed her attention on the ceiling. Matthew let out a dramatic sigh. It seemed this was not the response Matindi had expected. She crossed her arms, glaring. "What aren't you saying?"

"Tembi, could you give us a moment?" Matthew asked.

"You've already started, haven't you?" Matindi shook her head. "Your own little rebellion, just the two of you."

"Matindi, love—"

"Not just the two of you?!" Matindi threw up her hands. "And you never thought to tell me?"

Tembi and Matthew exchanged a glance. "You've said you don't want to be involved in politics anymore," Tembi ventured. "You've said that a *lot*."

"As recently as two days ago," Matthew added. "Over dinner, you told me that politics ruins your digestion, and you didn't want to hear a word about Domino, Lancaster, or the war."

"Well." Matindi said sharply, as if fury and resignation were in conflict. "Well, then."

"You used the phrase 'don't mention that bitch's name where I can hear it,' at least twice."

"I know what I said," Matindi replied, arms crossed.

"Do you want specifics?" Matthew said. "There's a small group meeting planned for later tonight."

"It's been postponed. Moto's still on assignment," Tembi said. "I think."

Moto was also a child of Adhama. He and Tembi had grown up on the same continent, in the same city. Despite the short distance between their two childhood neighborhoods, Tembi had gone halfway across the galaxy before she met him. He was several years older than she was, and worked as Domino's personal assistant. He was intelligent and kind and *gorgeous!* and he had been a friend to Tembi when she had needed one the most. He hadn't checked in for a few days, but that was normal for him. His job was...complicated.

"So Moto's involved in this conspiracy, too." Matindi moved to sit upon her old stone desk. "Kalais?"

Tembi snorted, and Matthew shook his head. "Not Kalais," he said. "He's too enthusiastic about doing whatever he can to help the Sabenta. But there are others..." He looked at Tembi, waiting.

"I'll leave," she assured him, and started towards the door.

"Large gods, don't tell me you've organized *cells!*" shouted Matindi.

As Tembi let herself out, Matthew began to rattle off a list of names. The moment she stepped over the threshold, the sound of his voice vanished: the Deep might not understand politics but it certainly understood secrets. When Tembi and Matthew had first begun planning their quiet internal rebellion, they had met on asteroids, or in small diners on the corner of nowhere. As time went on, the Deep grasped their desire for privacy, and now it spun their conversations away from outside observers.

She padded down the corridor, thinking. She was never sure how many Witches were involved in this...this...whatever it was. Matindi was wrong. It wasn't a rebellion, and it wasn't a conspiracy. If she had to give it a label, it was a...a reckoning of conscience in which a small number of Witches had come to believe that the prevailing philosophy of Lancaster was both outdated and amoral.

As members of a neutral trade organization, Witches could go anywhere, at any time. Their mobility kept the galaxy's principal supply chains humming along, as regular as orbit. It also meant that Witches turned a blind eye to war. In theory, this was...*appropriate.* It was appropriate for Lancaster to stay out of all forms of conflict. It was stated policy that the Deep would not be used for any purposes related to war, not for moving weapons or soldiers, or contraband across blockades. In theory, this helped keep war to a minimum, as what kind of fool wanted to strap themselves into pokey ships with FTL drives? Might as well be cavemen.

(In Tembi's opinion, if you wanted to go to war through hyperspace and brave the dangers of skipping across reality without reliable galax-caching processes, then you were truly committed to your cause.)

Except this war was different. Everyone at Lancaster knew how the Blackwing War had begun, even if the timeline of tiny slights that had snowballed into war had become incomprehensible for anyone but politicians and the inevitable pundits. It had begun the way wars always do, with petty grievances coming together in the form of murder. As Tembi had heard it, the catalyst was when a small local federation of terraformed planets with bioformed populations tried to negotiate for a better trade deal. The people who had money wished to keep it. Then, there came several generations of villains and heroes and would-be profiteers, and after that came war.

It had happened a thousand times before. It would happen a thousand times again. Except this time, the edges of the war had blurred. Local conflict became regional, with neighboring solar systems taking sides. Like a virus, this particular war kept *spreading!* infecting humans across the galaxy with various versions of a righteous cause. For many—for most—that cause was to define what it meant to be human.

Modified humans didn't fit into Earth's definition of "human." Earth first. Earth pure. No genes altered to improve survival on other planets (and let's all ignore how this allowed Earth purists to upgrade their babies for health and beauty and athleticism and intellect because "Earth pure" could be better phrased as "Earth perfect," and thus there was no need to ban all genetic tinkering completely because who wanted to raise an ugly baby?) That didn't mean that all modded humans were in danger. There were too many of them to eradicate completely, not without the galaxy falling apart. The Sagittarius Armed Forces simply wanted modded humans to relearn their place in the natural order. If Tembi kept her ears covered and Kalais didn't blink too hard at the wrong time? They could pass in Earth-normal society when necessary, and then go back to cavort like the freaks they were on their home planets. Modded humans like Tembi and Kalais weren't at risk, not unless they chose to fight back.

But people like Matindi...

The Blackwings had places to put people like Matindi.

Matindi's final fight with Domino had begun months before the day the ewer was shattered, when Matindi insisted that Lancaster must acknowledge how the Deep was done being a passive onlooker! A hundred small signs suggested that the Deep wanted to intervene on the side of the Sabenta, the loose confederation of modified humans who stood against the formal military of the Sagittarius Armed Forces. The Blackwings were purging entire civilizations, she said, and the Deep kept giving them signs that this shouldn't be allowed.

Domino had said no, no, never, and no. Not when Lancaster's independence kept the galaxy moving. They would help dispose of bombs and other threats in locations of shipping and commerce, and move Sabenta refugees out of the path of the thresher's blade, but that was all! Anything more would yank Lancaster straight into trouble, and the good they did for the galaxy as a whole would be lost within the crash of bloody war.

Matindi had said that the galaxy as a whole was about to be lost to the war, and they had the power to stop it. Why stand idly by when Lancaster could push for peace instead?

No, said Domino, and that is *final*.

It hadn't been final, not at all, but their relationship had gone downhill from there, and it had been pretty far down the slope to begin with, and on fire besides.

Later, after Matindi had gone into retirement, Tembi and Matthew had long conversations about morality, ethics, and philosophy in out-of-the-way diners. Others had joined in, small salons popping up in unlikely locations throughout the galaxy. Now, their rebellion that wasn't a rebellion was trucking along, with Witches trying to unknot the messy tangle of policy, protocol, and emotion that was Lancaster. They felt the Deep needed to be protected, and that its abilities should be used in the service of promoting peace instead of commerce. If this was to happen, they would need to change the belief that Lancaster's status as an independent entity was paramount to all else. It wouldn't be easy. It *wasn't* easy, but it wasn't imposs—

"—on your mind?"

Tembi jumped straight up, her bare feet smacking down on the marble floor as she landed. Beside her was a stunningly lovely woman with long black hair and plain blue robes, her head tilted to show the blue waves painted on her face.

"Bayle!" Tembi shook herself. "Sorry. Lost in thought."

"Oh, what *now?*" Bayle sighed.

"I don't know where to start." Tembi glanced around. The cavernous hallway was empty: most Witches didn't bother walking. Her best friend was an exception. Bayle taught some of Lancaster's introductory classes for junior Witches, and she wandered the halls during her breaks. "Where were you headed?"

"Home. I'm done teaching for the day." Bayle stretched, standing as tall as she could on her toes. She dropped her arms so they slapped against her sides. "What's happened?"

"Everything," Tembi said. "Let's go somewhere to talk."

Bayle nodded and jumped them, a quick trip which took them straight to the roof of the spiral nautilus. A short jump, yes, but Tembi couldn't help but wince. The Deep never felt the same to her when another Witch led the way. She had grown up with Matindi, so Matindi's jumps never set her teeth on edge, but Bayle's felt like she was plunging them both into cool, clear water. Which was more than fair, she supposed, as Bayle claimed that Tembi's jumps were like flying through a polite sandstorm.

The trip was worth it, though. The view was amazing.

The planet of Found was perfect. Simply perfect in every possible way. Twenty-five hundred years ago, the Witches had gone to the newly formed Earth Assembly and told them that they wanted to build their headquarters on Earth. And why not? Hadn't the Deep changed everything? Made galactic expansion a reality? Didn't the Witches who made it all possible deserve a prime location on Earth?

The Earth Assembly had laughed. No, they told the Witches. No. Earth is already bursting at the seams. If you are truly the masters of the galaxy, go and find a planet of your own.

So that was exactly what the Witches did.

They asked the Deep to find them a habitable planet. Not just any planet, no. Their planet needed to be the best and the brightest, where every single day felt like late spring, where the inclement weather of Earth almost never occurred, where the local flora never stopped blooming and any fauna were cute, small, friendly, non-toxic, and begged for belly rubs.

Oh! And beaches along the shorelines. Waterfalls, too, if that wasn't asking too much.

The Witches waited. Within the space of a day, the Deep said, ::FOUND::

Lancaster built the nautilus first, the living quarters for the Witches next. Then, around the periphery, a high wall to keep the rest of humanity's immigrants to Found away from Lancaster's golden grounds. Over the centuries, the campus sprung up within the walls, with Lancaster's own buildings bridged by thick lawns, dotted with wide lakes, and surrounded by a thick forest of evergreens. Last, beyond the walls and stretching for kilometers in all directions, was the city of Hub, prosperous from its proximity to the heart of the galaxy's transportation infrastructure.

"Look," Bayle said, pointing. Down in the center of the village square, Matindi's house was flickering in and out of existence as the other Witches argued. Then, the little house snapped into place as solidly as if it had been built there.

Tembi snorted. "Don't mess with Matindi."

"What happens if the old Witches all come together and ask the Deep as a group?"

"I don't know," Tembi said, as she sat. As soon as her butt hit the roof, her entire body reminded her that she was exhausted, and she gratefully flopped backwards to bask in the sun. "Do you think that'll ever happen?"

"No," Bayle said, as she tucked her long blue robes around her legs and sat beside Tembi. She stretched out her bare feet, twisting them in a swimming motion. Bayle's ankles were thicker than Earth-normal, and there was webbing between her fingers and toes. She kept her hands hidden and wore a pair of custom-made boots when she wanted to pass, but both she and Tembi agreed that footwear of any ilk was wholly the creation of greater demons and they avoided it whenever possible. "What's happened? The Deep keeps sending me an image of a broken egg."

"Oh, *gods,* how did I forget about the *moon?*" Tembi groaned. She checked the timer on the sleeve of her uniform: all of her jaunting about the galaxy had taken place in the space of three hours. *Give or take an hour for time travel,* she reminded herself.

Bayle poked her with a remarkably sturdy toe.

Tembi sighed and started from the beginning with the bomb, followed by the meeting with Kalais at the broken moon. At the right point in the story, Bayle hissed like a roach in an airlock: "He *didn't.*"

"He *did.*"

"I'll kill him," Bayle vowed, and then nodded towards the

distant village square where the dotting of Witches kept trying to convince the Deep to remove the cottage. "What about Matindi?"

"I told her about the moon, and she decided she was coming out of retirement again," Tembi replied. "Were you here the last time she did this?"

"You mean when she showed up with you? How old do you think I am?" Bayle nudged Tembi towards the edge of the roof with her bare foot as Tembi laughed.

Bayle might be older, but Tembi had been at Lancaster longer. The last time Matindi had come out of retirement, she had arrived at Lancaster with Tembi in tow. Tembi had been eleven, her face painted by the Deep with golden silhouettes of birds in flight. Their arrival had thrown Lancaster into chaos, as Lancaster had believed the Deep always chose adults to become new Witches. To think that this…this *child!*…had caught the attention of the Deep? Well! Obviously a mistake had been made somewhere along the way, and obviously Matindi was to blame. Or so went the gossip.

"Matthew's telling her now, about the…" Tembi let herself trail off as she gestured vaguely, hinting at insurrection, polarization, and everything else.

"Really?" Bayle draped her feet over Tembi's, and laid beside her on the roof. "Is that why you were walking around like you were in a stupor?"

"I'm just tired." Her eyes were shut tight, and the sun on her face felt good, a light pressure that bypassed her skin and soothed her like a warm blanket. It was still early in the day here on Found. There was a nap waiting for her, and maybe an oversized lunch—

The unmistakable sound and sensation of displaced air caused her to flinch. She was in no mood to have a conversation with anyone other than Bayle, and if one of those old Witches in the village thought she'd interfere with Matindi on their behalf, they had another thing coming. She was about to jump herself to her own bed when Bayle kicked her in the shin.

Tembi opened her eyes to see a rainbow.

"Scheisse!" she swore, unable to stop herself.

"No argument," replied Kalais. The sun was behind him, turning him into a streak of light dotted in color. He was dressed in the white and gold of Lancaster's formal robes, a multicolored array of badges and honorariums running in a vertical line from his left shoulder to the hem of the skirt. He sounded resigned and more than a little sorry as he added, "I've come to fetch you."

"No," Tembi replied. "I already reported to Matindi and Matthew. They'll brief the others." She glanced over the edge of the roof to where a tiny speck of green in white robes had appeared. The buildings nearest to the town square vanished, water and worse spraying up from broken utility lines until Lancaster's maintenance scripts shut them down. "I think it's going well."

Kalais shook his head at the chaos below. "They need you on Earth," he said. "Domino's requested your presence."

"Then let's go," Bayle said, as she stood and dusted herself off.

"Bayle, you're not invited—"

"Would you rather I make myself useful by heading into town and whoring myself out on a corner?" she snapped at him, blue eyes flashing.

Kalais looked away, beaten.

As Bayle moved, her robes changed from a casual sky blue to a cascading riot of the many colors of seafoam, pale blues and greens shading down to a deep ultramarine, the skirts dividing over themselves to fall in multiple layers, becoming formal robes which would have been at home on a princess. No Deep magic at work here, no, merely the usual blend of technology and absurd amounts of money which allowed Bayle to move from classroom to stateroom without pause. She looked at her bare feet and sighed; the Deep took over and a pair of black leather boots appeared.

For a brief blissful moment, Tembi wondered if she could simply let Bayle go in her stead. Bayle was a diplomat's daughter and had grown up speaking the language of power. Her home planet of Atlantis had quite recently proved to hold large quantities of a rare unpronounceable mineral essential to communication through the channels, which had elevated its status from a backwater nowhere to one of the wealthiest planets in the galaxy. Bayle had, nearly overnight, gone from fairly comfortable landed gentry to ultra-rich landed gentry, and people treated her accordingly. Tembi's early childhood had been spent picking pockets and rolling marks, and no matter how much time she spent at Lancaster, she knew she'd always have an accent. But she would never ask Bayle to fight her battles for her.

Bayle kicked Tembi again. As Tembi rose to her feet, she asked the Deep for help. Her dress robes smoothed themselves out, and the stains she had collected from rolling about on the roof disappeared.

Bayle pointed at Tembi's bare feet.

"No," Tembi told her. "They want me, they get me."

Bayle and Kalais glanced at each other, a quick communication which drove a dagger of pure fury into Tembi's stomach. She held out her hands, and a bright blue scarf appeared. She pulled off the white one and tied the new one up and over her hair in a practiced move designed to show off her ears, as she silently asked the Deep to swap out her tiny gold earrings for three sets of bright blue opals.

"Right, then," Kalais said, and opened their way through the Deep.

Tembi caught one last glimpse of the town square, its buildings newly returned but in disarray—*Small gods, is that store upside-down?*—and then they were away.

Chapter Five

Kalais opened the way, which meant the trip along the Rails was fast as the wind and devoid of any pleasantries. There was enough time for Bayle and Tembi to exchange a few ideas about the best spots to grab a quick lunch on Earth, and then they stepped out of the Deep in front of a set of doors crafted from rich, royal mahogany, the wood so old that it was mainly held together by 'bots, polish, and tradition.

"Ready?" he asked, but Bayle pushed ahead of him, Tembi following at her heels.

Too strange, watching Bayle shed her skin and become an entirely different person. The two of them had met during their Witches' classes, with Bayle nearly seven years her senior. Bayle had taken her on as more of a mascot than a friend, but Tembi knew the Deep, and she had shown Bayle how the Deep was more than a tool. Over time, that persistent awkward feeling of being less than Bayle, of her company being tolerated instead of enjoyed, had fallen away…except during moments like this, where Bayle was no longer her best friend but became more, when she was not merely Bayle but was also Lady Oliver, heir to the extraordinary Oliver fortune, future owner of an entire continent on the planet of Atlantis, and someone who dabbled in political gamesmanship for personal enjoyment.

Into the wolves' den, then, with Lady Oliver as the poisoned tip of the spear.

The chamber was enormous, lined in old woods and metals, the marble floor laid in patterns like the overlapping scales of a fish. At the front of the room, the Assembly was waiting. Not all of them. Officially, the Earth Assembly was formed from a delegate from each inhabited planet, and each of them had an equal say. But it was well-known that the true power sat in the hands of this very small Council comprised of the delegate from Earth, the delegate from Found, and another dozen from the wealthiest planets in the galaxy. These notables were sitting in the first row of the auditorium, their very presence a testament to the seriousness of the matter.

Behind them, trying to blend into the background, was another cluster of people, as no one of wealth traveled without an entourage. A dozen Witches waited with the secretaries and the security, personal chaperones to move these important Council members across the galaxy at their whim. They were dressed in Lancaster's formal uniforms to advertise how they had Witches at their command.

Tembi counted once...twice...yes, only a dozen Witches waited with the servants. Lancaster's representative opened her own way through the Deep, which meant one Council member did without entirely. Now, who would choose to go without the prestige of having a personal Witch standing ready to serve?

"Hi, Daddy," Bayle said, quite loudly.

"Hello, Minnow," Lord Oliver of Atlantis replied, also loudly.

Ah. That answered that.

Tembi was introduced, and asked to do a small presentation on the broken moon. Images were provided; a grammalight display of the moon hung in the air, noteworthy details edged in blue light. She recognized Kalais' work, as he had an artist's eye. *What a waste of talent,* she thought, as the moon spun above her.

She spoke of the Deep, and how it had brought her to the Stross cluster without being asked. This meant the incident was of some great importance to the Deep, yes? If she and Kalais were both called to duty, it had something to do with the war, yes? She did not mention time travel, as there was no need to mention time travel, and kept her eyes fastened straight ahead, her chin and ears high. When she was finished, she stood, fixed in place, waiting.

The Council's members had questions. Not many of them were about the moon, or the Deep. Mostly these were versions of "Why did you not report directly to Lancaster?" and "What are you hiding?" Tembi answered those questions as best she could. It was easier to stare into the middle distance than to focus on any of the people in the room. She even kept her distance from Bayle's father, who had given her the opals sparkling in her ears for last year's Solstice gift.

And Lancaster's own representative? For the moment, Tembi pretended that the woman in white with a hundred different colors braided into her hair didn't exist at all.

The interrogation ended. Tembi wasn't dismissed as much as she was summarily ignored, the conversation passing up and around her as if it were water and the Council controlled the tides. There was a chair over to the side of the podium; she sat, her bare feet sticking out from beneath her robes, her hands carefully knitted together to muffle any accidental sound.

Bayle and Kalais continued to stand. Now the questions were aimed at them, slowly, then building. Within a matter of minutes, the matter of the broken moon had disappeared altogether, with questions about the war taking its place.

"Could this be the Sabenta?" That, from Earth's own delegate, a gnarled lump of ego and venom. Tembi wasn't completely sure that Dame Idowu was a Blackwing sympathizer, but her loathing for modded humans was always plain. Dame Idowu's eyes drifted of their own accord down to Bayle's boots, and then bounced back up to focus on the girl's face.

"We don't know who is responsible," Kalais said, for at least the third time in as many minutes, and then the Council was off, issuing cold statements about why specific people shouldn't be allowed to have opinions.

Safely tucked away behind Bayle's robes, Tembi was able to watch the Council. Of the fourteen members in attendance, ten were genetically Earth-normal. The one who stood out was the representative from Chollhe, who was an utterly hairless person with pale blue skin, while the remaining three could pass by putting in a little extra effort. Bayle's father wore shiny shoes and cunningly crafted gloves, and Domino covered her head with a scarf to hide her ears—

Don't look at her! Tembi reminded herself, her eyes darting away from the Witch.

How old was Domino? Ageless, of course. The Deep had frozen her in time centuries before Tembi was born. She had the unlined face of an Adhamantian woman a few years older than Tembi, and carried herself with an unnatural eternal grace. Domino dressed in white and layered over this the colors of the Deep, as many colors as she could wear against her dark skin or thread into her long white hair, with gold and silver glinting in the edges between these.

She was beautiful. She was intimidating. She was as irritating as a million major hells.

Focus, Tembi.

Tembi sat, pretending to be furniture as she allowed herself to listen to conversations far above her clearance level. Plans were being made. Various covert actions would be taken: nobody admitted to having a spy ring of their very own, but their language danced around the fact that everybody did, and everybody else knew that they did, and they were all planning to release their spies to investigate what had happened to the moon. After that, representatives from the Sagittarius Armed Forces and the Sabenta would be called into a meeting. How the Sabenta could sit across a table and participate in a polite series of lies with the same people who were killing them, Tembi didn't know. Modded or not, all politicians possessed superhuman skills of their own, able to sit and talk with a clarity of detail that could be spun into arguments, and then woven into action.

How? Tembi didn't *know!*

"Are we sure a device caused this?" The discussion had finally returned to the matter of the broken moon. Even if she hadn't known Ambassador Marlowe, the set of his shoulders and the shine of his armor would have told Tembi that the speaker was from Camelot. Prickly bunch, those Arthurians. Tended to catch more than their fair share of bombs, which is why Tembi was passingly familiar with the ductwork in the central palace on the isle of Avalon. Nobody liked Arthurians, not even other

Arthurians: there were hundreds of civilizations based on Old Earth mythologies scattered throughout the galaxy, but Arthurians were the only ones who fell into planet-wide civil war every few decades. They had become a joke amongst other civilizations whose societies were formed from a common canon, but Camelot's vast wealth assured them a permanent spot on the small Council.

"What else could cause this?" Lord Oliver asked the question gently, as if asking a child to explain why the plate was suddenly empty of pastries.

Dame Idowu looked towards Kalais and Bayle, lingering on Tembi as she tried to stay hidden behind them. "What, indeed."

Lord Oliver began to reply—from his tone, it would be a cutting one—but as he did, the air in the chamber blew apart as the Deep opened. A short Witch appeared, accompanying a man in a bomb disposal uniform that was in worse shape than Tembi's own. He glanced around at the ornate Earth Assembly chambers, not a hint of emotion showing on his face as he stomped silvery moon dust from his boots onto the mosaic floor.

Tembi grinned. It would take more than an appearance in front of the most powerful people in the galaxy to shake Cooper. He was a rough twenty years older than she was, and wore every year on his face. He came from a modded civilization of artisans who had invested in eyesight and dexterity, and the two extra joints on each finger allowed him to manipulate tricky devices. If he couldn't defuse a bomb via manual labor, he was also an authentic tekker with a lift rating of fifty kilos. Cooper would admit he wasn't the strongest telekinetic in the galaxy, but he had better control over his abilities than the powerhouses who could lift a hundred kilos or more. Nerves of hyperdense plass, Cooper.

He saw Tembi and returned her grin. "Hey, kid," he said.

"And this is?"

"Hmm?" Cooper noticed Dame Idowu. "Manno Cooper. You told me to go out to the moon." Dame Idowu straightened in her chair, certainly on the verge of telling Cooper that she had done no such thing, but Cooper walked past her, right up to the front of the room where the grammalight display of the broken moon still rotated slowly in midair. He tapped on his personal wrist databand and the grammalight's image updated, resolving into large pieces of machinery. "Two devices," he said, the grammalight indicating the framework of a machine. Tembi recognized it from the fragments the Deep had pieced together on the moon. "The big one split the moon. Still don't know what that one is. Want to get back to it. Then they used a common compression bomb to blow up the first device."

"What else?" The representative from Old Georgia was quite sharp for a politician. When Cooper replied that there was nothing else at this very moment, as he needed more than two hours to work, the representative asked him a number of pointed questions about background radiation, evidence of recent FTL ship propulsion, and other possible considerations. Cooper answered grudgingly, his tone suggesting that he wanted nothing more than to be out of that room and back on the moon.

"Cooper," Dame Idowu said, pulling the questioning back under her control, "who sent you to the site?"

"To the moon?" He looked surprised. "Lancaster. I work for them."

"Do you?" Dame Idowu leaned forward. "Did they tell you that this was caused by a new weapon?"

Before Cooper could reply, a light cough came from Lancaster's representative to the Earth Assembly. It was a sound too soft to dominate the chamber but still loud enough to cause Dame Idowu to frown. Then: "Idowu, my dear friend, do you have something to say?"

Domino's voice was like the rest of her—unmistakably lovely, deceptively gentle, poison through and through. She was smiling at Idowu, patiently waiting.

If Domino was subtle as poison, Idowu was an old iron cudgel. "This man works for you, and your...*Witches*..." she spat, "...watched the disaster as it happened. I don't believe in coincidence."

"Nor do we, your Grace, but we serve the Deep." Domino was smiling as she spun her words into a web. "This event is of interest to us, and so we shall investigate."

"Not alone." This from another Council member, one Tembi recognized but had not met. They wore plain black robes and had their hair covered; they appeared to be Earth-normal, and could be from anywhere. "There needs to be an oversight process. If the Deep caused this—"

"My friends, please," Domino said, spreading her hands. "The Deep wants us to be aware of the event, but cause it? No. You know as well as I that the Deep does not engage in such actions."

"Anymore," the representative from Old Georgia said, and then added, "You mean, the Deep doesn't tear planets apart *anymore.*"

"True." Domino nodded, smiling sadly. "There were accidents, yes. Many thousands of years ago, when the Deep was new and none of us could truly speak to it. But have we at Lancaster ever failed you? Or your grandparents? Or your ancestors all the way back to your planets' founding?" She stood, a white cloud caressed in color, and moved to the front of the room. "You cannot put this on the Deep. Not when our history is long and storied, and unreservedly clean of events such as the destruction of moons. Is not it more likely—is not it wholly probable?—that what happened is precisely what Kalais and Tembi have said?

"Friends," Domino said, coming to rest in front of the three young Witches, shielding them from the rest of the Council. "There is no conspiracy here. The galaxy is at war. The Deep took two of its Witches to watch the workings of a new weapon. That is all."

A pause. Then: "Why?" Dame Idowu asked.

"I promise I shall have an answer for you, the next time we meet." Tembi could no longer see Domino's face, but there was a smile in her voice. "Investigate the matter of the moon, please.

Learn whether this was caused by the Blackwings or by the Sabenta. Or, perhaps, this is a third party announcing their arrival on the battlefield. But whatever you find, it will not be tied to Lancaster."

Domino bowed and moved towards the rear doors of the chamber, as if she meant to leave and give the others more room to fight. The discussion swelled again, returning to the structured reason of using conventional weapons to split a moon apart. Tembi's ears twitched as she followed Dame Idowu's muttered insistence that the Sabenta were sure to be at fault, and—

Tembi's eyes locked with Domino's own.

Scheisse!

She hauled her gaze away.

Too late.

"Tembi."

The whispering voice was in her head, almost imagined, with none of the mass and heft that accompanied the presence of the Deep. Compared to the wild reality that was the Deep, telepathy entered your mind as barely a breeze, a voice that might as well be your own watered-down conscience for all the good it did you.

Telekinetics? Pyrokinetics? Toss a rock and hit a dozen of those, although Tembi had wondered if some of those who had unreliable, untestable abilities weren't themselves gifted but had merely been in proximity to the Deep when it was in the mood to goof around. Telepaths, though? Despite visiting more planets and meeting more people than she could count, Tembi had met only one person who could be considered a true telepath. And that person just *had* to be Domino, didn't it?

"Tembi," the voice whispered again.

Tembi wanted to shut her eyes and run. Telepathy was far from an exact science, but eye contact helped initiate the connection. Sadly, once established, it was tricky to break. Even plunging straight into the Deep couldn't shake off an invasion from another mind...at least, not when that other mind belonged to a fellow Witch. Motion and other physical distractions could help break one mind away from the other. Tembi had found that singing worked better than anything else. Not that singing was an option as she sat here, on display, as motionless as rock.

Maybe she just needed more experience with telepaths.

"Domino?" Tembi replied, as if she had realized too late that the other woman was speaking to her. She straightened and looked towards Lancaster's delegate to the Earth Assembly. *"Is that you?"*

Was Domino fooled? Who knew? Domino stood, her posture a mirror of Tembi's own, with her chin and ears high. They were members of a found sisterhood, Domino had told her more than once. Perhaps she had meant it as a play on words—two women from the same homeworld called to the Deep's service on Found—or perhaps she was trying to be sincere. Tembi could never tell. Not with Domino.

Tembi shoved those emotions down, down, and concentrated on Domino's physical presence instead. Telepaths couldn't read whole minds, not the secret thoughts which crawled like worms beneath the soil. They could only pluck at the low-hanging fruits. She embraced how perfect Domino looked, how she was the only member of the Council with a sense of poise while the others fought and bickered like children—

"Come." The whispered voice sounded almost satisfied; Tembi nearly allowed herself to relax before Domino left the room in a swirl of white and color.

Leave the meeting? Tembi thought to herself. *Is that allowed?*

"With me? Yes. Come along, Tembi."

She went. As she left, she shot a pleading glance at Bayle and Cooper. Bayle raised an eyebrow, while Cooper chuckled.

Domino led the way, silently, gliding across the marbled floors on bare feet. No shoes for the daughters of Adhama, no, not when the stress of everyday life served them better than leather. She wore no headscarf, but an opalescent shawl fluttered in the breeze. They left the meeting chamber, and then the building, walking all the way. They passed some people who nodded to Domino, and several who stepped aside and bowed at the waist to her. A niggling idea tried to fight its way into Tembi's consciousness, where Domino was intentionally showing off her power—

Focus, Tembi.

The first time she had met Domino, Tembi had been awestruck. Domino was everything that Tembi wished she could be: she put lie to the stereotypes that Adhamantians were driven by anger. She was always calm, always present, a governing force at Lancaster's helm. That awe had quickly faded; Domino had shown Tembi that she held not a single iota of kindness in her soul, and while Tembi could overlook a lot, she couldn't overlook that. Since then, Domino seemed intent on winning Tembi over again. A head full of complimentary thoughts about Domino was usually the surest way for Tembi to escape.

Domino is so beautiful and graceful and—

Tembi always felt these encounters would go easier on the both of them if these thoughts weren't also true.

The foundation of Domino's robes was always white. Over this, she layered colors, bold and iridescent scarves fluttering in the breeze. Today, she wore ribbons along with the scarves. On anyone else, these would be knotted up before they were finished dressing, but Domino? Well, telekinetics weren't always telepaths, but telepaths were always telekinetics. She could waste a little energy keeping herself untangled.

"I serve Lancaster in all things," Domino finally said, after they had been walking for several minutes. A private café, small but dignified, and groaning in crystal and candles, was waiting for them at the bottom of a spiraling staircase.

"I know," Tembi replied, as she slowed herself to take the steps one at a time. "Matindi says you always put Lancaster first."

"I do." Domino nodded. The sealed doors of the restaurant slid open for the Witches. "The galaxy depends on us. We keep our organization healthy and strong, thus we serve the galaxy. It is a mighty obligation."

This last statement had been timed perfectly, allowing the

words to run through Tembi's head while the maître d' greeted and seated them. The table was spread in silver, with live flowers drooping artfully in the centerpiece. A glass of something sparkling was waiting for Domino, and Tembi ordered the same.

As the waiter left, Domino said, "Matindi has returned."

"Yes."

"She and I have not always shared the same outlook for Lancaster."

Tembi wasn't sure if Domino was still in her head, but as the other Witch didn't burst into outraged flames at what Tembi chose to keep to herself, it was likely their telepathic link had faded. When Tembi trusted herself to speak, she said, "I've noticed."

"I'm sure she's expressed her position to you. Today, you've seen mine in action. Dame Idowu would gladly do without Lancaster. Most of those on the Council would do the same. So, too, with the whole of the Earth Assembly. We are unwanted."

Tembi nodded.

"What they want is the Deep, but what they get is us." Domino said. Her eyes were dark brown, neatly matching the color of her skin. She had tinted the lids and her lips in matching hues of light blue, the same color of blue in the Witch's mark painted in prisms across her face. The room had no windows, leaving the candlelight to spark against the blue and cause it to glow. "Witches are a barrier to their goals. They would tear apart reality if they thought it would allow them to access the Deep—they've tried! Oh, Tembi, how they've tried. They've set their scientists to work. Three thousand years, they've tried, but the Deep lets only us in.

"Their reliance on us is the only protection we have against them. Do you understand?" Domino's hands were folded, her posture straight, but her long ears tipped forward to shout *attention! sincerity!* at Tembi. "It is the weapon we have to protect the Deep against them."

It was a good, solid argument, and if Tembi hadn't heard countless versions by eavesdropping on Matindi's fights with

Domino, it might have actually made an impact. As it was, Tembi merely nodded again, and tilted her own ears to signify agreement. Domino wasn't wrong, after all. The problem was that Domino assumed what was best for Lancaster was also best for the Deep.

"You agree?" Domino seemed surprised.

"Yes," replied Tembi. "I've always agreed with both you and Matindi."

Tembi's drink arrived, and the conversation paused for pleasantries and orders. When the waiter had left again, Domino said, "Tembi? Let me be honest."

Here it comes, Tembi thought. She tested her drink. Cider? No, something from berries, fermented and changed to white.

"I cannot manage the Council and a rebellion from within Lancaster itself."

"Rebellion?" Domino gave a very slight nod, her eyes fixed on Tembi's own, and Tembi was suddenly sure that Domino was still lurking in her head. She would find nothing she could use: Tembi had more than a decade's practice hiding her true emotions from the Deep, and misdirecting a human telepath was surely nothing compared to that! So Tembi kept her mind fixed on the truth of the situation—there was no rebellion, there were merely policy discussions over drinks, where friends came together and talked about what served as best practices at Lancaster. Much like this very conversation, as a matter of fact.

Domino rocked back in her chair, shaking her head slightly. "You're very good," she said in her implacable way.

"No," Tembi said. "I just know the truth."

"Oh, I wish I was as sure of that as you are," sighed Domino. "But the very nature of rebellion makes it difficult to understand."

"I'll pretend you didn't just insult my intelligence," Tembi said.

Domino smiled and gave Tembi a small nod. "I forget you are no longer a child."

"I wasn't allowed to be a child," replied Tembi. "Not since I was brought to Lancaster."

"That, at least, is pure truth." Their food arrived, along with someone to taste it. Domino waved them off. The perils of dining near the Earth Assembly meant there was surely some form of poison somewhere in the food, or perhaps the drink, or even the air itself. The trick was to know your own defenses were superior to the poison. Having someone taste the food was a sign of weakness.

(Tembi wouldn't have minded a taster. On Earth, she was a nobody of a Witch, and while nobody would try to poison her specifically, what about while she was in Domino's company? However, Domino knew poison better than anyone, and if she thought the Deep was able to pick out poison molecules from their food? Tembi could live with that.)

(She hoped.)

The topic of conversation moved from internal organizational rebellion to the war itself, mostly recent action reports about the bombs she had disarmed with the help of the Deep. As with all her meetings with Domino, Tembi knew she was being tested. She'd resent it—she did resent it!—but Domino was gently charismatic, and even though they had come from opposite sides of the same planet, it was always good to talk to someone else from Adhama. Whenever she spoke to someone who didn't use their ears as part of their body language, it felt as if a layer of depth was removed. *Adhamantians live in a galaxy full of small talk,* she thought, and Domino couldn't help but smile at that.

When Tembi explained how she had disarmed the bomb on the shipping station that morning, Domino's ears went straight up. "You did what?!"

Tembi steeled herself against the pain, and then held up the butter knife so Domino could watch her drag her fingertip through the dense ceramic.

"Small gods," Domino exhaled, as she reached out to take the knife from Tembi. She inspected it as if it might crumble. "I've never heard of a Witch doing anything like this!"

"I'm not the first." The Deep had made that clear, layering an image of Tembi over another human form, followed by another, and then another. She was the fourth, but she didn't recognize any of those other Witches it had shown her; she wondered if they were dead, and if so, how. "It hurts. It hurts a *lot*. I only do it when we have no other choice."

"And yet you showed me?"

"It'll be a few days before I fully recover." Tembi stared at her own hands. "This is the best time to show off.

"I don't know if every Witch can do this," she slowly began, groping her way towards an explanation she hadn't yet fully explored. "I think it's easier for me since I'm from Adhama, and working with bombs is all stress." She rubbed her fingertips together, and the sound of grating stone caused some of the other patrons to glance at their table in thinly masked disgust. "Since the nerve endings in my skin are already numb, there's not much pain. Starts to burn once it hits muscle, though.

"You could do it," Tembi added. Domino's skin was as smooth as polished marble, and probably twice as tough.

Lancaster's Assembly member stared at the butter knife in her hand, turning it over and over. "Perhaps later," she said with a shy smile, and set the knife back in its cradle. "There is still so much about the Deep we don't know. What a miracle it is."

"I don't like how we treat it," Tembi said. She tipped her chin up and met Domino's eyes, trying to punch as much meaning as she could into whatever telepathic link still existed. "We use it—we're *cruel* to it, and Lancaster needs to change."

Domino smiled. "Tembi, believe it or not, I agree."

Tembi blinked. "Really?"

"Aye," Domino said, still smiling. "One problem with living forever is that we forget how to see the world through another's eyes. I've fought with Matindi so long that it has become our routine. But when Matindi brought you to Lancaster, you were proof that the Deep was changing. I've been trying to change, too, ever since."

Tembi weighed this. "Matthew has said something like that.

How it's easy to get stuck in thinking that things are the way they're supposed to be, and it's hard to change."

"Matthew and I have discussed the situation." Domino reached out to touch the flowers in the centerpiece. They were going blowsy: any decent restaurant could invest in a vase full of live flowers permanently preserved at the peak of freshness; only the wealthiest ones could afford to bring in new bouquets. "We are...at odds. I think we need new insight to understand what it is we need to do to bring Lancaster into alignment with what the Deep wants."

Tembi watched Domino, wondering. Then, she nodded. "Too good to be true," she said, "but if you mean it...?"

"I do." Domino bowed her head. "I can't help but think that death serves a purpose, to clean out the old and make room for the new. We immortals? We might believe we know all from experience and time, but perhaps we refuse to see how we've just become clutter in the room."

Ah, there it is. It didn't happen often, but some Witches who were once immortal resumed the aging process. In whispers, Witches called it losing the Deep's favor. No one knew what caused it, but while the fallen Witch could still use the Deep to travel, they lost their status among their peers. No longer welcome at Lancaster, they took their centuries of amassed wealth to go to live out their remaining decades in anonymous luxury. Domino could go on about how death was a cleansing process, but if the Deep was changing its opinions about how Lancaster should be run, then she must have been worried about her own mortality.

(*And Matthew?* the nastiest part of Tembi hissed at rest of her. *How much of his willingness to help is self-preservation?*)

She sighed. *Focus, Tembi.*

"Have you talked to the Deep about this?" she asked Domino. "Maybe it can guide you."

"I have, but..." The other woman looked up, almost bashfully. "I was hoping, perhaps, you could help guide me, too."

Tembi, halfway through a bite of her curry, spent a few moments choking on her food. Domino waited, eyebrows arched.

"Do you need—" she began.

"No! No." Tembi waved her off. She hated when the Deep intervened in her bodily functions. A swallow of water goes down the wrong pipe, and the body knows how to manage it. A swallow of water goes down one way, disappears, and then reappears in the right place? Her body usually responded to that by hastily penciling an unplanned afternoon of vomiting into her schedule. When she had recovered, Tembi took another, cautious, drink, and said, "What do you mean?"

"It's easy enough," Domino dabbed at her lips with her napkin. "Matthew sits at my right hand. Matindi used to sit at my left. I have been without a left hand for too long. You can teach me new ways of thinking.

"Besides," she added with a conspiratorial smile. "I am left-handed."

Tembi chuckled in spite of herself. She knew she was being played. But this? This opportunity to slide into Domino's inner circle? This was an opportunity. If Domino was serious about wanting Lancaster to change, then she could work with this woman. Oh, yes, she certainly could.

"You've been doing well with bomb disposal," Domino continued. "Consistently high performances in crisis scenarios? That's what I look for in a lieutenant." She leaned forward, her eyes fixed on Tembi's, no doubt snatching up those low-hanging surface thoughts like ripe fruit. "I have another task for you."

Chapter Six

The study of dimensionals science—and never forget that *s* on *dimensionals*, as that was how you summoned an actually of pedants—was nearly as vast as the Deep itself, and about as well understood. Not for lack of trying, mind: for several centuries, efforts to distill the Deep into its component parts sucked the life out of every other discipline. An extradimensional entity that bent space to its whims? My goodness. Package *that* straight up for sale, why don't you?

They tried. Oh, how they tried! The dimensionals physicists had the Witches open paths along the Rails. They set up all manner of diagnostic equipment. A few of them fell so passionately in love with the Deep that it accepted them as Witches: at first, they thrilled at their access to forces beyond human comprehension; later, they got fed up at the lack of answers. Then they usually took up word puzzles.

Not that there weren't benefits of trying. Studying the Deep led to other discoveries. Faster-than-light travel was the hallmark invention of dimensionals scientists, followed closely by the ubiquitous entertainment and communications channels which moved data from planet to planet near instantaneously. And many said, without evidence, that it was surely not coincidence how the first quantifiable psionic abilities emerged during this early period of discovery, with the telekinetics running the gambling tables, the pyrokinetics burning everything down, and the rare telepath stoned to death in the street.

As for the Deep? Well, now. The dimensionals scientists eventually gave up and declared the Deep was a complete entity wholly unto itself, not something which could be distilled or replicated.

Thus Lancaster thrived.

Chapter Seven

Tembi walked over to the edge of the roof and looked down. The city below was so distant that it seemed small—*so* small!—and yet it also soared above her as she stood atop this mighty mountain of shipping crates, one mountain among many, boxes of plass and metal wrenched from the nearby docks and bolted together to form crude housing. The Deep hadn't stacked these, oh no. These slums had been shaped by human hands alone, slammed together into ridges and valleys, vast multicolored slices baking in the sun. They formed the streets of her home city: to the north was her old neighborhood, the one where she had spent eleven years, the one where people might still recognize her if she came around…

Adhama. An arid planet that was somehow also unbearably humid, its people with skin as hard as stone.

Home.

"You grew up here?" Bayle asked, staring open-mouthed at the slums below them while doing her utter best to pretend she wasn't staring at all. She looked vaguely fishlike, out of place and gasping. "You and Moto?"

Tembi nodded. "He lived just a few neighborhoods over from me, can you believe it?"

"Why does the Deep choose so many of its Witches from your homeworld?"

"Moto thinks it's because the Deep heard someone say that you've got to have thick skin to be a Witch, and the Deep took it literally." She sighed, and added, "But who knows?"

Moto. Handsome, smiling Moto, always ready with a joke or a shoulder to cry on, whichever was most in need. He had an earnestness to him that was undeniable, an honesty that drew you to him for comfort.

It made him one of Domino's most valuable spies.

And he had gone missing.

Which was impossible. Not when he was friends with a near-omniscient being who knew where each and every one of its Witches was at any given moment, down to the very location of (at least in Tembi's case, but probably in Moto's, too) the individual molecules in their bodies.

Witches didn't go missing. They couldn't. If you couldn't get your friend on the comm, you asked the Deep to jump you to them. If the two of you were in a snit and they didn't want to be disturbed, then you told the Deep with as much emotion as you could muster that you needed to see them, and eventually the Deep would relent and open the way. If you were a Witch with seniority, you could get the Deep to bend very quickly. As Domino was among the most powerful senior Witches—if not *the* most powerful—the Deep should have dropped Moto straight into her office, probably with a cup of her favorite morning coffee in his hand.

But Domino said that the Deep couldn't tell her where Moto was, and it refused to bring her to him.

Was he still alive?

Yes. The Deep was sure of this.

Go, Tembi, Domino had told her. *Go and find him, and bring him home to Lancaster.*

To Adhama, then, and Moto's childhood neighborhood. She pointed towards the valleys cutting through the metal mountains, far below. "That's where Domino says we should start looking for Moto," she said. "Says that if he's gone to ground, he might have done so at home."

"Do you think so?"

"Large hells, no!" Tembi hopped up on the low ledge of the shipping container's makeshift rooftop. "Moto's too smart to hide somewhere where anyone would think to look for him."

Bayle climbed up beside her. "So we're here because…?"

"Domino," Tembi replied. "You think she doesn't have at least one set of eyes on us?"

Bayle shivered. "I don't like the idea that she might be hiding in our minds."

"She's not that powerful," Tembi replied, as she shut her own eyes to concentrate on the sounds of the wind moving around her. "If she was, why would she bother with spies?"

Moto's gone missing. Domino again, smiling gently, easily, offering Tembi a bribe she couldn't choose to pass up. *Find him for me? I'm sure he's well, but I do worry.*

Find her friend, and slide into Domino's own personal council, all at once? Yes. Of course.

That's how she gets you, you know. Another internal voice, and this one sounded exactly like Matindi when she went into full mothering mode. *She gives you logical options with acceptable consequences, and there's no good reason to keep your neck out of the noose.*

Tembi sighed and rubbed her temples. It'd be easier if she were a telepath herself. Then she'd have a reason for all of this constant clutter in her mind.

Focus, Tembi.

Instead, focus on Bayle, standing beside her and shifting her weight restlessly from foot to foot. Bayle had asked her something: she waited until her friend repeated herself. "So we go through the motions of looking for him here, and then move on?"

Tembi replied by leaning forward and letting herself topple from the rooftop.

She couldn't feel the wind as she fell, but she heard it, roaring in her ears as she fell five stories, ten…twenty… She turned and looked over her shoulder; Bayle was right on her heels, her own eyes shut and long hair billowing behind her, smiling with the joy of it.

They spread their arms and let the Deep catch them, the air moving around them to slow their descent. They came down to earth as gently as blown feathers, bare feet alighting upon pavement so old and cracked it was merely a memory of concrete.

"The Witches have landed," Bayle muttered quietly, as the crowds around them pulled away, pulled back, disappeared into the dark of the stores, the shelters, the alleyways, leaving the two of them alone in the middle of the street.

"And now…" Tembi took hold of Bayle's sleeve and jumped them ten streets to the east. They stepped out of the Deep in an alley.

Bayle recoiled at the smell of the trash piled around them. "Let's go pretend to look for Moto," she gasped, as she unfolded a headscarf and wrapped it around her hair. "Good?"

"Good." Tembi adjusted her own scarf, making sure her earrings were visible. Before they had jumped to Adhama, they had stacked their fingers with silver and gold rings, and hung heavy chains around their necks, their hard currency on display. It was a siren's song of wealth, sure to tug at the smartest and bravest who lived within in the shadows.

Ten streets over, the word of their fall from the heights was spreading. The rumor that Witches were in town would keep them from getting popped or rolled. No one in the slums of Adhama was a fool. Witches had money, but you couldn't take money from a Witch. Not without enraging the Deep. But if you had something she wanted, you could con her for all the coin she carried.

They had come to Adhama to be conned.

Bayle reached up to touch her face, an unthinking gesture. She stopped herself before she could blur the paint. She and Tembi had washed the Deep's own paint away and had drawn their own versions of Witches' marks. Bayle's fake mark was a spiderweb, while Tembi's was a decent resemblance of the carnivorous pink rose from Matindi's garden. They were Witches, yes, but they were not themselves. For the length of the afternoon, Bayle would call herself Eliá and Tembi would be Selene, and anybody who tried to describe the two Witches who had come to town would run into problems.

Into the streets. The Witches ignored how the people pressed close, unnaturally close, testing the lines of their bodies for a purse. Sorry, friends, no coin or credit here, just the jewelry, and no pickpocket was good enough to slip away with a ring without the Deep noticing and bouncing it back to its owner's finger. This wealth must be earned.

A mention here, there. Do you remember Moto? Yes, the local boy who left for Lancaster. Has he been through here recently? Why? Oh, no reason. He's on vacation and we want to surprise him.

Lunch time. Meats of indeterminate origin on a stick, eaten while leaning against the wall of the market square. A far cry from their earlier plans of gourmet dining on Earth, but Bayle's eyes widened in astonishment and she went back to the vendor for seconds, and another small silver ring vanished into the old man's pockets as she showered him with compliments.

More walking. More talking. The children swore they've seen Moto! Just today! Come, come, we must hurry... A neighborhood elder stopped them before the children drew them off the street, clapping his hands and driving the urchins away with shouted threats, followed by apologies to the Witches. Children, *ach!* What can you do?

More walking. The neighborhood turned to ruins. There are no more children, at least none that they can see. They had been replaced by people who seemed carved from living stone. Tembi's skin, hard as it is, is still skin: it moves along with her moods. She could still smile. She could still frown. These people were petrified by the cruelty of their very lives. Cracks along their eyelids allowed them to blink; canyons along their cheeks allowed them to eat and speak; their fingers might as well have been rock with pliable clay for knuckles.

More walking. A storm had torn a path straight through the center of the neighborhood, and no one had bothered to put it back together. Maybe they couldn't afford to do so: a one-credit nail still cost a credit. They saw children again, playing on a chunk of rusted metal with a twisty bit that nearly resembled a playground slide.

Bayle was close to crying.

Tembi jumped them another ten streets north and east, and they started again.

The process repeated itself, except now neither of them had any appetite. They bought food and gave it away. The silver rings were spent; they had gold, but by then they had realized that dropping gold into this system would be like seeding it with tiny bombs, future disasters in the forms of robbery and murder.

Tembi conjured more silver from her stash back on Lancaster, and they bought food for the pack of urchins at their heels.

(Neither of them would admit that this was for them, and not the children. They both knew that no matter how many children they fed, there'd always be more they couldn't reach... couldn't even *see!* Suffering was like cockroaches in the sense that for every person in pain you saw, there were a thousand you didn't, and most of the time it was easier to pretend you didn't notice that first one than to do anything about it. At least these children could have a good meal, and their consciences could scream a little more quietly.)

They repeated the process again.

And again.

And then it was finally sunset.

"Ready to call it?" Tembi asked, thinking, *Please, please, please don't make me be the one who turns away from my own home.*

Bayle stared at her long enough to make Tembi wonder if, perhaps, her friend was a telepath after all, and said, "Once more. To be sure."

"To be sure," Tembi echoed, her stomach sinking as she said it.

Their jump to the northeast dumped them out in the doorway of a small tavern. Wordlessly, they went inside. The tavern was old, its walls made from stone instead of metal. The building had stood for so long that every object was slightly abraded from Adhama's frequent windstorms, and the walls were curling inward from a hundred layers of peeling paint. They fell into a booth at the back corner, not looking at each other. If they did, then one of them would have to bend, and then they'd end up back in the streets again. So, it was studious concentration on anything except each other.

Tembi ordered for the two of them, paying for their meals with yet another silver ring. They sat in silence, nursing drinks that were more fruit and ice than liquid.

"It wasn't all bad," Tembi said after a long while. "Growing up here, I mean. My mom and my sisters made sure I never went hungry. I had a good home. I was loved."

Bayle nodded, stirring her drink with an old long-handled spoon, *tink-tink-tink,* metal against plass.

"Although, you know, once I got out of here, I spent a long time wondering why the Deep didn't just come down here and fix…" Tembi waved a hand in the air aimlessly. "…this."

"Probably because that's our job," Bayle replied. When she saw Tembi's face, she added, "Not you and me. Everybody. All of us. Since we're the ones who made this."

Tembi nodded.

"That's probably why the Deep doesn't like war," her friend continued. "We keep killing each other, and it could stop it, but why bother?" Bayle was still stirring, adding a little more force than necessary, tink!-tink!-tink! the drink near to sloshing over the sides. "No matter what it does, we'll just find new excuses to start the next one."

A litter of sleeping kittens appeared on the table in front of them. There was enough time for one of them to wake up and let out a tiny squall before the Deep vanished them again.

"That's going to grow up to be one weird cat," Tembi muttered.

Bayle slid out of her booth and stomped off in the direction of the washroom.

Tembi put her head in her hands. "What a day," she said to herself. The bomb and the moon and the Council and then Domino and now a missing Witch when Witches *can't* go missing, and she'd probably been awake for at least twenty hours but once space lost all meaning then time was the next to lay its head on the chopping block, and after she found Moto she'd be dosing herself with meds to get back on Lancaster's sleep cycle—

"Pardon, Witch? Excuse me?"

Tembi looked up to find an Adhamantian standing beside the table. Their long hair was tied back by a headscarf. They wore no jewelry, and their robes were a couple of cycles away from threadbare, but they were clean and their dark skin moved in all the usual ways.

"I have a message," they said, eyes fixed on Tembi's cheek. "If you are a Witch."

Tembi sat up. "I am."

Their ears tipped down, a gesture which shouted louder than words about how they thought she was a liar. Tembi's own ears moved to lay flat against her head to show she had taken offense. An overreaction? Maybe, but this day just kept going and there was no end in sight. Matthew didn't like it when she went brawling in the streets, but she felt it was good for his health if he got to lecture her on conduct unbecoming a Witch at least once a quarter.

The messenger ignored her. "There is no shame in waiting for the Witch to return," they said, glancing towards the hallway which led to the washroom.

Tembi glared at them and stood, gathering her robes around her, and walked towards the rear exit. As she passed the washroom, she rapped on the door and called, "Clandestine meeting in the alley."

Splashing sounds answered her, as if the sink had been stoppered and filled, and an out-of-place woman from an ocean planet was trying her best to get as much of her body in the water as possible. Then, a muffled, "Be right there."

The back door of the café was locked with a length of chain, an old security 'bot clinging to the padlock with a set of oversized claws as an extra deterrent against anyone on the inside trying to open the door for would-be looters. Tembi didn't slow her pace, letting the Deep jump her from one side of the door to the other. The alley was almost pitch black, and there was a sharp drop on the other side where a staircase had rotted away; she stepped from the air to the ground, her robes billowing around her as she slowly descended stairs that no longer existed.

If Matindi had taught her anything, it was how to make an entrance.

A voice came from the shadows: "One of 'em's real."

A different voice, from a different pile of shadows: "Gallimore, did you get the other girl to come?"

"She is on her way," said Tembi's escort. "It won't be long."

"I'm just going to start hurling bobcats," Tembi grumbled to herself. Then, loudly, "I'm told there's a message for me?"

"For the Witch." The second pile of shadows moved, and as Tembi's eyes adjusted she could see the outline of a slim figure. There was a muffled clinking sound, and a short rod held loosely by their side bloomed in electric fire, vivid green sparks cascading from one end. "From her friend, Moto."

Moto. His name should have been a comfort, but Tembi couldn't look away from that sparking rod. She had been popped by the local law more than once as a child, and she had never been able to shake her lingering fear of popsticks. They could shock or stun or even *kill*—No, judge, I don't know how the settings got damaged! This is horrible and it's *all my fault!*—and she never trusted a person with a popstick. Never.

"May I hear it?" she asked, her ears high.

"If the Witch says so, yeah," they replied, tapping the side of the popstick against their thigh. The device was eight ways from bootleg; Tembi could see it sizzling away, its sickly energy turning the air around it into hot bits of plasma which sparked and flared out as quickly as they appeared. The air crackled like fat on a hotplate.

"What are we doing here?" she heard herself ask. There was a muffled, distant quality to her own voice. "Because it seems you're threatening me."

"No, girl, not threatening you, not at all," the first speaker said, staying well-cloaked by the dark. All she could see of them was illuminated by the thin light of the popstick. "But Witches? They'll turn me inside-out if I put a word wrong. Can't blame a soul for wanting to scar their hide before he goes, yeah?"

No, she couldn't. The Deep wouldn't intentionally kill anyone, no, and had not, not once in three thousand years. But there had been accidents, *so* many accidents, and there were drinking games among the young Witches at Lancaster, games that got *dark,* about how you *might* use something *like* the Deep to torture, to punish, to murder... A few hundred years ago, there was that serial killer who figured out a combination of 'bots and anti-grav plates to create impossible crimes. Crimes that were easy to blame on a naughty Witch and the Deep because no human should *ever* be that creative with intestines. Sensational story. Lancaster went to great lengths to keep it out of the public eye, which meant it would probably live on forever.

Oh, no, Tembi couldn't blame him for it at all.

"What can I do to get you to put that away?" she said, nodding towards his popstick.

"Think I'll keep it out," he said, still tapping away, pop-sizzle, pop-sizzle. "Until your Witch gets here."

The air in the alley blew itself to pieces as Bayle appeared. She dropped a half-meter to the ground, bare feet landing on the alley floor with a hard thump. "Our food's up," she said to Tembi.

The man with the popstick nodded to Bayle. "Witch-*nim,*" he said. "Do you want your companion to hear this?"

Bayle glanced at Tembi.

"They don't think I'm a Witch," she explained.

Bayle chuckled and reached out to touch Tembi's face. She held up her fingers, now slightly pink from the paint that had once been a carnivorous rose.

Tembi winced, and used the sleeve of her robe to remove the rest of the ruined markings. "Knew we should have used stick pens."

"Neither of us can draw for shit."

"Right." Tembi turned to face the shadows as she sent a silent request to the Deep. She couldn't feel its own paint bloom across her face, but the person with the popstick took a step towards her, pulling himself from the shadows. It was a man, tall and thin, touching upon middle age, and his skin rough but flexible.

"Those are birds…" he said quietly. "Are you Tembi?"

She nodded.

"This changes things," he muttered to himself.

And then he rushed her, popstick raised and ready.

Chapter Eight

What to do when you have an invisible guardian who watches your every move? One who, with the civilization-defining exception of events which follow an orderly schedule, quickly reaches critical failure when it comes to understanding most human interactions?

Moto had been the one who had taught her how to fight.

No, wait. Rephrase: Moto had taught her how to fight properly. Street brawls which kept going until someone was unconscious didn't count. Moto had learned how to fight in the streets of Adhama as she had, and later learned advanced techniques from spacers who knew where to draw the line. They had taught him how to punch and kick, and they used grappling techniques that had been invented in the low-grav settings of shipping docks. But if Tembi was to learn any of this, the Deep needed to let her get hurt.

The Deep hated when its Witches got hurt. And proper fighting meant that two of them tried to hurt each other? No. That could not be permitted. Here, have a cat instead.

Moto was patient. He was kind. He needed the Deep to understand that he was passing knowledge on to Tembi, so he had sat with the Deep and practiced singing, painting, all manner of art. He danced with it, in the Deep's private space between the worlds, with a young Tembi laughing at the two of them from the sidelines.

"Come," he had told her, and he had spun her up and taught her to dance, too. She had been twelve and he was easily twice her age or more, and he had ignored her fierce crush until she finally got it through her skull that he had adopted her as his little sister. Then, the two of them had slowly taught the Deep that there was a difference between fighting and...well...fighting. That one was aggression, violence with intent to cause injury or worse: that the other was a form of exercise in which skills were honed, and pain and injury were an unavoidable part of the process. They managed to teach it that proper fighting was, at its heart, a dance. And while the Deep still fussed and fretted when Tembi took a solid kick to her ribcage, it knew that she had missed a step in the dance. How? It all came down to intent: when somebody attacked Tembi, the Deep peeked inside their head to see if they truly wanted to hurt her.

This worked extremely well. Over the years, Tembi was able to practice against multiple sparring partners. Kalais, yes, as the soldier boy lived his life on the edge of fierce anger and bled it off through action. She had tried her best to teach Bayle how to throw a punch, and had sparred against those spacer friends of Moto's who showed up at the gym in their heavy uniforms. In all that time, the only tense moment had come when a man with a dark grudge went to take on Tembi and had ended up in the bathroom with his clothes on the roof.

Later, when she had started disarming bombs and bumped up against people who wanted those bombs to do their duty, the Deep would keep her safe. She wasn't sure what happened to her attackers: she joked about Assassins' Paradise because she couldn't imagine the Deep simply murdering them, leaving them to die of starvation along the Rails. But perhaps that was exactly what happened, with the Deep moving those threats away from her and into an alien realm in which they were instantly forgotten.

All of this history crashed against Tembi as she defended herself from the man with the popstick, unable to process what it might *mean*.

He was fast and the alley was dark, and Tembi couldn't shake her childhood fear of getting popped. That stick swung straight at her face; she turned, blocked, the hand holding the popstick was moved harmlessly to the side.

Disarm him. The half-heard thoughts of combat leapt from brain to muscle. If that gods-damned popstick was gone, she could—

Her arm up, her hand open, a quick grasp of his wrist. Her other hand swung like a club to bash the popstick away.

His bare foot struck the soft spot behind her knee, not to disable, but to discourage. She fell, kicking on her way down, her foot landing against his stomach and driving out his air.

He caught himself in a tight roll and came up, lunging towards her, the popstick in his outstretched hand.

He fights like Moto. That thought came and went as she rolled to the side, the popstick burning through the air where her shoulder had been a moment before, and then she wrapped the Deep around herself to jump behind him. A quick sweep of his legs, and the man fell, laughing.

"Cheating Witches," he said as he picked himself up, wiping the filth of the alley on his robes. He readied himself to strike again, and the glow from the popstick lit the lines of his face.

He looks like Moto, she realized. *Older. Harder.*

Tembi finally understood why the Deep had let this go on. She stood and forced herself to shake out her fists. "Are you his father?"

Confusion flickered across him, replaced by a sad smile. "Brother," he said, and then he added: "His younger brother."

"...oh."

The popstick sputtered once more, and went dark.

"Come," Moto's brother said as he turned away. "I have something for you, Witch Tembi."

Tembi followed. So did the two other Adhamantians.

Bayle paused, shook her head, and trotted after them.

Moto's brother led them on a short walk through the streets of Slate. His name was Cendo, the other man's was Obsenn, and the oh-so-polite messenger called themselves Gallimore. Other than that, there was no small talk.

"Not here," Cendo said. "Colors have ears."

Tembi glanced at Bayle, who gestured at her hair and then her robes as she mouthed the word, "Domino."

"Almost there," Cendo said, gesturing towards a nearby stack of shipping containers. The back entrance was concealed from

the street, a small lift on an anti-grav system, its mechanics contained within a weather cage to protect it from storms. There
was also a phenomenal amount of security. She spotted cameras, larger 'bots, and even a few predatory-looking avian creatures that smelled too gamey to be synths.

Tembi grinned. Cendo had money, and she doubted it came
from Moto sending his salary home, as she did with her own
first mother and sisters.

The lift rattled up to the fourth story. When the doors
opened, they stepped into what appeared to be a tiny warehouse crammed full of entertainment systems in brand-new
glossy packaging.

"All of this belongs to a friend of ours," Gallimore said.

"Your friend must be doing well," replied Tembi.

"He says running a small business is always challenging, but
it can also be rewarding."

Cendo chuckled.

There was a small room off to the back with a couch, a couple
of old chairs, and a table. Obsenn hit a couple of buttons on a
cluttered counter, and a section of the wall slid back to reveal a
crisper full of drinks.

"No thanks," Bayle said, then: "Oh!" She vanished, then reappeared a heartbeat later with two plain white bags. She handed
one to Tembi. "They packed our meals up for us."

"We're used to Witches in this neighborhood," Gallimore
said.

"No," Cendo said. He was holding a small metal box. "We're
used to Moto. Here," he added, as he handed the box to Tembi.
"He dropped this off a few weeks ago. Told me that if he ever
went missing to give this to you, and no one else."

"Did he say to beat me up?"

"Yeah," Cendo laughed. It had a crackling sound within it, as
if he had a cold he couldn't quite shake. "The Deep let you fight
me, didn't it?"

Ah. Tembi nodded. Faces could be altered, and it was possible
for someone to study how Moto moved and imitate it. But she

was terrified down to her marrow of popsticks. There was no chance the Deep would have let someone swing one at her head if it wasn't certain she wouldn't be hurt.

She opened the box, and—

"Whoa," Bayle said quietly.

A small, thin, beige wafer lay end-up in a fold of fabric within the box. With the exception of pocket lint, it was the most unassuming thing she had ever seen. If Tembi didn't know better, she'd have thought it was a stale cracker.

She'd have almost been right.

Tembi shut the box as carefully as she could. A heavy slab of inanimate meat had replaced her tongue; it took her two tries to form the words. "A Crisp."

Was she shaking? No? Good. *Focus, Tembi.*

She focused on her hands and not the Crisp. Definitely not the Crisp. Because there was no way on this world or any other that she should be holding one. Their manufacture was highly controlled and prohibitively expensive. Crisps were an order of magnitude more complex than the standard areotype, which did little more than gank and measure the localized atmosphere around a person to determine their identity. Areotypes isolated a person's scent, skin particles, and a dozen other minor physiological cues. Crisps? Those required location-sensitive data, the recipient's DNA profile, and a shared memory between the recipient and the sender. Crisps were for state secrets and mega-corporations, not...her. Nothing Moto could tell her would be *worth* putting into a Crisp!

Cendo leaned towards her and whispered, "Moto said you should take it at the place with the fish."

She nodded. "Okay." That seemed insufficient, so she added: "Did he..." *Don't ask don't ask don't ask don't ask he doesn't know and you don't want to know.* "...did he tell you how he got my blood?"

He shook his head. "Figured the Deep 'ported it straight from your veins."

Acceptable. Barely, but acceptable. Somehow that felt like the least of all possible invasions of privacy.

Gallimore coughed politely. She turned to see them holding out a knife, handle first. "Just in case," they said.

Tembi took the blade. Her hand still wasn't shaking? Strange. "Thank you."

"Good luck," Cendo said, grinning.

Bayle slid three gold rings from her index finger, and laid them on the counter, *plink-plink-plink,* before taking Tembi by the arm. "Where are we going?" she asked.

One deep breath...two... "The place with all the fish," Tembi replied, and opened the way through the Deep.

Into the heart of the ocean.

Not an ocean she knew well. Not even in passing. Moto had never bothered to tell her the name of this planet, let alone the name of this particular body of water. Was this planet inhabited? Was it even charted? Or had Moto and the Deep found this place and kept it a secret from everyone but her, just in case he needed to seed a message into a Crisp?

A million tons of ocean, all around, everywhere but beneath their feet, and the Deep pushing it away with the same pressure bubble that had allowed Tembi to walk across a broken moon. Below, the floor of the ocean, stark black rock instead of sand. The atmosphere of this planet was teal, and the water shallow enough to shine like an aquamarine. In this? Fish. Not like Earth-fish, no, not even considering their almost-countless strange forms. These fish were shaped like blades, pointed white daggers darting through the water in orderly schools of no more than ten. The light hit their skin and shattered into colors. There was no red here, or orange, and yellow was barely a scatter of light, but green and blue and purple and indigo cascaded around them.

Bayle gasped and spun in a circle, arms outstretched as she worshiped the water.

Tembi would rather have been back in the vacuum of space. She had wondered why Moto had brought her here, when both of them were desert creatures and they had done nothing but watch the water with suspicion. Now she knew.

"It's prettier at night," Tembi said, as she searched the black stone beneath her feet. She found Moto's mark, a small sigil of flame which matched the markings on his face the Deep had chosen for him when it had claimed him as its Witch, and tucked her robes beneath her as she sat atop it.

The box containing the Crisp rested in her hands, unopened, the metal surely warming from her touch. She wished she could feel its sharp edges, but it was nothing but a heavy lump to her.

Bayle tore herself away from the dagger-fish and sat down, facing Tembi. "Here?"

"Yeah." Tembi couldn't look away from the box. She would have preferred the business end of a popstick. That, she knew. "He brought me here a couple of months ago. Said he wanted to keep it a secret. Just him and me."

"And you didn't think that was strange?"

Tembi snorted. "Well, *now* I do."

Bayle reached out and tapped the box with a manicured fingernail.

"I know," Tembi sighed. "Have you ever…"

"…used a Crisp?" Bayle's eyes were wide. "No. Never."

Tembi opened the box. The Crisp lay on its fabric bed, unassuming and bland. Someone cleaning a room would throw it out and not think twice.

The perfect tool for the busy spy on the go.

"I don't know how he got this made," she said quietly. "Aren't these regulated down to the darkest hells?"

"Expensive, too," Bayle added. "That's two years' worth of Moto's money in your lap."

Tembi groaned, and reached for the knife.

Bayle slapped her hand away. "Could you not cut yourself with a knife you got from a stranger?" Another knife appeared, this one a meat cutter from Bayle's own kitchen cutlery set.

"Good point." Tembi accepted Bayle's knife and powered it up. She'd burn out its charge on her skin, but it was a Crisp and it wanted her blood, and—

She stared out at the fish as she slowly ran the blade over the tip of her tongue, opening a thin bloody cut. The pain was negligible. Almost enjoyable in its alieness. She couldn't remember the last time something had managed to cut through her skin.

She lifted the Crisp to her lips…

And then…

The Crisp was *right there,* and she couldn't bring herself to…

Bayle's hands clasped her knees. "I'm not going anywhere," her friend said, her blue eyes earnest. "I'm here. The Deep's here."

A light scent of blooming jasmine filled the sphere.

Tembi nodded, shut her eyes, and put the Crisp into her mouth.

Chapter Nine

How long does this take to work?
Is this how it's supposed to work?
Why couldn't he have just written a sossing letter?

The Crisp was taking its sweet time to dissolve. It tasted like processed sugar and rotting bread. She wanted to swallow and get it off of her tongue (and go and brush her teeth for maybe half an hour or an hour or maybe a nice round 24-hour cycle because the best-case scenario was that she was *sucking on her own stolen blood* c'mon, Tembi, focus), but it needed to recognize her, right? It needed to get the message into her bloodstream, and from there into her brain, right? That couldn't be an instantaneous process, right?

A glimmer of light, even though her eyes were still shut tight.

A man's face in the darkness. Handsome, or he would have been if he wasn't wearing exhaustion like a shroud. The brown skin and high pointed ears of Adhama's children. Nearly her own age, or just a few years older: the Deep might have stopped him from aging, but his dark eyes hadn't started to grow ancient in that frighteningly timeless way. He had shaved his head since the last time she had seen him, and this helped show off the red-gold flames cast in paint which ran up his cheek.

Hi, Moto.

"Hey, Tembi."

The background filled itself in. The image was a memory: Moto was talking to himself in his bathroom mirror. Behind him was the unmanageable mess of blankets he called a design element so he could avoid repairing the linen closet's broken door.

"I hope you never have to watch this. If you do, things have gone wrong."

What, no, really? Thanks, Moto. That's very helpful.

"If you're watching this, I'm—" He paused to laugh. It was not a wholly sane sound. He was sweating and shaking, a mild tremble which rocked his perspective in the mirror. "I'm in a stasis pod that I've asked the Deep to move two weeks into the future. Hiding outside of time is the only thing I can think of. I don't know if this will work. I've never tried it before. The Deep...I think the Deep says it won't bring me back unless I ask, and if I'm in stasis, I *can't* ask, so... Small gods, Tembi, I can't believe I'm doing this. The Deep is... Nobody else believes the Deep can manipulate time. It's the best way to hide. But..."

He swallowed.

"I've found something big. I can't tell Lancaster. If I do, it'll get back to the Council and they can't know that I've got this. Not yet. That means I can't tell you, or Domino might pick it out of your head. Except..." He paused and looked around, as if expecting Domino to pop into the bathroom behind him. "Except she always gets what she wants. So I'm taking the data with me when I hide."

Everything went dark. She felt herself begin to panic, but he reappeared in the mirror within a heartbeat. Ah. Moto had covered his eyes with his hands before he had caught himself.

"Something big is coming," he repeated. "If I'm not back by the third of Asteracaen, you'll see it for yourself. The Deep'll make sure of that."

The third... Today. That's today.

Oh. Oh no. He's talking about that moon.

That wasn't the worst of it. Like a flash of lightning burning through her cluttered brain, she realized that if the Deep had taken her to see the broken moon, then that meant Moto hadn't come out of stasis as he had planned.

Moto's memory-self was still talking. "If I'm not back by then, ask the Deep to bring me to you. You're my safeguard. The Deep trusts you, and it listens to you like nobody else. You might be able to talk it into bringing me home." He grinned, and a little of his exhaustion cracked away around his eyes. "I hope you never have to watch this. Or, after this is over, we'll go to the place with the fish and you can watch it in front of me. I'll be drunker than all hells when you do.

"I'm leaving this with my brother, just in case. You need the data I'm carrying. If you get me back and I'm…" Another long pause. "If I've died in stasis, give the data to Kalais. Make sure he gets it to his contacts in the Sabenta. They won't know what to do with it, but somebody who isn't in the Earth Assembly needs to have it. That's what I'm planning to do once I get back. By then, they'll *have* to listen to me, and—"

His face and voice vanished. Not a mistake of the hands this time. The memory had ended.

Tembi kept her eyes shut. Most Crisps were designed so the message would repeat. Not that she'd ever forget what Moto had said, but better safe than sorry.

Moto didn't reappear.

She felt a little annoyed that Moto had purchased what was obviously a shoddy knockoff Crisp, and then she felt more annoyed at herself for being annoyed at what was obviously her friend's moment of crisis. She opened her eyes. Bayle was eating, the white bags from the tavern on Adhama spread out around her. She handed Tembi a paper boat overflowing with a greasy brown mess.

"Thanks," she said, and started eating. It had gone cold. Silently, she asked the Deep to vibrate the gravy's molecules a bit, and the gravy in the boat began to steam.

Bayle raised an eyebrow. "And?"

"Moto's in trouble." Before Bayle could reply with a sarcastic comment, Tembi added, "It has to do with the weapon that destroyed the moon, I think."

"You think? You don't know? Wait, just start at the beginning."

"Hold on." Tembi said. "Let me see if I can get Moto back. Deep? Can you please pay attention?"

Drops of water fell from the roof of the atmosphere bubble. As they splashed against the black rock, the color shifted from teal to red.

"Buddy, do you know about the message that Moto left for me?"

More water. This time, the droplets shaped themselves to appear as faceted red gemstones, which caused Bayle to chuckle and carefully gather them together in a small pile.

"Is he still alive?"

More red gemstones. Tembi took the color consistency as a good sign.

"Can you please bring him here?"

The water stopped falling, and the gems in Bayle's hands turned teal before they fell apart and ran through her fingers.

"Deep?" Tembi paused. If the Deep felt as if it had done something wrong, it might panic. "I'm not mad, I promise, but I would really like to see Moto."

Moto appeared. An illusion, yes, but an illusion of Moto sleeping comfortably within a pure white stasis pod. Was this Moto as he appeared at this moment, lost somewhere in space and time?

Tembi wanted to punch the entire universe.

"Thank you, Deep," she said, forcing herself to grab on to *calm, calm, don't do anything which might scare the Deep into sending Moto away forever.* "Can you take good care of him for me until you bring him home?"

Another stream of red water, bursting into more gemstones on impact, and the illusion of Moto disappeared.

"Gimme," Tembi sighed. Bayle handed her one of the bottles that had come with their meals, and Tembi chased her anger away with cold alcohol and hot food. Between bites, she repeated Moto's message. It was easy; it had been burned into her mind. Stupid cheap Crisp. She hoped it hadn't done any damage to her own memories. She ran through what little details the Crisp had delivered, only leaving out the part where Moto looked like he had already been chased across half the galaxy and driven past the edge of panic. Bayle had a tendency to take in strays, and her perpetual crush on Moto didn't need any additional fuel.

Once she was done talking, they watched the dagger-fish while they finished their meals. It was a pretty sight, Tembi had to admit, especially as the sun was beginning to set, and the fish started to glow with bioluminescence as long hair-like tendrils extended from their sides to weave the schools together into a single massive organism. Tembi hadn't seen any nocturnal predators, but if hundreds of thousands of fish had evolved to mimic a single gigantic glowing creature the size of Lancaster's Tower, she could die happy never learning exactly what wanted to eat it.

Bayle kept her attention on the fish. If Tembi didn't know better, she'd have thought Bayle wasn't listening, but… Her stomach sank: Bayle was kneading that dense sourdough pause that always came before she invested herself in a conversation she didn't want to have.

She tried to head off the inevitable. "Don't say it."

Bayle didn't listen. "If we can't find Moto, we need to talk to Kalais."

"No."

"Tembi—"

"I'm not being stubborn," she sighed. "We have no proof. Of *anything!* We have Moto's memory inside my head, and Kalais and I are long past taking each other on faith."

"He'd believe you," Bayle muttered, as she turned away to watch the fish.

Tembi balled up the wrappers and shoved them into one of the bags. "How about this," she said. "Moto said he had data. How about we find that data and bring it to Kalais? We need to keep trying to get Moto back, so…" She hurled the bag at the wall of water surrounding them. It passed through the wall and stopped, and then slowly floated towards the monolithic dagger-fish, which ignored it except to provide holes for it to pass. "Moto told me just enough to keep Domino guessing, but he knows what's happening and we don't. We bring him home, and then he can handle the details."

Bayle wrinkled her nose.

"Am I wrong?"

"No," Bayle replied, as she packed up her own trash. "But there's a *war*, Tembs! If we can save lives by talking to Kalais, we should."

Tembi fixed her attention on the dagger-fish as she whispered, "Scheisse."

Bayle grinned at her, opened the jump, and they were gone.

A moment later, the ocean crashed into the void where they had been sitting.

A moment after that, the bag of trash Tembi had hurled into the water disappeared.

Chapter Ten

Change is the fundamental truth of the universe.

Then humanity gets involved and some truths manage to double down and find ways to fight back against change. A knife is a knife is a knife. It has been a knife for fifty thousand years before the Deep appeared, and will remain a knife until humanity fully divests itself from the tyranny of solids. A knife can be manufactured from different materials. It can receive a charge which allows it to zip through rock-hard substances. The design can be altered until it twists back on itself in impractical and dangerous spirals. But the fundamentals of what makes it a knife form its own truth.

Same with streets. Same with clothing. Same with pets and funerals and music, with swimming pools and medication, with lighting and vehicles and toilets. With tables, toys, and dinnertime.

Same with war.

Chapter Eleven

"I'm proud of you."

"I didn't think you'd approve. Thought you'd say Domino only offers traps," Tembi told her second mother. "I don't want to work for her, but getting close to her seems like the smart option."

Matindi grinned at her. "And you'd try to find Moto anyhow."

"And I'd try to find Moto anyhow," Tembi agreed. She paused, her eyes moving away from Matindi to her own cup of tea, staring into it as if it held secrets in the fragments of the leaves. "Bomb duty was a step in the right direction, but it wasn't big enough. I'll work on Domino. If she's sincere about change—" A snort as Matindi went to refill her own cup. "—then I'll have a voice in Lancaster's politics."

"In theory," her second mother replied, as she reached over to top off the hot water in Tembi's cup. "In practice? Remember that I used to have a large say in how this place is run, and all it got me was several millennia of bashing my head against the rocks."

"But you and I together? Plus Matthew? And Bayle?" Tembi was doing her best not to dance around in her chair. "Deep, you love Matthew and Bayle, right?"

::YES::

Matindi held up a finger. "Think carefully, Tembi. You wouldn't just be asking Lancaster to change its policies. You'd be asking the Deep to choose sides."

Tembi's excitement collapsed as if her feet had been kicked out from under her. "Oh."

"Oh, indeed. I haven't spent the last twenty-five hundred years doing nothing because it was easier. The Deep has favorites, but that doesn't mean it doesn't love all of its Witches."

"You ask the Deep to choose sides all the time! I mean,

you're here because..." Tembi waved her hand at her kitchen. It wasn't the same room as it had been when she left the house that morning. Then, it had been a mess stacked on top of a structurally sound layer of clutter. Now, the kitchen practically gleamed, the surest of signs that Matindi had moved in. Tembi couldn't find any real reason to object: the house had been Matindi's before she had retired, leaving it and all of her other belongings at Lancaster to Tembi. If she had known she would be having a houseguest, Tembi would have made some effort to clean. Instead, she had come home to learn that the other Witches had finally managed to convince the Deep to put Matindi's little cottage into orbit around Found, and Matindi wasn't getting it back until formal disciplinary meetings were held. So, Matindi had gone to her old house and began shoveling her way through the piles of dirty clothing and musical instruments which had accumulated in her absence.

"There's a difference between what I did today and what you're asking the Deep to do. Moving buildings around is a game, and I'm careful when I ask it to do that." Matindi replied. "Remember the Turtle Incident."

Tembi shut up as quickly as if Matindi had slapped her.

The Turtle Incident.

Nearly as soon as she had arrived at Lancaster, Matthew had taken her to visit the small museum at the base of the Tower to ease her into her new role. The place was for tourists, not Witches, with centuries-old exhibits drier than that Crisp. Even the exhibit about the Turtle Incident. That was polished testimonies and memorials, easily absorbed and forgotten, just a bunch of words about people who had died long ago. Later, back in the safety of this very house, Matindi and Matthew had sat her down and explained what those words truly meant, all of them sweetening the terror of a colony's worth of people turned inside out.

Tembi had been rightfully horrified. Matthew had brought a small grammalight display with him, in case she needed visuals to fully grok what had happened to the small colony on one of Neptune's more stable moons, but Tembi didn't want to see them. The very idea that the Deep—her kind, gentle friend who just wanted her to be happy!—could use its vast powers to rip a person apart had caused her to break into tears, right there at the kitchen table.

It hadn't been the Deep's fault, the two of them had assured her, as Matthew sat beside her, rubbing her back as she wept. It had been a mistake. Nothing more than a careless mistake. When the Deep first arrived, it didn't know how people worked. It had needed to learn that human bodies aged, that they could be injured. That they needed a balanced atmosphere to keep their insides on the inside.

That they could cease to exist.

It had been *our* fault, Matthew had said, many times. Not the Deep's.

That hadn't helped, not one bit. Tembi had been barely twelve, newly torn from her homeworld and thrust into a world of adults which had no real place for her. Learning that her best friend could be turned into a mass murderer with a misplaced word was too much. Her Adhamantian veneer had cracked, and she couldn't stop crying.

Later, once she was older, she had applied a teenager's grim curiosity to the Turtle Incident. There were very few visuals available: Lancaster maintained careful control over its brand. She had needed to ask Matthew to let her watch his grammalight display, and had gotten about halfway through the program before she decided that she had seen all she would ever need to see.

There hadn't been much more for her to learn. The Witch who had been held responsible for the Turtle Incident was never named. The very memory of her had been purged from Lancaster's records. All that was left of her was the story of how she had been playing a game with the Deep and had said something careless. It had been a terrible tragedy, but everyone agreed that space exploration was dangerous and much worse had happened. The Deep was blameless: the fault belonged to that nameless long-dead Witch, and to Lancaster. Now, let's all agree to pretend it never really happened.

Tembi still thought about it at least once a week, usually right before she started on the latest bomb.

She glared at her second mother, and then nodded, cowed. Matindi reached over and patted her hand. "The Deep thinks that moving ships and buildings around is fun," Matindi reminded her. "But we need to always remember how even that can be dangerous. Asking it to choose sides in a policy war? Who knows what might happen during *that* kind of game? I'm not going to lie to it with scenarios which make it seem like choosing one Witch over another is a puzzle without consequences."

Tembi shoved a fresh cookie into her mouth, grumbling.

"Don't rush into anything," Matindi said, as she gathered up her tea. "That's all I ask."

"Do I have to think about it for twenty-five hundred years?"

"Good night, dear." Matindi gave her a kiss on the cheek, then bopped Tembi upside the head. "Don't be fresh."

Tembi chuckled as she moved her dishes to the sink, took her usual handful of mini-meds to stitch her ulcers back together overnight, and ducked into her bedroom to get ready for bed. It had been a long day, and tomorrow promised to be much, much worse. All Tembi wanted to do was fall into dark, dreamless sleep. Her bed waited; soft, sweet-smelling, clean as anything.

She stared at it with great loathing.

"Deep?" she said aloud.

The taste of candied flower petals came and went.

"I need to sleep. Real human sleep. Just for a couple of hours, okay?"

There was no reply. Correction: there was no reply she could detect. Maybe the Deep was talking to her through methods which lay beyond the reach of her limited senses, and she'd fall into bed, thinking she could finally sleep, and the Deep would whisk her mind away.

"I'm serious, Deep. Please?"

"Oy!" Matindi, next door in the guest room, banged on the wall between them. "Deep, let the poor girl sleep!"

Three of Tembi's houseplants uprooted themselves from their pots and walked themselves out of her bedroom, closing the door behind them.

"I'll take that as a yes?" Tembi asked.

There was a pause, and then the pots disappeared.

Tembi wiggled into bed. The sheets were freshly washed and firmly tucked, their corners creased over to form a tight wrap around her shoulders. It reminded her of childhood, back when Matindi had managed her life. It was surprisingly soothing.

Sleep came quickly.

And then came the usual dream.

It always began with a crack in the world.

Which world? It didn't matter. One world was very much like another after humankind had their wicked way with it. A thousand habitable planets in the galaxy, a hundred times that number which could be habitable if the engineers tinkered with landmasses and genomes—and if you could afford an entire planet, why wouldn't you pay extra for the engineers to poke it, or you, into shape?—and this particular dream never came with a map.

So. One world.

One vague interchangeable world.

(One world which smelled a little too much like Adhama, an unmistakable scent of arid desert sands mixed with the hard brine of the nearby ocean, but Tembi did her best to never think about *that*.)

In the dream, there was a humming sound, the ground beneath her vibrating. As she ran, the world fractured beneath her feet, fast as a fruit cleaved with a knife. She ran through streets filled with screaming people, crumbling buildings, dust, dust *everywhere*, in her eyes, her nose, her mouth, her ears, and none of that made *sense!* She shouted for the Deep to come and help, to come and save these people, but the Deep was gone, the

Deep was—

What happened after that, Tembi didn't know, as that was when she woke, gasping, sheets yanked high around her neck, as if the sheets were trying to do her body's job of keeping the dust away from her.

Tonight, the dream began as it always did. The hum, the crack, the chaos, the nameless world turned to ever-blowing dust. A profound sense of loss, sweeping over her and pulling her down, down, down into nothing. But, instead of allowing her to wake in terror, the dream eased its grasp on her subconscious. She watched as the dust parted and the sky became clear, and two faceless beings clad in rainbow robes emerged, robes so bright and bold that Domino's were nothing but mud-puddle brown in comparison. These beings shifted form again and again, growing smaller as they shrank down to her own size, losing and gaining limbs, fur, feathers, *skin!*

The dream relaxed its hold again, and now it crumbled around her, pieces of colors squirming on the ground. She looked away from these and—

Oh.

She recognized this place.

The vague haziness of dreaming left her, leaving her as awake and aware as if she was walking around in her own body instead of as her dream-self. She had been in this dreamscape before. It was a dream of the Deep's own making, a dream where all Witches could come and touch the galaxy without the burden of physicality.

Tembi loved this place. It was reality without being real, an idealized version of what could (should?) exist in the waking world. The Deep stripped away nagging problems that tripped up the simple joys of experience. It wasn't complicated. It didn't need to be complicated! It was a world made up of small but meaningful things, like going on a picnic without insects, like lying in a grassy field to watch the stars without the evening damp seeping into your robes.

All Witches were welcome in this dream world, but few chose

to visit. Why bother? This dream world was a mirror of reality. Might as well jump from here to there in the waking world, where their money meant something and their status as a Witch was worth much more, and keep their dreams to themselves.

Tembi wished she had that option. The Deep brought her into its dream when it had something to show her, which happened often. For her, sleep was usually a portal to more work.

Tonight, the Deep had placed her one of the decorative court-yards which dotted the Earth Assembly's central pavilion. It was peaceful; the eager shrieking masses of the waking world had no presence here. She could take a moment to pause and look around, enjoy the grandeur of old Earth without the cloying presence of other people. It wasn't sleep, but it could be worse— *worse* was the dream of the fractured world that couldn't *possibly* be Adhama, really!—and she'd pop some 'rexies when she woke up to take the edge off her sleepdep.

In the Deep's own dream, the courtyard was green and gold, with vegetation dropped over its yellow stone bones. All of the plants were native to Earth. The stone, native to quarries in the region. The courtyard took up ten square kilometers in the middle of a city by the sea, on a continent that had been mostly desert until some light terraforming had dropped the planet's temperature by a few degrees. Now, it was paradise, with flowers draped across mammoth statues, and colorful birds darting about. Strange-looking creatures with long limbs and tails nipped back and forth within the trees, pausing in their business to scream at her as she wandered along the paths.

She was having a pleasant time until she found the posters.

One spot was much like another; the courtyard was designed to be a stately pleasure garden if you didn't know where you were going, the tranquil uniformity of the place broken only by its hidden delights. She found a frozen custard stand hidden behind a rock, a palette of Earth flavors waiting for her despite the lack of robotic servers. Chocolate was chocolate the galaxy over, so she passed that up and went for the local flavors that couldn't be found anywhere else. She was munching on a mystery blend of crushed berries in cream when she turned the corner and found a large glasshouse. There was garbage here, overflowing from bins and scattered across the ground, which was strange enough—Garbage! *Here!*—but posters had been pasted against the glasshouse's walls.

Tembi recognized them at once. Perfect smiling faces, their hands placed over their heart, right over left. Some of them wore uniforms of black so pitch that shadows couldn't catch the folds. There was text, but she didn't need to read it. She already knew what it said.

This had been the site of a Blackwing recruitment rally.

"No," she whispered, horrified. She would have preferred a battlefield.

The posters had been pasted against the glass. She gave a corner a tug and the yank adhesive released, the undamaged poster coming away in her hands. A souvenir for those who wanted one, she guessed. For those who wanted to remember the event.

It had reached Earth. No—it had reached the grounds of the Earth Assembly.

Or it had always been here, and they finally feel safe enough to come into the light.

A brief moment of panic, quickly replaced by anger.

"Kalais!" she shouted. "Get out here!"

The door to the glasshouse opened, and Kalais emerged, one hand in his hair as if he was slightly embarrassed. "How did you know?"

"The Deep doesn't like politics, and it wouldn't have stuck me in an Assembly courtyard unless it had a reason. Like someone asking it." She turned to leave. "Kalais, I'm exhausted. Talk to me in person. Tomorrow."

"No, Tembi, wait." He crossed the distance between them, tearing down another poster on the way. "I didn't stage this. The glasshouse is like this back on Earth. They left it up, Tembs! They meant for people like us to see it! They'll swear it was a maintenance error and the 'bots didn't get the cleanup request, but they left it up. They want everybody to know that the Blackwings have access to the Earth Assembly—"

"—and the Sabenta don't," she finished for him. "Yeah, Kalais, I get it. Believe it or not, I do understand what's happening."

Her memory kicked up the image of Dame Idowu staring at Bayle's boots, and—*No. Focus, Tembi,* she reminded herself, as she shoved that memory aside.

He waited—sometimes she *hated* how well he knew her!—until she could steady herself, and then he said, "I'm sorry for what I said today. It just fell out."

"I know." She opened her eyes and began to peel the posters from the glasshouse. Wasted effort, as they'd still be there in the waking world, but it kept her hands busy and it was deeply satisfying to tear those hateful things down, to rip away the bright Earth-perfect smiles and crumple them into small balls. "Help me."

He took a spot a few meters away from her, and they circled the glasshouse, tearing down posters in silent anger. Once they were done, they cleaned up the garbage on the ground. Dream garbage shouldn't be as nasty as real garbage, but the Deep was a stickler for details, and once they were done they found a nearby fountain to clean their hands.

"I don't know what to do," she finally said.

"I know," he replied. "But you can't do nothing. Or, maybe I should say..." He backtracked quickly and tried again. "...that I never know what to do, either. So I find something I can do, and work at it."

"Like the posters."

"Yeah."

She sighed. "I have something to tell you."

The words came easily. Talking to Kalais was always easy when they weren't at each other's throats. In a matter of minutes, she had told him about her afternoon on Adhama, and the message Moto had left for her in the Crisp. When she got to the part about the Crisp, he froze, motionless except for his fingers knotting into fists.

Once she had finished, he said, "He could have killed you."

She winced. "I'm fine, just—"

"Crisps soss with your head, Tembs! We're already barely sane. I mean—" He spread his arms to gesture at the dream world around them. "Even the best Crisp can malfunction! Do you want to spend the rest of your life seeing and hearing Moto talk to you in his mirror, no matter what else you're doing?"

Her stomach turned at the thought, but she pushed through it. "I'll let you know if that happens," she said. "What about his message?"

"I don't know," he said, shaking his head. "Moto doesn't panic. I've seen him in some bad situations, and nothing shakes him."

She nodded. People from Adhama had a habit of bottling up their emotions until it got them in trouble. Moto had been the one who had taught her how to control herself. The man in the Crisp wasn't the one she knew.

Kalais added: "I think something else might have happened to him."

"What?" Tembi started walking. As long as they were here, there was a pub a few shady pathways over. This was the kind of conversation—small hells, this was the kind of *day!*—that went better with a bottle or two of whatever beverage the Earth Assembly chose to tout to offworlders. Probably beer. Everybody knew beer, and what was familiar made for reliable sales.

"There's a rumor going around that the Blackwings are poisoning their enemies on the Council." Kalais knew where she was going, and he took the first turn towards the pub. "Not killing them. Slipping them a new mindfuck which knocks their resilience and intelligence down."

Tembi grimaced. Use of cognitive disruptors was routine, even in peacetime. The right blend could create whatever workplace disaster its user wanted. A common blend was used to heighten anxiety while also exacerbating aggression. Spike the drinks in a critical meeting with a few drops of that stuff, and then sit back to watch the chaos ensue. Except mindfucks were used so often that meetings were held behind a veritable gauntlet of air and water filters, all surfaces in the room were scrubbed before anyone could touch them, and there were legions of 'bots on molecule patrol darting away in the background. Not to mention that people in positions of power had to endure every conceivable form of biotest a couple of times a week.

A new type of mindfuck that didn't ping on the security systems? If it lopped a chunk off of intelligence and resiliency... *That* was a scary, scary thought! You'd have people in command positions making decisions without full control of their senses, and nobody would know it. Or maybe they *would* know it, or at least suspect it, and suspicion would fester like an open wound.

They reached the pub. Tembi found the taps, and pulled a couple of tall mugs full of beer for Kalais and herself. She leaned against the smooth stone surface of the counter and cupped her hands around the mug, wondering to herself if hydration in a dream might count towards self-care.

"We need to get Moto back," Kalais said. "If he did get hit with a mindfuck, we need to clear out his system so he can tell us what he learned."

"We need to get Moto back, full stop," she sighed. "Time's caught up with him. He's out there right now, still in stasis. He's alone and helpless."

Kalais spent a long moment busy with his drink, very obviously not shouting about how *the Deep couldn't move through time!* Instead, he chose to swallow and then said, very cautiously, "Yes, we need to get him back."

She grinned at him. "Where do we start? I've already asked the Deep."

"For advice?"

"No, but that's not a bad idea." Tembi pushed herself away from the pub's counter. "Deep? You know we want to find Moto, right?"

One of the pub's taps turned on. Another mug of beer floated over to the counter and joined theirs. Kalais watched it move in silence, eyes wide.

"Good fortune," Tembi said, as she held up her own mug, and tapped it lightly against the third. She gestured for Kalais to do the same, and he did, shooting his mug out and back so quickly that she feared the rest of his beer might whip straight across the pub. "Deep, do you understand that we're worried about Moto?"

The third mug bobbed up and down in the air.

"We know you're keeping him safe, but we're still worried." Tembi paused. She wished Matindi was here. Matindi knew what to…well, no, Matindi didn't know what to say to make the Deep understand, either. Nobody did. Probably not even the Deep. But she'd still feel better if Matindi were here. "We need to find him so we can take him out of stasis. Can you help us find him?"

Somehow, Kalais guessed what would happen. "Wait, Tembs, *no!*"

Too late.

There was a snapping sound as a stasis pod appeared, as if something in the local ecosystem had been broken. Tembi gasped, sick to her stomach, as Moto's pod cracked through the eggshell boundaries of the dream and clattered against the pub's sandstone floor. The world bent around them, a wobble in a manufactured reality, before it stabilized itself again with the pod in the middle of the room.

The pod. The pod was here.

Moto was *here.*

"Well…" Tembi said, once she had gotten the urge to vomit under control. She hadn't stopped to think. She hadn't thought the Deep would actually do it—no, she hadn't thought the Deep *could* do it! They were in a *dream world,* by all the little gods and devils! "Well, he's…safe."

"Safe?!" Kalais was clutching his mug as if he wanted to use it to smash open someone's skull. "Tell me this is another illusion!"

She shook her head even as she reached out to place her hands on the stasis pod. Its physical presence was a constant kick in the stomach, a slice of a different reality that had been wedged into a private corner of the Deep's dream that had been gifted to her and Kalais. When she touched the pod, she was shaken by the very truth of it. The posters on the glasshouse had felt solid, but they lacked the sensation of…of *fact!* that accompanied real objects. The stasis pod was a fact, and this made itself especially clear as her palms began to sting. The pod was cold. Cold enough for the chill to penetrate her skin. She snatched her hands away and tucked them beneath her armpits to warm them as she said, "No," she said, confirming it for both of them. "He's here. Don't touch it. Your hands will freeze right off."

"Okay…okay." She could see Kalais slide into military mode, the need to respond to a crisis triggering his training. He moved to examine the pod. "Okay. The pod's seal isn't broken."

"Should we open it?" She could barely see Moto inside the pod. The plass faceplate was smoky with soot. *Soot* and *cold? Where did the Deep park this thing?*

Kalais stared at her as if she had grown an extra eyeball in the center of her forehead. "We are not touching this pod until we get it back into the real world," he insisted. "Stasis is dangerous in controlled conditions, and he's inside a *dream?* How can that happen?!"

Tembi grabbed him by the wrist before he could spiral off into anger. "Kalais?" she hissed. "Shut up. Right this second."

"Deep?" she called, very gently. "Thank you so much for bringing Moto here."

Kalais settled his training around him. "Yes," he said harshly, as if the word grated at him. He glanced at the floating mug of beer. "Thank you. We were worried. It's good to know where he is."

Every table in the pub turned into a giant turtle and started walking around.

Kalais looked towards the ceiling. "I think I'm going to scream."

"No, you're not," she said, even as a turtle waddled straight towards the pod. She stepped in front of the turtle and nudged its shell to turn it aside. "We've got to get Moto back to the real world. Deep? Can you do that for us?"

One of the turtles turned back into a table and fell over, clattering against the floor.

"Deep, I'm ordering you—" Kalais began.

"Don't," Tembi said to him, as two more of the turtles became tables again. "Just don't. Deep, he doesn't have any orders. We're not angry. We're trying to figure out what's the best thing to do."

"*I'm* angry!"

"If you can't control yourself, you need to go," she told him. "We've got Moto back. That's a solved problem. If you scare the Deep so it thinks Moto isn't safe with us, it might take him and hide him again."

Kalais stared at her, his eyes white and furious.

"Go," she said. "Get out of here. I'll find you in the morning." He nodded, sharp as the edge of a knife, and vanished.

Tembi waited a few moments until she was sure he wouldn't reappear, and then she sat on the nearest turtle.

"Is this how you feel?" she asked the air around her. "Like everything should make sense but it never does, no matter how hard you try?"

The turtle swung its head towards her on its long neck, and said in the Deep's not-voice, ::*FULL BUCKETS*::

She sighed and began scratching the hard knots on the turtle's head. It leaned into her touch and began to purr like a kitten. "Can you bring Matindi here, please?"

There was a pause, and then Matindi appeared, dressed in her gardening robes. She took in the scene in the pub, shook her head, and took a seat on a nearby turtle. "Is that Moto in the pod?" she asked. Tembi nodded. "So you found him."

"No," Tembi replied. "The Deep brought him here."

"Have you tried getting him out?"

"Kalais thinks that would be dangerous." As Matindi's green eyebrows rose at the mention of Tembi's ex-boyfriend, Tembi explained what had happened since she had arrived within the Deep's dream.

Matindi slid gracefully down from her turtle and wove her way through the herd. She walked around the stasis pod, poking it once with a finger before Tembi could warn her. "Leave him here," she said. "He'll be fine here until you decide what to do with him."

"What? No, I can't!" Tembi laughed. "This's a dream, Matindi! Dreams don't last."

"This one does," Matindi replied. She reached out with her freezer-burnt finger to tickle a turtle beneath its chin. "Part of the Deep is always sleeping, aren't you, dear?"

::SLEEP:: the turtle replied with a smile.

"The Deep let me set up a room in this dream almost...oh, two thousand years ago," Matindi said. "Everything I've brought into it has stayed there. Including plants."

"There's a difference between plants and..." Tembi gestured to Moto.

"I agree. The Deep will never forget about Moto." She turned to speak to the turtle. "You'll keep Moto safe, won't you, dear?"

The turtle answered ::YES:: before it collapsed into a table. The other turtles followed its example, and within moments, the pub looked as it had before the Deep had flooded it in reptiles.

"Stasis can be really dangerous," said Tembi as she stared at the pod. "Viruses and bacteria still multiply in stasis pods. I don't want to leave him here."

"I know," Matindi said, as she went to pour herself a mug from the taps. "But if we don't know the agreement he's made with the Deep, this is the best place for him. Who's going to look for him in a dream?" she asked.

"Other Witches?" Tembi offered lamely.

"Where else would you put him, sweetling?"

Where else, indeed? There was an entire galaxy available to her—the place with the fish came to mind—but there were vulnerabilities with every possible hiding spot. Then the sensible answer asserted itself. "A hospital, to get him out of the pod and clean out the mindfuck."

"And if they can't diagnose this particular mindfuck? Happens all the time. He'll be stuck in the hospital until they do...

or he'll persuade the Deep to jump him out of there, and he may never trust you again, depending on how strong the mind-fuck is. If he starts jumping forward in time, we might never find him."

Tembi flinched. "Fine," she said. "I'll start looking for the source of the mindfuck." She went over to the pod and scraped some soot away from the plass so she could peer into the pod. "Moto said he brought documents with him. I'll bet the people who 'fucked him are in those files."

"Or it's a coincidence and every person associated with the Council has been hit, as has happened at least once a year for the past…oh…twenty-three centuries."

Tembi glared at Matindi, who replied with the beatific smile of a saint.

Chapter Twelve

The next morning, Tembi slept in. Someone else was handling bomb duty? She didn't need to be anywhere until a late morning meeting with Domino? *Delightful.* She woke when her ancient wreck of a cat gave up trying to scratch her awake, and draped himself over her mouth and nose instead. She coughed herself back to consciousness, and spent a few quiet moments petting Tabuu and telling him that he was just the worst cat ever while he purred and wiped his nose on her sleeve. Then, biscuits and coffee: Matindi was nowhere to be found, but the coffee she had left in the silver carafe on the kitchen counter was perfect in every way.

(Her second mother swore it took a minimum of five hundred years of practice to really *get* coffee, and she still didn't understand tea. As she had taught Tembi how to make coffee, and Tembi's own version was excellent but not exceptional, she believed her.)

Once showered, scrubbed, and clothed in a set of her better robes, Tembi stepped into the Deep. It was in a good mood, too: its colors flowed around her, its feather-fur soft and welcoming. As she settled onto its back for the quick ride to Earth, a burst of music turned the Rails a lovely shade of cobalt blue.

"All right, beautiful beast," she said, laughing. "We've got time. With you, we've always got time. What do you want to sing today?"

A small weasel-like creature appeared. Tembi didn't recognize it: the galaxy was full of life. Sentient? Possibly. Sapient? Definitely not. But it was full of beautiful glittering life all the same, and as it disappeared, it let out a surprised chirp like a little bird.

What to sing? Usually a song came to her, faster than anything. She had a fondness for ancient Earth songs—honestly, those songs were the only thing she appreciated about Earth—and she always had one at hand. This morning, she felt buoyant, with a small thread of melancholy and self-doubt making sure her good mood was safely tethered to reality. What song grabbed the glad mood of the moment and set it against a balance due?

...she began to sing.

The ballroom was filled with fashion's throng,
It shone with a thousand lights,
And there was a woman who passed along,
The fairest of all the sights,
A girl to her lover then softly sighed,
There's riches at her command;
But she married for wealth, not for love he cried,
Though she lives in a mansion grand.

It was a familiar song, one that she had sung with the Deep many times before. She started scratching the usual itchy spots on the Deep's back as they flew, and it started rumbling beneath her as it mimicked a purr.

She's only a bird in a gilded cage,
A beautiful sight to see,
You may think she's happy and free from care,
She's not, though she seems to be,
'Tis sad when you think of her wasted life,
For youth cannot mate with age,
And her beauty was sold,
For an old man's gold,
She's a bird in a gilded cage.

The prismatic world within the Rails shot by, colors plucking themselves from beneath the dark and splashing across them, the hues so bright they nearly had weight. Tembi began the final verse:

I stood in a churchyard just at eve',
When sunset adorned the west,
And looked at the people who'd come to grieve,
For loved ones now laid at rest,
A tall marble monument marked the grave,
Of one who'd been fashion's queen,
And I thought she is happier here at rest,
Than to have people say when seen...

The Deep sang along in its worlds-shaking voice: Tembi couldn't hear it, but she felt it through every molecule of her being, even down to the tips of her still-numb fingers. A series of jeweled insects appeared, butterflies and beetles and an assortment of small six-legged creatures they had never seen before, all of these flying around the Deep in tight buzzing arcs.

She pushed her hands into the velvet of the Deep's feather-fur, trying her best to feel it. And then—a small miracle!—she *did!* With a shiver, her skin went from unfeeling stone to all-over sensations, and there was a moment of exquisite discomfort where Tembi felt crushed by the weight of her own clothes. She gasped and dropped her face into the Deep's pelt, letting it swallow her up in its softness. Was it real, or was it an illusion in which the stress of her daily life hadn't tricked her body into wrapping her in armor? She didn't know and didn't care.

"You're the best, Deep," she whispered, and they flew on.

Light bloomed around them as the Deep swooped and soared along the Rails. Tembi had wondered about that name—the Rails? How *odd!*—to describe this space between the worlds. Matindi had told her that it was a holdover from an old method of transportation in which large machines used metal rails to glide from one place to another. Remove the machine from its rails, or the rails from beneath the machine, and both became useless. Put them together and they could remake whole worlds.

"Those machines were nowhere near as good as you, beautiful beast," she whispered, and the air filled itself with the glad scent of roses.

When the two of them had sung themselves out, the Deep opened the way and Tembi stepped into Domino's front office. Her skin settled around her like a shroud, all sensation leaving her again. *Appropriate,* she thought, as she announced herself to the office assistant and then took a seat in the waiting room. It was a remarkable room, with furnishings and décor worthy of Domino's positions at both Lancaster Tower and in the Earth Assembly, with views from two banks of windows. The office overlooked the Plaza, a wide paved park set off with seating and tasteful spots of flowers, and large enough to hold public assemblies of twenty thousand angry planetary dignitaries, plus food carts. Along the horizon was a stripe of blue: Tembi hadn't appreciated how near they were to the ocean.

A few minutes after she had nested down in a plush chair with a public channels display, another assistant appeared. Tembi knew him: a dour Witch named Douglas Frugal, his paint a dark swirl of red ribbons which appeared to split his face in half. "Witch Stoneskin?" He pressed a folded piece of paper into her hands. "Witch Domino is unavoidably busy. She wanted you to have this."

Tembi nodded, but Frugal was already gone, vanished through the Deep to manage whatever workaday chore needed his attention. She unfolded the paper; it was creamy and thick, with little wooden fibers blended into the pulp to suggest it was handmade. In the center of the paper, stark black letters stated: *Morality is the privilege of the comfortable.*

"What under the seven fat gods of Holt Prime am I supposed to make of this?" she swore as she folded up the paper and shoved it into her pocket.

A cough from the office assistant at the desk reminded Tembi she wasn't alone. The assistant gave a meaningful glance to the icons on a small shelf near his chair, and then turned back to his labors. The seven round spheres displayed on the shrine nearly got her to apologize, but she wrapped herself into the Deep and jumped away instead—religion made her itch.

The Deep waited as she considered her options. Tembi thought, and groused, and grumbled about semantics. "'Morality is the privilege of the comfortable,'" she quoted to the Deep. "What's she trying to tell me? That she's no longer reconsidering how Lancaster treats you? Is this her way of saying I'm a spoiled brat who focuses on the wrong thing? Or is it a coded message?" She pulled the paper from her pocket and held it up to the light spilling from the Rails. "Do you know what this means?"

Books sprang up around her, hundreds of them...*thousands* of them! Stacks of books reeking of old paper were interspersed among dedicated plass sheets with titles etched along the edges. Tembi took up the nearest one and made her way through twenty dense words about philosophy before she gave up. The Deep consumed an obscene number of books. She had no doubt that the Deep had memorized the contents of these books, and there was at least a sentence in each that would be directly relevant to Domino's message. Whether the Deep understood what it read was a different story (a-ha-ha) altogether, and she was sure the spontaneous library was its way of answering her multiple questions without needing to understand them.

Still, there was a way around this without hurting the Deep's feelings. "Good idea, buddy!" she said brightly. "Let's go to the Library."

The books vanished, presumably returned to wherever the Deep had found them, and Tembi stepped out of the Deep and onto a tidy gravel path. Around her was a dense hedge with boulders within the shrubbery, and above this was the distant spire of Lancaster Tower.

The Library was set within an ever-changing maze. The journey was said to teach the younger Witches a valuable lesson in humility, but its true purpose was to amuse the Deep and the Librarian. Young Witches who couldn't yet use the Deep to jump would approach the small stone cottage at the center of the maze, and find themselves on the other side of the building, staring at a new path through the thorns. They would shout and swear and eventually start kicking things, and the Librarian and the Deep would *laugh* and *laugh.*

(Practical jokes at Lancaster were extraordinary. Launching Matindi's small cottage into orbit was among the tamer tricks. The Deep loved to pull pranks, and its favorite was to lurk around Lancaster's holiday parties and wait until its Witches were good and properly drunk, at which point it could *take over their bodies!* It would use the Witch to utter a sentence or two, its choice of words slightly more coherent than usual, and then leave the Witch's body, taking the alcohol and mental inebriation with it. If the Witch didn't pass out from the experience, they were left acutely, almost painfully, sober, and the object of hilarity among their drunk friends.)

For Tembi, the Library had always been a place of refuge. Very few Witches used it. The building was more of an archive for the printed works of Witches than a proper lending library. The most valuable resource within its walls was the Librarian, a Witch named Williamson of immense age and an eternally youthful appearance which fit his personality about as well as a couture suit fit a starship. Williamson seemed to live in the Library: the building was always open, and he was always awake and sitting at the ancient wooden desk in the center of the Library's single room.

Today, Tembi knocked on the door and pushed it open. For a brief moment, she caught sight of a spacious kitchen with a patio which spilled out onto a lush green jungle, and then it was the usual small room with nothing but Williamson, the desk, and four closed doors

"Good morning, Witch-*nim*," he said, always proper.

Her ears perked at the Adhamantian honorific. "And to you, Williamson...ah...?"

"Hmm." Williamson glanced at the ceiling, as if ordering his thoughts. "My people did prefixes instead of suffixes. I suppose the equivalent would be Master Williamson, to indicate mastery of profession, but Witches as a group hold such rarefied sociocultural status that it might be closer to Lord Williamson.

"Which would make you Lady Stoneskin," he said, bowing to her from his chair.

She laughed, and returned the bow. "Old England, yes? They have lords and ladies on Camelot."

"Ah, that's right, you're a knight," Williamson said, his blue eyes bright. "Which would make you Dame Stoneskin."

"The Arthurians call me Sir Stoneskin."

"Conditionally gendered honorifics," he said, as he flipped on a plass tablet and made a note. "Ladies, but no dames. Need to trace the etymology of that division. Language is endlessly fascinating." He looked up at her and adjusted his glasses. "What brings you to the Library, o knight of Camelot?"

She set Domino's letter on the desk and pushed it towards him. He unfolded the paper and read the brief message. "I recognize this hand," he murmured. "What's the context?"

As Williamson was a core member of their certainly-*not*-a-rebellion against Lancaster, Tembi had no hesitation telling him about the events of the last daily cycle. She stopped short of letting him know that Moto was stuck in the Deep's dream, but everything else spilled out, her words practically puddling on the old wooden desk between them. As she spoke, Williamson's eyebrows kept going up, until they were in danger of vanishing into his close-cropped blond hair.

"...goodness," he said, when she finished.

"What does the letter mean?"

"Anything and nothing." At her frustrated sigh, Williamson held up his index fingers beside his own ears and tipped them forward to signal his own version of *mild apology*. Tembi grinned. "I would say that on its face, it means what it means: those who are fortunate enough to have their own needs met can then spend their time worrying about the needs of others.

"Morality is a need," he said. "But on the hierarchy of needs, it's below food, safety, shelter, and companionship, among others. It's only those of us who have sated these other needs who have the luxury of questioning possible moral failings. In that respect, Domino is calling those who judge morality in others—and possibly you in particular—spoiled brats." Tembi drummed her fingertips against the desktop in a staccato tempo. "But," he added, as he shoved his plass tablet beneath her hand to keep her from scuffing the desk's oiled finish, "it's more likely that Domino meant it to unsettle you, and nothing else."

"Why? She said she wanted my help."

The Librarian shrugged. "She's an immortal with an impossible job, Sir Stoneskin. If you're distracted, you're not bothering her." He grinned as her ears drooped, and added, "Work around her schedule. Take some of the burden from her. Prove you're worth her valuable time, and she'll set some aside for you."

"How?" Tembi shook her head.

"Get Moto out of the mindfuck," he replied. "Or take up some of Moto's duties until he's recovered. Or both."

Take up his duties... "You know what Moto does?" she asked, expecting some bland answer about administrative actions.

Williamson picked up the tablet and leaned back in his chair, and pretended to study its contents.

"Ah," she said quietly. Then, a small stray thought: "You were one of the first Witches, right?" She knew Williamson was older than either Matindi or Matthew, and even as Witches went, the two of them were considered old.

"No." He shook his head. "I'm of the second generation. I'm one of the first immortals. The Deep had to watch its first Witches die before it learned they could. Then?" He tapped himself on the sternum. "Forever young, and able to watch the galaxy unfold in a million new ways."

"And Domino?"

"Barely out of her nappies at seven hundred, but a precocious child. Determined to reshape Lancaster from the first."

Tembi's ears tilted to signal *distrust*.

"I didn't quite get that," Williamson said, "but I'll clarify. Domino came in, looked around, and decided Lancaster's culture was a gross distortion of the worst humanity had to offer. She cleaned the cobwebs out of the whole place, rafters to basement. We had..." He paused, appearing mildly embarrassed. "We had let ourselves believe we were better than we were. You know those old rotters down in the village, always angry?"

Tembi nodded.

"They're angry because Domino forced us to accept that we aren't divine. She did this nearly seven hundred years ago, but they still want to go back to when the galaxy worshipped them. Today, Lancaster is all about neutrality and gathering wealth, and..." He looked over his glasses at her. "That's *better* than how it used to be. But, perhaps, Domino's own story should remind us that we can always improve ourselves," he said. "Best of luck, young Master Knight Stoneskin."

She feigned a salute with an invisible sword. "And to you, Master Williamson."

"As we're colleagues, just calling me Williamson is appropriate." He turned back to his reading, his attention vanishing into his tablet as if a switch had been turned.

Colleagues. Tembi kept the smile off her face, but it took effort. Williamson had watched her grow up. She opened the front door, crossed the maze, and found herself in the great grassy fields of Lancaster.

What to do next? How to be of use to Domino—how to be of use to a woman she truly disliked—while also prodding her towards change? She mulled over her options as she started the long walk home through the tall grass. Focus on the problems in the order they appeared—

Right. The broken moon.

How did she keep forgetting that moon?

All of the hardest tasks came with checklists. If Tembi was to find the source of the weapon which had split the moon, she needed Moto. If she was to help Moto, she needed to find the mindfuck. If she was to find the mindfuck...

How did she go about locating the source of an illegal drug?

Kalais could help with that. He had access to the Earth Assembly, and he could suggest blood draws or whatever was required for testing. If they didn't consent...well, they still had another five liters of undiluted Motoblood in that stasis pod. He had snatched her DNA for the Crisp, after all. He owed her at least a couple of cubic centimeters of blood.

The idea of getting the Deep to pluck blood straight out of his veins still worried her, but it could be done. Other Witches used the Deep to empty their bladders. That, coupled with using the Deep to whisk the dirt from their bodies, meant that there were some Witches who hadn't seen the inside of a bathroom in a millennium. If she could make the Deep understand that she meant blood instead of urine…well, Moto had succeeded, so this was likely a manageable task, although she'd probably have to do an archaic blood draw with needles and tubes, followed by peeing in a cup for the sake of making herself perfectly clear.

Wait, no, she'd probably have to go into Hub for the blood draw. Lancaster's medical staff were exceptional but the majority were Earth-normal, and they fussed about her skin.

Except maybe they had already taught the Deep how to take blood without hurting the patient? It'd be worth checking—

The world split around her as the ground cracked open, liquid fire shooting up from beneath the lush lawns. She spun, falling, landing hard on her ass as Lancaster's white-gold Nautilus started burning, *burning*, fire running like water down from the top of the tower, cutting through the structure like plasma bolts, peeling it apart. A vast sound of humming, the sound rising up around her, with voices rising in screams, as if she hadn't been alone in the middle of an open field when the catastrophe began. Was she the one screaming? No, it was a chorus of voices, all of them in agony. The air reeked of burning flesh; there was heat strong enough to push against her skin. A slab of rock the size of her house rose up in front of her, one side still green from its recent life as a lawn. It hung there, nearly motionless, and then fell towards her like a tipping tombstone—

The vision broke apart, leaving Tembi breathless on the ground, staring up at the distant spire of the Tower. It was intact, still shining with its usual flawless beauty.

"Right," she gasped, her hands digging into the grass so hard that the smell of freshly bruised earth filled the air. "You're right, Deep. The first problem wasn't the moon. I forgot about the vision on the space station."

She stayed where she had fallen, wondering if her heart was about to hammer straight through her chest. The Deep sending visions to its Witches wasn't a rare event, exactly, but Tembi had heard that the majority of Witches went years (sometimes decades, or—*bliss!*—centuries!) without having reality wrench apart. While Witches like Tembi and Matindi had about two or three visions a year, they usually occurred when the Deep was trying to communicate something important, something specific…something necessary.

Something it didn't understand and needed its Witches to explain.

"I don't know what to tell you, buddy," Tembi whispered. "I don't know what's happening, either."

Tabuu popped out of the air and landed on her chest. The ancient cat, long accustomed to such shenanigans, let out an irritated squawk before stalking a meter away to clean his feet in meditative fury.

Tembi stayed flat on her back, staring at the distant tower, thinking. After a time, she stood, gathered up her cat, and jumped home.

Hours later, she was sprawled across the carpet in the central room, a constellation of digital data in orbit around her: Moto's information, retrieved from the stasis pod and displayed in grammalight for easy reading. The data was a chronology of the mindfuck taking hold. At first, each entry had been carefully prepared, showing the same purposeful sensibilities that defined everything her friend touched. But the entries soon devolved into rambling, turning Moto's detective work into a complex mess of disjointed statements, most of them about how the Blackwings were snatching tekkers off the street and filing them away for later.

It would be one thing, she thought, *if this involved a single location, or a couple of people. But no, he's decided to go poke about the entire Blackwing Army.*

Moto had been convinced the weapon that would split the moon was of Blackwing make. He had wisps of proof from here and there; apparently, he had spent quite a lot of time sneaking into different Blackwing facilities. However, there was no way she'd waste Domino's time with this information. Giant gods, no! Moto's data gave off smoke, but there was no fire.

(To be perfectly fair, Tembi believed it was a Blackwing weapon, too. The Sabenta's bombs were effective but were built on the scale of people who were hanging on to the edge of survival. It would take more resources than the Sabenta had to build a weapon like this.)

"...unless the Sabenta have been saving up and dumped everything they had into this project," she said aloud.

"Perhaps."

Matindi's voice caused Tembi to launch straight off the floor like a startled cat. Her second mother was leaning against an armchair, inspecting one of the data sheets. "How long have you been standing there?"

"Long enough to learn that Moto is in trouble." Matindi used a nimble green finger to spin a data sheet towards Tembi. It was among the last records in his files, and was barely coherent. "The poor boy. It might not be a mindfuck after all—he might be suffering from something worse."

Tembi nodded. She had had the same thought. Mindfucks were only effective when they were subtle. Moto's deterioration would have been noticed. It would have hampered his performance as a spy—

Wait.

"Why didn't Domino notice?" she asked Matindi. "If he was so far gone, she should have seen that. Helped him." Matindi murmured something under her breath, so low that Tembi could barely hear it. "What was that?" she asked, grinning.

"I said Domino probably did notice, and she couldn't be bothered."

What Matindi had said contained far fewer syllables and if

properly aimed could scorch the carpet, but Tembi let it slide. "If it's not a mindfuck, it'll be harder to help Moto."

"Or easier, if it's a physical issue."

"Should we take him out of the pod?"

"A different cause doesn't change the effect, sweetling," Matindi chuckled darkly. "As soon as we take him out, he regains consciousness. If he's not thinking clearly, he could jump and be gone forever."

Tembi sighed and began to flick Moto's data away. "What if we work together? You, me, Matthew, Bayle...even Domino. We'd make our meaning clear to the Deep then."

"At first? Yes." Matindi released her lock on the document she was reading, and the image dissolved. "But the longer it goes on, the more likely that Moto might catch the Deep when it's forgotten what we've asked." She waited, as if expecting the Deep to respond. Nothing moved; the Deep remained silent. "No offense meant, dear."

Again, there was no answer.

"Deep?" Tembi called.

This time, the grammacube which had displayed Moto's files raised itself into the air.

"Are we talking too fast for you to follow, dear?" asked Matindi.

::YES::

"Well." Matindi stood. "I'm going to see if the garden is beyond repair. Tembi will explain it to you."

A cushion pulled itself from the couch and floated over to nestle itself against Tembi's leg, and she glared at Matindi as she left to resurrect her long-neglected garden.

Chapter Thirteen

She had never been to Kadal before. The planet was a distant port on the main shipping lanes, with four moons barely large enough to deserve names. It was also simply lousy with lizards. She stepped out of the Deep in an alley a block away from the tea house where she was to meet Bayle, and found her feet and ankles swarmed with small green geckos.

Oh, well. She always did the reading before she jumped to an unfamiliar planet, and she had known to expect the lizards. She just hadn't expected so *many* of them! After a few cautious steps, she found they were quick to scurry out of her path, and she cautiously made her way into the city street, several lizards clinging to her robes. Most of the people she passed wore trousers with their cuffs tucked into their boots. They gave Tembi's long skirts and bare feet a puzzled look, only nodding at her once they spotted her Witch's paint. Along the way, some of Tembi's lizards hopped off and new ones hopped on, and she laughed aloud as she realized that humans served as their public transportation.

She loved her life as a Witch. Strip away the drama and the infighting, the politics and the odd explosive device, and you were left with an entire galaxy. One step, and you were inside the Deep. Another, and you were on a different planet ten solar systems away. Without the Deep, she might have lived and died in a busted neighborhood on a throwaway world. Now, she was learning about the travel habits of the descendants of old Earth's stowaway geckos.

What a *life!*

Except…

One of the locals glanced at her bare feet, and then her face paint. That should have been enough, except the wind chose that moment to give her headscarf a hard nudge, and it tore away from the tip of one of her ears. The local's lips curled in disgust.

She tucked her scarf over her exposed ear, and gave it an extra tug to ensure it would stay put.

What a life.

Bayle was waiting for her at a small table outside the tea house, staring into her cup. By way of greeting, she said, "This isn't tea."

The plass mug was clear, and Tembi could see an enormous quantity of small flecks of…stuff…suspended in the liquid. It could have been a trick of the light, but the stuff appeared to twitch. "Is it drinkable?" she asked.

Bayle fluffed out a paper napkin, stared pointedly at the glass, and waited. After a moment, all of the slightly shivering stuff appeared in a small wet pile in the center of the napkin. "Now it is," she muttered, as she balled up the napkin and tucked it aside. "Thank you, Deep."

Tembi chuckled as she shook the last of the lizards from her robes, and took the chair across from her friend. "Odd planet?"

"They're all odd. But some of them are more manageably odd," Bayle said, as a lizard climbed on top of their table and began to lick its own eyeball. "So, how do we locate Moto?"

"Speaking of odd," Tembi muttered, and caught her up on the events of the previous night. Bayle's usual calm demeanor dropped along with her jaw at the right points in the story. By the time Tembi ended with, "The current plan is to make sure we can cure the mindfuck before we take him out of stasis," Bayle was gasping like a fish left on a pier.

"I have questions," her friend said. "Too many questions. I don't… I can't… *I mean…!*"

"I know," Tembi replied. "But pick one and we'll start there."

Bayle waved her fists at the air until she decided on: "Fine. Do we have the time to follow this plan? If Moto knows something about the weapon, shouldn't we wake him up and get that information? You and Matindi can work together to force the Deep to keep him from jumping, and once we have it, we can put him back in stasis."

"I spoke to Kalais this afternoon. I found a way to get him some of Moto's blood, and he's already working to diagnose the mindfuck," Tembi told her. "If it is a mindfuck, we can play it safe for a day or two. If it's not, then we'll decide what to do. Besides," she said, as she handed her friend a data chip, "the Deep pulled what's on this chip out of Moto's robes. This is our job."

The chip was small, round, and gray. Utterly ordinary. The type of chip you would step over if you found it on the street, assuming whatever information it contained wasn't worth the minerals used to make it. Bayle tapped the chip against a bracelet, and began to thumb the air above the table as she scrolled through the data.

Or so Tembi assumed: the bracelet's feed was cued to Bayle's areotype, and she had it set so she was the only person who could see its projections. But Tembi had transferred the data to the chip herself, and she knew what part Bayle was reading when her blue eyes went wide.

When Bayle was finished, she thumbed off her drive and held out the chip to the open air. "Deep, could you return this to Moto's robes for safekeeping?" she asked. The chip blipped out of their existence. "Thanks, Deep," she sighed, and resumed staring into the depths of her beverage.

"Well?" Tembi asked.

"So that's why you wanted to meet here," Bayle said, her tone surprisingly mild. She refused to look at any of the people at the nearby tables.

Tembi nodded. "That was the last entry in his records that made any real sense. If something other than a mindfuck targeted to the Council hit him, it might have happened here."

"We're not qualified for this, Tembs."

"We're Witches," she replied. "We've got immunity."

"That's not the same thing as being qualified. You disarm bombs, and I teach classes in public relations. We're not detectives. As sure as all the minor hells, we're not spies. Moto…"

"…was more than Domino's assistant," Tembi finished for her.

Bayle nodded. "I know you want to do more to help the Deep and stop the war, but—"

Tembi pressed a finger against her own lips.

"Right, right." Bayle nodded, and then immediately shook her head in the same smooth motion. "You and I aren't qualified for… well…" She tapped her bracelet. "Tembi, Moto was trained, and look what happened to him!"

"I know," Tembi said, as she opened the Deep. "C'mon."

Still shaking her head, Bayle followed her into the jump.

One fairly heated discussion and a change of clothing later, they came out on the other side of Kadal.

It was darkest night here, or close to it. There were no happy lizards and no quaint tea houses a short block away. Instead, it was all stone and concrete, smashed into high and brutal walls that were lit in red, accompanied by a smell which rocked the two of them on their heels.

"Gods!" Bayle gasped, as she pulled the edge of her scarf free to cover her nose. "What *is* that?"

Tembi glanced in the direction of the blowing winds, and didn't answer.

There was a gate before them, humming with caged electricity. It was after hours. The guard box at the gate was empty, a glowing sign telling all visitors to come back in the morning.

She ignored it and marched forward.

They had changed into business robes: Bayle was in blue and gold, and Tembi was wearing the dusky colors of an Adhama sandstorm. There were shoes (sadly) and their hair was wrangled beneath their scarves, with Tembi's ears tucked safely away, and Bayle's hands shrouded within her long sleeves.

They were Witches. They had immunity. But that had been true for Moto, too.

Tembi stood before the gate, tilting her face to best display her Witch's paint. There was a clicking sound, and then the gate swung up, folding itself away within the edges of the building. A woman came out, tall in her Blackwing uniform but dwarfed by the sheer size of the gateway.

"Witches," she said, her voice flat. "Welcome."

"Lady Oliver of Atlantis," Bayle replied, and then she nodded to Tembi. "Sir Stoneskin of Adhama, as honored by Camelot."

The woman's face snapped from annoyance to suspicion keen as razors as she realized her unwanted visitors were both Witches and nobility. "Welcome," she said again, adding feigned warmth this time, and ushered them inside.

This was the guest entrance. All of the practicality of the building was hidden elsewhere. Here were nothing but the costumes of industry, with sales figures and products on display. They made durable goods here, after all, items that offered that handmade touch for the discerning buyer. Their guide chattered about production levels and shipping times and all the little details of moving products across the galaxy, a sales pitch that Tembi and Bayle had heard a hundred times before. This was what Witches did, after all.

"There are few on staff at this hour. We do have a guest suite," their guide said. "If you would like to meet with General Carroll, we would be honored if you would stay the night."

Bayle stared down at her, a tremendous achievement considering the other woman's height. "Thank you, but there's no need."

Their guide nodded. It had been an empty gesture anyhow. "Would you like to speak to the night manager?"

"We would," Bayle replied. "If they are all who are available to receive us."

Their guide's face showed nothing.

It took longer than it should have to reach the manager's office. The old delaying tactic was in effect, the one where unwanted guests were escorted along empty hallways until someone in a position of authority could perform a lightning cleanup and finish cramming stimulants into their bloodstream. After several minutes of walking and strained small talk, the guide's hand moved to her ear, and she gradually changed course to return them to an area near the guest entrance.

Then, the guide's eyes went wide, and she changed course

again. "Honored Witches," she said, as she picked up her pace. "General Carroll has made herself available to you."

"Yes," Bayle said, as she paused to inspect a piece of art hanging on a nearby wall. "Would you know anything about the artist? This is of quite remarkable quality, especially for a planet such as yours."

Their guide folded her hands together. "All of our pieces were donated by our residents," she replied. "They are for sale. Would you like me to inquire about this one?"

Bayle's hand leapt away from the painting as if it had opened a mouth and spit acid, but she said, ever so calmly, "That won't be necessary."

"Very well." Their guide resumed walking. Tembi caught a glimpse of the woman's self-satisfied smile in the reflection of a nearby window.

The three of them didn't speak for the rest of their short trip. Their guide deposited them in an overlarge office with its windows obscured by heavy fabric curtains, and offered them drinks. Tembi and Bayle refused; Bayle took a seat on a chair with her back to the windows, while Tembi went to lift one of those curtains so she could stare across the lot below.

"Gods," she whispered.

She had seen prisons. She had seen detention camps. This was different.

This was a block of stone and plass and metal, carved into buildings. All was black or gray, with the same red lighting that had greeted them at the guest entrance. There was no green or blue or orange, as nothing grew here. There was no brown; everything that had died or could give birth to new life had been scraped up and cast away. She doubted there were any other colors: someone with modded eyes had no doubt gone through and purged this place of all but red.

There should have been a sky of midnight blue overhead. Instead, she saw the flat gray of a weather cage, the largest cage Tembi had ever seen, one that stretched across the horizon. Fresh air could come and go, while wind and weather were sucked down to nearly nothing as they smacked up against the cage. Nothing else could enter it.

The buildings below were stark gray cubes, windowless and featureless, the foundational idea of a building before an architect gave it a soul.

She saw no people. That was the only good part about the view, that she saw no people walking about the featureless yard. There were bright spotlights casting their beams about the yard, but there was no suggestion that any other human creatures lived in this part of the world.

Even though this gray space stretched all around her.

There was no end to it.

They were already inside it.

"Impressive, yes?" Another voice, this one unfamiliar. Tembi turned to see a woman—*General Carroll? She's wearing the correct rank insignia.*—enter the room. She was taller and thinner than the guide, with moon-white skin, pale blue eyes, and platinum blond hair flowing past her waist. Her black uniform had three narrow red stripes starting at her left shoulder and running down her chest at an angle, as if the woman had been in a fight with a gigantic feline which had left her bloody.

And elegantly pointed ears which closely resembled Tembi's own.

"The Sagittarius Armed Forces have fourteen Hawk-class facilities," the blond woman said proudly. "This one is mine. Welcome to Camp Divested."

"General Carroll," Bayle said, standing. "Thank you for seeing us at this hour."

"We always accommodate Witches," the general replied, as she held out a graceful hand, palm up. Bayle covered it with her own, fingers held close together, and then moved to slide her hand back within the long fabric of her sleeve.

"Please, Lady Oliver, there's no need to hide. I know our reputation, but Blackwings welcome all," Carroll said, as she touched the tip of her own ear. She turned to Tembi. "I welcome you, as well, Sir Stoneskin. Are those the ears of a sister Tolkienite I see beneath that scarf?"

Tembi let the curtain drop as she turned to face the general. As she did, she pulled away her scarf, showing both her ears and her paint. "No," she answered. "I'm from Adhama."

The general's eyes went wide as she saw Tembi's golden birds. "I wondered if it would be you. Stoneskin is a common name among your people, but I've heard you are the only Witch who has taken it as her own," she said, her words measured. "To what do I owe the honor of a visit from two of Lancaster's most powerful Witches?"

"You honor us," Bayle replied. "We are young and barely vested, and thus have little power of our own. We serve at Lancaster's bidding."

"Of course," Carroll said, nodding. "I should not have presumed."

There was more of this jousting, most of which Tembi barely followed. The three of them eventually found their way to a small table. Carroll served them drinks, bowing so her hair hung like a fine white shroud around her face as she set each cup on the table. Wine, blood-red wine, in crystal cups. Her movements were alien in their meticulousness. No energy was wasted as she flowed easily from one gesture to the next.

Tembi wondered how many people the general had killed with those same fluid motions. Surely she must have gotten those perfect hands dirty at some point? Or perhaps she was like Bayle and her battles were bloodless.

"We are retracing the steps of a fellow Witch," Bayle told Carroll. "Moto Sanders, also of Adhama. His paint is of red flames." As she spoke, she triggered her bracelet. A projection of Moto's face appeared, visible to the three of them. He was calmer than he had been in the memory stored in the Crisp, and had black hair. He was also grinning, his dark eyes bright and seeming to shine out from within the projection.

Hey, Moto, Tembi thought. *We'll bring you the rest of the way home as soon as we can.*

"I've met him," Carroll replied. "Witch Sanders was bald, but those eyes? Unforgettable. We had drinks right here," she said, as she tapped the tabletop. "He wanted to know if our shipping needs were being met by our suppliers."

Tembi's ears went up. Carroll spotted this, and smiled. "My race on Tolkien has similar mannerisms," she said, as she moved her own ears to first indicate *attention,* then *surprise,* and finally *distrust.* "I've always found it lovely that your race and mine have parallel evolution in our communications. Do you feel as though you can never have a full conversation with the earless?"

"Sometimes," said Tembi, as she moved her own ears to mirror *distrust.*

Carroll's smile faltered as she nodded. "I see I must prove myself to you," she said, now somber. "How may I help you find your missing Witch?"

"I don't believe we said he was missing," Bayle replied.

"An educated guess on my part," Carroll said, waving one graceful hand to dismiss Bayle's comment. "Am I wrong?"

"Witches never go missing," Bayle said, as she pretended to sip her wine. "The Deep always knows where we are."

"Ah," Carroll said. Her smile returned, even as her ears called Bayle a liar. "Yes. The Deep."

Bayle had spent enough time with Tembi and Moto to understand the nuances of eartalk, but she didn't take the bait. "Retracing Moto's steps is an internal matter," she said. "There's no need to concern yourself with our reasons."

"Of course," demurred Carroll. "As I said, he came here to discuss shipping. How we move our goods off-world when Lancaster refuses to trade with us. Even though you choose to make those same services available to the Sabenta."

"We are not here to discuss policy," Bayle said. "Representatives from the Blackwings have already petitioned Lancaster to open the Deep to them. I'm sure they will petition us again. Your position is well represented."

"Of course," Carroll repeated, her tone flat as she went to refill her glass from a matching crystal flask. She glanced at the

Witches' glasses, ears dipping slightly towards *distrust* as she noted how the other women had only feigned companionable drinking. "I am merely repeating what Moto and I discussed. He agreed that the situation was…not wholly fair."

Tembi found herself nodding. Fair play? Yes, that sounded exactly like Moto. The Deep had been opened to the Sabenta only after the Blackwings had murdered them by the hundreds of millions. Now, when the Blackwings came to purge their planets, the Sabenta could call on the Witches to move non-combatants off-world and out of danger.

Moving Sabenta refugees and clearing bombs out of public places. That was the sum of the Deep's involvement in the war. It didn't touch ships outfitted with weapons. All of the Sabenta's fighting forces used FTL drives, as did the Blackwings. Exactly the same, except the Blackwings didn't have any refugees. The Sabenta might outnumber the Blackwings ten to one, but the Blackwings had old money and could keep all of the fighting contained to Sabenta worlds. Any Sabenta who couldn't escape in time was either killed or—

Tembi's eyes drifted towards the heavy curtains.

Not wholly fair, indeed.

Carroll spotted this. "Would you care to add something, Witch Stoneskin?"

"No." Her voice sounded cold.

"Where else did Moto go while he was here?" Bayle asked quickly. "I assume there was a tour of your shipping facilities?"

Carroll nodded. "I wasn't able to take him myself, but a member of my staff showed him around our facilities. Would you like to take the same tour?" She sighed as she made a show of checking the clock on the wall. "It would have to be in the morning. The buildings are closed for cleaning at night, and are dangerous."

And if we come back in the morning, whatever she's hiding will be gone.

"A generous offer," Bayle said. "We might take you up on that at a later time. For the moment, all we need to know are the details of your conversation."

"We spoke of the war, of course," replied Carroll. She peered over the edge of her wine glass, the reflection giving her blue eyes a small bite of red. "And how Lancaster's decision to aid the Sabenta instead of us reflects the priorities of your faith."

Bayle said nothing, did nothing. In the language of diplomats, this apparently was a breathtaking insult, as the general recoiled.

"Shall I be frank?" Carroll asked, placing her cup upon the table with unnatural grace. Somehow, the red hue of the wine stayed fast within her eyes. "I know you cannot speak of these matters with outsiders, but it may help if you know where I stand. I told Moto of my disgust with your leadership. You could do so much good, but you pretend it is prohibited."

Tembi felt pressed to speak. "The Deep doesn't like it when we use it in war," she said. "It's..." She searched for the words, and they crashed into her head, as suddenly as if the Deep had dropped them there. "It's scared of war."

"Don't insult my intelligence," Carroll said sharply. "There is no such thing as the Deep. Here," she said, as she gestured towards the windows. The curtains slid open, exposing the gray world of the detention facility. "*This* is reality. It is flawed and cruel, and if you have a problem with it, you should say so. Instead, you hide behind the image of a divine creature with supernatural powers, a religion like any other."

Tembi laughed, a chest-bursting sound that took all three women by surprise. "The Deep keeps the entire galaxy moving!" she exclaimed. "There's...how can you just *deny* it?"

"Lancaster and its Witches keep the galaxy moving," Carroll replied. "How? Technology, in all likelihood, augmenting your native telekinetic skills. Don't worry, Moto didn't tell me." She paused. "We did agree that Lancaster should never have chosen sides. You should have stayed neutral. The galaxy could have lived with your continued neutrality, though we would have hated you for it. When you joined yourselves to the Sabenta, you showed that your faith isn't constant. Your services can be bought.

"*We—*" she said, and it was clear she meant the Sagittarius Armed Forces and their allies. "—want to know your price. With your help, the war and all the suffering it has caused would be over within the week."

"Tembi," Bayle said, as she stood. "We will get no more information from General Carroll."

"Go," Carroll said, dismissing them with a wave of her flawless hand. "I had hoped you came to me tonight with an answer, but you children are useless. Tell your parents that the message I gave to Moto hasn't changed. We will pay whatever price Lancaster demands to end this war."

Chapter Fourteen

Tembi was fairly certain she was going to throw up.

Her arms were buried within the downy feather-fur of the Deep, her face pressed against its broad back. The rainbow space around them was touched in gray: the Deep knew she was upset, but it didn't understand why.

"Tembi?" Bayle was rubbing one of Tembi's shoulders with a single hand, a calm down gesture if ever there was one. "You're worrying the Deep. It's going to start bringing you cats to cheer you up, and this is no place for a cat."

"Scheisse," Tembi whispered, then nodded and took a breath. "Deep, I'm okay," she promised it. "I don't know how to explain to you why I'm hurt. It's…it's nothing you can fix. It's just an emotion I have to carry around until I know what to do with it."

She set her face against the Deep's soft pelt as the first tears began to fall.

It hadn't been Carroll's dismissiveness of the Deep that had stabbed Tembi straight through her soul. No, the belief that Witches was running a galaxy-wide grift was fairly common. While it seemed impossible to deny the very reality of the Deep itself—The human race had been reshaped around it! *The Deep was what made things go!*—people convinced themselves of impossible things every day.

The part that had cut her? That was the part where some people at Lancaster probably wished it were true.

Not Bayle. She loved the Deep as much as Tembi: Bayle had been on the path of most Witches when she had first come to Lancaster, attending classes which trained her to think of the Deep as a fallible, fragile component of the shipping industry that Witches-in-training had to master. Now, she was rubbing Tembi's shoulder with one hand, and the Deep's back with the other, trying to soothe both before a deluge of kittens appeared.

Bayle could no more easily deny the Deep than Tembi could.

But Kalais? Oh, Kalais! If he had a say in it, the Deep would be little more than a power source with a penchant for face painting.

Maybe that's all that the Deep was to him, anyhow.

Maybe that's all the Deep was to most of its Witches.

Tembi realized she was shaking. Not from the cold, although Bayle had opened the way so the Rails were as crisp as a plunge into an autumn pond. Anger—a slow-building furious anger, the kind that gave Adhamantians their reputation for violence—was beginning to chew its way out.

"I'm going back," she announced.

"What?"

She sat up, wiping her eyes with the sleeve of her robe. "Camp Divested. I'm going back. It was the last place Moto visited while he was still in his own mind."

"Are you well?" asked Bayle cautiously. "You have that look you get when you want to smash someone's nose all bloody."

Tembi nodded, and then she turned and screamed into the Rails.

It was catharsis, a technique she had found to help her maintain her Adhamantian composure even when she wanted to crack. Her voice was swallowed by the space, lost within the vastness of it. The Deep joined in, a slow lion's roar which grew and took on shades of red and black, shaking the Rails until color and sound blurred. She stood and let the vibrations scrub against her, arms outstretched as she joined her voice to the Deep's.

How long did this last? She couldn't say. It ended when her knees gave way and she crashed against the Deep's back, her throat raw from screaming.

Bayle had fallen into a tight ball, her hands pressed against her ears and her face hidden in her skirts. As the sound and lights faded, she uncurled and stared up at Tembi. "I hate it when you do that. It gives me such a deadly headache."

Tembi held out her hand, and the bottle of mini-meds she

kept for her ulcers appeared. She let one of the capsules dissolve on her tongue so the tiny army of medical nanobots could patch up her throat, and then handed the bottle to Bayle. "I hate these things," her friend said, as she shook one out, tapped it against her forehead to direct the 'bots, and then swallowed it. "I swear I can feel them crawling around."

"All in your mind," replied Tembi, as she rolled over to lie on her back. "Deep?" she asked, as she held up the bottle. "Want one?"

A chuckle shook the Deep's body, and the Rails settled into the colors of a warm summer night.

Bayle lay down beside Tembi. "Feel better?"

"Yeah," she sighed. "Sorry for your headache."

"It's smaller than the one I'd get if you dug up some back-alley parichone to give him a beating." Bayle paused. "Or if you went back to Camp Divested without thinking it through."

"Carroll is a parichone in need of a beating if I've ever seen one," muttered Tembi. "But you're right."

"To Lancaster, then?" asked Bayle.

"No," Tembi replied slowly, thinking more clearly than she had all day. Primal screams were an excellent way to jumpstart the brain. "And not Camp Divested. We need to learn more about what brought Moto to Camp Divested at the end before we run up against Carroll again."

With that, they knew where they needed to go.

They came out of the Deep in the small kitchenette above the warehouse in Adhama, with Cendo staring at them over a datascreen filled with bills of lading. Behind him, the walls were decked in star maps and narrow charts full of sums. He glared at the two of them, unease and anger wrestling on his face. Then, he looked past them and nodded.

Tembi turned. Behind her, Gallimore was slipping a popstick into their robes. They gave her a slow grin. "Might have worked," they said.

Tembi lifted an eyebrow. Gallimore looked decidedly different from the previous evening, with high flash in silver along the folds of their tunic and skirts, and a dozen earrings carved from stone dotting the ridges of their pointed ears. "The Deep would have dropped you somewhere cold," she warned them.

"Maybe." Their grin widened. "Maybe not."

"Gallimore," Cendo said, resigned.

Gallimore retreated, and sank into the old couch, still smiling.

Cendo flicked his fingers to dismiss the datascreens. The room dropped into its dull-painted self, with views of the room outside. The small warehouse was busy: it was afternoon on this part of Adhama, and people in work clothes were zipping along, carried by the speed of their tasks. "To what do we owe this honor, esteemed Witches?"

"Did Moto leave anything else for me?" Tembi asked. "A message about a Blackwing camp, perhaps?"

"Or…" she added, as the thought leapt up, unannounced, "or information about Domino?"

Cendo drummed his fingers on the old tabletop, a tapping-scraping noise which caused Bayle to grimace. He shifted to prop up his chin on his hand. "Apologies, Witch-*nim*," he said to Bayle. To Tembi: "Strange request, that."

"He's Domino's spy," Tembi replied, as she pulled out a chair to sit across from Moto's brother. Her anger was still riding high; she grabbed it by its hilt and willed it to behave, a sword with its point aimed somewhere between Camp Divested and Lancaster. "She trusts him, but I know he's never trusted her. She's a telepath; she must know that. So—"

"—why does she keep him around?" Cendo shook his head. "Are you detectives instead of Witches now, sleuthing through the underworld?"

"Moto gave us several mysteries," she replied, as she watched the workers in the warehouse stack boxes on an anti-grav lift cart. "We need to solve them. He's…he's not well."

Cendo relented. "I've noticed. What do you need?"

"To hit someone," Tembi muttered.

"You can have Gallimore for that," Cendo replied. "What

else?"

"Information, as we said. Those were shipping documents," Bayle said, pointing towards the bare walls where the datascreens had been. "Lancaster's seal wasn't on them."

"The Deep isn't the only mode of transportation in the galaxy, Witch-*nim*," he replied. "Lancaster charges a heavy price which not everyone can pay. I work here, on Adhama, making sure goods get to where they need to go."

"Except that shipping map runs through the Stross cluster." Bayle settled into the chair beside Tembi. "There's a moon missing, now. Does that make smuggling harder or easier?"

Tembi started to laugh: the answer to one of her mysteries was right there on the warehouse floor, and it rekindled her anger into full-bore fire. "Domino trusts Moto because of you."

Cendo inspected her face, and then nodded. "Yes, Witch-*nim*. Lancaster won't help certain people. Doing so would invite…complexities. Instead, they choose to ignore smugglers, and allow us to supply those people ourselves."

"Aren't you worried Lancaster'll call down the law?" asked Bayle.

Behind her, Gallimore chuckled. "The law loves us."

"The law doesn't love us; they love worlds with little trouble," Cendo clarified. "We fill a niche. We get items to people who can't—or won't—pay what Lancaster asks. If those people get what they need to survive, they don't cause much trouble. Since Domino needs people like me to service people like them, she needs people like Moto who can move information between us."

"And since you're his family, she knows he'll do right by both you and Lancaster." Tembi chuckled. It was horrible. Purely horrible. Domino owned Moto.

Cendo flicked his fingers and loaded his datascreens again. They covered the wall, orderly rows of facts and figures, with dates labeled in red. "Yes, and it's been a month since the last time I've seen him. That's an eternity in logistics. Any idea when he's coming back to work?"

"That's part of the mystery," Tembi said. "As I said, he's not well."

"Is he safe?" For a moment, the years fell away from his face, and Moto's little brother sat before her, small and scared.

"He is," she assured him.

Cendo nodded. His age shrouded him again as he began to page through his invoices. "What else do you need from me?"

Tembi was about to answer that she needed nothing, that she would now head off to Earth and shout at Domino until she felt better, but Bayle was faster. "Does Moto have contacts within the Sabenta?"

The smuggler's shoulders went back. "Why would you go chasing *them?*"

"Moto's last stop was at a Blackwing camp," replied Bayle. "He was gathering information."

"Lancaster's working with the Sabenta," Cendo said. "No reason for him to have his own contacts."

Bayle tilted her head to the side. "That's not what I asked."

"You're making my life difficult, Witch-*nim.*"

"I am a Witch. Such is my prerogative," Bayle replied, as serene as a summer stream.

Cendo sighed. "Gallimore, go introduce them around." When Gallimore chuckled, he added: "If you leave those Witches alone for as much as ten seconds, I will drop the weight of a thousand suns on your shoulders."

"Please," Gallimore said, as they stood and smoothed out their robes. "They shall be as safe as houses."

"Go," Cendo said, pointing towards the doors. "And send my brother home sooner than later: I've got twelve colonies that're about to run out of food." When Tembi's ears drooped, he asked, "What, you thought all I moved were entertainment sets?"

"No," she replied, then: "...maybe."

"I'd ask for your help, but then Domino would have a lock on you, too. Hard thing, to be a Witch with a heart." He gestured towards the doors again. "Go, go."

Tembi and Bayle followed Gallimore to a small washroom,

where they told the Witches to wipe the paint from their faces and change into casual robes. When they emerged, Gallimore inspected them.

"Good, good, you'll do," they said to Tembi. Bayle, however...

"I wore these robes yesterday," she said. "What's wrong with them now?"

Gallimore shook their head. "Not the robes, but the carriage. Here," they said, as they removed their scarf and used it to sweep Bayle's hair up and away. "This long, lovely hair means money. And try to slump a little, yes? You walk as if you own the world."

Tembi snorted. "Not *this* world."

Bayle nudged Tembi in the ribs with her elbow. "C'mon, I want to meet the Sabenta."

"Hush," Gallimore said. "None of that now, and not even when we're there. You'll scare them."

They gave Tembi an address half the city away. Tembi opened the Deep and led the way to the rear room of a small shop, the space around them cluttered in boxes of fabric. Gallimore led them, unnoticed, into an alley, and then another alley, and then another...

"Do you think we're being followed?" asked Bayle.

"No," Gallimore replied, as they looped an arm through hers. "I think we're having a glorious time!"

One arm around Bayle, another around Tembi, and Gallimore took them into the streets. Up and down, across busy markets and into quiet lanes. It was a middling part of town, close enough to the shipping ports so that the streets were filled with offworlders. Gone were the crowds of hungry children and towers banged together from old shipping containers. This neighborhood wasn't wealthy, but the buildings were planned and the food was plentiful. There was music drifting out of stores, and spacers walking by in their heavy boots, small bags swinging from their hands.

Somehow, Tembi had never considered that Adhama would have tourist districts.

Gallimore was laughing, telling jokes, escorting them from store to store, and getting more than a little liquor into them. Bayle was *enchanted*. Even with anger still wrapped around her heart like a hard knot of pain, Tembi couldn't deny Gallimore's charms. They even paused to braid a couple of flowers into Bayle's headscarf, a gesture so smooth that Tembi nearly missed how they were checking to be sure that Bayle's long hair stayed safely tucked away.

And then, the three of them were in a sniff store.

Bayle's nose flared at the boutique smells, and she moved towards a section which was painted in a dozen different shades of blue, with plass displays shaped into waves. She began opening vials and sighing happily at the aromas.

Tembi didn't notice much of a difference. To her, the shop smelled of spices, and more than a little soap. "Is this for off-worlders?" she asked.

Gallimore nodded. "Surprising—shocking—how the scent of your own homeworld can put you at ease." They pointed towards an alcove with a motif of sand, with hanging mobiles suggesting twisting windstorms. "That's Adhama, there. A nice souvenir to take back to the lovers and kidlings, to let them know what your trip was like."

Tembi couldn't resist: she started to explore the alcove. Most of it smelled of nothing special, except for one small jar which maybe, if she tried extremely hard, maybe smelled of a coming storm.

Gallimore swept it out of her hand. "On me," they said, smiling. They added it to a pile on the counter of Bayle's own selections.

"Can I help you find anything else?" the clerk asked.

"I have a friend coming in from the Batcho Nebula," Gallimore said. "Got anything to help them feel at home?"

The clerk flicked data back and forth, and Gallimore negotiated a price for a custom order. Credits exchanged hands, and the helpful clerk promised to have the package delivered to a restaurant across the street in thirty minutes. Then, the three of them were at a table, ordering offworld dishes at robbery prices.

"This seems…excessive," Tembi said, a finger tapping against the order display while she let her expression shout that she was not talking about food.

"It's how it's done here," replied Gallimore, as they pulled Bayle against themself.

"Is it, now?" Bayle asked, an eyebrow raised in mock suspicion as she snuggled closer, her curves aligning with Gallimore's own.

During their overpriced main course, a delivery 'bot zoomed in, dropped a package in front of Gallimore, and zoomed out.

"So fast!" they exclaimed, as they opened the package and held a small ruby-colored bottle against the light. "Bayle-*nim*, could you test this for me?"

As they spoke, they laid the bottle against Bayle's data bracelet.

"Yes…of course," said Bayle, as she watched information that only she could see. She went through the motions of sniffing and dabbing, pulling back her scarf to run a dab of oil along the pulse points of her neck.

"Show me what you smell like, lady," Gallimore said, smiling.

Bayle leaned back, allowing Gallimore to come in close, nearly touching. Tembi saw Bayle's lips moving, Gallimore's near ear twitching at what she said. Even the most ribald of bystanders would have flushed and turned away at seeing something so intimate spun out before them.

Within the span of time needed to pay the bill, the three of them were out the door and gone, with Bayle giggling and a high flush to her color.

Down one alley, and another, and finally, when all was quiet, Gallimore said, "Now."

Bayle opened the way through the Deep.

Chapter Fifteen

Witches, Tembi had learned, developed an instinctive feel for locations. Moving across the galaxy, across time zones, into space and onto planets? All of this spoke to a small part of the brain which remembered life as an ape, and took inventory as soon as the body was dropped into a new environment. So when Bayle brought them to the address which had appeared on her databand, Tembi knew they had come out in a room somewhere below the ground, and there was a good part of the planet above them.

"Ah," Gallimore said, as they reviewed their surroundings with a gimlet eye. "Yes, this would have been an inconvenient walk."

"Inconvenient?" Bayle's voice was a squeak. She was pointing at a dozen security 'bots, all of them closing in on long and spindly legs.

Gallimore spoke a series of letters and numbers, and the 'bots turned and left.

"Deep, where are we?" Tembi asked, her eyes shut so the Deep could sketch the edges of Adhama's maps in her mind. Her own home city, itself large enough to cover a fifth of a continent, shone bright, with a red dot pulsing near the shore. They were about a dozen klicks from the restaurant, next to the shipping docks.

"These used to be housing," Gallimore said, as they waved at the room around them. "An old cave system, found and explored when Adhama was first settled, and home to our ancestors until they got the terraforming settled and the storms tamed."

"I had no idea," Tembi said, as she paused to examine the walls. They were stone, but shaped with a plasma cutter to give them surfaces smoother than old glass. The floors had been left rough-cut, and were welcoming beneath her bare feet.

"Few people do." Gallimore stopped at the open door and knocked on the metal frame. "Incoming friendlies!" they shouted. "It's Gallimore. I'm here with Witches. Be aware."

"Should we—" Tembi began, but Gallimore held her back.

"We're guests in their house," they said.

There was a high-pitched buzzing, and a swarm of near-microscopic 'bots darted into the room. Tembi had a lightning-fast thought, there and gone, in which she asked the Deep to keep them off of her and Bayle, and the swarm landed on Gallimore as a dark humming cloud.

"They're searching for tags," Gallimore explained, as they turned and lifted their arms so the 'bots could reach their skin.

"The Deep wouldn't let a tracking tag through," Bayle said. "Not unless we wanted it. Or swallowed it."

Gallimore opened their mouth, and winked as the swarm zipped down their esophagus and back into the air. "Feels like nothing," Gallimore assured them. "If you want to meet the Sabenta...?"

"Fine," Tembi grunted, and asked the Deep to let them through.

It was all psychological, Tembi reminded herself. The 'bots were so small as to not cause any sensation, even as they sped through her nasal passages, her ear canals... She wondered about tags that had migrated to the stomach or lower, and that thought led to another, where a spy who had timed their digestive processes *just right* might have another opportunity for a listening device? No, there were easier ways to manage *that*... And was she *sure* all of those thousands of 'bots were being polite?

Then the swarm was out and gone, down the hallway, leading the way.

"Come, come," Gallimore said, as they followed the swarm.

The three of them left the small room and turned a corner. Tembi found herself in a massive hallway, dark as anything except for a single band of light coming from a slice in the floor.

No, not a slice: a corner. An edge, with the old lights illuminating the point where the ground fell away. The floor dropped down nearly a meter, ending in another floor with thick strips of rusting metal running its length.

"Train rails." Gallimore was peering over her shoulder. "Cheaper than anti-grav at the time."

"What's a train?" asked Bayle, and Gallimore obliged her with a description of thundering metal and plass, bearing down like enormous monsters into waiting stations before zooming out again, people stacked together within the shells as if a great divine hand had shoved them into messy bins.

Tembi whispered, "You're so much better than a train," and the smell of roses filled her mind again.

A scuttering noise of rock kicked across rock came from behind her. Tembi turned. Five meters away, a naked child stared back. His skin was a dull gray in the shadows, and Tembi had to squint to make out his features. Overlarge silver-blue eyes designed for a low-light planet reminded her somewhat of Kalais, but the child's fingers ended in deadly sharp fingernails.

"Hey," she called softly, as she crouched to sit on her heels. "What are you doing down here?"

The child backed away, then turned and ran, shouting at the top of his lungs. "Hide! Everybody, hide!"

"Ah, now, that's done it," Gallimore said. "Put your paint on, honorable Witches, lest you get shot."

"Shot?!" Bayle gasped.

"Shot," they confirmed, as they placed a firm hand on Bayle's shoulder to try to keep her from bolting.

Tembi sympathized with her friend. Guns were rarities, single-purpose weapons which couldn't be rationalized as anything other than what they were. Why carry a gun for self-defense when a popstick would do? Oh, right. That would be for the murders, or, at best, the psychological terror. She had been terrorized more than once while on bomb duty, and relished those times she got to turn that terror around on the gun's owner.

"What are we getting into?" she asked Gallimore.

Their ears dipped towards *uncertain*. "It changes, Witch-*nim*," they replied. "Please put your paint on. We do not want your mighty friend to hurt these people."

She asked the Deep for her Witch's paint and some good robes, and found herself dressed in a set of black robes she kept for semi-formal occasions, with gold trim along the sleeves to complement the rising silhouettes of songbirds on her cheek. Bayle was likewise dressed in her good blues and silvers, and while the Deep had left her shoes, her head was now bare and her hair hung in its usual long waves.

Gallimore nodded their approval, and cupped their hands to shout down the old rails. "It's Gallimore!" they called again. "I bring friends of Moto! Fail to welcome them at your peril!"

Slowly, cautiously, the shadows began to crawl as people stepped from them. They shared the boy's large eyes and sharp-tipped fingernails, but the color of their skin shifted from the dark of the shadows to that of the creamy gray-white of the tunnel's old halo lights. They were dressed in long robes of different shades of black and gray, with flashes of metal and cut-stone color concealed within the fabric to suggest each was wearing a large quantity of jewelry.

They were also breathtakingly beautiful. Tall, with their heads close-shaved, and utterly flawless skin, they seemed an alien race as they shifted between shades of gray, graceful clouds on a moonlit night.

"Chameleons," Bayle whispered. "They're Chameleons."

Gallimore nodded. "The last of them, smuggled off-world in small groups during the blockade."

Chameleon was a deadly world with unimaginably rich mineral deposits. In addition to a heavy atmospheric viral load which behaved as if it loathed humans, the majority of the animal species native to the planet were ambush predators, and resisted capture and killing. The settlers of Chameleon had invested in antibody profiles and chromatophore genome mods, and had slowly established small colonies to harvest the planet's wealth. Their world had been one of the first Blackwing targets in the war, ostensibly because the Chameleons were a major source of funding for the Sabenta. Money was certainly part of it, yes, but so were the Chameleons with their heavily modded bodies: the loudest Earth Pure pundits never failed to point out that interfertility between Chameleons and non-modded humans was abysmal, and this showed that Chameleons were on their way to becoming a separate species. Couldn't have *that!*

The Blackwings had kept a blockade around Chameleon for decades. Nothing went in, nothing came out, and Chameleon had to eat itself alive. Without access to off-world resources, extreme famine had resulted in civil war. After that, when most of the native Chameleons had died out, the Blackwings had occupied the planet in the name of peace.

All of this had happened nearly thirty years ago, long before Lancaster had agreed to move civilians affiliated with the Sabenta to safe locations. Today, the Blackwings held a wealthy world but could do nothing with it, as the problems that had required the first Chameleons to adapt themselves to their environment persisted and nowadays there was not a Chameleon to be found. At Lancaster, the genocide was spoken about in whispers. The Witches knew they could have helped, could have circumvented the blockade, could have evacuated the people from their planet. They could have done something. But, as the Chameleons had allied with the Sabenta as soon as the blockade appeared, Lancaster could—did—not.

Tembi had never seen a Chameleon. She had been told they were all dead, had died before she was born, and she had wanted to believe it. *Dead* meant past, gone, out of reach. *Dead* meant the problem had belonged to someone else, and that they had failed.

These people were alive.

"Tembs…" Bayle whispered.

"I know," she replied.

"We are in the most secure of the Sabenta's waystations on Adhama, honorable Witches," Gallimore explained. "The location moves beneath the city, hence the overcomplications in bringing you straight here. Cendo is their supplier, but he was not sure where they went after Moto disappeared, as Moto is the one who keeps track of their camps. If the Blackwings knew of their existence…" They allowed that thought to hang in the air, intentionally unfinished.

Bayle recovered first, bowing deeply before the Chameleons. "We are no threat," she promised.

"They are quite likely in need of food and supplies," Gallimore said. "With Moto gone, our direct access has been severed."

"Good riddance." A Chameleon man, tall and graceful, came forward. "Witches," he said to Gallimore cuttingly. "We finally rid ourselves of the one, and you bring more?"

"My new friends, come and meet Paisano, my old friend," said Gallimore, as they led the way down a long hallway. "He is usually a lot of fun."

Paisano was around Bayle's age, with long legs, large dark eyes, and skin that flickered in different shades of creamy gray as the four of them passed through pools of light and shadow. He had tattoos spiraling down from his head to beneath his robes, their colors mimicking his eyes in pale gray touched with silver. Around his neck was a jeweled collar wide enough to hang over his shoulders, and great golden cuffs covered his forearms. He wore his wealth and was likely rich beyond measure, except wealth had no measure when you were trapped in ancient tunnels beneath a third-rate city on a planet whose only purpose was as a waystation.

Gallimore turned into an alcove. It had been set up as an improvised temple, with pillows hugging the floor and an altar to the gods of Chameleon against the far wall. Here, again, was another display of massive wealth, as the altar was carved from a single pale gray moonstone. The top of the altar rose and fell in the shape of a tree canopy, with patterns of leaves etched into the moonstone's surface. The artist had decorated the individual leaves with different precious metals, and these shivered gently in the underground air currents. In the center was a forest god, a predatory silhouette cut from a separate gem, pitch black in color, full of sharp edges and wicked teeth.

Religion again, Tembi thought. *What a day.*

Tembi had no inclination whatsoever to spend any effort learning about imaginary beings or the wholly fabricated rules which governed them. The god—perhaps gods?—of Chameleon were alien to her. Nearly every god was. It was a big galaxy, and each planet tended to generate at least one dominant religion, usually more. No planet was a monoculture, and there were plenty of opportunities for multiple religions to spring forth and give birth to gods. She read up on local religions only when they bled into the legal system, and only to the extent which would reduce possible liabilities for herself or Lancaster, as some civilizations got viciously prickly when you couldn't be sossed to remember their respective gods' names. She chose to avoid religion altogether, except when she felt it necessary to throw gods around as the occasional curse.

Faith? That was a different. She didn't begrudge anyone for putting their faith in love, or honor, or a universal commitment to whatever they held to be pure. Such commitments, she believed, were embedded within human nature, which explained why almost all religions held them high as priorities. If somebody needed religion as a delivery mechanism for kindness? Well...she supposed that was acceptable, as long as they didn't insist on talking to her about it.

As Paisano moved to the edge of the alcove where a table with four chairs waited, the relief of not needing to discuss someone else's version of sacred lifted her up. He gestured for them to sit while glaring at Gallimore. "Moto was bad enough, cousin. You realize if I'm caught talking to Witches like this, then the alliance the Sabenta has with Lancaster could fall apart?"

"I made sure we took the most ludicrous road here. No one followed us." Gallimore chose the chair with their back to the open door. "We haven't been tracked or tagged, and the Sabenta know you are the liaison between your people and those who might help them, anyhow.

"So," they said, with a casual wave. "Begin. Liaise."

"I am not supposed to talk to anyone without a representative from the Sabenta—" he began, but Bayle pulled herself to her full height.

"Sir," she said, as she sat beside him and folded her hands on the table. "Thank you for coming. Gallimore is correct; we took every precaution in coming here. We would not jeopardize the safety of you or your people for a routine fact-finding mission."

Paisano glared at Bayle with sharp gray eyes, and then asked, "Who are you, really?"

"Lady Bayle Oliver of Atlantis," Bayle said, as she inclined her head to him.

"Large and vengeful gods!" cursed Paisano, standing so quickly that his chair tipped over.

"There's no cause to be dramatic," Gallimore said.

"Her father's on the Council!" Paisano was pacing. "Just being in the same room as her would be enough to inspire a whole fleet of rumors! Why not bring the War Witch himself while you're at it?!"

"He's my ex, and I'm rather angry with him at the moment," Tembi said. She was enjoying herself, probably a little too much, but it had been a difficult couple of days and Paisano flailed in a most hilarious manner.

He froze, noticing her paint for the first time. "Witch Stoneskin."

Tembi imitated Bayle's delicate head bow. It felt like a lie.

Paisano stood clumsily, unable to take his eyes from her face. He stumbled towards her and then knelt before her. "I'm no good at this," he said, still staring. "I'm…thank you. You've saved so many lives. Thank you."

"What?! No! Get up!" It was Tembi's turn to flail. "Stop! Bayle?"

Her friend came to save her, crouching beside Paisano in a swirl of robes. "Paisano?" Bayle said, very gently. "Could you come back to the table?"

"Yes, yes, it's—" He was flustered, still staring at Tembi. "You have to understand: Lancaster came to join the war only because you forced their hand. Without you, many among the Sabenta would have died."

"All we do is run transport for refugees," Tembi said. Her stomach was trying to creep out of her body by way of her feet. Who *knelt* anymore, really? Even when she was knighted, she hadn't been asked to kneel. "Besides, Kalais persuaded Lancaster to help the Sabenta. Not me."

"The War Witch has always given you the credit."

Really? This had become a full day of surprises. "He's being generous," Tembi heard herself mutter. *Kalais? But Lancaster hadn't done anything until he was chosen as a Witch. Why would he—*

"Perhaps we should concentrate on what brings us here today," Gallimore said, each word dipped in a hundred different flavors of bemused tolerance. "When all of this is over, we shall all go out for drinks together, yes? Paisano will buy the first round to show his gratitude."

"Good idea," Tembi said, as she shuffled around to the far side of the table, sliding its metal mass between her and Paisano. *Who kneels? Honestly, that's just sossing eerie.*

"What can I do for you, Witch Stoneskin?" asked Paisano, as Bayle escorted him back to the table.

"You know Witch Moto Sanders?" Gallimore asked. "Cendo's brother?"

"Of course. He's our..." Paisano paused, unable to keep himself from looking at Tembi.

"We know what Moto does for his brother," Bayle said, gently. "He keeps lines of communication open among persons involved in transport."

Tembi kept her face still. Only Bayle could tidy up something as consistently messy as language.

"I...yes." Paisano nodded. "Witch Sanders isn't involved with moving refugees. He does make sure that the Sabenta has access to material goods...without Lancaster," he added quickly. "He's..."

"He puts the Sabenta in touch with people like Cendo," said Bayle. "And he makes sure that Lancaster provides space for people like Cendo to help the Sabenta."

Paisano glanced at Gallimore and then sighed, a deep gray sigh which floated up and expanded to fill the room nearly as well as if the Deep had been involved. "There are no secrets from Witches," he said quietly.

"You might have noticed that Moto was unwell?" Tembi asked.

"Yes," answered Paisano. "A tremble to his hands, a nervousness to his manner. The Witch had always embodied strength— I took those as signs that he had betrayed us. For many days after he left, I kept my people on the move. We settled here a week ago: we are tired, and when you're tired it's easier to accept how there's no running from Witches.

"When you arrived, I thought you had come to end us," Paisano added, nodding to Tembi. "If Gallimore had not been with you—"

Tembi cut him off. "If Gallimore wasn't with us, the Deep would have been. The Deep always is with us. It's safer if you remember that."

His eyes moved to the shrine, and he gestured with both hands in a well-practiced ritual motion. "I will remember, Witch Stoneskin."

Bayle changed the subject. "We came from a meeting with the Blackwings," she said, as she tapped away on her bracelet. An image of Carroll's fortress appeared. "At a Hawk-class facility. We received a rather one-sided sales pitch, and no evidence of what might have happened to Moto."

"We're also trying to find the weapon which split a moon in the Stross system," Tembi said. If she hadn't been watching him, she would have missed it. But there it was, a quick flicker of tension as his eyes darted to hers and away. "Would you like to tell us anything about that?"

"No, Witch Stoneskin," Paisano said. His skin took on a slightly darker cast, as if he was retreating into familiar shadows. "I wouldn't."

Tembi leaned forward. "I disarm bombs," she said. "Day in, day out. All kinds. Pressure, pulse, shear, distortion, acid, toxin, vapor, mass… You know what they have in common?" Paisano was watching the doorway of the alcove, as if she wasn't speaking, as if he was waiting for someone more important to come and to join them. "Massacres cost money," she continued, rapping her fingertips on the tabletop with a sharp *clackclackclack*. "The Blackwings are unmatched on matters of scale. All the Sabenta can afford to do is detonate and hope they get lucky.

"Adhama's next door to Stross," she continued. "This is a busy shipping system. Plenty of traffic. I'd think the Sabenta on Adhama would be busting themselves to find out what happened to that moon."

"Unless they already knew," Bayle said.

"I'm not the one you should ask," Paisano said, his attention still aimed towards the door. "I'm a refugee on the run, and responsible for the last of my people. I'm in no position to help the Sabenta." Tembi stared pointedly at his elaborate shoulder collar, and then nodded towards the altar and its blend of artistry and riches. At first, Paisano pretended not to notice, even as his skin shifted from gray and began to redden. "What do you want from me?" he finally snapped, a rush of blood turning his face a dusty rose. "Yes, the Sabenta build bombs! They sabotage and terrorize, and if we're lucky, the right people die! But the Blackwings? They've built whole cities to warehouse the Sabenta before they kill them! Now they're slicing into moons? How do we stand against *that?!*"

Tembi couldn't help but notice his minor slip. "You don't," she said. "You can't."

"We're dead," Paisano said, his energy spent. "All of us, dead. *You'll* be fine," he said, with a quick flip of his hand towards the Witches. "The rest of us… You think it'll stop? If the Blackwings get an official seat on the Earth Assembly, if they keep running their programs… Even after we're gone, they'll say 'Never again' and do it again anyway, and again and again—"

"Easy," said Gallimore. "You're among friends."

"Am I?" he snapped. "The Sabenta are losing—*losing!*—and the Witches could fix all of it, just magic the Blackwings away! Easy and done!"

"I believe we're at the intersection of anger and nowhere," Gallimore began, but Tembi placed a hand on theirs. "Wait," she told them. To Paisano, she said, "We need to help Moto. He might have information that can help the Sabenta."

"Might?" Paisano echoed. *"Might?"*

"We won't know unless we find him. Officially, the last place he went was the Blackwing facility," said Bayle. "Unofficially?"

"Fair, fair..." Paisano angrily rapped his knuckles against the table, as if thinking. He glared at Gallimore and said, "Start Downriver."

Chapter Sixteen

If Bayle had come along, it would have been a different kind of trip. Bayle would have fidgeted all over the cab of this short-range zipcraft, pretending they weren't awash in rotting food and the stench left behind from what could have been livestock. She never could convince anyone that she didn't mind substandard cleanliness, but it was always entertaining to watch her try. Sadly, her students and her schedule couldn't keep without asking the Deep to break even more laws of physics, so today it was just Tembi and Gallimore rocketing through the stars.

Gallimore was violently embarrassed.

"Again, I am sorry," Gallimore said, as they bustled around the cab, sweeping trash into a bin.

"Don't clean up on my account," Tembi replied. She had moved her chair so she could rest her head against the ship's hull and listen as the sounds from its engines purred along the curves of her skull. The song of an FTL ship was a toneless substitute for the Deep, but it was a kind of music nonetheless. An image of the Deep flying alongside the zipcraft as it cut through spacetime appeared against the backs of her eyelids: she wondered if it was her own imagination, or if the Deep was truly playing with the ship, swooping around and above it in great invisible arcs.

"I bought this craft new three years ago," Gallimore said, followed by the sounds of more garbage being stuffed into the bin. "Brand-new. I knew it wasn't to be mine, and I bought it with Cendo's purse, but my hands were the first on the sticks. I coaxed it through its maiden flight, heard its body creak as it came to life… This—*this!*—is what has become of it?"

"Are all smugglers so prissy?"

Gallimore snorted, and Tembi opened her eyes to see them toss the bin into a corner still ankle-deep in trash. "Obviously not." They sighed and kicked the nearest chair, which rocked on its antigrav rollers before bobbing upright. Gallimore sat, and pushed against the floor until their chair came to rest beside Tembi's. "We should take pride in what we do and what we own, don't you think?"

Tembi reached up to touch her ears, where shards of dyed ceramic had replaced her usual gold rings. She felt a vague sense of loss, even now, even when all she needed to do was ask the Deep to exchange clay for gold. "Sometimes."

"What would you do, if you had not become a Witch?"

Kalais rumbled through her memory. "Probably live and die on the corner," she grumbled, half to herself.

"You?" Gallimore laughed. "No. Some are born for the street, and others for the stars. Luck might start you on your way, but I feel you would have made your own luck and made it there regardless."

"Perhaps." Tembi thought of her own family, her first mother and her three older sisters, all of them living in an old tatty shipping box which rested within a stack of other tatty shipping boxes, the four of them clawing money together so she could spend her days at the local school instead of working or thieving. "Were you born into luck?"

"Can't say," they replied, tipping their head back so their ears brushed against Tembi's headscarf. "I hold dim memories of my childhood somewhere, I am certain, but I have never gone looking for them."

"So you've made your own luck?"

"Best as I can." Gallimore waved a hand in the air, and the ship's viewscreens came online, turning the roof and walls from featureless white panels into a vast starry sea. "I did so by putting myself in debt to Cendo, which can be seen as another kind of luck. He protects me as long as I have value to him."

Tembi stretched up, up, her fingers brushing against the viewscreen. The ship had dropped out of FTL, and the solar system bloomed around them in slow-moving light. "You don't work for him?"

"It's complicated. A story for another time." Gallimore pointed. "We're here."

She stood, slowly, eyes wide.

Downriver.

She had heard of it, this thieves' paradise hidden a million klicks from nowhere. Some called it the black market, but from here, it was anything but black. The markets were tacked within dark blue asteroids, all moving in the same slow orbit, their forms cast in shadows and silver from the nearby stars. There were so many of them, each turning at different rates, stone waves lapping against space.

A river indeed.

"Here," Gallimore said, as they sat up and slid their chair back to flush with the control panel. "Come and fly us into dock."

Tembi began to laugh. "I think not! I've never flown as much as a hopper."

"Time to learn, then." They patted their lap.

She shook her head, grinning, and used her own chair to bump Gallimore's away from the controls. "What do I do?"

A bobcat appeared on the console, hissing.

"Well, that's a thing," said Gallimore dryly.

"One moment." Tembi shut her eyes. "Deep?" The smell of the rotting barnyard in the zipcraft increased. "Deep, I don't want to fly the ship. Gallimore and I are flirting."

"Oh, are we now?"

Tembi hushed them. "Deep, this is a human game. I'm not replacing you, I promise." The bobcat hissed again. Tembi opened her eyes and moved away from the controls. "All yours," she said to Gallimore.

Gallimore pressed the back of a hand to their temples. "I will never pretend to understand Witches, but explanations are welcome."

"Oh, the Deep gets jealous." Tembi reached out to tickle the bobcat. It turned its back to her and began grooming a hind leg. "It doesn't care when Witches have relationships with other people, but by all the gods large and small, never let it catch you at the driver's seat of an alternate form of transportation." She picked up the bobcat and stared into in its golden eyes. "I love you. Not this silly machine."

The bobcat grumbled and disappeared.

Tembi sighed, and flipped her legs over Gallimore's knees. "Fly us in, valiant smuggler."

"Yes, Witch-*nim*," they said, the image of decorum as they tugged Tembi's robes down to cover her exposed calves.

The zipcraft glided through the asteroid belt, its path as clean the cut of a laser. There were no nervous moments. The small craft had proximity buffers to keep the smaller asteroids away, and Gallimore's skills allowed them to dart safely around the ones the size of moons. An asteroid appeared, one of many, one no different than the other giants within the cluster. A twist of the controls, a blue horizon before them, a crack within the ground beneath them...and then they were inside.

They went slowly, the zipcraft plodding down the center of old mine tunnels. The walls glowed as they passed, the dark rock reflecting their craft's safety lights. Several kilometers fell behind them, dropping away into lifeless black silence.

Before them? At long last? A swelling of gold and gleaming color, cloaked within the deepest parts of the abandoned mine.

"Welcome to Downriver, Witch-*nim*," Gallimore whispered, leaning towards her, their lips against her cheek. Tembi flicked an ear to smack against their nose, but allowed herself to curl against them, delighting in the rush of color which had swallowed their ship.

Downriver was a smaller market as such things were measured, but it was nevertheless large enough to show the bounty of a hundred worlds. Stuck in an asteroid belt which circled the edge of the Stross cluster, it was a captive moment of commerce. On Adhama, the saying was that if you needed it, go Downriver.

Tembi had never come here. She had the galaxy open to her—why would she come *here,* with its shady reputation and prices hovering around extortion? Just as well pop off to the source and avoid the smugglers' surcharge. She had assumed it would be loud, crowded, filled with people clinging to the edges of morality. It was all of these, certainly, but she hadn't thought it would be beautiful, too.

If you were being generous, you could call Downriver a city. It had buildings made from the husks of old starcrafts strung together on gold and silver wires, bobbing together in the low gravity. Rainbow-hued bubbles surrounded these, their plass shells coated filled with a green riot of plants.

Airdogs, she thought. They were still too far away for her to see them clearly, but the semitropical plants were every spacer's best friend: they sucked in pollutants and blew out clean oxygen faster than any other organism yet discovered. They were highly regulated. Airdogs grew so quickly that they were considered a dangerous invasive species, as several planets had undergone a second wave of terraforming when airdogs got loose and sucked temperate climates down, down, down into a new ice age, the freeze finally ending their rapid life cycle. Most habitable spacecraft and offworld shipping ports had their airdogs penned up in a heavily controlled section of their gas exchange processes, and the excess growth was dehydrated into powder as soon as it was culled.

As she watched, one of the bubbles grew a small hole, and a tiny humanoid shape flew up towards a second bubble. A tangle of greenery broke loose and followed them into the unprotected mine shaft outside. A passing zipcraft flew through the fresh green cloud, no doubt pulling a few stray airdogs along for the ride.

Gallimore circled the great central cavern once, twice, and then took them out of traffic and down a side tunnel. The zipcraft settled into a holding pattern above a smaller bubble marked in red glyphs.

"Here," Gallimore said, as they released Tembi's legs. She silenced a sigh. It had been a long time since anyone had touched her, and Gallimore knew how to coax feeling from beneath her skin. There was something to be said for dating a fellow Adhamantian. "Come, Witch-*nim*, we must make ourselves present-able."

She stepped into the bathroom stall and changed into an old spacer's uniform, the pants and heavy boots clinging to her legs and feet like a cloying film. A breather collar, which Gallimore said needed to stay active at all times, and gloves to hide her fingerprints. No headscarf, and no golden birds along her cheek: Gallimore was a familiar face in Downriver, there to wine and dine and show off their contacts to an unremarkable new client, nothing more.

Tembi met Gallimore in the airlock. They bowed to her, and tapped the thin collar around their neck. She did the same, and the breather flickered over her face. Gallimore took the two of them outside, into the low gravity, and down to the bubble which opened to welcome them. Inside was a humid dissonance of plants, and they fell through those into a screaming tangle of color and sound as this small eddy of Downriver swallowed them up. The shell of an old mine stripper had been hollowed out, a marketplace built within its husk, artificial gravity wells set to keep the component pieces of this miniature world in their proper places. A good marketplace was its own ecosystem, with resources coming in and out: Gallimore told her about those who worked in this slice of Downriver, those who lived and loved and raised their families, building a bright slice of community alongside the criminals who patronized it.

"Luck is fickle," Gallimore told her. "Even when some make it to the stars, they go no further. They find what they've been looking for...or not." As they spoke, they stepped over a woman lying prone on the sidewalk, a pool of blood seeping into the depleted rock of the mine.

Tembi glanced over her shoulder. "Should we—"

"No." Gallimore said, somewhat sadly, as they took her by the elbow and brought her back to their side. "No, we should not."

There was no law here, no designated bodies occupying the streets. There were peacekeepers in the form of mothers, fathers, business owners, those who had an investment in in order for the sake of their families or pocketbooks. When Tembi looked back a second time, she saw the woman's body was being rolled into an antigrav cart by a couple of rough-looking teenagers, who laughed as they hauled her towards a nearby broker who advertised composting services.

"Best not to eat anything local," Gallimore warned Tembi, and a cold shiver charged down her spine.

Into the thick of the market. Gallimore was recognized; shopkeepers waved and offered samples. People appeared, made small talk, and vanished into the stalls again. From time to time, Gallimore stopped to call the office, and would then relate news to various customers. Tembi watched, learning, as they kept Cendo's networks alive, pausing only occasionally to ask Tembi how she was faring.

Then, so fast she nearly missed it, a uniform within the crowd.

Once she had spotted the first, the other Blackwings appeared as easily as if she had mastered a trick of the eye. Earth-normal, all of them, from their bare heads to their heavily booted toes. Their uniforms marked them as foot soldiers and low-level nobodies, but they acted as if they were each Somebody, walking as if they were on holiday without a care in the world. Laughing, sometimes singing, always bullying their way through the marketplace with broad shoulders.

And once Tembi had noticed the Blackwings, she noticed how Gallimore was deftly steering the two of them away.

"Breathers up, always," they told her, pointing towards their own face mask. "Oxygen aplenty here, but there are areotypes hidden all over the market, as *some*—" here, they nodded towards the Blackwings, "—would gladly purchase a list of known persons who came Downriver. Confirmation of your presence here would fetch a sweet price."

"I'm a Witch," she said quietly, grinning. "We're everywhere."

"Literally, yes," Gallimore sighed. "However, practically speaking, can we try to avoid giving poor Paisano a coronary? He can barely manage a meeting a kilometer beneath the surface of a planet. Imagine how he would shout if you were found here."

She laughed, and let Gallimore move their hand to just below her waist. "Then why did he send me here?"

"Ah," Gallimore said, leading her into an alley. "There's a question."

"I thought we were retracing Moto's steps."

"Are we?"

She nodded towards the market. "Where else would he get a knockoff Crisp?"

Gallimore chuckled. "Anywhere and everywhere, Witch-*nim*. Things are never as easy to acquire as when they are controlled."

Tembi's mind shaped a quick reply, but the words died on her lips. She moved away from Gallimore, not quite hearing their questions, and found herself staring at a market stall groaning under old books.

"Taste for the rare?" the clerk asked. It must have been a trained response, as his nose was firmly fixed against an ancient tablet.

"That book," she said, pointing towards an embossed spine.

A small mistake: the book leapt from the shelf and smacked into her open palm.

The clerk, a man far too young to be selling antique books, finally looked up. "You need to pay for that."

Tembi barely heard him. She yanked off a glove with her teeth, and worked a stack of gold rings from her thumb, letting the Deep toss them through the air to land on the clerk's tablet. The part of her brain that would always live in poverty shouted at her for overpayment, but she couldn't truly care, not with this book in her hands. It was old but in good condition, its cover and pages made from a retired form of rubberized gel that was just beginning to go to crumbs around the edges.

And the title? The words had glowed once, probably, before the book's power source had failed, leaving only a smooth reflective pattern within the bumpy texture of the cover. *Death Count: The Turtle Incident and Other Deep Lies of Lancaster.*

"I see what they did there," Gallimore said as they read the title from over her shoulder. "The author should be ashamed."

Tembi hushed them, turning the book around and around in her hands, as if to convince herself it was real. "Do you know what this is?"

"I hope it's worth disclosing your status," they replied, as they carefully shoved Tembi into a secluded corner.

"Telekinetics are cheap, and they're all showoffs." Tembi began to page through the old book. There were pictures. Photos of Witches, photos of—

"Oh," said Gallimore quietly.

"We don't talk about it," Tembi whispered, as she lingered on the scenes of Neptune's moon. "It's been sanitized. Lancaster monitors the datafeeds and the channels, and sues people into oblivion if they try to put out books like this. When they do get out, they have the Deep to collect them for destruction. I don't know how this one escaped."

"Perhaps it was in a Witch's private collection."

"Maybe." Another page, another set of images. This was much more detailed than Matthew's sanitized educational grammalight program. This was—

Tembi had to shut the book to keep herself from gagging. The smell of blood rose around her from an unseen source, an unmistakable sense of sadness pressing down, down— "I know," she whispered. "You made a mistake. It happens. You see me make mistakes all the time. But we need to learn from our mistakes to keep them from happening again."

Gallimore was staring at her, concern riding them. "Moto is easier to manage, Witch-*nim*."

"I'll be sure to tell him you said so." Tembi went to wipe away a tear, her hand thumping against the invisible shield of her breather before she could touch her face. "Show me where he bought the Crisp, and then we're out of here."

"We're not here for a Crisp," they reminded her, and moved her into the thick of the market.

Word had spread of the telekinetic who could summon books to her hand, and children were clattering around her feet, begging her to perform tricks. She grinned at them, and silently asked the Deep to lift the smallest child a half-meter into the air. The child giggled and danced before she asked the Deep to set him down, and then the other children *pounced!* each of them begging for their turn. Tembi laughed and told them no, no, her telekinetic lift rating was barely twenty kilos, and lifting one book and then one small child had bled her dry.

"You're good at this," Gallimore told her, as the children fell behind them, fighting amongst themselves over what they had been denied.

"I hadn't realized how often I pretend to be something other than what I am," she said, and was about to mention something about her evenings on the town with Bayle when the atmosphere quickly dropped. Gallimore grabbed her by the sleeve and pulled her off the road, into the doorway of another shop. Most of the children disappeared, vanishing into the strange mess of streets formed by the busted machinery. Those who remained were older, bolder.

"Go," Gallimore whispered to those children, pointing back the way they had come. "Quickly. *Go!*"

The children scattered.

"What's happening?" she asked as the two of them moved into the store, Gallimore holding the bottom of the beaded curtain so its heavy falls stilled and settled.

Gallimore hushed her. "Paisano did not tell you to go Downriver to retrace Moto's steps," they whispered, as they made sure the windows were covered. They put their back against the glass, and pulled Tembi close. "He sent you here to witness cruelty."

Tembi glanced around the store. It was a mishmash boutique, a little of this, that, and the other. Pieces of security 'bots were scrambled in bins across the floor, while one wall was dedicated to small animals in stasis cages, their paws and noses pressed against the bubbles. The animals were as silent as stones, waiting.

"*Shhh!* Girl, *hide!*" She turned to see a large woman with blue hair in tight braids. She was gesturing frantically. "Gallimore, hide the lady!"

"Come, Witch-*nim*," they whispered, as they crouched behind a bin of plass motors. "You said you wanted information. Come and watch, and learn."

She knelt beside Gallimore, tucking the book beside her for its safety. The windows had been plastered over, but small holes had been chipped around its edges. Gallimore pointed to the largest of these, and she pressed her face against the plaster so she could see. Outside, the narrow street was silent.

Gallimore tapped her shoulder, and pointed towards a number of objects floating in the air. "Could you?"

"Right, yes," she said quietly, and shut her eyes.

Deep?

A nervous scent of flowers, jasmine jittering into lilac.

I don't know what's happening here, either. We need to watch and learn together. Do you understand?

There were clicks of metal on metal as the small garbage constellation settled.

Good. Thank you. We can do this.

The floral scent straightened out into peonies growing beside an ocean.

She opened her eyes, smiling, and saw the first murder as a Blackwing soldier swung her popstick into the meat of an old man's chest. He howled once, fell, and she jabbed him again, discharging a full charge straight into his neck.

"Giant gods!" She nearly leapt to her feet, but Gallimore was there, hands steady on her shoulders. They pressed rough fingers against the shield covering her lips, their ears tipped out and held fast in place: *Stop!*

Tembi nodded as she moved her own ears to *firm attention*, and turned back to the window.

More soldiers. More residents of Downriver. The uniformed soldiers came along, laughing, pushing their captives along. Not one of the soldiers paid attention to the old man's body save to step over it.

Every soldier looked Earth-normal. All of their prisoners did not.

"Where are they taking them?" Tembi whispered, once the soldiers had passed.

"There's a meeting square in the center of the bubble," Gallimore replied. "Only a few of them will be killed, as slaughter is terribly bad for business. This is merely a show of force to remind all who shop at Downriver that the Blackwings hold power here." They let her stand. "If you need further proof, we can go watch, but…" they moved to the curtain and pulled it aside to frame the old man, lying on the packed rock of the asteroid. "I would rather not, myself."

Tembi stared at the body. "How did you know this would happen?"

They met her eyes with a sad smile. "This always happens, Witch-*nim*. How do you think that first poor woman we saw in the street became a corpse?

"To more fully answer your question," they added, "I knew there would be a large raid today, and I made sure we would arrive ahead of it so you could watch."

"There's a big raid here twice, three times a month," the shopkeeper said quietly from her spot on the floor. "Different bubbles each time. Gallimore, if you knew, why didn't you warn us?"

"Politics," they answered, as they set a credit chip upon a nearby table. "Thank you for your hospitality, Jack. If I have done my job today, this will be the last time the raids come to Downriver."

The woman stared at the chip, then at Tembi, and gave Gallimore a tight nod. "I'll keep my mouth shut, but not for money."

Gallimore returned her nod. "The galaxy runs on favors. I'll remember you to Cendo."

The woman bowed to Tembi, blue hair sliding forward to shroud her face. "Mistress Witch."

Gallimore pressed a finger against their own lips, and drew Tembi from the store, her book tucked carefully beneath their arm.

"Quietly, quietly," they said, searching the street.

"Do you want me to jump us back to the ship?" The old man's body was lying face up. The popstick had done terrible things to his eyes.

"I wish we could, but there's one last thing we must do," they said, as they began to walk back the way they had come, keeping close to the walls.

Quietly, quietly... Tembi concentrated on her steps, on keeping her robes pulled tight so the fabric wouldn't snap around her legs, trusting Gallimore to keep them out of danger.

She wasn't expecting the sharp shout, the hand on her shoulder.

The owner of the hand spun her around, and she was face-to-face with a woman in a Blackwing uniform.

"Hey hey, another!" The soldier was broad-shouldered and Earth-normal, with skin the color of loamy soil and dark freckles across her cheeks. "Missed you in the sweep, girl. Let's go join the fun."

Tembi twisted sideways and broke the soldier's grip. "Stop," she said. "This is a warning."

"Warning?" The woman barked, as she tried to flick one of Tembi's protruding ears. The breather's shield blocked her; the woman grabbed the breather collar and snapped it off. "Who the fuck do you think you are, girl?"

Tembi held out her hand. Her breather disappeared from the soldier's grasp and reappeared around her own neck.

"Oh, that was *fast*," growled the soldier. "I couldn't even see it. You're a tekker, aren't you? Hard bite of one, too."

"Yes," said Tembi, her ears high and her anger climbing. Breathers weren't designed for clean breaks. If it hadn't been for her skin, she'd be seeping blood. "And proud of it."

"Then why hide yourself?" Another Blackwing soldier, another large woman with a hard face and pinched expression. If the second woman didn't have the cold eyes of a predator, the two soldiers could have been twins. "Why lie?"

Gallimore was at Tembi's arm in an instant. "No trouble, my

friends," they said, somehow once more transformed into the polite yet otherwise unremarkable person Tembi had first encountered in a tavern on Adhama. "My client and I are not locals. Please take note that we would be missed."

Gallimore's calming words seemed to be just so much fluff in the air. "Another mutt," the first soldier growled, as they reached for Gallimore's breather collar and snatched it away.

Tembi's ears flatted back against her head. She wasn't in danger of being trapped Downriver, but if things went bad and she got separated from Gallimore, they might not be so lucky.

Gallimore squeezed her arm, their ears moving quickly out and then holding in place—*Stop!*

Tembi stopped, took a calming breath, and allowed her ears to ease back to their normal position.

"Look at you," said the soldier with dangerous eyes. "Nothing but animals."

"Perhaps," Tembi said. "If so, you might ask yourself why you think it's smart to corner us."

The market was suddenly quiet enough to hear Gallimore let out a near-silent sigh, and Tembi realized she had just provided the Deep with yet another excellent example of how everybody makes mistakes.

"Fuckin' tekker!" The first soldier slapped Tembi's hand away; the second soldier's own hand went to her side, and the high-pitched whine of an overclocked popstick split the air.

"Enough!" Gallimore put themselves between Tembi and the soldiers. "She's a Witch!"

The word was a protective talisman. The soldiers froze, eyes first wide, then narrowing in suspicion. "Proof," said the predatory one. "Now. Or it won't matter what you claim."

They all but trembled as Tembi's golden birds appeared, as her junky spacer's uniform shimmered into her black-and-gold dress robes, as a Witch—no, as Tembi Stoneskin—emerged before them.

"*You!*" shouted the first soldier. "The Sabenta bitch!"

"You're confusing me with the War Witch," replied Tembi.

"I'm the Lancaster bitch who keeps soldiers in the Sagittarius Armed Forces alive by stopping the Sabenta's bombs."

Silence, cut only by the hum of the popstick. The second soldier thumbed off the device.

"She comes here to shop," Gallimore said, holding up the book they were carrying. "Hard-to-find items one might be reluctant to sell to a Witch."

There was a pause as all eyes turned to the book. The scandalous book, one that no shopkeep in their right mind would sell to a Witch for fear of some vague, possibly supernatural, punishment. The soldiers had no choice but to accept their story, slight nods begrudging Tembi's win. The collar was returned, with Gallimore adding that the Witch-*nim* very much liked her shopping excursions in Downriver and would be extremely distressed to learn if anything dreadful was to happen to it, or to its citizens. Tembi kept her mouth closed, allowing Gallimore to patch the hole she had kicked through Downriver's society.

As Gallimore turned Tembi away from the soldiers, the first swellings of guilt rose up within her. "I've ruined your reputation here," she told them.

"Oh, Witch-*nim*," they replied, gesturing towards the marketplace. People were emerging from the stores, staring. "You've helped me today. What better reminder of Cendo's reach than a Witch? More, a Witch who is not also Cendo's brother? They shall break their own necks to prove their worth.

"And the attacks might stop," Gallimore said. "These raids? They are done because the soldiers enjoy it, dancing through such playgrounds where they can kill without consequences on their days off. You have shown them that is no longer the case."

She glanced at Gallimore. They were intent on the market coming back to life around them, and their eyes were cold, as cold as anything, and she realized she had been used in a way both hideous and noble.

Chapter Seventeen

The next day seemed to start so well. Other than a quick stop in the dream's tavern to make sure that Moto was still hale in his stasis pod, her dreams were sweet and meaningless. But then, over breakfast in her freshly scrubbed kitchen, Tembi finally gave voice to what was bothering her: "I don't know what I'm doing."

Matindi didn't bother to look up from her reading. She had seized the ill-omened book from Downriver as soon as Tembi had returned home, and was devouring the pages over and over. "That's nice."

"Matindi!"

"Tembi!" her second mother whined back at her, and then she sighed and shut the book. "Fascinating," she muttered to herself. Then, "Domino doesn't want someone who knows what she's doing, dear. That's why she chose you."

Tembi blinked.

"Didn't think of that?" Matindi got up, carefully set the book aside, and started cleaning. "A skilled spy goes missing, and she assigns an untrained soldier to track him down? Don't make that face, dear," she added, her back to Tembi as she pushed the dishes through the cleaner and returned them to the cupboard. "You *are* a soldier in a war. A peacekeeper is a soldier nonetheless."

Matindi finally noticed her face. "Oh, sweetling," she sighed. "Domino leads one of the most powerful organizations in the galaxy. She has near-infinite resources at her disposal. On top of it all, she's hundreds of years old. You're a mewling child in the cradle compared to her. Why would she send you after Moto?"

Matindi's words were an assault. The answer, when it slid out, even more so. Tembi rolled forward, feeling as though she had been kicked in the chest. "To distract me."

"Yes," Matindi said, as she covered Tembi's hand with her own. "Now, ask yourself why she'd go to such lengths."

This time, the answer eluded her. Tembi stared at Matindi's hand and wished she could feel the softness of it. Then, slowly, as events rolled together into a timeline… "It had to be that moon. She had no real interest in me before that."

"Right and wrong," Matindi said. She was almost smiling. "She's always had an interest in you."

Tembi's hand beneath Matindi's knotted into a fist.

"Good," Matindi said. "Stay angry. You're a soldier, so think like a soldier." She let Tembi go, and stood, glancing around. Her eyes lit upon the silverware bin, and she yanked this out and dumped the contents on the counter. Then, her head came up, green eyes burning. "I take that back—don't think like a soldier. Think like a general on the battlefield and outmaneuver the foul cunt."

"Matindi!"

"I hate her," Matindi said, slamming spoons into a noisy pile. "I truly hate her. Lancaster could be so much more than—" She caught herself, staring at a single spoon as if it were a piece of her sanity. The spoon went down, gently. "I have myself to blame," she said, very quietly. "I was here long before her; I allowed this…I allowed *her*…to happen."

"Do you want to talk about it?"

"No," Matindi said, as she shuffled the knives to one side and began to sort through them. "Not at all."

"Did you know about the Chameleons?"

"I thought you said they were geckos."

Tembi blinked. Her second mother was as sharp as shattered glass, but she had as much guile in her as a box of newborn puppies. She had told Matindi all about Camp Divested and Downriver, and she had thought she had mentioned that Paisano was from a lost race, but perhaps she had skipped over that part. Or maybe she had mentioned it, but that book made for highly distractible reading.

…or maybe Matindi was so furious at Domino that this

would be an exceptionally bad time to suggest that Lancaster could have played a minor role in a genocide.

"Right. Geckos." Tembi nodded. "We have them on Adhama."

Silence claimed the kitchen. Frustrated and feeling more than a little like a coward, Tembi went outside to bask in the sunlight on the front stoop. There was birdsong and Matindi's excellent coffee—*Did it truly take five hundred years to master coffee?*—and the unmanageable invisible weight of knowing that Domino was easily, handily, professionally moving her around like the insignificant pawn she was.

How was she supposed to think like a general? That felt like the wrong question. The right question? Hmm…that felt more like a combination of insurrection and self-improvement. How was she supposed to go from a woman who took bombs apart to someone who could…could what? Take down Domino? Was taking down Domino the right course of action? Despite her machinations, Domino was valuable. The Witches needed someone like Domino to handle their dealings with the Earth Assembly, and all gods both large and small knew that person shouldn't be Tembi herself.

Matindi, though…

Tembi grinned at the thought of the tiny green woman in that too-elaborate Assembly room, smiling serenely at Dame Idowu. Ah, but no. Matindi would fight that position tooth and nail.

Matthew, though…

Now, there was an idea!

Could it work? Gods knew Matthew had twelve lifetimes' worth of experience as an administrator and a politician. If she managed to toss Domino, someone would have to step forward and take over Lancaster's place on Earth—

A shadow, a cold voice, her own name as a statement: "Witch Stoneskin."

She snapped upright. Before her, a tall man in a Blackwing uniform, five thin red claw marks sweeping across the black cloth from shoulder to sternum. He was as bald as an egg and wore glasses. Beneath one arm was a large white box, a thin stack of books resting upon its lid. At the end of the path were soldiers in formal dress, milling about as they inspected Matindi's front garden.

Tembi scrambled to her feet. She knew this man, by constant exposure from the channelsluts if nothing else. "Wallis—Admiral Wallis, I didn't—"

"My time is precious," he said, nodding towards her house. "Invite me inside. We don't want to do this out here."

"I don't..." Words slipped away. The public figurehead of the entire Sagittarius Armed Forces was standing on her front stoop, his toe all but tapping in impatience. Resistance seemed pointless. "Come in. Please."

Wallis stepped past, a twist of fabric hanging from his waist whipping against Tembi's legs as he moved. The door opened before he could reach it, Matindi waiting in the curved hollow of the front hallway.

"Good morning, Admiral," Matindi said, smiling, nodding over her clasped hands. "Welcome to our home." She had changed from an old nightgown into robes as white as clouds, with green branches with flowers embroidered along the sleeves. Behind her, the house was tidy—no, it was immaculate! Not a fleck of dust nor an errant fingerprint marred the sterile beauty of the place. The artwork was on display with refreshed lighting, and fresh flowers draped the common room in a light floral perfume.

A true Witch's home.

Tembi was caught somewhere between amusement and horror. Efficient though her second mother may be, there was no chance this had all happened in the time she had drunk a cup of coffee: Matindi had asked the Deep to *clean!*

Wallis stared at Matindi, and the house, and then back at Tembi. She couldn't be sure, but she'd put a couple of credits on a bet that he couldn't decide whether to talk to the Witch who was obviously competent but bright green, or the Witch who was obviously outclassed but appeared closer to Earth-normal.

Tembi wiggled her ears at him.

The Admiral turned to Matindi. "Two of my own threatened Witch Stoneskin yesterday. One reported the incident. I regret to inform you that I must present her apology on her behalf." He bowed low, and set the box and books at Tembi's feet.

"Please, Admiral, come," Matindi said, a saucer and cup appearing in her hands. Tembi didn't recognize it; the delicate bone china looked ancient. Matindi pressed it into his hands, smiling. "Earth coffee. I made it myself."

Matindi ushered him into the greeting room, and seated him in a chair in a sunbeam, all the while making soothing conversation while she sipped her own cup of coffee. In the silence of the white noise, Tembi picked up the books and the box, the large stack shifting in her—

A *thump* as the contents of the heavy box rolled to bump against the side. A noise somehow familiar, somehow hard and soft and also wet. Oh, she knew this sound, or sounds exactly like it. The sound of cleaning up after a shear bomb, of meat and bone packed up for disposal, freshly cut.

And yes, the Admiral was watching her, watching as she moved the box, watching to see what she'd do.

Tembi glared at the Admiral, and then opened the box.

The Blackwing soldier with the predatory eyes stared back at her. At least, her head did. The box was relatively small, and she had been very large.

Calm, Tembi reminded herself. *You've seen worse. You've held worse. You've caused worse. And you have to stay calm, or the Deep will know something is wrong, and it'll whisk the Admiral away forever and there will be an intergalactic incident and then on top of it all it'll fill this place with cats.*

Tembi replaced the cover, placed the box on the table beside her, and began to thumb through the thin stack of books. It was difficult to read when her brain was beating *CALM CALM CALM* or perhaps that was the sound of her heart, over and over, as the man who had just handed her *a severed human head* was still looking right at her. She thought—she was *sure*—

the books were more of the same as the one she had found yesterday, books about the Deep and associated conspiracies, but the titles slipped across the edges of her sanity and drifted away, meaningless.

Books in hand, she found her way into the common room, and sat.

"Gifts," she said to Matindi, as she set the books on the conversation table. "This was what I went shopping for in Downriver. And…" Tembi chose the chair across from Wallis. "…was she from Kingsrow?"

Wallis nodded. "Strange customs on that planet. I don't believe in them myself, you must know, but when a dishonored soldier's head finds its way up the chain of command, you cancel your plans and see it home."

Matindi's cup made the slightest sound as it rattled against its saucer.

Tembi nodded. "What will satisfy her honor?"

"Couldn't say," the Admiral sniffed. "I've heard that most of Kingsrow has evolved out of this level of barbarism, except in extreme circumstances."

Such as insulting a Witch. Such as threatening her life. This woman is dead because of me and—

Focus, Tembi.

"We will respect her wishes," Tembi replied. "I would like to speak to her second, if I could."

The Admiral's silence answered for him.

"Ah," she replied. "How?"

"Dropped off the package to her superior officer, told him the story, and killed herself before they could arrest her." He glared at Tembi, his hands knotted into fists. "Her second was the other soldier you met in Downriver. She swore to us the mistake was theirs. They didn't mean to threaten you."

"No," Tembi replied quietly, ears high. "They meant to threaten me—they meant to do worse. But they didn't mean to threaten a Witch."

Wallis was as silent as the grave.

Manners often served in place of conversation. "Thank you for your time," Tembi said, a ritual response, the politest one she could find. She needed to get this man out of her house before the shock wore off and she started screaming. "And for the books."

Wallis nodded, stood, allowed himself to be led back down the hallway. Tembi had to do it; Matindi seemed unable to move from her chair. At the door, he paused. "May I offer some advice?"

She nodded. It was easier.

He stared down at her over the rim of his spectacles. "Keep to Lancaster, to the pretty places," he told her. His voice was somewhat kinder than it had been when he had arrived. "War is ugly. If you want books, send someone to find them for you." He nodded towards the box on the counter. "Witches cause collateral damage.

"Good coffee," he added, as he set the cup and saucer on the table beside the door.

Tembi shut the door behind him. She did not slam it, no, nor did she allow it to make a sound as it sealed out Admiral Wallis and the soldiers waiting for him. There was no reason to make a fuss; he was only doing his job.

She stared at the box, aware that she now needed to do hers, still wholly unaware of what that job might be.

"I'm proud of you," Matindi said. "You handled that extremely well." She was once again dressed in sleepwear at least four decades old. Around her, the house was drifting back into its usual state of disorder, piles of get-to-it-later clutter reappearing on flat surfaces, fingerprints along the glass...

Ah, right, she hadn't asked the Deep to clean, not really, she had asked it to sweep everything under the allegorical rug until the Admiral had left, a small touch of stage dressing for unexpected company, oh, and there's the cat, and he's sniffing the box and I'm about to start screaming—

Indeed, Tabuu, Tembi's ancient but immortal cat, had managed to haul himself onto the counter and was exploring the white box, his nose immersed in the scents that were no doubt slipping out from beneath the lid.

"Tembi..." Matindi swallowed and tried again, eyes fixed on the box as Tabuu started to paw at it. "Tembi, this is your house now, but if you plan to honor a dead woman by keeping...by keeping that—"

"It's gone," Tembi promised her. "Just...I just need some time to think."

Tabuu let out an irritated *mrrremph!* as she swept him up and carried him back to her bedroom.

A shower, interrupted by a quick scurry to the toilet when the last fifteen minutes crashlanded in her stomach and demanded a quick escape. Various bathroom peripherals began to circle her in cautious orbit, soaps and cosmetics and the universal bottle of mini-meds, as the shock finally wore off and the Deep tried to heal a wound it didn't understand.

"It's okay," she assured it. "It's okay," over and over again, a monotonous chant which blended into the sound of water raining down against the backs of her ears. "Human stuff. I don't understand it, either."

Not true, not true at all, you know exactly why there's a woman's head in a box in your kitchen, she's dead, her friend's dead, it's all your fault, Wallis is right, collateral damage is all you're good for and—

She scrambled for the toilet again.

When she finally managed to pull herself together, she walked into a peaceful scene: Matthew in the greeting room, Matindi wrapped in the shelter of his arms. They stood in sunlight, her head pillowed against his chest, their eyes closed and speaking softly to each other.

Tembi watched them for a few moments, and then stepped into the Deep.

The white box came along.

"I don't know what to do," she said, her face pressed into the Deep's downy feather-fur. "How do I change this? How can I change *any* of this?"

The rainbows of the Deep's pelt blurred into gray. Around her, the colors of the Rails fell apart, weeping away in damp, blurry lines.

Focus, Tembi.

This, at least, was collateral damage she could fix.

She wasn't in the mood to sing. Which, as she had told Bayle countless times before, meant she needed to do it. Singing purged the mind and cleared the soul, and she needed that now. A ditty, a sea chanty, something easy and utterly devoid of substance.

Morality is the privilege of the comfortable

"Well, I'm uncomfortable as all manner of hells," she muttered. "I should have punched Gallimore when I had the chance."

Now that she thought about it, she should have snuck a solid punch into that last conversation with Gallimore! After they had spiked her straight into Downriver as both weapon and shield, they had offered to fly her back in Cendo's small spacecraft. Tembi, furious, had coldly announced she hoped to never see them again.

"As you wish, Witch-*nim*," they had said, bowing at the waist. "Know that I did not act out of malice but in service of the greater good."

"And that's supposed to make me feel better?" she had snapped.

"Yes," they had said, somewhat surprised. "More people will live who would otherwise have died."

That was enough to get her into the ship for the ride home. The conversation was dark, with none of Gallimore's usual wry humor to cut it. At some point, she had mentioned that she had received a cryptic message from Domino—

"Ah, yes," they had laughed. "That babble about morality and comfort?"

"What?" Tembi had asked. "You've heard it?"

"Domino said the same to Moto, back when he began working for her," Gallimore had replied. "Kept him grinding in place for days."

Hmm. Out of all the options she had considered, a timesink wasn't among them. "What did he do?"

"He talked to his brother about it. Cendo said it was nonsense, as all that we do can be thought of as either moral or amoral if framed as such."

That didn't sound much like Cendo, and she had said so.

"Well, to quote, he said that Moto needed to pull his head out of his ass and do what he could to help those in need." Gallimore had stared at her, ears back and eyes hooded against the storm. "So, Witch-*nim*, with all due courtesy, pull your head out of your ass and help me save those who would be murdered."

She had briefly considered having the Deep drop Gallimore into the heart of the nearest sun and then yank them back to the ship unharmed, but had nodded instead.

"Good," Gallimore had said. "With that in mind, Witch-*nim*, let's talk about the Chameleons."

And so they had, and for a time Tembi finally felt as if she had a real direction...at least, she had until the severed head had appeared. Now, she wondered if Gallimore was wrong, and violence begat violence and Domino was right to stay out of it.

"Gods, everything is a nightmare," she sighed, as she flopped face-first into the Deep's feather-fur, her body lying just far enough away from the white box so she could pretend it wasn't there.

::SING:: it replied.

"You sing," she said, tickling its back. "Pick a song. I'll join in."

There was a long pause, and then a single slow note sounded. It was familiar, made by a rodent-like creature on the planet Guilford which had a voice far more beautiful than science and logic required. The song grew as more individual voices joined in, each unique, all of them streaming together into a symphony. She let the Deep sing alone for a while, delighting in her friend's ability to harmonize with itself, and then joined her own voice to its chorus. They cut their way across the Rails, singing a duet made from a thousand and one voices until the pain of the morning had eased.

"I'm sorry if today was confusing, Deep," she whispered into its feather-fur, even though she wasn't sorry, not at all. She felt knocked flat by the enormous weight of things she wanted to say to it, explain to it, force it to *see!* And then the Deep would understand and it wouldn't be such a burden and she could—

No. She would go to her own grave knowing she had spent her life dabbling in accidental cruelty, and even that was drawn out of her as seldom as she could manage.

(Ex-boyfriends didn't count.)

"You and me, buddy," she sighed. "Everybody wants something from us, and we have no idea how to make them happy."

A beetle and a butterfly crashed headlong into each other, scattering colors like confetti as they toppled away and plunged into the Rails.

"Going to take that as an agreement." She reached out to check if the box was still behind her. Yes, sadly, it was still there. There would be no pretending it had fallen into the hollows between the worlds, oops, gone forever, she was too careless to be trusted with dismembered body parts. "Next problem."

The beetles landed on the top of the box, their small hooked faces pointing towards her, patient.

"Yeah, we've got to..." She tapped the box, and then had a thought. "Deep? What's Blackwing policy when an officer is given something they can't accept?"

The beetles piled on top of each other for form a pyramid and made a rude noise.

"I can't be the first one to have gotten a...gift...like this." Tembi was having none of the Deep's usual delaying tactics. "You've memorized the contents of entire libraries," she reminded it. "What's the official protocol?"

A thin plass tablet dropped onto the Deep's broad back. Tembi picked it up and waited for it to adjust to the rainbow-hued light, and then read aloud: "'Chapter 8, Section Two, Nature of the gift...Unconditional monetary gifts cannot be accepted by...' oh it goes on like this for pages!" She skimmed the next paragraphs. "Custodian responsibilities…Conditions of acceptance…okay, here we go, Circumstances to decline acceptance."

And then she groaned.

Chapter Eighteen

By 2500 AD, personnel transportation within the Solar System was primarily driven by the Deep. The Turtle Colony was established on Neptune's largest moon, Triton, in 2518 AD. The colony was established as a waystation between Earth and the heliosphere, and was used to facilitate deep-space study and exploration. On 8 June 2529, all 2,361 persons within the Turtle Colony biosphere were discovered to have perished. At trial, the Witch who oversaw shipments to Turtle Colony reported that she had used an inaccurately worded statement when talking to the Deep. This misunderstanding resulted in conditions inhospitable to sustaining human life. The victims of this avoidable tragedy are honored each year on Turtle Day, and the Witch's name and rank have been struck from Lancaster's records.

While the Turtle Incident was significant in terms of overall loss of life, it was not the only tragedy humanity has faced on our journey to the stars. Other notable disasters include the Soyuz 1, *the* Soyuz 11, *the* Apollo 1, *the* STS-107 Columbia, *the* STS-51-L Challenger, *the* FG81-6 Griffon, *the...*

Chapter Nineteen

Above all else, Witches-in-training learned control. Witches made mistakes, not the Deep. They learned if a Witch made a mistake, disaster would follow. They were told the Deep was infallible. That the Deep *couldn't* make mistakes. That training, routine, and policy helped preserve the perilous relationship between small foolish humans and the vast unknowable Deep.

All of that was a marvelous pile of chicken shit and salesmanship. Any Witch who took the time to speak with the Deep, rather of simply ordering it around, would recognize the Deep as a bundle of nerves the size of the known galaxy, badly in need of reassurance. The Deep made mistakes like any other sapient creature. It had dreams, emotions, goals…it was a person.

People make mistakes.

This, Tembi thought to herself, as she stared at the main gates to Camp Divested, the white box tucked beneath one arm, *is definitely one of them.*

She waited until she was certain the monitors and soldiers standing guard had registered her presence, and jumped past the doors.

The entrance hall was as empty as it had been the other night. All of this space, for nothing but a first impression. There were two soldiers in uniforms minding a desk, and another standing around with a large popstick slung over his shoulder, looking pretty. Tembi walked up to the desk as the commotion started, feeds bursting to life as they tried to keep up with a Witch on the move.

"Let General Carroll know I'm here to see her," Tembi said as she swept past the desk, her bare feet slapping against stone. No shoes, not this time, and the last few days had exhausted most of her supply of expensive Witches' clothes, so she was wearing the same headscarf and casual robes she had thrown on that morning. She was certain she came across as one shabby-looking piece of dross.

Focus, Tembi.

The soldier with the popstick lurked on the edge of her peripheral vision as she retraced her steps from a few nights before, moving steadily towards Carroll's office. Walking was a courtesy, really, as Carroll's entire garrison had become a blur of motion, rushing to get everything presentable before the Witch passed by. It took a while before Tembi got the feel of the twisting hallways, all of which doubled back upon themselves as if making it more difficult for an enemy to reach the vulnerable core. However, she was a Witch: a sense of direction was her sole purpose. She pulled apart the knot of corridors in her head, and found herself before Carroll's doors. They stood open, the arch framing Carroll at her desk.

The general was glaring at her. "Witch Stoneskin."

Tembi blinked. There was something different about Carroll, something *better*, something—

She cackled aloud.

She couldn't help it. Carroll glowed. It was faint—barely noticeable at all!—but the general literally *glowed*, a halo of celestial light gently spinning around her. With her near-white hair and skin, it gave her the appearance of a gods-touched creature from old Earth, divinely manifest.

Carroll's eyes tightened.

"I apologize," Tembi said, bowing her head to the general. "I didn't realize we had caught you without your makeup the other night. It surprised me.

"Camouflage 'bots?" she continued, moving closer to the general's desk. Another soldier with a popstick moved to intercept; she jumped past him, still staring at Carroll. "Set to illumination, and opacity dialed down to almost nothing?" She found the chair in front of the desk and sat, one bare foot balanced across her leg, the white box in her lap. "We used to wear them as kids when we went dancing. Cheap way to look fancy."

Carroll said nothing, even as her fingers tapped against her databand. The faint illumination faded, leaving Carroll clad in her uniform and her own natural beauty. Finally, she sighed. "I'm extremely busy, Witch Stoneskin."

"I won't keep you," Tembi said, as she held out the white box to one of Carroll's guards. "But I was given a priceless gift by a Blackwing soldier, and I cannot in good conscience accept it."

Carroll nodded to the soldier, who opened the box and—

"Careful," Tembi said, as she asked the Deep to catch the box and hold it aloft. "Someone did me a great honor, and I would not see her disrespected."

The soldier nodded as they gingerly pushed the floating box towards Carroll, and kept nodding even as the box settled beside her before leaving to go be quietly sick in the corner.

Carroll nudged the half-open lid aside and peered into the box. A sharp breath, followed by a hard swallow. Then: "Won a duel with a Kingsrow lass, did you?"

"You could say so," Tembi said. "I would like to see her home safely."

"And you've come here as I have her genetic tags on file," said the general, as she shut the lid and turned the white box back into something ordinary. "Any high-ranking Blackwing officer could get you this information."

"I am on speaking terms with you and no other," Tembi replied, and tried to ignore how her stomach felt as if it had already decided to leave this confrontation, with or without the rest of her. "As we left our last meeting in such poor faith, I thought a dialogue of how to right this particular wrong would be of use to both of us."

The general stared at her, long ears tipped out, as if trying to catch the words that Tembi wasn't saying. She turned to her soldiers and said, "Leave us." As the door shut out the rest of the world, Carroll asked, "Where is your friend, the politician?"

"Lady Oliver of Atlantis has prior commitments." Now that the others were gone and she was left alone, staring up at this golden creature, the realization that this was a tremendous mistake hit her anew. "It is up to me to see this soldier home."

Carroll sniffed. "The head's yours," she said. "The body will be buried by her kin with honors, but the head is now your property. They won't take it back. If you try to force it on them, they'll think that the original insult hasn't been resolved. If they're traditionalists, then trying to return it will only create more of…" She laid a hand upon the box. "…this."

"Ah," Tembi said, nodding, as if such a concept was wholly sensible and not a swiftly moving exponential nightmare of severed heads. "Even if I explain that their concept of honor isn't compatible with my own?"

An ear twitched, tugging a strand of fine blond hair backwards. "Most of Kingsrow now considers this type of behavior to be barbaric. You happened to find a soldier from one of the holdout colonies. Congratulations." Carroll netted her fingers together. "What else may I help you with?"

Bayle always said that silence and a simple smile were a diplomat's best friends. Tembi did her best, but found herself leaning forward, her ears tilted in the Adhamantian signs of *watching, waiting, ready…*

Adhamantians and Tolkiens shared enough body language to communicate her unspoken purpose. "Clever. No one could fault you for coming here, not with *that*." Carroll nodded towards the box. "Who brought it to you?"

"Admiral Wallis."

Carroll's eyebrows lifted. "Moving up in the galaxy, I see."

"It came to him, and so he came to me."

"Wallis knows who you are. Impressive." Now Carroll leaned back, smiling. "Have you thought on what I said?"

"About ending the war? Oh, yes. Very much so."

"And?"

Tembi bowed her head in a motion which might be mistaken for a nod. "First things first."

"Of course." Carroll's ears twitched, first down and then up: *amusement*. "If you do not wish to display the head in a place of honor in your own home—"

"I do not."

"—then the next best outcome would be to entomb it within your own family's ancestral burial site."

"I have no family burial site," replied Tembi, as she added yet another item to her to-do list. Ghastly, yes, but she had come to terms with the notion that her first mother and sisters would likely die centuries before her, and she would rather not think about the specifics while mourning them. "My family does not come from wealth. I could pay for a cremation or a grave."

Carroll made a sour noise. "That's no good. It's got to rest in a place of personal value." She paused, and added, "I would like to offer a kindness to you, Witch Stoneskin."

Tembi allowed her ears to perk up: *firm attention!*

"My family has a large tomb on Tolkien." Carroll grinned slyly, as if confessing a secret. "I am in excellent health and have no intention of dying any time soon. Let me offer my space to inter the soldier's head for a period of no more than five years. During that time..."

Tembi picked up on Carroll's meaning and nodded. "I will establish a permanent place of rest worthy of her sacrifice."

"A lovely plan. No family of a soldier could find fault with a general's own tomb." Carroll waved one graceful hand in the air. A voice replied: "Sir?"

"I am leaving with Witch Stoneskin," she replied. "I shall be back within the hour."

A pause. "Yes, sir."

Carroll rose, hands out, as if asking Tembi to come into her arms. "I have never done this," she said, a confession. "How does one travel through deep space?"

Tembi stood and reached across the desk to place her hands upon Carroll's. "Like this."

The Deep wrapped them up, and they were gone.

The Deep's back was wide enough for them both (and a large dinner party besides), but Carroll's face was fixed into a polite smile as she looked straight down, down... "How long will this take?"

"Not long." Tembi ran her fingers through the feather-fur.

The Deep's pelt was thoroughly shining in rainbows; it loved showing off for strangers. "Short jumps are near-instantaneous. Long distances require a little more time...or maybe not. I think the Deep could make it shorter, but it likes the company. We went across the galaxy, once. It took eighteen minutes."

"Eighteen minutes." Carroll shook her head. She was still looking down, as if expecting to fall. "Eighteen minutes to move across the Milky Way. So brief, and yet an eternity—how do you manage the dark?"

The Rails sang around them, bright and cheery, with the near-infinite colors of the Deep below. But this was not the first time Tembi had brought a stranger into the Deep; not everyone could see it, hear it, feel the rainbow rush of the galaxy around them. "It's not dark for me," she replied, even as the color dimmed and the scent of an irritated musky animal filled her mind. "It's beautiful. Every color you can imagine, and the Deep loves to sing."

"Ah," Carroll said softly. "The Deep."

Tembi grinned. "If you close your eyes, it's not as scary."

Instead, the general pulled her long hair into her lap and began to plait it, forming a complicated pattern which resembled waves upon the water. Tembi took note: Bayle would want to learn it. "Tolkien is a large planet. How do you know where I want to go?"

"Best as we know, a Witch tells the Deep she wants to travel, and the Deep parses the destination from either her or her companions." Tembi leaned back, arms out and sprawling against the thick pelt. "There's loads of research on brain waves, telepathy, and the Deep. Very little of it conclusive, of course."

From her vantage point, she could see Carroll nod politely. "Of course."

"Even here, you don't believe in it?" Tembi propped herself up on her elbows. "We're traveling back to your home planet in a pocket dimension! I'm human, yes? How could I do *this*?"

"Perhaps this is a discussion for a later time," Carroll said, braid forgotten and hands clasped in her lap. "I am at your mercy, and do not wish to antagonize you."

Tembi snorted. "Fair. But the Deep is a miracle." She flopped backwards, the feather-fur drifting around her. "It's a shame you can't appreciate it."

"Oh, I do," Carroll said.

"Right. That's why you're here."

The general took a breath, as if preparing a response, and then they were standing in a wide meadow, green-gold grass all around, with a crystal blue pond shaded by a single large tree.

"Ah," Carroll sighed, almost satisfied, as she straightened her flawless dress trousers. "That was quite fast."

If this was a graveyard, it was unlike any Tembi had visited before. Not a marker or a memorial marred the pastoral landscape. "Are we in the right place?"

Carroll nodded absently, tapping on her databand as she walked slowly forward. "East by north-east. It should be right… ah." She stopped, and uttered unfamiliar words in a light, lilting tongue. As she spoke, a veil parted and a building of pure white stone emerged, as if Carroll's words had drawn back a painted curtain. Beneath their feet, the grass withdrew, fine-honed blocks lifting themselves to provide a path to the crypt.

"Stay close," Carroll warned her, her eyes alighting upon Tembi's ears, her face. "There's security here, and it might mistake you as unwelcome."

Tembi stilled her hands; no fists, not here. Besides, she'd drop the box. "What do you mean?" she asked, as wide-eyed and innocent as any person could be.

Carroll was pressing against the stone, her attention set on a puzzle which served as a lock. "There are several races on Tolkien," she replied. "Mixing does happen, but responsible parents take their children offworld so as to not offend. With your ears…" There was a click, and a panel of the door slipped into itself. "If you were taller, it would not be an issue. But please, Witch Stoneskin, stay close."

The door opened, sliding apart as if it was a silver-wrought necklace coming undone. As the pieces fell away, Carroll stepped into the dark of the tomb.

"Come," she called to Tembi. "Come."

Tembi looked at the box, shut her lips to trap a sigh, and then followed.

The inside of the tomb was quiet, thick pieces of colored plass turning the golden meadow light into chunks of solid reds, blues, purples... *No yellow and no orange,* Tembi noted, with a mere smattering of green in the corners of each window. "It's peaceful," she admitted, as her eyes searched every cranny of the room for corpses.

"I used to come here as a child," Carroll said. She nodded towards one bare wall made from the same white stone as the building's shell. "My mother lies there. She passed when I was but five and two." The general's voice had changed, an accent peeking through its surgically clean edges. "She died in an accident. I never saw her body; I eavesdropped on the funeral and learned she was maimed beyond recognition, and I spent much of my childhood believing they sealed her behind stone to preserve the memory of her beauty."

She glanced at Tembi and her cheeks colored ever so slightly. "Not in so many words, of course."

Tembi smiled. "Children are complicated. We're smarter than we understand. I was eight when the Deep took me, but even then I realized how Lancaster used it."

"Lancaster..." Carroll sighed, fingers resting against the wall where her mother lay. "Yes, you have been poorly used, haven't you?"

"The *Deep* has been poorly used." She realized she was grinning, and quickly wiped her face of all expression. "As all of Lancaster is trained in how to use it, but not with kindness."

"As you say." The general bent her head towards where her mother lay, and then turned to the wall below it. She whispered a word to the stone and it opened for her, shaping itself into a wide ledge long enough for a tall woman to rest. "Here, Witch Stoneskin. Our soldier can sleep here for those five years you'll need to establish your own family tomb. It will rest in stasis, eternal from this day forward."

The white box slid easily into the niche. Tembi had a moment of What Next? paralysis: *Do I need to take the head out of the box? Do I need to display it? Do I need to vid it and send it to the family as proof?* but Carroll touched her forehead, then the box, and then the wall, which obliged her by melding shut into a solid face of smooth white stone again.

"I shall have the caretakers send notice to her family, with my family's seal upon it," Carroll said. "We provide stipends to the survivors of those killed in battle. With your permission—"

"Let me think on that," Tembi quickly said. "There are implications of defining this incident as a battle."

"Of course." Carroll's smile didn't touch her eyes. "But most soldiers do not come from money, and their families would surely welcome the gesture."

Oh, and it seemed to have been going so well! Tembi thought she had been in control of the situation, but no, no, she was still far out at sea with no rescue in sight. She paused, as if thinking, and then asked, "Would the stipend be split, or would each family get a whole?"

If Carroll realized she had been caught, she didn't show it. "We are generous," she said. "Each family would receive a whole."

"That is most generous," admitted Tembi. "I will consider it." She turned away, pretending to show respect to the blank wall of stone where the soldier's head now lay, until she no longer felt the urge to shout, *"I did not mention a second soldier!"* like an actor delivering a crushing blow.

Chapter Twenty

"Do you think Wallis had them *killed?*" Bayle was wide-eyed, properly horrified.

Even after hearing the story of the beheading, Kalais was not. He made a sour sound at Bayle, who returned it by lobbing a bottle of beer at his head. The bottle vanished before it hit him, reappearing in Bayle's hand.

The Deep wouldn't allow harm to come to its Witches even in its dream? Ah, well.

The tavern where they had left Moto's stasis pod was untouched, likely abandoned save for Tembi's brief examinations of the pod. She and Bayle were sitting as near as they could to Moto, while Kalais sat across from them, leaning against the bar with his own cold bottle of beer balanced on his knee. "Of course not. Carroll didn't expect Tembi to come ask her for help, either. I'll bet her morning briefing contained a mention of the incident in Downriver, and when Tembs showed up, she saw an opportunity."

Tembi leaned back to rest her head against Moto's stasis pod. The sharp electrified feeling of a real object shoved into a dream had dissipated, but the pod had remained too cold to touch until she had realized that it would never come up to room temperature if it wasn't in an actual room. After she had told the Deep to warm it to a comfortable 26 degrees, it now gave off enough heat to feel welcoming. She was drowsy, rolling on the very edge of unconsciousness, but if she fell asleep here in the Deep's endless dream—*or fell into...more sleep? A Deeper sleep? a ha ha ha ha oh **gods***—she wondered if she'd wake rested, or if she'd have to spend twice the energy to pull herself out of the dream.

"Carroll doesn't know I tipped to her," she said, talking mainly to stay awake. *(Alert? Aware?)* "I played wide-eyed child the entire time." After their visit to the tomb, the general had suggested a friendly meal. Tembi had brought them back to Camp Divested, and they had dined in the officers' mess. The food had been wonderful, until Carroll let her know the produce was farmed on worlds that had been recolonized by Earth-normal populations once the Sabenta had been... Carroll had paused, waved a hand, and allowed Tembi to change the topic.

It had been a feint. If Tembi returned to meet with Carroll again, it would likely become the first of many, as the general attempted to tap away at Tembi's opinions on the Blackwings' ideology, or perhaps her faith in the Deep.

"I can't go back." She shivered, remembering how the complex flavors and textures of the meal had turned to sand in her mouth. "Politics is not my strength."

From her perch on top of Moto's pod, Bayle snorted. "That's sossing nonsense, Tembs. You're a born diplomat. Paisano was all but dancing to your tune."

"You have to go back," Kalais said. "My contacts analyzed Moto's data. The Blackwings weren't testing a bomb when they cracked the moon."

"What?" Tembi's ears twitched at that. "No, they're wrong. I've seen shear bombs before. That was a shear bomb swiped up for scale."

"It was turned into a shear bomb, maybe." He was staring into his bottle, eyes white and vulnerable. "But it began as a test to see if they could open a way to the Rails."

Tembi and Bayle swore, and then couldn't help but laugh. Around them, the dream shivered in color.

"Oh, that's rich!" said Bayle. "You can't get into the Deep without...you know..."

"...the Deep!" Tembi finished, chuckling. She reached over her shoulder and rapped on Moto's pod. "No human can do what the Deep can. Like any old sossing three-dimensional mammal could ever find a way to shove reality into a dream."

"Probably not—probably never—but they do want access to the Rails," Kalais said. "If they can find a way onto the Rails without the Deep, they can cut out Lancaster."

"Unlikely," Bayle said with a sniff.

"Plausible, though," admitted Tembi. After she had returned from Camp Divested, she had skimmed the books Wallis had brought. One was an old treatise on the practical physics of the Rails. The author had written at length about its so-called "gate-keepers," with scorn trimming each sentence, word, syllable, and letter. "They've tried before."

Bayle's bare feet dropped to rest on Tembi's shoulders. "Who's 'they'?"

"Soldiers. Opportunists. Scientists." Kalais went behind the bar to find three fresh bottles. He opened these, paused, and then opened a fourth bottle and left it out on the bar. "Anybody who wants to use the Rails without Lancaster's involvement."

"Didn't end well," Tembi mused aloud. "Next to impossible to open a hole into another dimension. Lots of accidents. Lots of explosions."

"Bet some of 'em looked like shear bombs," Kalais said, as he handed Tembi her beer. She took the bottle but didn't reply. "Want to know the scary part?" he added.

"Definitely not," Bayle muttered.

Tembi shushed her. "What's the scary part?"

"That this was a large-scale test."

The significance took a moment to circle and land. When it finally did, Bayle shuddered. "Then they must have gotten smaller tests to work."

"Maybe," Kalais replied. "Logic says yes, that you wouldn't set anything up on such a large scale if you hadn't gotten it to work on a smaller one. Moto thought Camp Divested was a test site for the smaller portal. That's why he was sniffing around, trying to make inroads with Carroll."

"No." The logic was sound, but the story didn't make sense to Tembi. "The Deep would have told us if someone else was using the Rails. Right, Deep?"

The mirrors over the bar opened five sets of midnight blue eyes and said, :: *MOTHER FATHER* ::

"Oh no," Kalais sighed. "Here we go."

"Quiet," Bayle told him. "Deep, whose mother and father?"

The fourth bottle of beer disappeared.

There was a pause. When nothing else happened, Kalais said, "Should I start looking for a parent company, then?"

"Don't be an ass," Tembi told him. "I'll ask Matindi to talk to it. She knows how to get it to open up."

"You should take it singing," Bayle said. "It likes to talk with you while you sing. I think that's when the two of you share the same bandwidth."

"Then you need to come along." Tembi patted the floor of the dream. "The Deep may be talking, but it's hard to hear when I'm singing."

Above the bar, the blue eyes shut and sealed themselves into the mirror with a single multi-octave musical note.

"Everything's gone sossing weird again," Kalais sighed. "I'm off."

"Wait," Bayle said. She tapped her toes against Moto's pod. "What about the mindfuck?"

"Could be anything. Could be nothing." He shook his head. "Moto's tests came back negative, but that might mean there's a new drug out there and nobody's caught it yet."

"I don't like leaving him in the dream," Bayle said, as she scrubbed a little more soot from the pod's faceplate.

"Same," Tembi said. "But now that we know he hadn't discovered a bomb but a portal, we can see where that leads us."

"Straight back here," Kalais muttered darkly. "Stuck in one place and talking in riddles."

"Didn't you just say that I need to go back to Camp Divested?" snapped Tembi. "Now, why would you tell me that, I wonder?"

"Right, right." He sighed. "Tembs, Carroll is going to try and recruit you. She's already started. If you let her, she'll give you more access to the camp."

"Why?" Tembi was close to laughing. The idea of going back and spending more time in that mass grave shaped like a fortress with a woman who lit herself in gold? Absurd. "If they've already gotten a portal to work, then why would they care about an actual Witch?"

"You're not just a Witch, Tembs. You're famous. If Carroll manages to befriend you, it'll be a sign of their strength."

"Besides, they still need the Deep," Bayle said. "They didn't get the large portal to work, did they? They tore up a perfectly good moon in the attempt, too."

"Which is probably why they tested it where they did," Kalais said, nodding. "We thought it was a bomb. The Council did, too, for the same reasons. Bombs are used to make statements; hiding a giant explosion would make us suspicious."

"Let me think about it," Tembi said, eyes closed. "I've got to meet with Domino tomorrow." Her friends groaned in sympathy. Beneath her, the floor buckled and honked like a large bird. "Stop that," she said, patting the floor. "We're allowed to think Domino is scary."

The floor twitched, rumbled, smoothed itself back into tiles.

"How do you always know what that thing is saying?" muttered Kalais.

"We start by not thinking of it as a thing, and we proceed from there," Bayle said, scratching the side of her beer bottle as if scratching a cat behind the ears. The bottle giggled and began to purr.

Kalais hastily set down his own bottle and held up his hands in defeat. "I'm out. Message me with the next time you want to meet."

"May you have wide and wild dreaming, broad as the sea, glad as the tides, soft as the shore," Bayle said.

Tembi pointed over her shoulder at Bayle. "What she said."

Kalais rolled his eyes and vanished.

"He would have made the perfect general," Bayle sighed. "But he makes a terrible Witch."

"He's a wholly average Witch. That's the problem." Tembi shook her head. "And I don't know if he'll ever get over...you know."

"Mmhmm..." Her friend nodded at the unspoken reference

to a certain Solstice party three years ago. The Deep had used appalling judgement by hopping into an incredibly drunk Kalais, danced around the room once, twice, and then cracked his foot so hard against a coffee table so hard that everyone in the room had heard the bones snap. Worst of all, when the Deep had fled in embarrassment, it had purged the alcohol from Kalais' body as it went, leaving a suddenly sober man with five broken toes roaring in pain and anger on the carpet.

Tembi patted Bayle's knee. "We should go, too."

Bayle sighed dramatically and draped herself across Moto's pod. "Now must I to the monument alone, and within three hours will fair Juliet wake."

"Do I want to know?"

"Not unless it's set to song." Bayle rolled off of the pod and landed beside Tembi. "Want me to come with you when you meet with Domino?"

"All gods large and small, yes," Tembi moaned. "But."

"But." Bayle dropped her hair over Tembi's lap. "That woman reads me like a book."

"Yeah." She smiled at her friend and pushed Bayle's hair away from her eyes. Blue as the sea, naturally, and always. "Get some sleep. Happy ocean water…stuff."

"Such a poet," Bayle said, grinning. She stretched, yawned, and disappeared.

Tembi stood and leaned on Moto's pod. Bayle had brushed off enough of the soot to show all of Moto's face through the plass. He looked silent, still, not even breathing.

"We can't leave you here," she whispered. "It's safe but it's not… It's not right."

Morality is the privilege of the comfortable.

She had been turning that message over and over again in her mind. Everybody had an opinion, but none of the answers truly grabbed her.

None save Gallimore's, where, with all due courtesy, she needed for her to pull her own head out of her ass and go help those in need.

Tembi swore and punched Moto's stasis pod.

The pod rocked and tilted sideways before the stabilizers righted it. She checked to see if Moto's eyes had opened like the pivotal moment in a drama on the channels: no, he was still perfectly preserved. If humanity ended at this very moment and the Deep persevered, it would be just Moto, here in the eternal dream, forever.

"This isn't *right*," she muttered, and set about purging Moto and the pod of all possible incriminating evidence.

The next morning, she arrived at Domino's office. Lancaster's Earth Assembly member was actually there this time, and her mouth dropped open in something very near surprise when Tembi announced that she had found Moto and she needed help bringing him home.

Domino, regal as always in her costume of whites and rainbows, gestured to the nearest chair. She locked eyes with Tembi; the feeling of Domino climbing into her head was unmistakable. "Tell me everything."

Tembi did. She was utterly straightforward and truthful, beginning with her tour of Adhama and the Crisp, to Moto's brother, to Camp Divested, to Gallimore and Downriver, and finally to the final resting place of the severed head. The lies were in omissions: the second tour of Adhama went unmentioned, allowing her to skip over the Chameleons. She couldn't forget them completely, and when she thought of how Lancaster had helped to vanish them, she allowed the bloody image of the soldier's severed head to fill her. Domino flinched on Tembi's behalf whenever she allowed herself to remember the moment when she had opened the box.

She ended by plunking Moto's data on Domino's desk. "Kalais says this proves the Blackwings are trying to find a way to use the Rails without the Deep. They're doing an end run around Lancaster, and they split that moon in the Stross cluster with their last attempt."

Domino couldn't seem to close her mouth. Finally, she said, "Goodness."

Tembi was working very hard to not delight in how Domino was so off-balance. She kept her thoughts fixed on the goal: "Moto is safe in the dream, but we can't leave him there. He needs medical attention to purge the mindfuck or whatever it is that's caused him to misfire. How can we tell the Deep that he needs to be in a hospital, and stay there?"

"Let me manage that," replied Domino. "It's not the first time a Witch has suffered this nature of trauma. The Deep can be convinced."

Good enough. Tembi sent a silent request to the Deep; Moto's stasis pod appeared in the middle of Domino's office. "Ah," Domino said. "We're doing this now?"

"It's wrong to keep him in there longer than we have to." She paused, and forced herself to move. "And I want to go back to Camp Divested. Carroll thinks I'm a useful idiot. If she has information about the machine they're using to open a way to the Rails—"

Domino's head snapped up. "No."

Tembi had expected some resistance. "I know I don't have much experience, but this needs to be done."

"I agree," Domino said, standing. She came around the desk, her dress a cloud lined in color. "I agree on both counts, which is why you should not be the one to do it." She laid her hands upon the stasis pod and peered through the plass to see within. "You've accomplished so much in such a short time—three days since the moon was split!—and if I had no other options, you would be my choice to pursue this.

"But I do," she said, looking up. "I have others I can call with more experience, who can slip in and out of a Blackwing camp without being noticed." Domino moved towards the windows and stared at the wide expanse of the Plaza below. "And I'm beginning to think your skills might be wasted on spycraft," she muttered, as if to herself.

"Come," Domino said, as if she had decided something critical. "Let's go for a walk."

Tembi reached out and tapped the pod. "Moto first."

"He will keep—"

"Yes, he will!" Tembi couldn't keep herself from snapping. "That's not the *point*."

Domino, her eyes half-hooded in the way of an Adhamantian preparing for a coming storm, stared at her before nodding. "As you wish."

Frugal, Domino's assistant, was summoned. Instructions were given: Moto would be moved to a quiet medical suite in a hospital on Found, and brought out of stasis, a Witch posted with him at all times to make sure he was kept from jumping. This hadn't seemed sufficient to Tembi, so she had moved inside the Rails with Domino, the two of them speaking quietly and sternly to the Deep that Moto needed care and *must not be moved*.

"He will be fine," Domino assured her. "The Deep listens."

"I know, but the Deep doesn't remember," she said, and wrinkled her nose as her bobcat synth appeared and chirped angrily at her.

"Be satisfied," Domino said, her tone suggesting that she was at the end of her patience.

Tembi nodded respectfully to the bobcat. The automaton flipped its tail at her and turned into a sour smell which hung heavy around their heads.

"Now it will pout for the rest of the day," Domino murmured.

"Take it singing. That's its favorite thing," said Tembi, as she scratched the Deep's feather-fur. "Isn't it, beautiful beast?"

The smell dissipated with an irritated huff.

Domino watched, silent.

"I figured out your message, you know," Tembi said, surprising herself. If she hadn't been here, safe within the Deep itself, she probably wouldn't have mentioned it, ever. But she was never alone with the Deep. "You know? *'Morality is the privilege of the comfortable.'*"

"Oh?" The other Witch raised an eyebrow.

"If you put in the work—*real* work—you'll never be comfortable, because then you're forced to face how there's no such thing as a purely moral action."

The other eyebrow went up. "Let's take that walk now."

They came out of the Deep in a quiet section of the Plaza, that vast open plain in the center of the Earth Assembly's pavilion. It was an amphitheater, an ancient design to channel sound from the speaker to the far corners of the crowd. The stone was older than any Witch; tiny plaques positioned all about the place made note of its origins on a distant island, and how it had been disassembled, moved, and reassembled here after Earth's last big war for its own good. No one came here unless events were scheduled, as it was too much effort to reach without a reason and there was too little around it to hold interest. If you wanted to sit on a pile of old rocks, there were more pleasing piles with better views down by the beach.

"I come here to think," Domino said, as the two of them walked around the amphitheater, bare feet hard upon the old stone. "I appreciate the perspective."

Tembi silently wondered if that meant perspective on age, or space, or the significance of such vast silence in a place designed for sound.

Domino replied, smiling, "All of it."

Into the Plaza. Enormous, artful in places, brutal and sterile in others, the result of competing visions across millennia. They said a city could fit within the cradle between the buildings. The waking world's version of the glasshouse she had visited in the Deep's dream was here, about a kilometer to the west. Nearby was a garden, plants from throughout the galaxy chosen for the same colors and forced to find ways to live together. (Or not. Matindi always had a ready lecture on how plants enjoyed murdering each other when they toured the Plaza, and the gardeners were always busy.)

They paused and bought crushed ice to ward off the heat of the day. Domino waited until Tembi had taken a nice soothing swallow before she said, "Tell me about the Chameleons you've found," and waited patiently, sipping her own drink, until Tembi's coughing fit was under control.

She thought she had been doing so well, with every thought of Paisano and his people tucked carefully away. A reminder that she should always be on her guard? Certainly. "I'm not fond of telepaths," Tembi told her, allowing an Adhamantian's honest anger to fill her thoughts.

"Nor should you be. We're insufferable," replied Domino. "Would you like to hear the story?" When Tembi nodded, Domino tapped her databand to wrap them in silence, and then asked, "First, how many are in the group you found?"

"I don't know," she replied honestly. "I think it's somewhere around a hundred."

Domino slumped, eyes closed and fingertips against her forehead. "So few?"

"There could be more in hiding."

"There are," the older Witch replied. "I myself have moved several thousand others into different cities across the galaxy."

Rather than endure endless coughing fits, Tembi dumped out her drink into a planter and threw the cup into a nearby bin. "Start talking. Please."

"Not much to tell," Domino said, "save that it is easier to preach that Lancaster is impartial than practice that lesson. If it eases your conscience," she added, "I did not break the blockade. I paid smugglers to find and move those Chameleons caught off-planet, and to pay for surgery to help them pass for Earth-normal."

"Does that ease *your* conscience?"

Domino stared at her until Tembi had to look away.

They resumed walking, with Tembi trailing after her because she had no idea what else to do. After a long uncomfortable silence, Domino said, "I'd like to formally offer you that job on my staff."

Tembi tipped her ears to *attention.*

"We'll be at odds for some time, I believe," Domino said. "Possibly forever. But, unlike Matindi, I believe the two of us can work with each other for the greater good of both Lancaster and the Deep. Am I correct?"

"Yes." Not a lie. She most certainly would work with Domino, even if the two of them developed permanent limps from subtly kicking each other at every opportunity.

"You are…" the Witch paused, certainly searching for favorable phrases, "…ill-suited for espionage. Too driven by that conscience of yours, I fear. You would be better suited for a job where I can weaponize your moral compass. Lancaster has invested in many charities throughout the galaxy. I want you to oversee these, improve their efficiency, and recommend new venues and opportunities."

Charity work? Tembi let the idea wash through her. It wouldn't be nothing. Lancaster was *so rich* and *so influential,* and managing its investments would be life-changing for *so many* people! Except that meant—

Domino stopped and placed a hand on Tembi's shoulder. "I know your true goal is to change Lancaster itself," she said. "Spending some time in this work will give you experience and perspective, and you are lacking in both. Better to learn now and plan for the future, than to rush into problems, no? Humanity's fatal flaw is how we can only imagine new versions of what we already know, and we both want more for Lancaster than to be caught up in endless retellings of our past failings. Do you agree?"

Yes, *of course* she agreed! That was the problem! And Domino would send her on one merry chase after another, each of them wholly worthy of Tembi's time and attention, and the rot at the core of it all would never be addressed.

The telepath plucked all of this from her thoughts: "Fifteen years," she promised Tembi. "That's all I ask. Barely a blink in the life of a Witch. Enough time for you to learn what you must, to learn what is right and what is possible, and how to blend these.

"We'll start with more training for you." Domino began to make notes on her databand. "Finances, protocol…and infiltration and espionage, of course, as you'll be meeting with some rough people and I don't want you to stumble into another dangerous situation by accident. When Moto wakes, I'll have you shadow him.

"But while you're being trained," she added, "I want you to find a safe home for those Chameleons on Adhama." Domino glanced in the direction of the distant sea. "Somewhere safe. A place no one knows about, including myself. Somewhere that will eventually form a home for those Chameleons I've moved into hiding. I wish this to be secret and deniable, as this is more than moving Sabenta refugees. If the Earth Assembly learns of this, we risk our neutrality. This is a duty, and I'm putting it on you because you are young, and I can blame youthful transgressions if you are caught.

"Do you understand?" Domino said, resting a hand upon Tembi's shoulder.

For a moment, Tembi's heart leapt within her.

For a moment.

Then came the memory of Cendo, reminding her that it was a hard thing to be a Witch with a heart, and she knew that if she did this, Domino would own a piece of her as much as she owned a piece of Moto.

She looked up at the tall Witch clad in rainbows, and said yes.

Chapter Twenty-One

They came out of the Rails on a pastoral planet beneath a red-and-blue sky. Nearby were the ruins of a small settlement, long abandoned and stripped bare of anything of value. Pools of water splattered across a dense landscape of gold and green, with patches of flowers and small flying creatures. It reminded Tembi of the cemetery on Tolkien, except the living had a right to be there. Beside her was Paisano, dressing down in a silver-gray tunic and pants, a small jeweled collar, and thick but plain metal bracelets.

She had to ask. "Where do you shop?"

Paisano, staring all around them as if he had never seen a world in the sunlight before, said, "I don't. All I wear belonged to my father, and his father before him." He paused, as if he had finally processed what she had said. "Chameleon used to be able to buy anything it wanted. Now, all we have are castoffs and antiques."

"Do you want to buy this?" Gallimore, their arms wrapped around Bayle's waist, stepped out of the Deep. It was a fair question. Lunair was lush and close to Earth-normal in all but sunlight, as one of the planet's two suns was in the latter stages of dying. The abandoned settlement was located on an island several thousand square kilometers in size. Not far across the sea was a city of three million settlers, serviced by a small starport. Lancaster rarely came here, and the Blackwings had no need to do so, as the planet had no hidden wealth and the majority of its settlers were Earth-normal. Lunair was, quite simply, a nice starter planet if you couldn't do better, and a terrible one if you could.

The Chameleons' leader began to walk, slow and graceful, along the memory of a paved road. His skin was mimicking the color of dark clay, near to gray but with a little red thrown in to bring it closer to Tembi's own, and the silver in his tattoos had changed to gold. Strange, to think he was using her as camouflage. "Nobody wants to go to the refugee camps," he said. "They're filth, dropped on continents or planets nobody wants. They are so far off the chains that there's no way to get any resources in, no buyers for anything they make, and you Witches won't touch them. Here, we might have some degree of comfort and have time to prepare for a better future."

He removed his collar and stared at it, his thumb caressing the gemstones. "Go," he said, hastily pressing it into Gallimore's hands as if worried that one of the two of them might change their mind. "Buy me an island."

"Paisano?" Bayle asked, as she exchanged a weighty glance with Tembi. "There are other worlds available. You don't have to take the first piece of land you see."

"We are used to castoffs and antiques," he said, gazing towards the settlement. "I like this place. I think we can thrive if we rebuild upon these bones."

Tembi looked to the sky. "And the sun?"

"When it goes, we have a spare," he said, and grinned at his own joke.

It was the first time she had seen him wear anything but a frown, and it transformed him, elevating him from a near-alien creature of shadows to a gorgeous human man.

"Do that more often," Gallimore said, and Bayle had enough time to meet Tembi's eyes and fan herself dramatically with one hand before the two of them stepped back into the Deep, leaving Tembi and Paisano alone.

"Do what?" Paisano asked them as the air closed itself with a small thunderclap, and then he asked the same question of Tembi, who shrugged in feigned ignorance.

The two of them walked towards the settlement, Paisano taking the lead. "A plague took these people?"

"A treatable plague," she said. "They chose to not treat it."

"Why?"

"Religion, I think." Tembi looked around at what remained

of the small colony. Nothing but overgrown foundations and scraps of standing plass were left. "This place has been avoided since then. The locals say it's cursed."

Paisano made a ritual gesture, touching first his forehead and then his heart. "Let's find where they were laid to rest. We will build a memorial, and we shall give them whatever honors we can." When Tembi raised an eyebrow in question, he turned his gesture into an embarrassed shrug. "I know very little about this universe, except that we are at its mercy. We do what we can to avoid its wrath."

"That's a...pragmatic philosophy."

"I agree, but I've yet to be proven wrong," he said, as the old road turned towards the ruins of the settlement. They explored as best they could through the overgrowth, startling a great many naturalized old Earth honeybees in search of pollen. Several alighted on Tembi's bare arm, and Paisano went to remove them. "Here, let me. I don't react to venom if they sting me."

"Leave them," she laughed. "They can't sting me."

"Ah." Paisano seemed to notice his hand against Tembi's arm, the colors close enough to match. He coughed, and his skin shifted several shades closer to its usual gray, with the gold edging in his tattoos moving towards tarnished silver. "Apologies," he said. "It's mostly unconscious. Think of it as a compliment; we tend to model ourselves after the most powerful person in the room."

"It's not an issue," replied Tembi, flushing slightly. "And Bayle outranks me by a matter of magnitude."

"That's not what I meant," he said, smiling gently.

Tembi's flush grew and threatened to evaporate everything south of her hips. She turned and moved deeper into the ruins. "How much control do you have over it?" she asked, as she clambered over the pieces of a tumbled plass wall. "My skin reacts to stress. Physical, psychological, emotional...the greater the strain, the harder it gets.

"Also rougher," she added. Better he learn now than at a completely inopportune time. "My people measure our lives by our grit."

Paisano was silent for a few moments. Then: "Mine have forgotten green."

"Hmm?" She turned to look at him.

He had picked a frond from a plant and had laid it against his own arm. "I was born off-world, in hiding. Same with all who are younger than me. Green was the first color to go." His skin beneath the plant was guttering through different shades of blue. "I also can't do orange or yellow, but that's hereditary among the men in my family. There's no reason why I should not be able to master green." He sighed and let the frond slip to the ground. "No one took the children out of hiding. The first time I saw a large quantity of green, I was past the age where I could easily learn new colors."

"That's terrible."

"I suppose. I do find it very sad." Paisano stopped and gazed at the sky. "Our eyes are different from Earth-normal. I see a wide range of distinct colors, and can mimic most of them. Green feels like a loss I'll never fully understand.

"I want more for my people," he said, as they walked into the middle of what might have once been a small town commons. "I want my children to grow in a place like this, and learn more colors than those of rocks and shadows. But I don't want them to be in hiding forever. If we can't rejoin the galaxy as ourselves—as Chameleons!—we should have stayed in the tunnels. So we will come here, and establish ourselves in some rarified trade, and our children will learn green."

"How will you rebuild?" Tembi asked, a little bit of dread rising. If Paisano didn't want to stay in hiding, the Blackwings would be on this place like cats on murder. The Chameleons were their quiet success, their best example of what would happen if they were crossed. A small number of survivors might be allowed, living reminders to wander the galaxy, lost. A colony of them, though, rebuilding their lives? No. Oh *no*. That must be stopped. That must be *crushed*.

"Slowly," he replied. "Carefully. And we shall not be alone.

There are many among the Sabenta who also see no future in the refugee camps. Gallimore has suggested that we add three Sabenta for every one Chameleon. They will give us a different form of camouflage."

She chuckled at that. "You've thought this through."

"I've done nothing but," he said. "All I haven't planned for is the possibility of hope. Your head Witch? Domino? Was she telling the truth about other Chameleons in hiding?"

"I think so." Domino had told the Deep to take Tembi to a colony on the edge of a nearly-nothing solar system. The planet was colder than Tembi liked, and most of the settlers wore thick clothing. Still, she had seen some of them display the same unreal beauty she had come to associate with Chameleons, and some of the men had tattoos on their hands and necks with gilded edges. "She says there are several thousand survivors, hidden in different locations. Once you're set up here, I'll give you the coordinates and you can decide how you should proceed."

"How to proceed?" He laughed. "I have no idea! We've lost nearly all of our civilization. I've never set foot on our homeworld. I might not recognize what they brought with them when they fled. I might not recognize *them*."

"Do you want to go?" The words were out before Tembi could catch them. "To Chameleon, right now. I don't know how much time we can spend there without getting caught, so we'll have to be fast, but…"

She trailed off as Paisano stared at her, tears in his silver-gray eyes. "I have misjudged Witches," he said, taking a careful step towards her. "You've been villains I can blame. But you, Witch Stoneskin, have done nothing but try, and that makes you more a hero than almost any other soul I have known."

She stared up at him, somewhat amused and more than reasonably aroused, as he gently touched her bare arms, her shoulders, her face—

The air blew apart beside them.

"Paisano, my good friend!" Gallimore stepped from the Deep,

with Bayle a half-step behind them. Gallimore saw Tembi step away from Paisano, and their ears tipped forward in a wordless apology before they turned back to the Chameleon. "Cendo needs two months to put all of the pieces in place, and then you will be the anonymous owner of this pleasant chunk of Lunair."

The Chameleon bowed at the waist, and Tembi grinned at Bayle as he took the opportunity to adjust his tunic. Ah, well. Since she had started bomb duty, all she allowed herself was the occasional kiss. No one in possession of a decent balance of common sense and self-preservation wanted to cuddle up with an actual rock.

The four of them took a moment to celebrate, with Bayle conjuring sparkling wine from one of Atlantis' best vineyards. They laughed and danced and got decently drunk, and after Bayle and Gallimore snuck away into the bushes, Tembi shared a small kiss with Paisano. It was sweet but short, with her pulling away before he could introduce anything more complex, and then turning away so he could check his lips for abrasions without either of them feeling guilty.

After that, the real work began.

How did you rebuild a civilization? A secret civilization, with barely enough surviving members to form a viable gene pool? Carefully, cautiously, each decision made with the welfare of the future colony in mind. What outsiders could be introduced? Soldiers who could no longer fight, and the families of dead Sabenta heroes.

Loyalty. Trustworthiness. Careful section and evaluation, each step of the way.

They'd have to be careful, especially for the first few years. Yes, the island had been purchased by new settlers. There was no choice but to accept that information would get out, and that the locals would drop in with Lunair's version of pies and casseroles to welcome their new neighbors. The Chameleons would be forced to blend in to the Sabenta colonists, to pass as members of the new population and not the primary reason for the colony to exist. They had two things in their favor: the galaxy was sure they were dead, and they were Chameleons. Blending in was what they did.

A slow procession of tasks, each more important than the last, began to swallow their lives. Bayle managed most of the logistics and paperwork, while Tembi had strange, often irritating, clandestine meetings with ranking members of the Sabenta, most of whom wanted her to explain *precisely* why the refugee camps that were good enough for the Sabenta weren't good enough for the Chameleons.

"We should trade jobs," Tembi had said to Bayle. "You're so much better with people than I am."

"I agree," replied Bayle. "That's why I know there's no way in all of the greater hells that I want to do yours."

So Tembi spent half of her time meeting with angry people, and the other half meeting with exceptionally skilled people, as she began to learn what it would take to manage Lancaster's charities. Finances, certainly, and her lessons weren't too different than what she had gone through when she had trained with Cooper, where an experienced professional recognized that investing a little extra time in Tembi would save them whole shiploads of work in the long run. She had always possessed a good head for math, and she already had a Witch's education in logistics, so the pieces of Lancaster's charitable investments scattered throughout the galaxy quickly came together. Her tutors were eager to help her. None of them were Witches themselves, and the Witch who once held Tembi's future position had gone on sabbatical several years before, leaving no clear plan to return. There were moments when she thought her tutors would have been happy to shove any old Witch into that management void to save them from needing to fill that role themselves.

However, mastering the practical skills needed to oversee Lancaster's charities was only part of Tembi's training. She wasn't sure it was possible to cram common sense into someone's skull, but Domino appeared to be hells-bent on keeping her from repeating her mistakes with General Carroll. Tembi had never before considered how the gritty tricks of politics were put into play: Domino set her to lessons with teachers who knew how to manipulate courtrooms, financial institutions, and an assortment of seedy underbellies. She had thought that her own childhood meant that she wouldn't be surprised at cruelty, but she couldn't have been more wrong. Life at Lancaster had caused her to go soft—how she had laughed when she had realized that!—and the people who showed her how to navigate the different arenas in which Domino's personal contingent of Witches moved were *brutal*.

All those skills she thought she already possessed? Compared to her new teachers, she knew nothing: she didn't know how to fight; she didn't know how to move within dark corners of the galaxy; she didn't know how to slip in and out of dangerous places. These new teachers didn't care enough about her to throw her the occasional compliment. It was sink or swim, and she sank to the bottom like a rock. She spent a lot of time on the Rails, screaming out her frustration.

At least she wasn't in danger of dying. The Deep was, as always, her ever-present guardian. When these new teachers forgot she was a Witch and set out to break her down, the Deep would remind them, often by flinging them across the room, or sending their clothing to the rooftop. It never hurt them: those new teachers didn't want to kill Tembi, so the Deep didn't send them to wherever it sent those assassins who had come after her while she worked on bombs. Proof that the Deep was still picking through her assailants' thoughts to determine appropriate punishments, although Tembi developed a minor fear that some of these teachers might get fed up and send a hypnotized assassin against her, some generally innocent person who thought they were at a recreational firing range or something equally banal, and they would empty an entire battery into her before the Deep realized that the bubbling puddle of goo on the ground had once been Tembi.

(Or maybe this had already happened and the Deep had wiggled with time to prevent it, and this twisting of what had-been and what-was caused Tembi-the-*not*-goo to spend entire nights staring at her bedroom ceiling, wondering.)

There were also some cross-disciplinary skillsets in effect, as Tembi quickly learned that dealing with angry people would be a mainstay of every part of her professional life, clandestine or otherwise. Someone was always furious with the situation, and since there was no use in getting mad at war or money, that meant someone was always furious with her.

Two months. Angry people, deadly people, and Tembi caught in the middle.

Through it all, Moto slept.

She and Bayle would go to his hospital room and watch him, his chest rising and falling in a slow unchanging rhythm. It was good to see him out of the stasis pod, and his dreams were gentle enough to allow the physicians to manipulate his skin.

But.

Frustration boiled up, up, into the stress of the day. Bayle still needed to teach classes at Lancaster; Tembi had taken over Moto's duties with Cendo. They were exhausted, short-tempered. They snapped at each other more than they should. There was never enough time, and Tembi sometimes came close to asking the Deep to wiggle more hours into her day…but no. She didn't know how that would go, except for badly.

Then, finally, a last clandestine gathering in the tunnels beneath Adhama. Paisano stood among a collection of anti-grav crates, the hundred-odd Chameleons clustered around him. A young child clung to his legs, shaking.

"It will be good," he promised her, as she began to cry. "There will be two suns, and a sky full of stars."

Tembi couldn't take it. She reached out and joined hands with Paisano, and spun them away, all of them, children and crates and three generations' worth of suffering, into the Deep.

Chapter Twenty-Two

The colony on Lunair still had no formal name, so Tembi opened her heart and showed the Deep the ruins of the old village and the spectacular ombre of the blue-red sky above. Instead of opening onto the memory of the road, the Deep set them down in the middle of a damp field. Tembi had no idea why until she realized that the nearby village was a hub of activity, construction crews moving up and down fresh-made streets. There was no room for two Witches and a hundred Chameleons to drop in unawares. They slogged through the muck towards the village until Tembi had the bright idea to let the Deep lift them in the air, and then it was a game in which the children giggled and raced each other around the sky.

Paisano watched one large-eyed girl as she stopped and stared at the open world around her, and then began to cry as she struggled to climb down to the ground. "Ah, my heart," he said quietly, and went to rescue her. As soon as he reached her, the girl buried herself in his arms, as if the sunny day was a monster she couldn't face.

As they came upon the town, voices cried out in shock: was this a Blackwing raid? There were weapons brandished, but Paisano was known to some, and Tembi was recognized by most. Soon, it was a celebration: there were Chameleons in the galaxy again, they were here, and they were safe.

Safe.

What a wonderful concept.

Safe was certainty. It was knowing where your next meal came from, and there was a reasonable expectation of regular meals after that. Safe was lying down in a bed of your liking at night, knowing that when your eyes were closed, the world would pass you by and let you wake to rejoin it on the morrow. It was trusting that those around you would catch you if you fell, and hold you up when you couldn't move on your own.

If you had safety—true safety, with all the quibbly bits managed—you could want until your eyes fell out, but you would need for nothing else.

Providing safety and maintaining it in the face of all challenges was the most enduring form of love.

There was a moment where Tembi, standing next to Paisano, had to take him aside as he folded over himself. She slipped an arm beneath his shoulders and pulled him away, into an unfinished building, and watched as he wept.

"We can never repay you," he finally said, as he wiped away his tears.

"Never think you have to," she replied.

He stared at her, his dark eyes earnest and far too similar to Kalais' for her to safely lose herself in them. She gave him a smile and a firm pat on his shoulder, and left him to rejoin the celebration.

It was too easy to stay on and help the colony. The Sabenta had so many needs, and so many of those were about moving: moving people and goods in, moving information around, moving water and earth and plass and stone, moving the natural world around to make way for humans. Tembi might have been reluctant about helping them, except the Deep loved building towns. It was poor with the fine details, such as plumbing and cabling, but the town was to be made from prefab plass shells like Matindi's quaint country cottage, and their foundations were ready to go. (They were also kitted with dehydrating packbins for waste, so at least there would be no toilets zooming into the stratosphere this time.) As long as Tembi and Bayle could ensure that each building went to its proper location, the colony's technical laborers could attend to the rest, and so the town sprung up around them, as fast as if a clever child was playing with a favorite set of blocks.

Besides, it wasn't as if she and Bayle could just abandon these people. They had sworn to do right by the Chameleons, to do what Lancaster had not. So, the two of them jumped between their duties on the far side of the galaxy, and came back to the hidden colony when they could sneak away. Sometimes, Matthew asked her why it was that she was avoiding Lancaster. She wasn't. She was killing herself to keep to the schedule that Domino set for her, those ongoing meetings with financial tutors and all-purpose assassins. But she was *so* tired, and her attendance at their little non-rebellion had suffered. She didn't know how to explain how she was doing something real instead of merely talk, talk, talk, and so she let that part of her life slip away. He didn't press her. Why would he? She and Bayle were still young, and the young were notoriously unreliable.

Matindi, on the other hand?

It was a pleasant evening and the air smelled of early summer and rain. The mood of the colony was high, with nearly all its members present at the nightly communal dinner in the village square where everyone came together at the end of another day of hard labor. The town was nearly finished. The main road was established, the group habitations completed. All that was left were the small homes for individuals and families, and as the town had been planned and built out from the center like the hub of a wheel, these could be completed at a slower pace. Tembi and Bayle were sitting at one of the wide tables with Paisano and some of the other community leaders, laughing even as they made plans for tomorrow. Then, Flury, a former Sabenta colonel who was sitting across the table from them, stood up in shock.

Tembi and Bayle turned to see Matindi stomping towards them, robes flapping from her pace. "*This* is where you are?" she shouted. "*Here?!*"

"Excuse us," Tembi said to the table, and she and Bayle pretended not to scurry as they went to meet her.

Matindi was furious, just burning with anger. "How *dare* you?!" she hissed. "The *ego* of you two selfish children! The Blackwings will make an example of these people to punish Lancaster!"

"Matindi—"

The small green Witch threw out an arm, and the Deep pushed the girls into the shadows of a nearby building so quickly that their feet scraped across the ground as they flew backwards. "You had *no* right! Their deaths will be on *you*."

"Matindi—"

"We've got to get them to a safe—"

"Matindi!" Tembi shouted. "Look!" She pointed towards the tables in the village center. The three of them were the center of attention, nervousness pouring from the community in tremulous waves. The crowd was coming together, slowly, with the Chameleons in the center. The adults and older children couldn't shake off the shades of gray that had defined their lives, but the smallest children were turning brown and green to blend in with the landscape.

"No," Matindi whispered as her hands slammed across her mouth. "Oh gods, no."

"They're the last. The Sabenta have been sheltering them," Tembi said. "They couldn't move them onto a ship to get them to a colony, not without separating them for safety. When we found out, we wouldn't leave them, and once we got them here, we…" She didn't know where that thought was headed. How did you package hopelessness and empowerment in the same word?

Bayle took over for her. "Domino knows," her friend said. "She knew there were a small number of them left, and she told Tembi to help them"

"Does Matthew—" Matindi stopped, unable to continue.

"We think it's just Domino," replied Tembi. "She had to keep it close to keep it quiet."

Matindi nodded, and then kept nodding, as if the motion was helping her brain process the rediscovery of an entire lost race. Tembi couldn't help but grin: she had never seen her second mother so shaken. "All right," Matindi finally said, and smoothed her robes. "Introduce me around."

After that, the new colony had the help of three Witches.

It was an idyllic time. The small colony thrived, and as the phase of building things ended and the phase of building lives began, there was real joy to be found. Almost all of those in the colony had been refugees, and the stability and security of a true home was so strange that it was itself a cause of stress. Some couldn't manage, and they left, disappearing into the fields or hopping out with a supply run. The rest relaxed into the new status quo, unpacking bags for the first time, or removing their valuables to store them in their houses.

There would be crime, of course, someday in the near future. Crime and anger and pettiness, and most likely violence, once their needs seemed less important and their wants came forth. For now? They were safe, and that alone took up so much space in their lives that they could not make room for anything else.

Sometimes people broke into song.

It was hard but hopeful. Tembi and Bayle were tired, but it was a good exhaustion. For the first time in her life, Tembi felt whole. It showed in her very skin: once, she tripped and fell and skinned her knee, and the sight of her own blood caused her to weep in relief. After that, she went to the nearest garden and pressed her face into the flowers to feel the petals against her skin, and after *that*, she went looking for Paisano.

All in all, it had been a very good four months.

The only bit that gnawed at her was Winter.

Tembi had found the old woman by accident. She had been walking along a side road, snacking on a plate of truly substandard chips. A nagging impulse kept poking her in the stomach, reminding her that the best chips in the galaxy were at that little seaside booth on Tatumn, a quick five-minute round-trip—

"Witch."

Tembi stopped, chip in hand. Everybody called her a Witch, but they said it like it was an honorific, a curse, or caught between those, not...

Not like they *knew*.

There!

A woman, lounging in a pile of garbage ready for transport. Sprawled across the top of a hundred different kinds of filth, using it as her throne. She was ancient, a piece of dog-gnawed leather which had gained the ability to walk. Her head was bald save for a few strands of silver hair, and her clothing was rags, rags, a dense tangle of rags, rags layered so thick she could barely move, as if she had taken to wearing an album of her entire lifetime wardrobe on her body. She looked Earth-normal, but she must have been from one of the desert planets and modded for its climate, or she'd be baking herself alive in the heat.

"Jig off to Tatumn, would you? Get yourself some of those chips?" The old woman grinned, showing a full set of pristine white teeth. Tembi doubted they were her own. "Good stuff, yeah? Can almost taste 'em meself."

Another psychic! The only true mind reader Tembi knew of was Domino. She couldn't resist: she stopped beside the old woman and set her basket down.

"What's your name?" Tembi asked.

"Ah, you're a raw one, y'are…" The old woman stared at Tembi with eyes the color of mildewed sewage. "Tembi Moon? No…" The old woman caught herself. "Stoneskin now. Changed your name already, but it doesn't suit you."

"Oh?" Tembi's hands were still rough, the tiny impacts of daily life ensuring she would always have hard calluses. She ran her fingers over her thumb, stones over sandpaper, and the sound crumbled in the air between them.

The old woman cackled. "Skin deep, you absolute pudding." She peered through those sickly eyes to see Tembi's face. "Birds? Ah." The old woman shook her head. "Before I formed you in the womb, I knew you, and then I marked you like cattle in the pen."

Tembi sighed and gathered up her basket. The woman was cracked through and through. Any insight she could have given into Domino's abilities would be tainted with the batty rabble churning in place of her brain. "Do you need anything?" Tembi asked her. "I can get you clothes, some food… Would you like some of those chips?"

The old woman started laughing, a deep frog-croak of a belly laugh. After a time, she sighed. "You have a good soul," she said, wiping tears away with a filthy thumb. "But souls can be corrupted, girl. Better learn who you are before someone tells you elsewise."

"I'll keep that in mind," Tembi said, but before she was two steps into her escape, Matindi appeared in a flurry of brown robes.

"Tembi, can you—" Matindi began, and then her voice cracked and froze at the sight of the old woman.

The old woman, who had finally let her froggy laugh fall away, renewed her croaking.

"Do you two know each other?" Tembi asked Matindi.

Her second mother stared at the old woman. "I've never seen her before," she whispered, voice all but gone.

"H'llo, Matindi," the old woman managed, before she toppled flat on the ground in uproarious laughter. A pedestrian carrying an oversized bucket stepped around her, shaking their head in disdain.

"You sure about that?" Tembi asked.

"Yes," Matindi said, as she began to climb the garbage pile to reach the quivering pile of rags. A little of the usual metal had returned to her tone. "Quite sure. Run along, dear, I'll take it from here."

"Uh-*huh*." Tembi inspected the trash. There was a clear path up the far side which would take her straight to the old woman. She started to climb, toes squishing in the damp. "I don't think so."

The woman cackled. "Witches, Witches everywhere, and not a one who thinks!"

"Tembi?" Matindi's usual no-nonsense voice was back. "Leave."

Stray pieces of garbage began to shake themselves loose from the pile, up, hanging in midair. Was it the Deep? Or...no. If the old woman was a telepath, she was also telekinetic.

"Tembi, dear, I'm serious."

"I don't want to leave you," Tembi replied, as the garbage began to fly in slow circles, a solar system of trash all centered on the gravitational pull of one ancient crone. "Deep?" she said, speaking loudly so the old woman couldn't help but overhear. "You got this?"

The old woman laughed all the harder, and the shivery scent of unripe pomegranates filled Tembi's imagination. She wasn't sure what that meant, but she got the feeling the Deep was laughing, too.

"Go, Tembi," Matindi said firmly. "I'll be fine."

Tembi went. Fifteen minutes later, when she returned from Tatumn, a filmy plass baggie of hot chips and sauce in one hand and a bundle of clean clothing in the other, she couldn't find either Matindi or the old woman. The Deep was no help; it was in a good mood, and bounced her across the colony following false leads until she got fed up and ordered it to just *go ahead and send these to Matindi, godsdamnit!* When the chips and clothing disappeared, she dusted her hands clean of the whole affair and went back to work, assuming she'd never speak to that old woman again.

She was wrong.

Throughout the next few weeks, the old woman kept appearing and disappearing along the periphery of Tembi's life. She would pop up, mutter a strange comment or two, and then vanish into the colony again. This shouldn't be too unusual; the colony didn't have more than a couple thousand settlers in it, after all. You tended to see the same faces.

It would have been fine if Matindi hadn't been glued to the old woman's side. They were inseparable. The old woman—"She calls herself Winter," Matindi told her—was everywhere, with Matindi by her side. This caused problems: Matindi walked away from her job as a teacher, leaving a classroom of distraught children. And with a Witch as her protection, Winter was *everywhere!* bouncing across the colony, charging into locked rooms and closed meetings, and generally making herself into a public nuisance. She was a wrinkled, laughing ball of chaos, a bottle of alcohol never far from her hand. There were other substances, too; Winter wore a scarf which reeked of ptarch. That particular drug killed its users sooner rather than later, burning through their skin and their central nervous system with unseen chemical fire; Tembi had no idea how a person of Winter's age could use ptarch and survive.

She also had no idea why Matindi permitted Winter to twist the colony up into knots. When pushed, all Matindi said was that Winter was a philosopher. Tembi, who was certainly having none of that, pushed harder.

"She's studied the Deep, all right?" Matindi finally snapped at her. She had developed a new habit of toying with a bracelet made from live moss when she was feeling tense, and she yanked it this way and that. "She's got fascinating ideas, most of which I hope are wrong, some of which I'm terrified are right." The two of them were standing at the edge of a field, aggressively pretending that Winter hadn't pulled her pants down and wasn't urinating on her own legs. Matindi sighed and held out her hands; a bucket of soapy water appeared. "I think she's testing me. She wants to know if I'm worthy before she tells me everything. It's…it's fine. This is fine."

The urine vanished and Winter spun around, grinning at them with those immaculate out-of-place teeth.

"Pants, Winter dear." Matindi sounded exhausted. The bucket disappeared, and Winter hauled up her pants before she teetered into the nearby field.

"Do you need help?" Tembi said, somewhat shocked. Matindi rarely used the Deep to clean. Human waste? She would have thought Matindi would never, ever ask the Deep to manage that. "I can watch her if you need a break."

"No." Matindi paused, arms crossed, and looked out across the fields. The grain—*wheat? sorghum? something else?*—was gold tipped with green; Tembi had heard the farmers talk about the harvest starting in another month. "Give me time," Matindi said. "Her thought processes are a mess. I've got her on meds, but digging through them takes work. She's forgotten so much—"

"Forgotten what?"

Matindi hopped up on her toes so she could kiss Tembi's cheek. "Soon," she said. "Once I get my notes together. This is too important to rush."

"I hate it when you ask me to wait before you drop ten kilos of truth on me."

"Such is life when one doesn't want to appear foolish," Matindi said, and she followed Winter into the golden fields.

Chapter Twenty-Three

There is still divinity in the galaxy.

Here we have a piece of plass, a chemical compound which can be spun into various levels of durability and clarity. Renewable, recyclable, repairable, a miracle substance which has replaced most conventional building materials. Not quite glass, not quite plastic, closest to rock. Amber, perhaps, tree sap turned ancient, except amber is natural and plass isn't. Except nearly everything across the settled galaxy is made from plass, or was made with plass, or contains a core of plass in its hidden innards for strength. For humans, that might make plass the most natural compound in the galaxy. Plass should be considered divine.

It's not, though. Neither is carbon, which should be worshiped for its life-giving properties. Hydrogen, likewise. More common than dirt, and treated as such: the divine is saved for what is precious and unattainable, not what exists at the tip of a finger.

Humans have shit for priorities.

Chapter Twenty-Four

Paisano slept hot and hated it, so the windows to his room were always open at night. Tembi didn't mind. It meant Paisano had a bedroom to himself, a rarity among the Chameleons who usually chose to cluster together for heat. She had found a downy blanket nearly as soft as the Deep's own feather-fur, and she kept herself wrapped within it as she curled against Paisano's naked back. Having a sense of touch was just bliss.

She reached out and ran the beck of her hand down Paisano's arm. *Velvet,* she thought. *Why do the books all say skin feels like velvet? It's like...* The comparison escaped her: the closest she could get was the feel of a clod of freshly ploughed earth, warm from the sun and ready for planting.

(It was possible she had gone a little wild lately, running around the colony and touching everything she could. No regrets about that! A sense of touch was such a fleeting luxury for her that she was willing to act the fool. Not for the first time, she wished she could smack her ancestors for not making the distinction between physical and psychological stress when they had paid to get their genes adapted, but she supposed they had been operating at the mercy of a tight budget like everybody else.)

Paisano stirred in his sleep, the colors of his skin shifting towards a deeper shade of gray. He was changing, too, now able to integrate some different shades of blue and purple into his camouflage. He had confessed that he didn't think he'd become comfortable enough to blend into their new planet's bold golds and greens, but the youngest Chameleons had already learned how to blink in and out of the background. Games of tag among the colony's children were epic.

Hands knit behind her head, Tembi stared out the window. There were so many stars! They brushed against the nearby rooftops, lighting the town in pale white. Paisano had chosen a house in the second circle of the town, and said it was large enough for him and eight others. There were only three bedrooms, but the Chameleons had lived in small cramped quarters for so long that they felt most comfortable when they were packed tight together. It reminded Tembi of her own childhood, with her mother and older sisters all sharing a couple dozen cubic meters back on Adhama, and the ever-present knowledge that there were layers upon layers of unseen human beings pressing against her on all four sides. She hadn't realized she missed that kind of forced community.

Was she happy? Was this *happy?!*

Tembi grinned.

Her databand chirped. She slapped her wrist to silence it, but the chirping continued: Lancaster would not be denied. They had been especially pushy lately, yanking her this way and that, asking for more of her time. It was as if Lancaster was trying to bring her back to heel without forcing the issue. It was the same for Bayle, and had gotten so bad that her friend had given up her room in the colony and started sleeping in her own home on Found again, just because she was tired of being summoned to the Tower for ridiculous reasons.

Tembi leaned over to kiss Paisano's shoulder, and made the short jump from bed to the street below, asking the Deep to grab her robes on the way. Dressed and decent, she slapped the databand and opened the channel. "Good *night*," she said, crunching down on the word.

A small grammalight projection appeared before her. A man's face, his brow pinched. "Can you get here?"

She blinked. She hadn't talked to the other members of her old bomb squad in months. "Cooper?"

"We need you. Right now. Can you—"

"Yeah," she said, as she asked the Deep to swap out her robes for her bomb uniform. It was spotless: Matindi must have found it and given it a good wash. "Pressure bomb?"

"We don't know."

"On my way." She broke the connection and stepped into the Deep. It was a long trip, about five minutes along the Rails. The Deep had sunk itself into her mood so there were no bright colors, only the sharp nervous anxiety of moving towards a dangerous unknown. Cooper had trained her in the fundamentals of demolitions and explosions, and had worked with her as she and the Deep had honed their skills. He had—quite grudgingly and while very drunk—admitted she could do things which he and his team of specialized 'bots couldn't. If Cooper needed her now, it didn't necessarily mean all was chaos and flame, but it meant things were certainly close.

The Deep opened onto what must have been a small colony on a moon with a paper-thin atmosphere. Cooper was waiting for her in a breather and grav gear.

"Gods! Always jealous of you Witches," he said as she walked towards him. "Takes me a year to get kitted up."

She grinned. "Good to see you, Coop."

"Same. This way," he said, gesturing towards the colony. As with Downriver, there were atmospheric bubbles around clusters of buildings. "They called me out here an hour ago. Bernie is evacuating the locals."

Tembi hissed. Bernie was the Witch who usually got tapped to move Cooper across the galaxy. If they had left Cooper alone to evacuate the colony, things were bad.

"Tell me about it," he agreed, and turned to the atmospheric equipment which adjusted the climate within the colony's bubbles. "It's over here."

The device in question was smaller than her bobcat synth, and was standing apart from the rest of the machinery. It was obvious why the colonists had reached out to Lancaster for help: shaped from sleek matte gray plass, cut into hard angles, and plumbed all over with tubes, there was a sinister quality to the device. You knew just from looking that it was meant to *do* something, and that *something* was most certainly not benevolent.

Except...the device looked...familiar? There was something

about it which strutted around her subconscious, looking for something to kick. "Are you sure this is a bomb?" she asked.

"Not at all," answered Cooper. "Never seen anything like it. The locals said they noticed it a couple hours ago. Called their investors and their equipment suppliers to learn if it was an addition to the usual gear. Once they confirmed that nobody knew where it came from? Well…"

"…chaos," she finished for him.

"Yup." He glared at the device. "Might be a prank. Might not. I don't trust it."

"Have you poked it?" she asked. Cooper had explained his telekinetic abilities as an extension of his sense of touch, where he could feel objects without laying hands on them. Much like she used the Deep's own extraordinary senses to help her explore unfamiliar objects, Cooper could move his mind across a strange bomb from a distance.

"Lightly as I could," he admitted, arms crossed. "Didn't want to poke it too hard, in case it responds to tekkers."

Tembi shivered. Some people (*cough*cough* the Blackwings *cough*) didn't approve of telepaths and telekinetics, and had developed mechanisms which responded to extra-sensory intrusion. *Can't keep out Witches, though,* she reminded herself as she sat down and shut her eyes. *Can't keep us out of anywhere.*

A deep, centering breath…another…another… Unlike Cooper, she needed to lay hands on a bomb before the Deep could feed the pieces into her mind, but maybe if she took a moment to herself, centered herself and focused on the device, the reason for its familiarity would make itself clear.

Where have I seen this before? Those angles, those sleek materials. Her subconscious kept telling her it was too clean, too perfect. And far too small. The last time she had seen something like this, it was a mess. A giant mess.

Sometimes bombs go off. Sometimes I only get to see them once they've blown. Think bigger, Tembi. Think about ruined bombs. Think about broken—

"Scheisse!" Tembi shouted. She leaned over to seize Cooper's foot and wrapped the Deep around them and—

Everything stopped.

They were caught in the blink of a moment between real-ity and the Deep. Cooper was frozen in time. Behind him, the strange device had begun to activate, twisting in on itself, the strange design folding sideways to open a portal. In that portal were colors, brilliant, bright colors—*The Rails,* she thought. *It's a gateway to the Rails*—but all of them losing cohesion as soon as they appeared.

The machine couldn't contain it.

You can't have the Rails without the Deep!

Whiplike cracks of light appeared, lashing out from the cen-ter of the portal. The device pulled away from the ground, fragmenting, the uncontainable energy of the Rails lifting the device and the atmospheric machinery around it. Sound was starting to catch up with light, a gathering roar of destruction which would do as much damage as the coming explosion. Tembi threw all of her strength into hauling Cooper towards her, into the safety of the Deep, and then—

Darkness.

Silence.

Then, a small fleck of gold-white light, which grew to illumi-nate the Rails and the broad feather-furred back of the Deep. And Cooper, lying beside her, teeth clenched and trying not to scream from the loss of most his left leg.

"Gods! Coop!" After the roar of the device, Tembi's own voice sounded like the squeak of a mouse in her ears. She tore off her headscarf and wrapped it around his thigh, yanking it tight to slow the flow of blood. "Don't move. Don't move!"

"Not...not planning on it." He let out a small half-laugh. "Left leg?"

"Yeah."

"Good, good." He was gasping from shock. "That knee was bad. Thought about sawing the sossing thing off myself."

"Stop talking," she said. She needed to calm down. She need-ed to *focus.* The colors of the Rails were wobbly and the Deep was miserable and there was a chirping noise she couldn't place and there was *so much blood, oh gods!* "Deep, take us to a hospital…" Which hospital? So many of them, but not all of them had the equipment to regrow limbs. "The hospital on Found!"

Her bobcat synth appeared and squalled at her, all of its fur standing on end.

"Deep! The hospital!"

The cat lunged at her face. Tembi fell backwards, astonished, and shrieked as she rolled off the Deep's back and straight out of the Rails. She landed on solid ground, her breath knocked out of her body and more nauseated than she had ever been in her life, vaguely aware she had landed in the middle of a quiet pastoral town square.

"Tembi!" Matindi's voice. Small green hands around one of hers: Matindi was kneeling beside her, checking her pulse. "Where did you come from?"

"What?" Tembi could barely hear herself. She had hit the ground hard. Her ears were ringing—*chirping?*—and she was sure her stomach was about to pop out through her mouth and begin walking around on its own. "Where's Cooper?"

"Cooper? Is he here? Why are you bleeding?" Matindi tried to help her sit up. Tembi made it about halfway before she had to curl up in a ball, but in that moment she had noticed where she was, her landmark a house directly across the square from them. Paisano's house: the Deep had brought her back to the Sabenta colony. Matindi began to pull Tembi's robes aside, searching for the source of the blood. "Tembi, where are you hurt?"

"Not mine." Tembi rolled onto her side and threw up. She wiped her mouth on her sleeve, tasted copper, and then threw up again. "The blood…it's Cooper's. He called me out for a bomb…it went off…" She glanced at her databand and realized it was the source of the incessant chirping. Messages were flooding in, one after another, the display blinking up every few moments. "I was trying to get him to a hospital, but the Deep threw me out here."

"He's on the Rails *alone?!*" Matindi sounded horrified.

"I'll find him." Blearily, she saw a dark-skinned woman appear in the street in front of Paisano's house. A moment, two, and then the woman changed clothes in a heartbeat before she vanished into thin air. Once she was gone, Tembi instantly felt a million times better, as the fog that had been clogging her thoughts vanished, and her stomach stopped roiling. She stared at the spot where the woman had stood, and whispered, "Oh, *that's* not good."

"What?" Matindi grabbed Tembi's chin and peered into her eyes, as if checking to see if she had a concussion. "Sweetling, you're scaring me."

"The Deep brought me here—" Tembi realized her mistake as soon as she said it, and she found her feet. "No! Matindi, the Deep brought me to *now*. This moment! Why?"

The two gentle slaps across her face didn't hurt; Matindi never had the heart to truly hit anyone, and Tembi's skin was already going hard again from stress. It did shock her enough to freeze her in her tracks. She stared down at her second mother, finally realizing that Matindi was terrified. "Tembi," she said in a calm, gentle voice. "You're scaring me. Stop moving and explain."

Tembi shut her eyes. *Where to begin?* she wondered, and then started by prodding her databand to stop the message notifications. "Do you remember the device that split the moon?"

"Yes."

"Cooper found another one. When I got there, it activated. Matindi..." she paused. "Matindi, it opened a portal to the Rails."

Her second mother's jaw dropped. "That's not possible."

"I know what I saw." The memory of the bright colors turning sickly was burned into her mind as clearly as if it had come via a wonky Crisp. "The Deep got us out of there, but not before we saw the device start to... I don't know if it exploded, or if opening a way to the Rails tore everything apart. It sliced straight through Cooper's leg—*gods!* Cooper's still out there!"

"Tembi, finish your story, or so help me, I will smack you

again."

She glanced across the way towards Paisano's house. "The Deep brought me back here. It brought me back in *time*. I just saw myself leave."

"Oh, that's not good," muttered Matindi.

"Right?!" Tembi looked around, searching the dark shadows of the colony for whatever the Deep wanted her to find. "Something's happened. Or *will* happen, here."

"Then we must—" Matindi stopped, her words hanging on a single breath. Before Tembi could ask what was wrong, Matindi's body flew apart into a million sharp-edged fragments.

There was no warning: it was impossibly sudden. The space between Matindi standing in front of her and Matindi spread across five square meters in jagged pieces took up less time than a heartbeat. The cuts were as clean as that which had severed Cooper's leg. Nearly as bad was the sense of unholy *wrong*-ness Tembi had felt when the portal had opened to the Rails was back, only devoid of light and sound.

Tembi screamed.

Then—and only then—did the Deep act.

The fragments of her second mother came together, pieces of a puzzle fitting together. They aligned perfectly, cleanly, and Tembi could see their edges seal. Matindi was staring at her, eyes unfocused but flawless, as if the damage had never happened.

Then she toppled lifeless to the ground.

"Is this a vision? It's got to be another vision—" Tembi knew she was wrong even as she dropped to her knees and turned Matindi over. The Deep would shatter illusionary planets and pretend to dissolve strangers into nothing, but Matindi? It would never hurt Matindi! She was sure it couldn't even imagine hurting Matindi! "Deep! *Help!*"

:: GRANDMOTHER ::

:: FIND GRANDMOTHER ::

The Deep's voice roared around the square, sorrow and rage in its purest form, echoing from every corner. Plass shattered; rock turned to dust. Heedless of all else, Tembi held Matindi to her and began to cry. Another wave of nausea came over her, this one from the stark realization that she was holding her second mother's body. The grief of it settled into Tembi's bones, becoming part of her, bonding to her soul.

And the night sky broke into warships.

Sleek predatory dropcraft blinked out of FTL, cracking the air from displacement. Their bellies split open; Blackwing soldiers in dark gray body shields and grav kits fell in controlled arcs towards the small village, popsticks burning with cold white fire.

Pure rage caught Tembi as she realized she and Bayle had been tricked off-planet—*that Matindi had been assassinated!*— all to keep the Witches from fighting back when the colony was purged. Ears flattened against the noise, she placed Matindi's body on the ground and then stood to face the invaders.

"Let's do this," she whispered to the Deep, and it howled around the square, readying itself.

Tembi hit the ground, the back of her head throbbing. She glanced up in time to see Winter bring a heavy bottle down on her skull again.

Winter peered down at her. "Don't kill the poor girl," the old woman said, as she lifted the bottle a third time.

All went black.

Chapter Twenty-Five

"Tembi! C'mon, Tembs, get up!"

A familiar voice.

No, an annoyingly familiar voice: Kalais.

Wait, no. Kalais? Why is he here?

She managed to get one eye open, and the world flopped over sideways. She really wanted to throw up again.

"Tembs, get *up!*"

Definitely Kalais. "Matindi? Winter…she hit me."

There was something wrong with that. Winter hit her? No. The Deep wouldn't let anyone hurt her.

But the Deep let Matindi die. It knew what would happen and it did nothing.

There was something wrong with that thought, too. It didn't do nothing. The Deep had brought her back through time to be with Matindi at the end, so Matindi could—

A hard jostle. There was a shoulder tucked under her arm. "Here, take her."

"Where's she injured?" Another familiar voice: Paisano.

"Can't find a wound, and her skin's too hard to cut. I don't think the blood is hers. Hide her until she can jump you out. I need to help with the evacuation."

"Kalais?" Her skull nearly split with the word, but she had to know. "Where's Matindi?"

"She's here in the colony?" Tembi opened her eyes to see Kalais shake his head. "Haven't seen her. She's probably jumping people out."

"…no…" She couldn't explain, couldn't ask why he had found her but not Matindi's body.

"Keep her awake." Kalais was talking to Paisano. "Use this on her, even if she shouts at you to save it for someone else. She's how you escape."

"Yes, yes." There was a hiss, followed by a soft weight draped across her forehead. She had enough feeling left in her skin to know that the object shifted temperature and began to act as a cold compress. A medical nanopack, the emergency version of her usual mini-med pills. A million microscopic 'bots were no doubt zipping through her system, diagnosing her injuries, swarming the damaged tissues and repairing them, but all she felt was cold.

Tembi was passed from one set of hands to another, and then another. Paisano left, the man who replaced him as her nurse soon followed him. Their voices reappeared from time to time, always talking softly to her to keep her from slipping back into unconsciousness. Slowly, Tembi's thoughts began to clear, letting her puzzle out the circumstances: they were in hiding, and the adult Chameleons were darting naked into live fire to locate and rescue their fellow colony members.

She opened her eyes. Around her were some of the colony's children, crying in absolute silence. Not all of them. Not even most. There should have been five times their number. Most were Chameleons, sitting still and blending into the walls so closely that they were almost invisible in the gloom. The older Chameleon children were standing with their backs to the windows, their skin the same shade of mottled gray as the room itself. Anyone taking a cursory glance through the plass would think the room was empty.

"What's happening?" she whispered.

"Blackwing raid." The speaker was Chime, a young woman fairly high in the colony's hierarchy. She had been a Sabenta soldier before she had lost an arm; repairing missing limbs was prohibitively expensive for most refugees. "Paisano asked you to take the children to safety as soon as you're able."

Tembi tried to nod, and found her head no longer felt like a shattered egg. The med 'bots were doing their job. "The War Witch is here?" she asked.

Chime hesitated. "He says the Deep brought him to you."

"Oh." The medpack beeped softly, its cycle complete. Tembi

sat up. Save for a grave sense of sorrow and a bone-deep weariness, she felt normal. Wide dark eyes followed her every move: she wondered if the older children would have been out assisting with the rescue if she hadn't been knocked flat and left defenseless. When she got her hands on Winter, she was going to sossing murder the old—

Focus, Tembi.

She opened her arms. "Come, children."

They rushed to her, Chameleon and Sabenta alike, and she folded the Deep around them. They moved across the galaxy wordlessly. Tembi knew she should have been chattering to keep up their spirits, but she couldn't make the effort. The Rails were gray: the Deep shared her sorrow.

The Deep opened into her own living room at Lancaster. It hadn't been a conscious choice, but the Deep had picked a longing for home and security from her emotions, and Tembi's house met those needs. She snapped off the lights, drew the shades, and told the children not to leave the building. Then, she was back into the Deep.

Cooper came next.

Tembi knew even before she found him. The Deep twisted in on itself when she asked about him, and the gray of the Rails turned black. The Deep took her to his body, now nothing more than a corpse floating alone in the dark, all of his nimble brilliance spilt along with his blood.

What a way to die.

She gathered up his body, too numb to cry and unwilling to say anything to the Deep to put it at ease. She knew it was miserable; she knew the Deep knew that she was angry. She also knew there was nothing that would come out of either her mouth or her mind that could be kind, and so she forced herself to say nothing, think nothing, feel nothing at all.

They came out in the same shadowed room in the colony. Chime was surrounded by another dozen children. When they saw Cooper, they began to moan quietly. She laid him down against the far wall and whispered, "I'm sorry." Then, again,

Tembi opened her arms and took the children back to her house at Lancaster. This happened twice more, until there were no more children waiting in the little house, and after that she moved the adults.

"Keep them safe," she told Chime, and gave her a code she could use to ping Bayle's databand. The children were all sitting in tight clumps across the central room, staring at nothing. Soon, a new clump of problems would arise—Sheltering Sabenta children from a Blackwing raid in her own home? What was she *thinking?!*—but for the moment, no one would look for them here.

Back to the little colony.

Her anger was high, a brutal song within her veins. No hiding in the quiet room this time. She stepped out of the Deep in the center of the village. There were bodies all around, some left where they had fallen, some stacked into a rough pile and burning. A nearby Blackwing shouted at her, pointed a popstick at her...

Tembi didn't bother to raise a hand as the Deep blinked the soldier out of her reality.

"Enjoy your time in Assassins' Paradise," she muttered, as she walked into the battle.

Soldiers closed on her. The hot song of her rage lashed out, again and again, taking those who would kill her and sending them away, away. Where? She didn't care. The Deep mourned along with her in a burning wind which lifted the soldiers and hurled them aside, away...

Would the Deep kill for her? Oh, yes, *yes!* Gladly! It knew she was hurting and it would do anything to heal that.

A Blackwing came at her, and she wondered if the Deep could fragment the faceless soldier into a million sharp-edged pieces, just like—

The smell of roses. The taste of the galaxy's best coffee. Warm, clean sheets wrapping her up at night.

"Stop," she whispered to the Deep. "Don't kill them. Matindi wouldn't want that."

Instead, she punched the soldier in their throat, right below the protection of their faceplate, and then kicked them to the ground.

She kept kicking them.

The Blackwings knew there were Witches here.

Another soldier came at her from the side. A foot behind their knee, a tug to put them on the ground, the same foot straight into their faceplate to drive them back.

They had a way to kill Matindi. The Deep knew it would happen, but it couldn't stop it!

The reflection of green sparks against the polished black of his shielded armor. She turned and blocked the popstick before it could touch her, tossed it aside, and kicked the soldier in the stomach.

If the Deep couldn't stop it from happening...

She hissed with realization: *the Deep wanted me as witness.*

The soldier staggered back, and then barreled forward, shouting. They were massive, a human-shaped avalanche bearing down on her. Tembi snarled at them as she lifted the fallen popstick.

Bayle and I kept getting yanked back to Lancaster. It annoyed Bayle so much she started living at Lancaster again, and if I wasn't getting laid—

The popstick flashed as she jabbed it straight at the soldier. Unlike the others, this one appeared to have a little more than basic combat training; the popstick slid across the armor of their arm as they blocked, and then they threw a fast and heavy punch at her face.

Cooper called me out to defuse a bomb.

She dodged and raised the popstick again, all set to drive it straight into the solder's ribs to hurt and hurt and hurt! Gods, she was so glad the Deep was letting her fight!

Cooper works for Lancaster.

Tembi stopped, the shock of realization nearly freezing her in place.

She threw the popstick at the soldier and wrapped herself in the Deep, this time asking it to jump her to a nearby rooftop where she hid behind an overhanging ledge. From there, she stared down at the village, forcing herself to slow down instead of letting her rage drive her. There were connections she didn't want to make, didn't even want to consider.

Pause. Breathe. Take in the battle.

The action was winding down. There had been two soldiers for every villager, and as the raid had started in the dead of night, the colonists had had no chance of winning. Some of those who had fought back had been killed, but the majority had been stunned, captured, and herded like livestock towards waiting FTL transport ships. It would have been over ages ago if it hadn't been for the Chameleons and their camouflage, and Tembi would have bet every credit she owned that their slim advantage had lasted until a Blackwing soldier had remembered to flip on the infrared.

She leapt across the rooftops, running on the night air when she couldn't clear the distance between buildings, searching. There were people in the colony she couldn't abandon, not even for the forty-plus children crying in her living room on Found.

Paisano!

There, below, hiding behind a row of tall bushes which resembled chunks of seaweed blowing in the night breeze. His camouflage was mottled gray to resemble the shadows cast by the bushes. She wouldn't have spotted him at all, had Kalais not been crouched beside him, cloaked in an atmospheric bubble cast by the Deep to hide them from scans.

Into the Deep and out again, kneeling beside Paisano. He gasped, or would have, had Kalais not whipped a hand across the other man's mouth. "Shhh," Kalais cautioned, and nodded to Tembi.

"Matindi's dead," she said. The words sounded absolutely unreal. "She was killed as the raid began."

"Oh, Tembs." His lenses were up, allowing him better clarity in the dark. Tears welled up in his pale eyes. Even when the two of them had been at their worst, Matindi had shown him love, too.

"Later," she said, peering through the shrubs. "What kind of weapon fragments a body into sharp pieces?"

"Sharp?" Paisano whispered. He hadn't turned to look at her, instead keeping a watch on the people being loaded into the nearby dropships.

"Yeah. Clean edges, like broken glass. Matindi was—" Tembi took a deep breath. "She was shattered. The Deep put her back together almost as fast as it happened, but she was already dead."

"The Deep didn't stop it?"

Tembi glared at Kalais, but it was an honest question instead of a perfectly aimed arrow. "No. I don't think it could. Instead, it brought me back to bear witness."

At least her second mother hadn't died alone. A blessing in the form of a trauma, but she hadn't realized it until now. Gods, the poor Deep was probably so confused!

"A weapon that can kill Witches." Paisano sounded almost in awe. He turned to Tembi: "I'm glad you're safe."

She smiled at him, so sadly. Less than a half an hour had passed since she had been curved around his sleeping back. And now—

"Yes, well," Kalais whispered quickly, and pointed at the ships. "What to do about *that?*"

"My people are in there," Paisano said. "I can't leave them."

"Some of your people are in my house," replied Tembi. "Almost half of your children. Consider that before you charge the ship."

Paisano's shoulders slumped. "Shadow spirits, I don't know what to do."

She looked to Kalais. "No," he said. "I want to tear those ships apart, Tembs, you know I do. But—"

"Lancaster is pulled straight into the war." She shut her eyes. There had to be something they could do, some trick of the Deep's to salvage the situation. She could yank out parts of their engines, or jump out captives one by one as soon as they were loaded.

Focus, Tembi. They know there're Witches here. They probably have taken precautions—by every dark hell, they killed Matindi! You're not invulnerable any more.

Oh, now there was a sobering thought! She hadn't given herself time to process how she might actually die here.

Focus, Tembi.

"I have an idea. You're not going to like it," she said to Paisano. "You'll spend it doing childcare while Kalais and I rescue the others."

"Tembi—" Paisano's lips curled back, exposing his sharp teeth.

"Fight the right people now," Kalais reminded him, a hand gripping his shoulder. Paisano closed his eyes tight and nodded.

"C'mon," Tembi said, as she laid her hand atop his and jumped them.

He wanted to talk; she couldn't. The colors of the Rails were black in utter misery. "Give me a moment," she told him, and shut her eyes. "Deep? I understand now. I'm not angry with you. I'm sad, too."

Cooper died alone so Matindi didn't have to. It was a half-formed thought which she packed up and shoved away, as there was no way she could manage all of this at once. Instead, she held on to those last precious moments with her second mother, where Matindi wanted nothing more than to help her, even if she didn't know how.

That had been the essence of Matindi, always. From the moment the Deep had brought the two of them together, Matindi had tried to help Tembi. She had faltered and fallen more than once, had run from their problems, had tried to help by hurting—*the last time Matindi touched me was to hit me, oh, heartbroken gods!*—but she had always wanted to help.

"Matindi was so much like you," she said to the Deep. "All she wanted was for things to be better."

The Deep sang a mourning dirge in greens and golds and

shadows.

A few moments later, they stepped from the Deep into her house. Bayle was there. She received a quick hug, Paisano got a gentle kiss, and then it was back to the colony to rejoin Kalais in the bushes.

"Now what?" he asked, as the last of the colonists were loaded and the cargo doors were shut.

"Now we pick a ship and stow away on it," she said.

"Tembs, no," he protested. "We can jump inside the ships but we can't take people out without being noticed. And if they spot us jumping in, we're done."

She nearly grinned. "That's not what I said."

Chapter Twenty-Six

As they had no way to know where the prisoners were being taken, the two of them took shifts clinging to the side of a ship, living barnacles which couldn't be shaken by multiple jumps through FTL. It was necessary: the hulls were designed to repel tracking 'bots, and while the Deep *might* remember some of the colonists, and it *could* remember a particular ship, this was not the time to gamble on its attention span. Thus, Tembi and Kalais rode the ships. Soon, they had to bring Bayle into it, and then Matthew, too: Bayle came in to relieve them, as Tembi and Kalais needed time to perform their usual duties for Lancaster, and after Matthew was told how Matindi had died, his cold anger had demanded he take an active role. And then, after word had spread that Matindi had been murdered by the Blackwings, all the members of their tiny not-resistance joined in, taking turns riding the prisoner transport ships as they crawled their way across solar systems.

As they flew, they plotted.

For the first week, anger drove them. FTL was *so slow!* and there was ample time to nurture their anger. Anger over Matindi's murder; anger over the Chameleons and the lies which had erased them. And, as the reality that they lived in a world of lies and murder finally penetrated the thick skulls of the older Witches, there was anger directed towards Lancaster.

Word spread. Witches who had never considered Lancaster to be in the wrong denied the accusations. That lasted just long enough for a Chameleon to make an appearance. Some denied their eyes and required genomic tests before they would believe.

(Tembi was sure that some never would.)

By the second week, anger had been replaced by confusion and sorrow, and a sudden flare-up of accountability. Tembi was grateful that so many of the older Witches had come around, if only because she had somewhere safe to stash the colony's children. The Witches in Lancaster's picturesque central village had opened their homes and taken in the refugees, convinced that the act of offering shelter to a fellow human being counted as doing something good.

The third week after the raid on the colony, Tembi realized that their little non-resistance had become an actual resistance. She had been talking to Williamson as the two of them shared a shift, a small bubble of atmosphere encircling them and a couple of comfortable armchairs. The Librarian had brought beer, which he preferred to drink at room temperature; Tembi opened her bottle and asked the Deep to slow the beer's molecules to chill it, and then took a deeply satisfying drink.

"Domino's in on it," Tembi told him, and not for the first time. "She has to be. She hated Matindi."

To her surprise, Williamson nodded. "Did she make sure you and Bayle wouldn't be there when the raid went down? Probably."

"That's the first time you've acknowledged it," Tembi told him. This conversation had happened time and again with any Witch careless enough to stand still around her, and none of them had been willing to commit to Domino's involvement.

"Hold, Sir Stoneskin." Williamson held up a hard-used scholar's hand, ink crusted beneath his nails. "She likely played a role in the raid, but not to the extent of your accusations. What's more likely: that she murdered Matindi, or that the Blackwings approached her as a courtesy, told her they were planning a raid, and asked her to remove her wayward Witches from harm's way?"

"Domino poisoned Matindi once." That fact was Tembi's final word in every argument. It had happened when she was a child and Matindi was raising her at Lancaster, so it was a fairly recent salvo in their infamous war.

Tembi's usual closer had little effect on the Librarian. "She didn't mean to," Williamson said, as he went to open a second bottle of beer. "A sedative for one modified human can be toxic to another. Say, instead, that Domino meant to drug her, which is a crime and a moral failure, but one not on par with murder." He leaned forward, as if trying to push the meaning of his words into her mind. "Most of us are here, Sir Stoneskin, to learn how the Blackwings murdered a Witch. If we can save some good people along the way, so much the better for our consciences, and we all want justice for Matindi. However, Sir Stoneskin, self-interest is a powerful motivator for us old immortals, and I beg you to remember that."

She nodded, grudgingly, not yet ready to ask Williamson why he was here. She was sure, completely *sure*, he was here to help the colonists…but.

Regardless, a large number of Witches were now committed to riding these ships to their destination. And once they arrived…

Well. They were all sure they would do something, even if the specifics were lacking.

Except Paisano was not convinced of that. There had been a fight, the kind that could not be patched over with gentle words. Two weeks after the raid, Paisano had started to ask questions:

Why *couldn't* Tembi just—

Why *wouldn't* Tembi just—

Why was she leaving his people on the ships?

She tried to remind him about Lancaster and neutrality. Paisano wasn't hearing it, called her excuses weak, demanded she put deed to word and rescue the prisoners.

They had been standing in her kitchen, sharing a tense meal where politeness could easily go sour. She forgot what had catalyzed Paisano's anger, but the spark never mattered when the gas lay thick all around and was also toxic. Tembi was accused of holding him a captive, of crimes beyond her power. All of Paisano's anger at Lancaster roared out of him, crashing against Tembi, and then he shouted that her inaction had resulted in her *killing Matindi!*

That was whole-cloth bosh, of course. Neither direct nor indirect action on Tembi's part had caused Matindi's death, unless you went all the way back to the beginning where Matindi would still be alive if Tembi had simply minded her own business and left the Chameleons to *soss off and manage their own rotting selves!*

Then, a cold moment between them in which both knew they must apologize and neither would, so Paisano knocked a stack of books off of her kitchen counter and stomped out the front door.

Tembi had given herself the luxury of a long-overdue cry, taken a shower, and hopped over to the hospital to see Moto. He was still motionless, still unconscious. She had pulled a chair over to his bedside and resumed crying, and most likely would have stayed that way for much of the afternoon had she not felt another's eyes upon her. She looked up, and—

Domino.

The tall woman's ears were set to *sorrow*. She had nodded to Tembi, and vanished.

"Here once a day." A medical professional had swept into Moto's room, touching various devices. Tembi didn't understand what they meant until they clarified: "Domino is."

"Truly?" Tembi had wiped her eyes on the bedsheet. She couldn't cram a bedside manner into her view of Domino's personality.

"Truly." They had picked up one of Tembi's hands uninvited, testing the hardness of her skin. "Same planet?" they asked, nodding towards Moto.

"Same neighborhood, practically," she had told them, grinning. Doctors always thought Adhamantians were fascinating specimens of genetic engineering. Half-assed engineering, but still.

The specialist had released Tembi, and turned to test Moto's cheeks. "Your friend," they said. "Soft skin. Good dreams."

"You still don't know what's happened to him?" she had sighed.

They had shaken their head. "Not mindfuck. Sedative? Maybe. In his cells, like chiithen, drinking vitality, *theeet theeet theeet.*" To emphasize that last point, they had pursed their lips and made a sharp sucking sound.

"Chiithen?"

They had paused, and then extended their hands a half-meter apart. "Sharks?" They shook their head as they searched for the right word. "No. Leeches. They fly."

Tembi had decided she wanted no part of whatever planet they were from. "Can you wake him up and ask him where he's been?"

They glared at her. "Sedative, child? Means he is sedated. Sleeping."

"I know what—" She had caught herself. "Thank you. Yes. What if you stimulate him enough to wake him?"

The specialist had patted her on the shoulder and left.

"I thought it was a good suggestion," she had muttered.

And so she had left Moto once again.

Now, alongside Williamson, riding the transport ships towards their unknown destination, Tembi wanted...

She had no idea what she wanted, and she said so.

The Librarian passed her another beer. It was a start.

Traveling in FTL was a series of overlapping grays. There were no colors or features to be seen, and the hum of the ship's engines was a quiet drone, barely audible within the bubble. Bayle had called it a pulse, the sound of blood in the ears when the head was pressed against the pillow at night. Maybe, maybe not; Tembi considered Bayle's sense of hearing adequate at best. Although she did agree that the ship sang a lullaby of sorts, a slow-moving rhythm which traveled up and down in soothing scales.

"I never imagined my life would be like this," Williamson said. She looked over to see him watching the silver-black blur of space over the dark line of the ship, his own bottle of beer pressed up against the small rim of atmosphere surrounding them. "Glory, always glory, called to service and given every possible gift in exchange."

"Do you want to die?" she asked, surprising herself. "Is that why you're here?"

"What? No," he said, amused and horrified. "Never. I could live a million years and not even begin to understand what it means to be alive."

"Then you're here because you don't want to die?"

He smiled at her. "Your moral code is a small glory on its own, Sir Stoneskin, but perhaps you don't need to invest as much of yourself in exploring the motives of others."

"I just need to *know!*" It came out close to a snarl.

"Why?"

"Because nothing makes sense! Nothing matters unless we make it matter! It's blood and chaos until we decide it shouldn't be, and we can't even agree on how to do that!" There was more in there, about the purpose of life being the act of crafting meaning from nothing, but there were no words—there would *never* be words!—to articulate it.

"A true philosopher," he said, grinning. "I've read about you, but I've never actually met one before. See? There's always something new to learn." There was a good chance she would have hurled her bottle at him, save that the gray of FTL began to shift into different colors. "Ah," said Williamson, as he began to pack up his travel kit. "I believe we've finally arrived. You stay here and I'll pop off and get our team, yes?"

Right, yes. Their team. Three weeks of preparation, anger, wondering... They weren't battle-trained, and Kalais refused to teach them, saying he would be sending Witches to possible slaughter. The compromise was that they would slide Sabenta operatives into the prisoner population during the transfer. Several teams had been left on standby, ready to go as soon as the ships arrived. Williamson jumped from the ship to pick up their team, taking the armchairs and beer with him. Tembi settled herself on the ship's hull to wait, thinking about the complete uselessness of philosophy.

The Librarian returned in minutes with four Sabenta spies, each indiscriminate in manner and appearance. They sat down upon the hull, talking quietly amongst themselves. What plans did you make when you were about to sacrifice your freedom? Voluntarily going into a prison, with no promise of escape. Tembi fixed their features in her mind, hoping that would be enough if she had to ask the Deep to yank them to safety. But one human was so very much like another to the Deep, and it only seemed able to remember its Witches.

No, she thought. *That's not true.* There had been many times when the Deep had sent her images of people. Specific people, some of galaxy-shaking importance, while others were so small and insignificant in the scale of things that they had never needed to exist at all. The Deep knew them. It remembered them!

But Cooper died alone in the dark.

Kalais had stuck them behind a monitor array, believing that in the unlikely event that the Blackwings were equipped to detect life signs on the hull, their proximity to the sensors would be interpreted as equipment error. The spies clustered together, two still in quiet conversation, the third praying over a small white icon, while the fourth stared off into the multihued reaches of hyperspace.

Tembi sat beside the fourth, a woman in tattered, somewhat smelly robes.

"Witch," the woman said, nodding politely.

"I understand if you need silence," Tembi said.

The Sabenta spy seemed to silently weigh several answers before replying: "No. I've made my preparations." She extended a hand, palm up. The ends of her fingers had small adhesive pads. "Gych."

"Name or greeting?"

The other woman grinned. "Name."

Tembi gently pressed her palm against Gych's own. "Tembi."

"I know." Gych nodded. "What do you need?"

"Nothing." She was suddenly sure that forcing herself on Gych had been a huge mistake. "I'm sorry to bother you."

Gych sniffed. "You've taken my bombs apart, you know."

"Eh?"

"My bombs. Careful ones. Good ones! I know you've disarmed at least four."

Tembi stared at the spy, unsure whether she should be angry or just give in to the urge to start laughing hysterically. "I'm sorry," she offered, substituting bland manners in place of sincerity.

"No hard feelings." Gych patted her on the knee. "You did your job. Now, back me up so I can do mine?"

All of those flecks of carbon, twisting into nothing, forever.

"Sure," Tembi said woodenly.

"We get the children first. Then, as many adults as we can." Gych pressed both hands against the hull, rocking back and forth. The pads on her fingers stuck to the surface. "You take them away from the camps before we blow the solar batteries."

Somehow, Tembi had never fully realized that she was aiding and abetting a Sabenta sabotage team. Her stomach knotted. "Is this the plan?'

Gych looked at her as if she had sprouted another eyeball. Definitely a stupid question. "No, Witch Stoneskin. This is an opportunity. Infiltration during distraction. Then, rescue and demolition. The plan is to take the whole compound down at the end."

"How long will this take?"

Ah, she had certainly sprouted a fourth eyeball with that last question. Gych was all but looking for a child's toy to distract her. "Rescue phase takes longest. Coordination within the camp, make sure everyone knows to be at the right point at the right time. Do it slow, do it careful. Rush it, we're caught, we're dead.

"Once that's done? You know how fast things can burn." Gych nodded, an absent-minded gesture. "Yeah, you do."

The strange auras of hyperspace fluttered and then stopped as the ship dropped from FTL into orbit around a green-and-yellow planet. The ship cruised lower, pulling through the atmosphere, the dotted colors of the planet resolving themselves into deserts and marshy plains. From the ship's perspective, the rim of the planet was touching the night, and off in the far distance was a large city ablaze in lights. Tembi thought that the ship was moving towards that distant city, but it curled in the air and moved towards a dusky patch of grassland where a mammoth building waited, an armored shell protected beneath a weather cage. As the details of the building became clear, she wondered…no. It would be too much of a coincidence to have the ships end their journey at Camp Divested. They had reached a different Hawk-class facility, another city-sized mess of hideous plass-and-stone blocks, the lot of it cast in the blacks and grays and reds of loss.

The Sabenta spies had clustered together again, trying to isolate which of the fourteen separate structures would be used for processing. One spy had a databand embedded in the radius bone of his left arm, and was using it to chart constellations.

"Deep?" Tembi asked aloud. "Where are we?"

A vision appeared, six planets in orbit around a sun, with rings around the second and third planets, and the fifth lit with a golden halo.

"Andromeda Four," the Librarian said, surprising her.

"You can see this?" she asked, gesturing towards the Deep's vision hanging before her.

Williamson nodded. "If we're on the fifth planet, we're in A-Four."

Gych had been listening. "Camp Investment," she said to the others. "Hawk-class processing facility on the planet Thunder Bay." The one with the databand grinned; the other two traded quick hand gestures. She turned to the Witches to explain. "Camp Investment is third-gen. Lots of security holes in third-gen Sagittarius Armed Forces installations. They think it to be state-of-the-art, but it's easier to move around in here than in older facilities."

"All right," Tembi said, nodding. "How do we get you in?"

"You don't," replied Gych, as the ship slowed and turned towards a landing strip cut along a bare patch of plass. "We get ourselves in."

"Easy enough." She settled back on the hull, waiting. The vibrations cutting up through the ship were almost unbearable, even with the Deep providing a shield around them as protection. She shut her eyes and tried to find the music in it, but there was none to be found in the sound of the antigrav engines as they hauled the great mass of the ship around.

Then, a gratifying *thump!* as the ship clicked into its port, followed by the sound of powering down.

More waiting.

On the ground, the landing crews scrambled around, prepping different receiving areas for the prisoners. The Sabenta spies watched intently: the chaos between the moment when the prisoners stepped off the ship to the moment they were processed would be used for infiltration. One pulled up his shirt and opened a small sack glued to his stomach, and then began to pass small, nearly invisible eyekits to the other Sabenta. There was an extra set; he handed it to Tembi, who dropped the small lenses over her eyes and looked around, her vision magnified.

She was honestly surprised at how long the landing process was taking. She was used to the relative concepts of *here* and *there,* and was usually long gone when ordinary humans sank their resources into the transportation process. It seemed as if you had whole weeks to waste on FTL travel, you'd quite logically invest that time planning the most efficient and effective disembarkment processes so your cargo would be off the ship as quickly as possible—

Gods! Hiding on top of a prison transport ship and she was still thinking about logistics. You could take the Witch out of Lancaster and all that.

Focus, Tembi.

Across the landing pad was a second ship. She wasn't sure why the Blackwings had brought multiple ships: the colony hadn't been large enough to fill one ship, let alone two. The other ship had landed before theirs, and their crew seemed more organized. The doors opened, and the prisoners were being funneled from the hull to the ground.

The eyekit focused on those other prisoners, allowing her to spot individual faces. Oh, she knew so many of these people! She had shared meals with them, read stories to their children, helped them build their homes. Names and memories cascaded through her mind, ripping into her stomach, shredding her already-thin composure.

And then, the unexpected, as a withered old woman emerged from the other prison ship. Tembi sat, stunned, jaw slack as if she had taken a hard punch to the face. She had asked the Deep to bring her to Winter a dozen times, and relented only when she assumed the old woman had died in the raid. Why else would the Deep refuse to listen to her?

Williamson had noticed her confusion. He reached over and plucked the eyekit from her face, adjusted it beneath his glasses, and began to search the prisoners. "What am I looking for?" he asked.

"Bald head with strands of white hair," Tembi gasped. "Old woman. Really, really old."

"Hmm." He had already spotted her, his head tilted as if he was grasping at a memory. "Do you know her?"

"That's Winter! She was there when Matindi died!" No, that wasn't quite right. Winter had shown up after the Deep had put Matindi's body back together. She knotted her hands and knuckled her forehead, trying to remember. "Scheisse! I thought she was dead."

"Do you think she killed Matindi?" Skepticism in his tone; Winter's journey across the galaxy in a prison transport had not helped her appearance. Or, likely, her smell, as even with the refugees crowded together and moving forward, there was a small gap around her.

"No!" Tembi hadn't, but now she was rethinking everything. "Matindi swore Winter knew more than she let on. She kept trying to get her to talk. Maybe…maybe she knew Winter was dangerous, or maybe…" She gave up. Nothing she said felt right.

She turned to the Librarian. "We've got to get her out of there."

"We yank her out, and we risk telling the Blackwings we're here. No one at Lancaster will thank us for wasting their time."

Or the Sabenta. Gych and the other spies were watching them as if they expected them to set fire to the ship.

"What if she's the one who murdered Matindi?" Tembi asked him. "Are we just going to let her escape?"

"Lots of good people died in that raid," muttered one of the Sabenta.

"Including my mother!" she snapped at him. "Can you bring Winter out with you?"

Silence. Then, Gych said, "No promises."

"But—"

"We're not choosing between as many babies as we can save or an old esorohing."

Tembi closed her eyes at the brute force of their logic. "Gods," she whispered. "All right. I'll go in with you. I'll get Winter out myself."

One of the spies snorted. "No."

"Yes." Williamson leaned forward, the eyekit in one hand, his glasses in the other. "She goes with you." He turned to Tembi and gave her back the eyekit. "Get in, get out. If Winter killed Matindi, find out how and why."

"You are children," said one spy. "You will get us all killed."

"Tembi's a child, but she has training in espionage," Williamson replied. "I, on the other hand, do not. However, I am twenty-eight centuries old, and I have long exceeded my life's stock of patience.

"Relevant to your concerns," he said, leaning forward, "if you want your mission to succeed, you need to make me happy enough to want to be here when you get out."

The Sabenta protested. They argued. They tried calm reason. None of it worked: they didn't have time to make it work. "What do I do?" Tembi asked Gych.

The spy had already resigned herself to the inevitable. She sighed. "Realize you have no power."

Chapter Twenty-Seven

Home, for a change of clothing. Faster to go herself then have the Deep bring the contents of her hamper to the ship. The Chameleons and the Sabenta were gone from her own small house, but they had left a mountain of castoffs and garbage. They had tried to be good guests, but there had been so many of them, and so many of them had been children besides, and she couldn't be sossed to care about anything as trivial as mess after Matindi's murder.

Mixed blessings, she told herself, as she dug through the clothes that had been left behind. In the middle of the mountain was a pair of pants which fit quite well, and over against the wall were an old pair of shoes only one size too large. Over these went the top half of a robe covered in bloodstains, and thus came together an outfit which matched any of those worn by the prisoners caught up in the raid.

What else? What else? Tembi zoomed through her house, kicking her way through trash, asking the Deep for quick jumps around the rooms. Her search was directed by instinct as much as anything: she was looking at days or weeks or maybe months of pretending she wasn't a Witch, and she wasn't sure what she'd need. A quick stop in the bathroom so she could pop a dozen mini-meds to do battle against her ulcers, and another in the kitchen to suck down calories. As she ate the most decadent things in the stasis box, her eyes wandered, searching for something she could scrub through her hair to make it match her clothes. She settled on a finger's worth of good old fashioned butter, and there was a nearby open jewelry box, small and delicate, full of dirt. Tembi dumped the dirt into her hand and ran it though her hair. Then, she belatedly asked herself why there was a box of dirt was on the kitchen counter, and if it was even dirt at all. A moment's inspection found a small note tucked inside the box.

Witch Matindi,

Apologies for disturbing the peace of your home. I did not know who you were.

Admiral Wallis.

Tembi snorted without humor. She had wondered where that bracelet made of living moss had come from. Wallis had done enough belated research to give Matindi a gift she'd actually appreciate.

Back into the Deep, and out again to crouch beside Gych. The Sabenta spy stared at Tembi's new clothing before nodding.

"I brought some for you," Tembi said, sliding a bundle of the colonists' old clothing towards the other spies. Their outfits were visually identical to those worn by the prisoners below, but the spies thanked her and added them to their own clothing as an extra precaution if the Blackwings used any direct chemical detection 'bots.

"Here," one of the men said, and held out a breather. "They'll have areotypes. Keep that in, and it'll change your profile enough so you won't be you." This breather was wholly different from the one she had used in Downriver. Instead of resting comfortably around her neck, this machine went inside her mouth and sucked tight against her soft palate, invisible. Tembi had to sit quietly with herself for a few moments to relearn how to breathe. No helping it, though. There were countless surveillance technologies, but areotypes were the least expensive and the hardest to deceive, and were thus always in use.

Beneath them, the ship groaned as the doors along the hull opened. Gych and the other spies slid to the side and went over the edge, moving carefully along the rim of the hull to stay out of sight until they could drop to the ground and blend in with the prisoners.

Williamson watched them go, and then turned to Tembi. "You sure about this, Sir Stoneskin?"

"Not at all," she said, shaking her head.

"Here," he said, and handed her a small smooth piece of quartz. It felt warm through her skin, as if Williamson had carried it in his pocket. "The Deep knows this is mine. Send this back to me if you need me."

Tembi smiled, touched. The rock was a kind gesture when all she needed to do was ask the Deep to send Williamson to her. She was slightly shocked as he reached out and pulled her into a hug. "Stay safe," he told her quietly. "Please."

"I'll be okay," she whispered, and before she could let her resolve crack, she slid from his arms and went over the side of the ship.

The Deep hummed along her skin, its sensations nervous but...excited? Yes, it was excited. It knew she had been training for something, and Tembi had been maintaining such a concentrated blend of anxiety and novelty over the last few months that it was willing to let her push herself.

From a distance, the transport ships seemed to form single large, smooth curves. Up close, the hulls were plated like a fish, scales and ridges folding over themselves. She followed the same path the Sabenta spies had taken, cheating only slightly by letting the Deep slow her descent so her skin wouldn't grate against the plass. There was a hard drop of thirty meters from an exhaust port to the landing pad, and she used the Deep to cling to the hull like an insect as she scuttled. Then, she was hanging upside down above a set of doors with prisoners streaming out and there was a single moment of sheer unthinking terror when she was sure there were no Blackwing soldiers around as she let her feet fall over her head and flopped forward, falling... falling...

Tembi stood, surrounded by colonists. There were small gasps as she was recognized; a few people said her name, shocked, and quickly silenced themselves. They moved around her, swallowing her into themselves. Not one of them spoke to

her, but more than one person touched her shoulder, her arm...
She could barely feel them but each small contact whispered of
hope.

She fell in with the motion of the slow-moving lines, head
down, letting her ears fall to the sides as if she had no energy
left to lift them. The stench of the people around her made her
want to gag: unwashed bodies, human waste, and more than a
little blood and decay hanging heavy around her. Anyone with
a modded sense of smell was likely screaming internally.

Processing came next.

When they were planning the escape, this had seemed another logistics problem: why not save time and process the prisoners while they were on the ships? Kalais had said no, that the
Blackwings had found it was cheaper to process the living and
dispose of those who had died, rather than processing them
at the beginning of the journey and then weeding through the
survivors at the end. At that, Tembi had stopped talking and
had stared off into the colorless grays of FTL space, doing her
utmost best to think about nothing at all, especially not thinking about what might be happening in the cargo holds of the
ship a few meters away.

We could end all of this with a word.

That same thought now kept rolling through her head as
she walked. "No power," she whispered to herself. "I have no
power." And she fixed her mind on that instead, to quiet both
herself and the Deep.

Context was everything: a thousand people wasn't that many
people, but it was also a lot of people. On a broad sheet of plass
under a gray night sky, it felt like more people than Tembi had
ever seen in her entire life. That was wrong, totally wrong: there
were easily a thousand people living in a single mountain's
worth of homes on Adhama. Here, with them standing around
her, they felt like the sole inhabitants of the entire galaxy.

Blackwing guards ahead, grinning at each other. Tembi expected cruelty—for her, Downriver had defined them—but
no, they were all but ignoring the colonists, moving them into

queues of consistent length for easy processing. It would have been easier if they had been cruel! She would have *understood* if they were cruel! This methodological processing, though…no. She couldn't grok how this could be just another job.

Separated from those around her. Shunted into a queue. Head down, shoulders slumped. Nervous and twitching, but not too often; it was a long flight and the colonists had little left in reserve. Then, her legs bumped against a table. A Blackwing guard opened her mouth, inspected the interior with a little light, and made her breathe into a tube: Tembi was extremely glad that the Sabenta had invested their sparse resources in breather integration tech.

"Name, age, planet of ancestry, and race," said the woman at the table, her fingers moving over a chunky plass tablet.

Tembi said quietly, "Selene Tamber-Tren, twenty, and I'm from Adhama but I'm half-Tolkien." Hopefully that would help explain any genetic confusion caused by the breather. She'd have to remember to thank General Carroll for the convenient cover story the next time she saw her.

"Skills?"

Before she could reply, a loud cackle from a nearby queue caused the Blackwing guards to turn. Tembi kept her eyes down, but turned an ear to follow the sounds of Winter causing her usual chaos. She had flipped over a table, leaving small objects to levitate in the air around her.

"A sossing tekker," a nearby guard spat, and Tembi wondered if her ruse was already over and she'd have to reveal herself to rescue Winter.

"Put her with the others." That voice had the note of command; Tembi turned to see a soldier in a uniform with a single red stripe running down across his torso. "We need every tekker."

Could it be that easy?

Yes, apparently it could: when she was asked to sign a final document, Tembi asked the Deep to pull the tablet towards her, as if she had summoned it to her hand out of habit. As the

Blackwing soldier was still holding it, she couldn't help but feel the tablet jerk before she clamped down on reflex.

"Tekker?" she asked Tembi, eyes narrowed.

Tembi nodded. "Rated for 10 kilos, but I make up for it in dex."

"Show me," the guard said, and tossed a handful of desktop detritus into the air. The Deep caught it all, and Tembi guided them through one of their old classroom exercises to fix the objects in simple orbits around her.

The soldier at the desk leaned forward, almost eager. "How long can you maintain that?"

"Ten minutes," she replied. Cooper had told her that thirty minutes was the goal for professional tekkers, as long as you could sustain it for fine detail work. Ten minutes seemed more realistic for a colonist who had done nothing to try and escape from a prison ship.

The soldier wrinkled her nose. "Good enough. Experience?"

"Solar arrays," replied Tembi, wincing as she realized a moment too late that this sudden golden opportunity to get access to both Winter and the Sabentas' target shifted her involvement from that of a getaway driver to that of a co-conspirator.

The soldier tapped her data into the tablet. Tembi, dismissed, was moved aside from the front of the queue. A few minutes later, another soldier moved her over to an open space where other colonists milled around, waiting. Winter was among them, but so was another person whom Tembi recognized, a former Sabenta soldier named Gillian. He saw her thrown into the pen and rushed over, gripping her shoulders in his culture's version of an embrace.

"You never told me you were a tekker," she said, loudly enough for the nearby Blackwings to overhear. She took him by his shoulders and leaned in close, quickly, whispering, "Call me Selene."

They broke apart. "Never came up," he replied, his eyes darting towards their captors. "You, too?"

"Yeah." She watched Winter out of the corner of her eye. The old woman had removed her clothing and was waving various body parts at the guards, who ignored her. "Were you on the same ship as Winter?"

"She's a popstick, that one," Gillian said dryly. "They'd'a thrown her out the airlock on the way here if she wasn't a valuable tekker. They're doing experiments on telepaths." He leaned in close again, and whispered. "Don't go near her until we're alone."

Tembi nodded. Winter would out her as a Witch without a thought. They turned away, Gillian shielding her from Winter's view. "What kind of experiments?" she asked.

"Don't know." He made a gesture with both hands that she couldn't place. "Started about ten years ago. Telekinetics are cheap; telepaths are pure platinum. They go into a Blackwing camp and they don't come out."

Tembi made a noncommittal sound. Moto's notes had hinted that he had been poking around Camp Divested for similar reasons, trying to learn why the Blackwings had been whisking up telepaths, and how that might be connected to the device which opened a gateway to the Rails. Somehow, all of this cycled back to that machine which split the moon.

The two of them sat, Gillian using his own body to hide her from the direct line of sight of the colonists and the Blackwings alike. Either news of her arrival had spread, or the tekker pen was always a subject of interest, as people kept turning to look at them.

"What's the game?" he asked, very quietly.

If he thought it was safe to talk, it was, but Tembi shut her eyes and reached out to the Deep anyhow. *Hey, Deep?*

The smell of roses filled her senses, a massive relief from the odoriferous miasma coming from the colonists.

Everything is okay. This is where I need to be.

The smell of roses strengthened, and the nervous tightness that Tembi had been carrying behind her breastbone eased. She asked the Deep to make sure she could talk to Gillian about secrets without anyone overhearing them, and the sound and feel of a tiger's resonate purr washed through her.

"Okay," she said to Gillian, but as she opened her eyes, she caught Winter staring at her. The old woman grinned, spat out a brownish clod, and turned away. Tembi waited, holding her breath...no, Winter was done with her, at least for the moment. "Okay. Here's what's happened..."

Halfway through her story, his head fell. When she had finished, he whispered, "I'm sorry."

"No, I'm sorry! We had to leave you on those ships."

"That's just it," he said. He couldn't seem to meet her eyes. "We thought you did. All of us thought...We thought you had been biding time on Lunair...playing a game, really. And when it'd ended for you...you'd abandoned us.

"I'm so sorry about Matindi," he added. "I didn't think Witches could..." He trailed off, unable to finish.

"Yeah," she replied, her voice thick. "We've had to play it safe. I need to talk to Winter before anything else goes wrong."

"And then what?" Gillian asked. "You disappear while we wait for rescue?"

Tembi watched as the first colonists were herded towards the high plass fence which served as the perimeter of Camp Investment. As they walked through the massive weather cage that encompassed the facility, their bodies appeared to blur ever so slightly, as if they had passed from one world into another. "I don't know."

The next week was like no other in Tembi's life. She was moved into the tekker barracks, a large building populated with heavily modded humans. Their only shared characteristic was some degree of control over extrasensory abilities. Telekinetics outnumbered the others by twenty to one: there should have been an equal number of pyrokinetics and psychometrics, but the first were usually too dangerous to let live and the second tended to scream themselves senseless after a few days in the camp. Those that did survive in the barracks were meek little things, always cowering in corners, and Tembi couldn't coax them to talk to her.

There were no telepaths. Winter had been swept away into a different part of the building, and Tembi was kicking herself for failing to talk to her when she had had the chance. But, oh, it was hard to think about that when she was inside the larger machine of Camp Investment! Gych had told her to believe she was powerless, but she knew—*knew!*—she could escape at any time, and so she felt *wrong*, like a visitor, like a tourist who had gone for a walk around a bad neighborhood for the thrill of it.

(By all gods large and small, she kept comparing it to the walk she and Bayle had taken through Adhama's slums, and her heart felt near to breaking.)

It didn't help that the tekker barracks were mostly closed away from the rest of the camp. Tekkers were more dangerous than normals, certainly, but the size of the barracks meant there was no need to move the Tekkers into the general population. Work detail was on the ground floor, which was divided into multiple factory units where the tekkers were put to work mass-producing specialized tech. Above that were rest barracks, and even a small recreation facility. There were no windows, and only a single giant door on each side of the building to permit movement. A prison, certainly, but…not a terrible one? They were fed and had access to sanitation. 'Bots kept the place clean, and the weather cage over the facility kept the environment the monotonous temperature of a warm late autumn day. It wasn't pleasant, but she had braced herself to expect Hell itself, and it wasn't that, either.

By the end of the first day, Tembi had decided she had made a mistake to brand herself as a tekker. By the end of the first week, monotony had set in and she had decided she needed to start taking risks if she was going to locate Winter. She was seriously considering walking through an exterior wall so she could pretend she was a new kind of tekker if caught, except that was when a guard called her name and tapped her to do some work on a nearby building's solar arrays. Something had gone dreadfully wrong inside the core processing unit, the maintenance 'bots were a special kind of useless, and it was either crack the processor's case or bring in a tekker who was familiar with the system.

Well, scheisse. She hoped the insides of a Blackwing solar array resembled a bomb, otherwise she was out of luck and would never leave the building under someone else's power again.

The Blackwing guard put her on an antigrav cart, shackled her hands to a bar, and sent her off, alone. A small section of the east door opened before her, a small hole peeling away from its shielded maw, and she was outside for the first time since the ships had landed.

What should she do? Right, yes, she was a prisoner. What did prisoners do once they were alone and outside? She looked around as she pretended to test the restraints holding her to the cart. Camp Investment appeared to be almost exactly like Camp Divested, with the omniscient grays and lack of anything living. There were smokestacks on half of the buildings which punctured the great dome of the weather cage, but otherwise the facility was unmistakably similar.

And there were no people. None. No guards, no prisoners. She had the impression that if she somehow escaped from the cart, the very wrongness of her presence would set off every alarm in the place.

Hold on, that makes no sense. Her Witch's training kicked in, forcing her to truly look at Camp Investment, to analyze how it functioned. Not the security side. No, she didn't know enough about security to assess that. But she knew logistics down to her very core, and a facility of this size would require all manner of supplies. Without teleportation, that meant standard transportation was in use. And if there was nothing she could see…

Tembi looked down. Yes, there, along the sides of the buildings were overlarge soffits and exhaust pipes. The real action was under the facility. No wonder they kept the prisoners off of the ground floor except during their heavily guarded work shifts.

She grinned. Gych had said that Hawk-class facilities were easier to move around than other, older Blackwing camps.

Tembi would wager a large chunk of credit that once you were inside the underground infrastructure, security was minimal.

Good. She could work with that.

The antigrav cart puttered along at a pace slightly faster than Tembi could walk. Now that she had figured out Camp Investment's infrastructure, she found she was actually bored. The camp was massive and gray, gray, gray, with little to distinguish one building from another. Unable to get enough slack from the shackles to sit, there was no real opportunity for her to rest, and her temper was starting to grind away at her patience.

A small eternity later, the cart turned towards the perimeter of the weather cage. The cart passed through the shielding, and Tembi was suddenly basking in the warmth of a glorious morning. She tipped her head back to take in the sunlight, and—

The smell slashed across her senses like a knife. It was fetid, *rotting*. She turned and vomited off the side of the cart, an involuntary response which did nothing to help. *Gods!* The stench! Suddenly, the Deep was there, wrapping itself around her, sheltering her from the smell within her own private atmosphere.

Tembi hauled herself up by the shackles, letting them support her. Her eyes were shut: she knew that smell, and she didn't want to see.

Focus, Tembi.

"Oh, gods," she whispered, and forced herself to open her eyes.

Bodies, yes, of course there were bodies. The infamous mass graves of the Blackwing prison camps. She had thought—

She hadn't thought. If she had, then she would have realized the facility was too clean, too well-organized. There were no problems, because the Blackwings had one method of dealing with problems, and apparently the Blackwings were too busy to shovel dirt over the bodies once those problems were solved.

No, she thought, as she stared across the open pit to the distant fields beyond. Those were torn in multiple places, as if dirt had been removed and later replaced. *It's all about efficiency. It's easier for them to leave the pit open until it's full.*

It was such a carefully planned process that Tembi folded over herself as far as her wrist restraints would allow, hugging her own stomach. This was evil—no. This was worse: this was corporate, a straightforward line item assessment of human beings. Add operational or financial value to the Sagittarius Armed Forces, and you were kept alive within a relatively comfortable prison. Subtract it, and—

"I can't do this," she whispered to herself, even as she had no clear notion of what she meant by it.

"No one can." Tembi squeaked and tried to leap from the cart, but the wrist restraints held her fast. The antigrav cart lowered and rebalanced as Winter climbed up to join her, and then continued its slow trek towards a pair of solar arrays in the middle of the ruined fields.

"Where did you come from?" Tembi gasped. The Blackwings had been at the old woman with hygiene 'bots. Winter's usual stench had been cut in half, but she was still offensively ripe. She was standing within the Deep's atmospheric bubble, and it was murder on Tembi's already abused nose.

Winter was grinning at her. "Look at you," she said. "Woody meets Buzz, all shiny and new from his package."

I don't have time for this. Tembi glanced around. They were alone. Not another living soul was near the open graves, but who knew how long that would last? "Winter?" She dropped her voice and spoke smoothly, calmly, trying to emulate her second mother's patience. "Do you know what happened to Matindi?"

The old woman cackled. "Foolish girls."

"Winter—" She wanted to reach out and grab the old woman by the shoulders, maybe shake her a little. *No. Be kind.* "Winter, do you remember Matindi? The green woman from the colony?"

The old woman rolled her eyes, and then aimed her attention at the restraints. They snapped open and clattered to the ground. "Come," she told Tembi, as she toppled backwards from the cart.

A momentary pause while Tembi tried to weigh out the pros and cons of—

"Ah, soss it," she growled, and stepped from the cart, letting it continue on its preprogrammed path without her.

The old woman was walking straight towards the graves. Tembi ran up behind her, all set to grab her to keep her out of the open pit, but Winter turned to her, tears streaming down her face. "Did you know it would be this bad?" she asked. "They talk about it—they always talk about it! But knowing it's out... *there...*" Winter gestured vaguely towards the sky. "...is different."

The edge of the grave was before them. Winter lowered herself to the ground and sat motionless, staring at the raw horror of it. "I'm very old," she said. "I've done terrible things. But I've never seen anything like this before. Does that make me lucky?"

Tembi couldn't bring herself to look at the grave. That one glance had been enough, broken bones and torn flesh and crumpled bodies that didn't resemble anything that had ever been alive, with eyes torn from cracked skulls and the very flesh moving, *moving!* from an infinite press of insects and scurrying creatures—

"I think it does," she whispered.

"You should go," Winter said, patting Tembi's foot. "This is no place for good little girls."

"It's no place for you, either," Tembi said, kneeling beside the old woman. "Please come with me. I'll take you somewhere safe."

Winter didn't look at her. "No."

"Why?" When Winter didn't answer, Tembi took a different approach. "Matindi told me you've studied the Deep."

That earned a small giggle from Winter. "Do you think it understands?" she asked, pointing.

"Understands murder?" Tembi forced herself to keep her eyes on Winter. "I don't know. I think it barely understands death. I know it doesn't understand why we choose to be cruel to each other."

"Do you want it to understand?"

Cooper, bleeding out alone on the Rails... "Sometimes. But it'd be wrong of me to try and force it. Matindi and I thought the Deep might be a young child, so that's how I try to treat it."

"Good girls." Winter patted her foot again. "Good girls."

"C'mon." Tembi tried again. "Let me take you somewhere safe."

The old woman ignored her. "If it's a child, it needs to be protected."

"I try to do that, too." She slipped a hand around Winter's wrist, and then reeled backwards at the sudden shock against her cheek: Winter had slapped her! "Hey!" she snapped, temper rising. "It's time to go."

"Then go!" Winter shoved her. *"Go!"*

"I can't leave you here!" Tembi shouted. Winter turned towards the open grave and curled up in a small ball, shaking, hands pressed against her ears.

Tembi snarled a knotty curse at the sky. What was the value of one old woman when weighed against an entire colony of Sabenta refugees? She might as well be aboard the ship, arguing moral certitude with Gych and the other saboteurs. How many eyes were on them at this very moment? How many snoop 'bots were riding along within the folds of their clothes? What was she risking with this delay? She glanced over her shoulder at the antigrav cart, still slowly scooting across the ground towards the distant solar arrays.

It was crossing one of the plowed-over graves.

Without warning, the edges of her vision went red.

Tembi was never truly sure what caused her to crack. When she was a teenager, it was a general mix of classes and dating. These days, she could keep her stoic Adhamantian composure in place by screaming her rage into the privacy of the Rails. But the Blackwings hadn't—

They didn't—

They couldn't take five seconds to tell an AI to respect the dead?!

Months of bottled frustration broke open within her. Tembi

stood, her hands going to fists, and looked—actually saw!—the open grave before her, all of that violent death turning to jellified rot below her feet. For that brief moment, the gruesome details were just that, details, and none of them necessary for her to grok the Blackwings' true crime: they had killed people. *People!* Murdered in the thousands by an army focused on the most efficient ways to solve problems.

People should not be problems!

"Tembi?"

She looked down. Whatever was written on her face caused Winter to shy away, but the old woman whispered, "Don't use the Deep to kill."

Tembi turned to stare into the grave again. "I don't need to."

Chapter Twenty-Eight

Time to impose order. Winter, now obedient from fright, was jumped to safety. Tembi left the old woman in her own bunk in the Tekkers' quarters with instructions to stay quiet and hide. Then, down to the ground floor. Multiple jumps were required to avoid the guards, but the Deep was glad to be doing something more than wiggling small objects in the air, and each small jump left Tembi with the echo of bold, brassy music singing in her ears. She had asked the Deep to swap out her prisoner's tunic with a Blackwing guard's uniform, and she tucked her ears and her wild riot of hair beneath a matching scarf. Around her neck was a breather collar designed to resemble a torque necklace.

Did she have a plan? Not really. But if she had learned anything of consequence over the past two years, it was that nearly everything could become a bomb.

Through an internal door, heavily warded by 'bots which were easily tricked by the uniform and a stolen security token. Then, a wide industrial lift brought her down, down, into the hidden infrastructure beneath Camp Investment.

She nearly laughed. It was Camp Divested all over again, with stark gray walls covered in extravagant artwork. There was wealth here, quite a lot of it, and the former child pickpocket started categorizing the most portable objects with a practiced eye.

Focus, Tembi.

She thought back to her visits to Camp Divested. General Carroll had shown her around the public areas, but she had also spoken at length about the research facilities, the hydroponics kits, the factory floors...

She had never mentioned what they did with children who were too young to work.

Would there be a nursery? No, not in a place such as this. Not for the Blackwings, who were all about efficiency—

Tembi stopped, hand flat against the nearest wall to hold herself up, as she realized the Chameleon children were likely already dead and oh *gods*, Gych and the others would have known that.

This had never been a rescue mission.

In a place such as this, unoccupied supply closets were easy to find. She kept herself moving long enough to find one, and then slid inside and barred the door from within so she could sit on the floor, shaking. Now alone, the Deep began to bring Tembi her usual comforts as it tried to soothe her, her ulcer pills and a cup of coffee from a favorite shop on Found, and then there was a small squall as her cat appeared. Tabuu stalked around her in a rusty circle before he dignified himself to rub his cheek against hers, and then settled in an old, bony heap in the hollow of her lap.

"Thank you, Deep," Tembi whispered, as she went into the pocket of her uniform and came out with Williamson's rock. She held it tight for a moment, and then offered it out to her friend. "Can you take this to the Librarian? I need to see him."

The small stone disappeared. Tembi stayed on the floor, her back against a stack of plass crates, trusting the Deep to keep her safe in case of accidental discovery or security sweeps. Her cat purred, making biscuits against her calves. Her thoughts were still adrift in the space beyond rationality: she idly wondered what would happen if she smothered him. Would the Deep finally allow the poor creature to die?

He's not in any pain, she reminded herself, stroking the hollow beneath his chin as he blinked at her with green-gold eyes. Small gods, she loved this ridiculous cat. She couldn't be angry at the Deep for not realizing that cats aged, too, not up until Tabuu's years were about to end and the Deep froze him into feeble immortality so Tembi would never have to mourn him. He was here with her now, a million klicks from home, and that itself was a miracle.

She felt herself begin to calm, her Adhamantian composure returning. By the time Williamson stepped out of the Deep, she was able to smile at him.

It didn't fool him at all. "Tembi, what's wrong?"

She pressed her forefinger lightly to the tip of Tabuu's nose, and asked the Deep to take him home. Once the cat had disappeared, she looked up at the Librarian. "We were set up," she said. "The Sabenta used the raid as an excuse to get us to bring their best saboteurs inside the camp. The Chameleon children are…" She couldn't finish that sentence, so she tried a different path. "There are mass graves to the east."

Williamson removed his glasses, and pressed the sleeve of his robe against his eyes. "I'm sorry," he said.

"I didn't see their bodies, but I wasn't looking. The Deep can take you there if you need proof."

"Gods, no," he said, and sat beside her, head in his hands. They sat in silence until he asked, "What do you suggest we do?" She gaped at him, jaw slack and ears flat, so he added: "You are the knight and the philosopher, Sir Stoneskin. Not me."

She shook her head. All of her anger was gone, as if she had screamed out her rage along the Rails. In its place was the certainty that no matter what else happened, all of this was wrong, and she would no longer be a part of it. "I don't think I'm coming back to Lancaster," she told him.

"Sir Stoneskin—"

"I can't keep doing this," she said. "Balanced on the edge, pretending we don't know what's happening? Tell Lancaster…" Her words tripped over themselves as she began to unknot her thoughts. "Tell them I came here to find out how Matindi died. That's true enough. When Gych and the others take this place down, I'll get as many people out as I can. Then I'll just…disappear."

"Tembi," he said quietly, as he took one of her hands in his own. His blue eyes were earnest and clear and *oh* so old, a blue that could only be found in a morning sky on Earth. "It's not like you to run away from your problems."

"It's not running if you can't solve anything by staying," she said, slightly coolly, as she tugged her hand away. It would be such a blessing if people would stop trying to assess her mood by her skin. And she couldn't remember the last time the Librarian had called her by her first name. Had he ever? "Lancaster might change. Someday. But even if I'm driving change, it'll take too long for me. If Lancaster wants to stay neutral, I can't be part of Lancaster."

He stared at her, and then nodded. "You are remarkable, Sir Stoneskin," Williamson said. "I wish I had more time to get to know you."

"The Deep won't let me die, Williamson. Not if it can help it." She took a deep breath. "But don't tell anyone back at Lancaster that I'm still alive, except Matthew and Bayle. Let the others draw their own conclusions."

He smiled sadly at her, and brought his fingers to stand against his own ears in *agreement*. Then, he held his rock out to her. "Here," he told her. "In case you need me again, or would just like to see a very old friend."

A fast hug, and Williamson was gone.

Tembi stayed in the supply closet for the better part of an hour. Options, options, too many options, and none of them realistic. The wise choice of action would be to pursue Gych and learn the details of their timeline, but Camp Investment was the size of a small city, and she couldn't just ask the Deep to jump her to wherever Gych was hiding without causing problems.

Narrow it down to two options, then. First, she needed to make sure the children taken from the colony were…well, maybe Camp Investment could still surprise her with its lovely daycare and adoption programs. All she knew was that she couldn't live with herself if she didn't investigate. After that? If this place was like Camp Divested, it had research facilities: she might be able to find out how Matindi had died, and she still needed to learn how the Blackwings had opened a portal to the Rails.

Once done, she would cause as much chaos as she could on

her way out.

"Wish you were here, Moto—wait, Deep, no!" she whispered, catching herself in the act. "I don't actually want Moto here. It's not a real wish."

A box of random plass objects tipped over and assembled themselves into something resembling a houseplant. It climbed down from the stacks of stuff and perched itself on her knee. She started stroking it under a fake frond, like she had with Tabuu's skinny chin.

Maybe Bayle would let her move her house and all of its contents to Atlantis, and she could spend the rest of her eternal life pretending she enjoyed seafood. No, she should go to Camelot instead: she was already a Knight, and there were long stretches of Camelot which were still open for purchase. She would be landed gentry. Sponsor a village and manage a few hundred square kilometers. She would have a small palace with a garden, keep goats and chickens, and grow brutal green roses.

That thought sounded good. *Shockingly* good!—a part of her she had never acknowledged craved the peace of the land.

No, she reminded herself. *That's running away...running to delay. I won't run from a future I already know.*

She blinked: she knew what was coming? Now that she thought about it...oh. Yes. Yes, she did. A future as a smuggler, somewhat like Cendo but with reach. It made her smile. Maybe Gallimore would allow her to steal them away. She certainly needed someone around to remind her when she needed to pull her head out of her own ass and focus on larger goals.

The houseplant chirped at her.

"Yeah, buddy," she assured it. "You and me, doing good for good people. Would you like that?" The houseplant paused, came apart in small pieces, and reassembled itself in the shape of a sphere. A moment passed as it slowly rotated in the air, and then it split in half.

Tembi smiled. "I understood that," she said. "Yes. Let's search this place. If we find anything about the weapon that broke the moon, we'll give the evidence to the Earth Assembly."

The plass pieces fell to the ground with a smell reminiscent of a ripe fart.

"I didn't understand *that*."

The smell grew stronger.

"Fine," she complained, and shut her eyes to visualize the other side of the compound. "Find us another storage closet like this one." When she opened her eyes, the closet was the same, save for a different shade of gray paint on the walls and the overhead illumination strips weren't fully lit. She stood, dusted off her stolen uniform, and grabbed an official-looking plass box from a nearby shelf before opening the door.

The hallway was cavernous and nearly empty. It was a straight shot: she could cruise east or west until she disappeared over the horizon. A main route, then. Very promising. There were small antigrav boards propped up at charging stations beside closed doors, and she grabbed one of these, tossed it to the ground, and stepped aboard. After a few minutes of travel, more people began to appear via large side tunnels, all of them in Blackwing uniforms, all riding similar boards. A few minutes after that, people on foot started to clog up the tunnel, walking in both directions. Tembi hopped off her platform and left it in a convenient basket, and joined her half of the crowd as they continued their journey.

The tunnel ended, finally, in a hopper station. She pulled into a small alcove with a large map displayed against the wall, and watched a fellow traveler as he tried to make sense of it.

"Place is a maze," he said. He appeared to be Earth-normal, but his accent reminded her of Bayle's.

"Tell me about it," she said, and held up the plass box. "You know where Research is?"

"Which one?" He shook his head. "No, don't say, I wouldn't know. The Research compound is to the north," he said, gesturing towards the map with his fingers held tight together. "Do you know where Central Agriculture is?"

That, she knew: General Carroll had bragged about her food supply over their single meal together. Tembi directed him towards the hydroponics facilities, and watched him walk away in boots that were overlarge around his toes and ankles.

She turned towards the station and boarded the third hopper. It was in excellent condition, large enough to fit a dozen passengers, and flew down the hopper tunnel at tremendous speed. She disembarked at the third station, ducked into a bathroom, and asked the Deep to jump her to a similar bathroom in the area the Atlantean had indicated. She came out in yet another overlarge gray corridor and followed it north. And then, at last, there was a sign on a door that read RESEARCH, BUILD. 4, and she took that lift up, up, to enter the top-secret research facilities of Camp Investment without a single problem.

Even with the shape of Tembi's entire life defined by her near-omniscient friend, it would have been too much of a coincidence for Gych to have been the first person she saw. Instead, Gych was the third, standing somewhere a little off in the distance behind a receptionist's desk, chatting away as if she had been born and bred for life in that particular office.

Tembi walked up to the receptionist and announced she had a delivery for a genetics lab on the third floor. Gych, laughing, came up behind him. "Baruu, this is probably Dr. Pearson's order. Mind if I walk her up? He'll eat me alive if I don't get this to him."

The receptionist waved her through with barely a scan of her stolen credentials. Gych went through the niceties of offering Tembi her fake name and a cup of what the Blackwings deceptively referred to as coffee before taking her to another lift. Once inside and alone, Gych looked at Tembi, her eyes dark. "Come to take apart more of my work?"

A hundred different questions wanted to be first in the queue, but Tembi pressed them into order and started small. "How did you know where to find me?"

"Tracker in your breather," Gych said, and tapped her arm until an embedded databand pushed an image into the air. An overlay of Camp Investment appeared, much like the map that Tembi had studied down in the hopper tunnels. Five bright white lights were concentrated in the Research compound, with dozens of blue lights scattered throughout the rest of the large facility. "When you went on the move, so did we." She typed quickly, her hands covered by light gloves which matched her Blackwing uniform, and then whispered, "Acquired," before closing the display.

A long pause. "Well, Stoneskin?" Gych finally said, still staring at her with hooded eyes.

The next question in the queue was the only one that truly mattered. "Are the Chameleon children alive?"

"None of the Chamelons that were taken are still alive," Gych scoffed, "and neither are the children."

The full meaning of her words failed to register until they did, and Tembi found herself clinging to a safety rail. "No," she whispered. She felt the Deep push against her, helping her wobbly legs to hold her up.

"Gather yourself, Witch," Gych said, and opened the lift's door. The two of them came out in a bright corridor, and Gych led them into a small private office. Once there, she held out a small silvery packet. "Data for you. All we could get about the research the Blackwings have done on Witches. I hope it leads you to your second mother's murderer."

"Thank you," Tembi said, and silently asked the Deep to hide it in her stashbox at home. When the packet disappeared, Gych asked, "Did you find your old woman?"

"Yes."

"So you can leave now." The Sabenta spy wasn't asking.

Tembi needed to know. "Was any of it true?"

"A difficult trick, embedding agents in these camps." Gych paused before adding: "Harder to get them and their data out before the bombing starts."

A painful twist of her stomach, and Tembi said quietly, "Oh."

The Sabenta spy nodded. "You've helped us with a rescue mission, Witch," she said. "Apologies if it wasn't the one you believed it to be."

Tembi closed her eyes. "And the prisoners?"

Gych paused. "A fair planet, this is," she finally replied. "Lots of land. Good climate. We will make sure that many will survive to enjoy it."

A whole city's worth of prisoners... "How can I help increase those odds?"

"Witch?" A gentle pressure against her hand; Gych was trying to be comforting. "Witch, go home. Your people have made it clear that this is not your fight."

"How can I help?" Tembi asked again, and this time her voice came out as hard as rock. When she opened her eyes, Gych had tilted her head to the side and was inspecting her anew. "You saw the graves," she said.

Tembi nodded. "I knew they were here, but I didn't understand what that meant."

"Good," Gych said, still patting Tembi's hand. "Understanding is good. But I have no time for you, Witch. I have responsibilities. Please, Witch, please leave, and let me focus on them. These are *my* people here. I want them to live; I will do whatever I can to save them. So, please leave. That is the best way for *you* to save as many as possible," she added, stressing the 'you' hard enough to bruise Tembi's ego.

A thousand different arguments raged within her, but...

"I'm going to warn my friends, and then I'll take the old woman with me and go." It was the most difficult thing she had ever said, and Tembi thought less of herself even as she said it.

Gych gave a small and happy sigh. "Thank you," she said. "It is the right thing. You want the satisfaction of blood and explosions, but that...that is not for you. Not this time." She leaned forward. "If I live, I will send you a message," she said. "If you want, I will train you, and then next time, it *will* be for you."

Tembi's stomach twisted again, and she rose to leave without another word.

She backtracked the slow way until she had left the Research compound, giving Gych the benefit of whatever cover she could. Then, she jumped across the compound to the tekker building. The Blackwing uniform and her headscarf let her blend into the background on the factory floor as she moved among them, searching for Gillian. She was recognized; some of those who knew she was a Witch saw her moving in their enemy's clothing, and their expressions ranged from surprise to fiery excitement before they turned back to their labors.

The guards along the edges of the room nodded to her as she passed: the single red stripe slashing across her uniform gave her rank and respectability. Still...

They *had* to know she was gone by now, right? That Selene Tamber-Tren, low-rated tekker captured at the Chameleons' colony, had managed to escape on her way to the solar arrays? There should have been some fuss, some accountability, some turmoil in the building.

Maybe prisoners escaped all of the time. Maybe all of the security and walls and weather cages were theater, and she had become just another number on a tally. She had been questioning the wisdom of leaving Winter in Selene's own bunk, but if nothing was happening, if all was normal, then all was—

Tembi turned a corner and saw, standing in the center of the hallway, General Carroll in all her glowing splendor.

If Tembi had been prepared? Perhaps she could have caught herself in time, turned away, pretended to be someone else. It was a large galaxy, after all, and one person could look so very much like another. But she had grown comfortable sneaking around Camp Investment, and to be caught so suddenly, by someone so unexpected, struck her from ears to toes in astonished terror. The Deep seized upon her emotions, flaring to life and rising around her in a cloud of loose objects, writing instruments and furniture and shards of plass—*oh gods, are those pieces of the floor?*—all of it aimed at Carroll, ready to crush her or stab her or perhaps sweep her into the tunnels below.

Carroll required a moment to gather her composure. That was what saved her: if she had been lying in wait, Tembi was sure the Deep would have either unleashed its hovering arsenal or simply swept Carroll off to Assassins' Paradise. Yet as she stood there blinking in astonishment, her mouth slightly slack,

Carroll seemed as surprised to see Tembi as Tembi had been to see her.

"Ah," Carroll managed, nodding. "This explains everything."

Calm, Tembi thought at the Deep. *We're caught.* Sweeping anxiety was replaced with a question, and the image of chess pieces on a grammalight display: the Deep was asking her if this was a game. And how could she answer that without alarming the Deep, or removing her best defense?

She couldn't. Instead, she asked the Deep to swap out her clothing, and stepped forward in her robes—her best robes, the ones she almost never worse, with raw silk in dark teal, and swirling garnet patterns glowing along the skirts—and her Witch's paint of golden birds, with her hair unbound and her ears high. There were the usual gasps and shouts, but these were hidden within the unfamiliar sounds of a large number of weapons coming free.

Well, now, Tembi thought, her Adhamantian calm wrapped around her as tight as a shroud as she took in the two dozen soldiers standing around Carroll and another high-ranking Blackwing officer. *I didn't even notice her army. How careless of me.*

"General Carroll," she said, bowing slightly to the Tolkienite. She channeled her best inner Domino as she gestured gracefully towards the soldiers and their armaments. "Such a shocking greeting! I thought you offered me welcome in all Sagittarius Armed Forces camps."

"Are we truly doing this?" muttered Carroll, and when Tembi answered her with a serene smile, she sighed. "Yes. Welcome, Sir Stoneskin, honored Witch of Lancaster." She turned to the man standing beside her in a ranking officer's uniform. "Have you met my counterpart, General Baldwin? Camp Investment is his to command."

Baldwin was an older man, his hair a violent black and his face a worrisome red. "Carroll? Explain."

"Why don't we go somewhere more pleasant to talk?" replied Carroll. She pointed towards the solders. "Bring the prisoner."

Prisoner? The objects floating around her reoriented on Carroll before Tembi asked the Deep to settle them back into their places. *We are not prisoners,* she promised it. *Carroll isn't talking about us.*

No. No, she certainly was not, as the soldiers behind Carroll and Baldwin parted, and revealed Winter.

The old woman was wearing a pale blue circlet around her head, a piece of tech which pretended to be jewelry. Around her hands were multiple bracelets in the same color. Tembi had seen those before on some of the tekkers with high lift ratings. They were suppression devices used to quell psionic abilities, and the stronger you were, the more dampers were needed to bring you down to normal.

Winter's arms were *layered* with them.

"The most powerful tekker I've ever had the pleasure to study," Carroll said proudly. "She escaped from Camp Divested around the same time your Moto Sanders went missing. I thought the two were connected, but had no proof.

"Now," she said, smiling down at Tembi, "here you are. Lancaster rescues its own."

What could Tembi say to that? An admission would be a lie; a denial would sound like one. She kept her mouth shut and followed. Down the hallway and into a large conference room, the soldiers lining the walls as Tembi was given a place of honor at the head of the table, Winter sitting beside her. The old woman's head was bowed, tears slowly leaking down her cheeks.

"We haven't harmed her," Carroll assured Tembi. "My researchers were sequencing a cognitive repair agent for her, and she disappeared before we could administer it. I brought it with me. It clouds the mind while it works. When it's done, she will be...Gods!" The Tolkienite laughed. "I cannot wait to see what she'll become!"

"Don't get too attached." While Carroll had taken the chair across from Tembi, Baldwin was standing with his arms crossed.

"Camp Divested has the best psionic research facilities," Carroll told him. "My team has already established her genetic profile and tested her abilities."

Baldwin made a sound that was a clear denial, and Carroll's ears tipped back to show *annoyance* as she rolled her eyes where he couldn't see, and then winked at Tembi.

I am drowning in the shit, Tembi thought. Beside her, Winter let out her usual cackling laugh. This time, though, it kept going, that first sharp burst rolling around the room and trailing into misery.

"Shut her up," Baldwin told one of the soldiers. The soldier unhooked her popstick and discharged it into Winter's shoulder. The voltage must have been low, as Winter kept laughing, a dry and broken sound. The soldier looked at the popstick in confusion, thumbed up the voltage, and moved to shock the old woman again.

Tembi held up her hand, snatched the popstick out of the air, and laid it flat on the table in front of her.

Carroll leaned forward, her smile predatory. "Escalation," she said. "Good."

"I won't let you hurt her," Tembi said, as she rested a hand on Winter's shoulder. The old woman was still laughing, the sound grating on every nerve in hearing distance.

"What will you give me?" Carroll's smile widened. "Perhaps I haven't just injected her with a brain booster. Have I poisoned her? Or does she sit here as she knows she is full of 'bots that will slice her apart if she fights me?

"What will you risk for her, Stoneskin?" Carroll leaned back in her chair, catlike and *so* very satisfied with herself. "Quite a lot, I think, if Witch Sanders, and then you, have come to free her."

Tembi glared at Carroll, her thoughts racing. She believed to her very core that Carroll would have stuck slow murder into Winter's veins if it would benefit her. Could she jump out of here with Winter and…stick her in stasis, maybe? Or could the Deep—

"Are you done?" Baldwin snapped at Carroll. "I want to know why the Witch was running around my compound in a soldier's uniform."

"Hah! You're right!" Carroll laughed brightly. "I had forgotten!" She turned to Tembi, her predatory smile reborn. "Who else were you meeting in Camp Divested, Stoneskin?"

Winter's cackling laugh became a howl, miserable and sobbing. It was that sorrowful sound that finally drove the truth of Gych's words into Tembi's heart: *Realize you have no power.*

She could run, but it would save her and no one else.

She could fight, but it would define Lancaster as part of the war.

She could surrender, but the war would tick on around the voids left by her, and Winter, and Gych, and the others she would drag down with her as she fell …

Tembi realized she was staring down at her own hands and their impenetrable skin, and wondering for the first time in her life why it couldn't protect her.

Winter gasped, a hitching sound, and her howl became a near-inhuman wail.

"Shut her up." General Baldwin moved around the table, looming over Winter.

"Don't touch her," warned Tembi, rising to her feet. She couldn't do anything for herself, but she would *not* let anyone hurt an old woman, not while there was life in her body.

"Children," said Carroll with another roll of her eyes. "Settle down."

Baldwin yanked a small cylinder from his pocket and aimed the open end at Winter's tear-streaked face. She looked up at him and stopped crying as realization wiped away her misery.

::*NO*:: Tembi shouted. Her voice was devoured within the roar of the Deep, a mighty sound which came from her own throat and boomed throughout the room, down the hallways, throughout the building and down, down, to the foundations of Camp Investment. The world itself seemed to twist, a sharp torque of reality.

She fainted.

She came to on hard stone, staring up at a crumbling building. It made no sense at first, and then she recognized the architectural backdrop of Earth Plaza behind the ruins. The amphitheater, she thought. Oh gods, the Deep had swept her out of Camp Investment and back to Earth! *Winter...what happened to Winter?* Feeling as if she had been run over by a hopper, an unholy stench crushing her into pieces, she got her hands and legs beneath her and tried to stand.

No. Even as her senses felt honed to a razor's sharpness, nothing else about her body wanted to work. She fell on her face and felt the Deep catch her, lower her back to the ground so her suddenly sensitive skin wouldn't rake itself across the pavement.

"Thanks, Deep," she whispered, and realized she could barely hear herself over the clarity of the sounds around her. Breaking plass, rocks clattering across the stone of the Plaza... And the screaming...there were so many people screaming! Was this her dream again? Was she caught in the vision of the broken world and couldn't escape?

"Tembi!" A welcome voice, audible over the cacophony. *"Tembi!"*

"Kalais?" Still flat on the warm stone, she pressed her hands flat over her ears and begged her head to forgive whatever abuses she had committed. Beside her, his familiar hands were helping her to her feet, holding her up, strong and comforting.

"Tembi, what did you *do?!*"

"Kalais, what...?" Her sense of sight had become as clear as her sense of sound, and he was staring at her, his eyes wide and horrified and also somehow delighted, his features striking in their crystalized perfection. She was unable to process it all, and instead asked, "What's happened?"

He laughed, a near-hysterical noise, and turned her so she could look around at—

At Camp Investment?

Yes.

No. *Oh* no!

Camp Investment. It was there. All of it, right there in front of her, a goodly distance away but still *right there.* She had always heard that Earth Plaza was large enough to cradle a city, and yes, there it was, an entire Blackwing prison compound nestled in the hollow bowl of the galaxy's central power structure.

She looked down and realized the smell was coming from the mass grave beside her.

"Oh," she whispered. "Those came, too."

And she blacked out again.

Chapter Twenty-Nine

The aftermath took weeks to resolve. Tembi spent most of it next to Moto's bedside, as she had been ordered to stay on Found until the inquisition was over. Uneasy and unwelcome at Lancaster, she had learned the hospital was the only place the channelsluts couldn't bother her if she wanted to get out of her house.

Her house. Which Matindi had so carefully cleaned before she was murdered, and all of her second mother's work undone by a battalion of terrified Chameleon children—

No. She couldn't go home. She slept in her bed and showered when she remembered those were options, and the rest of the time was spent in the hospital or in Matindi's gardens. There was newfound joy in gardens and in gardening, her hands in the rich soil summoning an elusive peace hiding deep in her soul, but even Matindi had needed to go inside and enjoy regular breaks from her plants.

What was she supposed to do?

"You will stay on Found and be the very picture of obedience," Domino had told her, when Tembi had tried to object to home imprisonment. "You owe Lancaster."

Did she, though? Did she really?

For the time being, she thought she did. She had yanked a whole playground of horrors into the light, and there was no hiding the truth of it. The Sagittarius Armed Forces had tried. They truly had. At first, they said Camp Investment was private property and no one could trespass. Well, that didn't work, especially as the Earth Assembly needed to send in security teams to ensure the facility didn't pose any health risks besides the... well, besides the whopping huge mass graves. Then, the Blackwings tried to limit access to certain areas of the compound. This failed for the same reasons. And once the research facili-

ties had been cracked open and the vids and gramms taken
by the security teams started to sneak out across the channels,
it was a *deluge,* a *flood,* a mighty crashing *tsunami* of invasive
channelsluts breaking down the walls, pushing cameras and diagnostic 'bots into every tiny port and uncovering all of the
filthy secrets that Tembi had managed to avoid on her brief self-
guided tour.

The Blackwings then tried to say that Camp Investment was
an aberration, that they had had no idea the conditions were
so poor in this new third-gen facility of their own design and
ownership. That lasted just as long as it took the channelsluts to
break into the other Hawk-class facilities and report back that
conditions were as bad there, and much worse in some of the
older camps. (Nobody ask the channelsluts why they couldn't
have flown a couple of 'bots over these facilities long before
now, since those infamous mass graves had always been outra-
geously infamous.) Finally, once everything seemed to be calming down, the bookkeepers appeared and used the Blackwings'
financial records to lay bare a whole new set of horrors.

Tembi kept her mouth shut throughout it all. Better for her
to be called a hero or a villain, to be torn apart time and again
by people who had never met her, who had never even learned
how to pronounce her name, than for them to learn the truth.

She had to tell someone, though, and so, once they finally had
time to sneak away to the place with all the fish, she had told
Bayle, still whispering despite being the only humans around
for hundreds of millions of kilometers, that the Deep had been
the one who had made the decision to take Camp Investment
to Earth Plaza.

"No," Bayle had whispered back, blue eyes wide in fright.

"It wasn't me. I didn't ask it to do that! I *swear,*" Tembi had
said, and had then started to name things she held as sacred to
force her friend to believe her. Bayle had silenced Tembi before
she could finish the first words, and had pulled her into a hug
and let Tembi weep.

If the truth ever came out…

It couldn't come out. The Blackwings hadn't been defeated, but their reputation had suffered mightily thanks to the Deep. And while Kalais had been shouting about how the Deep had supported the Sabenta's cause for years, the very idea that the Deep would do something so dramatic, so irresponsible, so wholly reckless on its own—

No. It couldn't come out.

There had been a public statement about her involvement. She admitted guilt, top to bottom. The Council and the channelsluts had kept asking why, so she had given them the Chameleons, and enough of their bodies had been unearthed from the graves to prove her words true. Paisano was trotted out and became a celebrity in his own right, a king in exile. Chameleons from across the galaxy began to find their way to him, as did offers of safety and new permanent homes. Paisano and the Chameleons, at least, were well on the way to a happy ending of their own.

At least Tembi had finally gotten some answers from Domino.

Matthew had come to that meeting with her. He had lost weight since Matindi's death, with new lines burned into the edges of his eternally young face. The painted branches on his cheek were bare of all greenery. Exhaustion lay thick over him and his shoulders were bowed, even as he stared at Domino with fresh loathing. "You sent the Blackwings to Lunair," he said to her as soon as they appeared in her office.

"No." Domino didn't try to dissemble. "But I received word they would soon raid the colony, and I attempted to pull Tembi and Bayle from danger without becoming involved. Had I known Matindi was there, I would have called her away, too."

"We don't believe you." Tembi echoed her second father. "Cooper said he needed my help disarming a bomb right before the raid began. That hadn't happened in months. It wasn't coincidence."

Domino spread her hands, all grace. "I was not the one who made that call," she replied. "I believe someone in the Blackwing Army built that gateway to the Rails, and made sure it would be used to distract you, and to ensure you would be off-planet before the raid began. Your involvement would complicate an already serious situation. My research team is delving into the data that the Sabenta spy gave you. I'm sure they will tell us that weaponizing the Rails may be the most likely way to murder a Witch. Perhaps a smaller version of that gateway is how Matindi was killed.

"However…" she paused, knitting her hands together in her lap. As she did, the room took on an icy cast, all warmth slipping away. She locked eyes with Tembi, and the now-familiar sensation of Domino sliding into her thoughts took root. "However, we are not here to talk about *my* motives. Tembi, why did you do it?"

"I didn't." She sat in the chair across from Domino and folded over herself into a small, anxious ball. She had been sitting on this for days—only Bayle and Kalais knew the truth—and it hurt to keep it to herself. "The Deep did."

Matthew inhaled sharply. "Tembi—"

"She's not lying, Matthew." Domino had leaned forward, still staring intently at Tembi. "Or, she believes she is telling the truth, and Tembi's thoughts are always among the least complicated I've ever experienced. She is as straightforward as a song."

"Oh, sweet gods," said Matthew. "Tell us the story again, and this time, don't leave anything out."

So she did, starting from the time when the ships had landed at Camp Investment. When she reached the part where Winter was weeping silently in the conference room, with General Baldwin's strange weapon pointed at her, Domino told Tembi to stop.

"What happened to this woman, Winter?" she asked.

"I don't know. I lost her on Earth." Tembi glanced towards the windows, where Camp Investment was tucked away behind the silken curtains. "She's here somewhere."

"Likely rounded up with the rest of those who escaped," Domino murmured to herself, jotting down a note on a nearby tablet. "And it was at that moment the Deep chose to jump the camp to Earth?"

Tembi nodded.

"And you're certain you didn't make the request, or suggest anything that could be interpreted in that manner?"

"It never even occurred to me," she said truthfully.

Matthew looked at Domino, who nodded. "I can be misled," she told him. "I can be lied to. In this instance, Tembi is doing neither by intention."

He shook his head. "Oh, kiddo. You let this land on you and it wasn't your fault?"

She grinned sadly at him. "The Deep doesn't make mistakes," she said, echoing her old lessons from Lancaster's early training. "Only Witches make mistakes."

Domino suddenly sunk in her chair, her queenly posture sagging, and she pressed her face into her hands. "We can't help you."

"I'm not asking you to." Tembi and Bayle had already gone over the options, all of which were middling-bad to terrible. "It's been a little less than three thousand years since the Turtle Incident. Lancaster is due to make an example of a misbehaving Witch."

And so, as Lancaster's elder Witches went through the motions of defending her before they reached the inevitable conclusion, Tembi performed her duties as best she could. She avoided the channels, but the stories still reached her. How she had moved a thousand buildings and a million people—living, dying, and *dead!*—to the Plaza. How she had put the innermost workings of the Blackwings' processing camps on display. How Camp Investment, removed from its moorings and repositioned beneath the eyes of the galaxy, had been subject to scrutiny, followed by outrage and a great shift in public opinion against the Blackwings. It was one thing to know that people were being interred and murdered in prison camps. It was another thing entirely to see this laid out before the eyes of the galaxy, with the greedy channel crews and their spokesluts dripping hot juicy access all over the Plaza.

Very hard for Lancaster to claim it wasn't involved in the war. Not unless it sacrificed one of its own, this young Witch with more power than she should have had. Mistakes had been made, yes, but this time, the Witch didn't kill anyone!

It didn't hurt. Not as much as Tembi thought it would. During her brief stay in Camp Investment, she had already decided she needed to leave Lancaster. If this was the last thing she could do to help Matthew, then it's what she'd do. Besides, excommunication from Lancaster didn't mean she would never be with the Deep again, after all, and even if she never made another credit, her investments were chunky enough so she'd never hurt for money. The opportunity to change how the other Witches saw the Deep? She'd never forgive herself for sossing that up. And she'd miss the Library, of course, and swimming with Bayle in one of the campus's many ponds. The holiday parties where Lancaster Tower was lit in crystal, where Witches often drank enough for the Deep to sweep into the unoccupied space between their ears and use them to speak and walk around, and then swooped out of them in a great rush which left them as sober as—

Tembi snapped upright so quickly that her tablet fell from her lap, beeping at her in protest as it clattered on the floor. She barely noticed, her attention fixed on Moto.

The Deep's party trick of dropping into a drunk Witch's body for a few moments and then leaving a fully sober and embarrassed Witch as it jumped out… Could it work? Probably not. Alcohol and whatever was in Moto's system were both sedatives, but cats and chickens were both animals and she had seen the one happily eat the other.

But when the Deep had spoken through her at Camp Investment, it had rocked Tembi to her soul, had made the world as bright as fire. Could the presence of the Deep burn the impurities out of Moto? There was no reason in the world—any world—not to try.

She leaned forward, close enough to whisper without the chance of being overheard. "Deep?"

Nothing.

"Deep?" She tried again, louder, this time holding the mental image of a Witch in their holiday finest and speaking in a voice so rich and melodious that it seemed impossible that it could come from an ordinary human throat. "Deep? Can you talk to me?"

::TEMBI?::

The Deep spoke, not through Moto, but through the reflections of every surface in the small room. Around her, Tembi could hear the hospital wing's equipment flare to life in response, even as the workers and patients stayed unaware.

"Through Moto," she whispered, eyes shut tight, willing the Deep to understand. "Talk to me *through Moto!*"

A pause. Then, Moto's chest fluttered with a deep breath, and he sat up.

::DARK:: he said in a voice that was Moto's own, but also not.

"Open your eyes," she said, and he did, looking around the room as if he had never before seen the inside of a hospital. He saw Tembi and his head tilted towards her like a small but curious predator.

::YOU ARE SMALL:: he said, as he poked her on the cheek painted in golden birds.

"I know, buddy," she said, grinning. "Thanks for talking to me. You can leave Moto's body now."

::SAD:: the Deep replied, and Tembi barely had time to wonder if her otherworldly friend wanted her to know that Moto felt sad, if being inside Moto made it feel sad, or if humans as a species were simply pathetic before Moto toppled forward onto the hospital bed.

Face-down in the sheets, Moto groaned and slowly dragged one arm forward to push himself upright, and Tembi began to laugh.

"Did it work?" she said, as she helped him up. "Are you *you?*"

He blinked at her, dark eyes wet from the light. "Tembs?"

"Don't jump," she told him, as she wrapped both hands around his nearest arm. "Promise me you won't jump, okay?"

"I..." He scrubbed the sleeve of his hospital robes against his face, stopping with a jolt and staring at the fabric before he tried it again, more carefully. "How long have I been asleep?"

"You can feel that?"

"Not happy about it," he said, grinning at his lie. It was the old Moto grin, half-wicked, half-kind, and she nearly broke out in tears from relief. "I've been out for a while, haven't I?"

"Promise me you won't jump first."

"That long?"

"Promise me!"

He submitted, his ears moving forward in acquiescence. "I promise. Can I use the bathroom?"

"Yeah," she said, "but I'm going with you while you do."

"Hey!"

They compromised with her sitting outside the door to the hospital room's small toilet closet, talking loudly to him and also reminding the Deep every other minute that *Moto can't jump yet!* The story of why he was in a hospital was a long one. About a third of the way through, Moto exited the bathroom and joined Tembi on the floor, his hands entwined with hers. When she reached the part she couldn't tell—the part she still *needed* to tell, *needed* to force out of her, the necessary catharsis of purging that moment when Matindi shattered into sharp pieces—Moto pulled her against him and let her cry herself out. He smelled of medical cleansers and, beneath that, of home.

"Is that the end?" he asked quietly.

Tembi shook her head and let her head rest against his chest as she told him about Camp Investment in a whisper low enough to reach his ears alone. When she finally finished, she let him process in silence, listening to him breathe.

After several minutes, he said, "Earth."

"Yeah."

"In the *Plaza?!*"

"Yeah."

Moto exhaled slowly, and then asked in a low voice, "You're sure you didn't ask the Deep to move the entire compound?

Not even by accident?"

"I'm sure," she sighed. "The Deep made the decision, not me."

"That doesn't sound right." He shifted his weight and gently moved Tembi into the crook of his arm, and then stood with ease. "It doesn't understand politics. There's no way it would have understood the…the *value* of putting the camp on Earth!"

"Slow," she reminded him as he began to stretch. "The 'bots kept you fresh, but you've been asleep."

"For how long?" he asked her again, and she gritted her teeth and told him. "Eight *months?!*"

"You weren't thinking clearly when you went into stasis," she said. "We couldn't wake you up. At first, we thought you'd been hit with a mindfuck, but then you just kept sleeping, and they couldn't find a cause."

Moto rubbed his face, pausing again halfway through to glance at his own hands. "That's so strange," he muttered, as he turned to examine his face in the mirror. "I think I was hit with a mindfuck," he added, as he tugged at his cheeks. "I don't remember a lot of the last few months. The ones where I was still awake, I mean, last year. I'm really sorry about that Crisp. It seemed like such a good idea at the time! Gods, it was so expensive, too." Tembi hurled a pillow at him. Her friend caught it and tossed it back to her, still smiling. "Sorry I've put you through all of this, Tembs."

"It's fine," she said with a shrug. "I'll be excommunicated from Lancaster, but they can't force the Deep to abandon me. That's all that matters."

He froze, staring at her. "What?"

"I mean…" He was *staring* at her, his ears frozen as if she had said something so unforgivable that he wouldn't allow himself to hear it. "I mean, Moto, they can't blame the Deep! Planting a death camp on the Earth Assembly's pavilion is nearly as bad as the Turtle Incident. If I take the blame, say I told it to move the camp? Everybody will still trust the Deep."

"Tembi, you sodding—" He stopped and rubbed at his eyes again. "You went to Domino with this, didn't you, and she agreed to let you take the blame." It wasn't a question, so she didn't bother to answer. "All right, we've got to fix this," he muttered, as he began to search the room. A pile of folded robes in browns and reds appeared on the bed. "Thanks, Deep. Tembs, none of this was your fault. I'm not going to let you protect her. Not after what she did."

She stood to face him. "What did she do?"

"I don't know how to tell you this," he said. "Not after Matindi—"

"What did she *do?!*"

"Domino helped the Blackwings build that gateway to the Rails."

Chapter Thirty

There was a circular room at the top of Lancaster Tower that was beautiful beyond measure. Witches did not enter this room by way of the Deep, oh no. To enter *this* room? The seat of power at Lancaster? That meant passing through doors of green metal pressed into golden wood, all of it carved in starbursts. These were centered on the image of a single rising sun, with golden rays twisting from its surface. The sun was banded through the center with a long stripe of gold set with fiery red gemstones. Those doors opened slowly on a room of blue, a beautiful deep sapphire in color—quite possibly in fact, too, as the whole of it was cut from a single giant dark blue gem.

The Oratory. The celestial heart of the galaxy, as the heart is an engine and what was decided in this room made that engine go. Admission was for Witches alone, for if you could reach the top floor of Lancaster Tower and open those gilded doors, then you were a Witch indeed.

The Oratory had no draperies, no carpets, nothing to distract from the walls and ceiling, and the floor of golden marble spread out in repeating starbursts. The only furnishings were chairs of carved wood with cushions of white silk brocade which lined the walls like thrones. Some were larger and more splendid than the others, but each would be at home in a palace.

The largest chair was shrouded in a fine translucent cloth which had been painted in rainbow colors. Domino sat, waiting for them, the edges of the cloth wrapped around her bare arms.

Matthew entered the Oratory first, Tembi by his side. Behind them came Bayle, Kalais, and Moto, followed by Williamson and a hundred other Witches, some of them holding Chameleon children by their hands. All members of their small rebellion, their worst fears realized.

All of them furious.

"You killed her!" Tembi shouted, causing those ancient Witches to murmur. Undignified behavior? Yes, but Matindi had been her second mother, and Tembi was still thought to be barely out of diapers by the same Witches who allowed her to take point. She could—and would—give voice to those emotions they considered beneath them. "You helped them make the tech that *killed* her!"

"I believe I did," Domino said, nodding.

"Why?" Matthew sounded calm, but his hand on Tembi's shoulder was shaking.

"You know why." Domino was utterly still, a dark statue in white-and-rainbow robes. "Lancaster must stay neutral. Our hand was forced when we offered our assistance to the Sabenta. I brokered a deal with the Sagittarius Armed Forces to maintain the balance: sixty months of my assistance to help them study the Rails. The terms of our agreement ended twenty-one months ago. When my service ended, the Blackwings were still collecting data. I have no proof that it was my aid which gave them the ability to develop a door to the Rails, but the timing is more than coincidental.

"If Lancaster stops, the galaxy stops," she added. "This is not an excuse; it is my governing principle. My sole purpose is to make sure that Lancaster continues."

The quiet murmur of the old Witches swelled as they picked Domino's argument apart. Matthew pushed forward. "You bartered data?" he asked.

"It seemed safe enough," replied Domino. "The Deep and the Rails have been studied before, and my time was the only commodity at risk. In exchange, the Blackwings promised they would not seek reprisal against Lancaster." She nodded to Moto. "Tell them what you learned."

Tembi turned to see Moto's ears flicker out and back: he hadn't expected this. Still, he walked forward until he was level with Matthew, and then turned to face the gathered Witches. "The Blackwings threatened to attack us," he said. "Not us, not directly. They'd go after our partners, those on the lower rungs of the shipping chains."

"Be honest with them," chided Domino. "They had already begun." She looked to Tembi. "Do you think those bombs kept appearing in shipping waystations by accident? Each one was a message. They slowed when I agreed to barter my time, but were renewed when our agreement ended."

Tembi's anger flared—*All of those bodies? Nothing but a message for Domino?!*—and felt dark elation when Domino flinched. Actually flinched, her eyes darting away and her ears flashing at Tembi to *stop!* It was the first true emotion she had ever seen from that woman, and Tembi couldn't help but push forward, thrusting the images of what she had seen in Camp Investment, the bodies, the unholy smell, as if she held a knife pointed at Domino's mind.

Around her, distantly, she was aware that the memory of the smell she held in her head was flooding the room, a dubious gift from the Deep. "Thank you, buddy," she whispered. "Make them understand."

She took another step towards Domino. "They lied to you!" she said loudly. "The bombs kept coming. And Bayle and I went to another Blackwing camp." She was shouting now, her Adhamantian rage breaking through. "There, the general—General Carroll—she told us that the Blackwings still thought the situation was unbalanced. You gave them what they wanted, and it didn't change a thing!"

"Wrong." The word was harsh, almost military in nature. The Witches rumbled in unease, the ones nearest to the doors parting to make way for a small bald man in a Blackwing Admiral's uniform, a dozen soldiers wearing honor colors behind him. Behind the soldiers came Domino's assistant, Frugal, his face red from embarrassment, and two of the more popular channelsluts and their grammalight crews to put the whole sodding mess on display for the entire galaxy. "What she gave us opened the Rails. That's useless to us. Worse than useless. We still can't move around in the bloody place. It tears us to shreds."

"Admiral Wallis," Domino said, nodding to the newcomer.

"You are late."

"I'm not one of your Witches," he retorted. "Don't snap your fingers and expect me to appear."

"And yet, you are here," she said, smiling slightly.

"To deliver another message," retorted Wallis. "You promised you'd limit Lancaster's involvement to the refugees. You lied. And you?" he said, turning to Tembi. "I warned you to keep to the pretty places. You should have listened."

"You killed Matindi," Tembi said, heartbroken.

He laughed, a cruel laugh which lifted up and shattered against the gem's ceiling, fracturing into hard echoes.

"Do you deny it?" Domino's voice, soft and soothing, moved within the room as she tried to heal the damage of that laugh. Who would admit to killing a Witch? Certainly not a well-known representative of a major political party. That way lay the collapse of all things.

"No," Wallis replied, and Tembi closed her eyes as the known order of the galaxy broke around them. "I gave her a gift, and it lay in wait to kill her."

"Explain yourself," said Domino, the softness of her voice gone to stone.

"Our research into the Rails yielded a few tricks that work on a different level of spacetime," he replied. "Asymmetrical molecular fragmentation is one of them. Pulls apart an object in random stages instead of all at once. Impossible to predict the order of how it will happen. We tested it on tekkers to be sure. We thought Witches were the same, and we were right."

Tembi realized she was blinking back tears. They had torn Matindi apart in pieces, so many and in such an odd manner that the Deep hadn't known how to stop it. The Deep had seized those pieces and put her body back together, but she was already dead.

Wallis moved to the center of the Oratory. The Chameleon children tagging along with their new guardians pressed their faces against the Witches' legs, shivering. "Matindi was supposed to be our warning," he said, turning in a slow circle so the crowd would hear him. "An unwanted Witch no longer associated with Lancaster would be the only casualty. Those two other Witches were supposed to be safe during the raid, and you," he pointed at Domino, "would heed our reminder to keep your people in check. No more helping our enemies avoid consequences.

"But then you moved Camp Investment," he said to Tembi. "You put our practices on display. Public support has rallied to the Sabenta. That cannot be allowed."

"What's done is done," said Domino calmly. So very calmly. "We cannot unwind time. We will negotiate a new—"

"Stop!" Wallis slapped his hand against his thigh. The sound cracked against the gem again, harsh, unyielding. "You made us look weak before the entire galaxy. There will be no negotiation. Just a message."

"No!" Kalais sucked in his breath. "Stop him!"

"Perceptive, War Witch." Wallis nodded to him, smiling.

"Deep!" Tembi shouted. Wrong, it was all wrong! She was no longer sure why they were here: this was a reckoning, but it was not meant for Domino alone, and Wallis wore a skull's stark smile.

"Ah, Sir Stoneskin." Wallis glared at her, his eyes red behind his glasses. With those eyes and his too-tight grin, he looked as if he had developed a terminal addiction to stimulants. "Your Deep can't help you. We've set the bones of this project for years, every time we've come to Lancaster."

A low keening sound came from beyond the Oratory, slow, droning, like a hive of bees hidden within the forest. It was familiar in a terrible way, a sound Tembi heard when she was on the edge of dreaming and the planet that wasn't quite Adhama tore itself into pieces. "Stop," she whispered. Then, to Wallis: "Stop!"

"There's no stopping this. Domino showed us that your Deep can't work with what it doesn't understand." He smiled at her, arms out as if expecting a hug, and then used both hands to gesture to the windows. "And neither can you."

Tembi staggered towards the windows. She knew she should have fallen, but the Deep was lifting her, holding her up, keeping her standing.

Keeping her in the Oratory.

Where she was *safe*.

Time slowed. Beneath them was the small world of Lancaster campus, its perfect manicured paradise. She heard Wallis talking, a distant voice saying that the Blackwings had been seeding their tiny weapons throughout Lancaster, just in case. They were all over, buried within the earth, stuck within the masonry, embedded inside the plass, waiting. Waiting.

There was no need to destroy the whole campus, he said. The picturesque village and the small town square where the Chameleons had found shelter would do.

Let me go, she begged the Deep. *Let me help!*

::STAY:: the Deep told her—told all its Witches—its voice loud enough to fracture the gem and the stone walls of the Tower. The soldiers around Wallis fell to their knees at the sound; two of them began to weep. Witches from the village began to fill the room, unwittingly torn from whatever tasks had occupied their afternoon during their peaceful retirement. They complained, were silenced by their friends, were drawn to the windows with the heavy gravity of foreboding.

The world took on a dreamlike quality as the small village below was torn apart.

Wallis laughed, delighted, as the older Witches began to wail about those left behind…their pets…their workers…the children in their care. "How many dead?" he asked. "Your Deep can put it all back together again, but can it return the life to a corpse?"

Tembi started to move towards Wallis, but the popsticks came out, blocking her path. "Retribution!" Wallis shouted over their electrified buzzing. "We do not accept the dishonor you've forced upon us!" He came towards Tembi, leaning across the popsticks. "Submit, girl. Show the galaxy that even Witches cannot stand against us.

"Stop this. Here. Now," he added, glaring at Domino. She had seized the arms of her chair as if using them to hold herself in place. "Let these deaths be your last, and stand as a warning to all. None will interfere in our righteous cause."

Tembi found that she felt perfectly calm, the softening blanket of shock wrapped around her as tightly as the Deep. Down there, where the village had been, the ground was still floating, great clods of grass and stone raining up, up. There were bodies caught in that earthy haze. Lancaster's employees. Those Chameleons who had chosen to stay. Maybe even a Witch or two, the ones the Deep hadn't bothered to yank to safety.

I should be angry, she thought to herself. *Why aren't I angry?*

A howl split the air, echoes ringing off the blue gem hard enough to hurt her ears. The Oratory shook from the Deep's rage—

No. Not the Deep's rage.

"You *dare?!*" Domino roared, launching from her throne. "You dare attack *Lancaster?!*" She came forward, her hair flying, her fingers curled into claws. She reached out with both hands towards the soldiers, then gestured towards the sides of the room, splitting the group into two, hurling them aside.

Wallis stood before her, still laughing.

She jabbed at the air between them, her hands bound together into a stone knife. The air twisted, stabbed straight into Wallis' chest. There was blood, bone. He didn't seem to feel it, laughing at Domino even as she sliced him in half.

The soldiers came to their feet, rushing her, popsticks swinging.

Now Tembi found she could move. She threw herself at one soldier, tackling him around his waist. Around her, some of the other Witches did the same, either bringing the soldiers down themselves or using the Deep to sweep them up and hurl them into the walls and ceiling of the gem. Injuries? Oh, yes, those popsticks were *cranked.* Tembi took three hits to her face and shoulders before the soldier simply vanished, off to a new life in Assassins' Paradise or wherever, his popstick sputtering out as it spun across the marble floor. Similar disappearances were happening all over the room as the Deep caught up with events, snatching up the Blackwing soldiers and warehousing them somewhere else.

Bayle was there, holding her, shouting something as she pulled Tembi onto her lap. Tembi couldn't hear her, couldn't feel her, numb from the heavy-duty shocks.

And Domino?

Standing tall above them all, still flawless, still perfect, even with the body of Admiral Wallis in pieces and bloody at her feet, with the hem of her white robes soaking in red, and the camerasluts drinking it all in.

Chapter Thirty-One

The house was a disaster. Matindi had been the last person to lift a finger against the inevitability of filth, and it felt slightly evil to overwrite that memory of her second mother by cleaning, even if she couldn't reach her own bed without jumping through the Deep. Yet here, now, as she was on the verge of leaving her life at Lancaster behind her, Tembi gave herself over to an unfamiliar urge to clean.

First came dishes encrusted with dried food, stale breads that hadn't made it into the stasis cabinets, various condiments from her travels which should have been used before they had separated into assorted smooth and chunky strings of goo. Then, a thorough scrubbing of every surface she could find, moving the suckcloth around the room until it couldn't hold another particle. It went into the bin with the old, and out of the box came the new, and thus continued the wasteful cycle of cleaning in which filth leapt from one object to the next but was never actually conquered.

Was she crying? Oh, yes. But she refused to move the house to Bayle's backyard on Atlantis until every trace of Lancaster was gone.

The Witches' village was back in its original state. As soon as the Blackwings' hidden machines had finished their work, the Deep had put the pieces back together as neatly as it had done for Matindi's missing corpse. The picturesque village was as clean and idyllic as usual, albeit chock full of the dead. In total, sixty-seven people had been caught up in the Blackwings' vengeance. Most were workers, but there had also been two Sabenta refugees who had escaped the raid on Lunair only to be massacred on Found, and five Witches.

Dead Witches. No, *murdered* Witches!

Those particular Witches hadn't been well-liked by anybody,

said the rumor mill, not even by the Deep. They hadn't started aging again, but they surely checked the backs of their hands and the skin of their necks at least once a day, looking for evidence that the Deep had finally forgotten them. Leaving them to die when the rest of the Witches in the village were pulled to safety was certainly that. But now that they were dead and gone, the Deep was in mourning. A crooning sound kept shaking the windows across the campus, the whole of it soaked within a thick bank of fog. Tembi and Bayle had already agreed they'd spend that night along the Rails, holding each other and the Deep as they slept.

The tears kept falling, and she kept cleaning. Order from chaos. She had no control over anything but the objects in front of her, and she would scrub them into submission.

There was no reason to stay at Lancaster now. The old Witches wouldn't throw her out, but she had become a pariah, her and Bayle and Kalais and even Moto. Someone needed to carry the blame, and consensus among the Witches was that none of this would have happened if these four young rebels had followed millennia of established policy and stayed out of the war. And don't you dare start poking holes in that logic, as someone *must* pay for this tragedy!

Domino? Yes, obviously Domino should be the one to pay. You couldn't murder the public representative of an entire army and get away with it. But when that crystallized moment of Adhamantian rage had passed, Domino had seen what she had done, and…*fled*. Up and disappeared into the Deep, and no one could find her. (To be fair, nobody was looking.) The channelsluts bantered back and forth about whether Wallis' death had been murder or an act of war. They mashed all possible appropriate consequences into a fine polemic goo. But the fact of the matter was that nobody wanted to be the one who tried to punish her.

Tembi did. Sort of. She wanted to ask Domino if she had used the Deep to tear Wallis apart, or if she had one hell of a tekker's lift rating. Once she had the answer to that question, she planned to ask Domino if she had been the one to slip Moto the mindfuck, and if her regular daily visits to Moto's bedside were to ensure he stayed sedated. It wasn't enough motivation for Tembi to hop around the galaxy searching for her, but if she ever bumped into Domino in a bar? Oh yes, she'd ask her questions, and then the two Adhamantian Witches would learn which one would crack first.

In the meantime, Matthew had taken over Domino's position as Lancaster's representative on the Earth Assembly. Witches from across the galaxy had been summoned back for a truth-and-reconciliation meeting, in which Lancaster's organizational decisions would be assessed, and operational policies were changed. In the meantime, Matthew was using Lancaster's newly tarnished reputation to its advantage: keep your word to the Witches, or your choices were to vanish into oblivion or die a gruesome death.

Tembi paused in her scrubbing, as a nagging thought demanded her full attention. She poked at it…was it about the war? About Domino? Yes, all of this and more…the war itself was all but over. The Sagittarius Armed Forces' camps had been shut down. Both the Blackwing and Sabenta armies were starting to slip away, the Blackwings due to a temporary lack of internal cohesion, the Sabenta due to a lack of enemies. The war would flare up again, surely, but that might be a decade or more away—

And then, as if she had been hit over the head, Tembi realized she had all she had ever wanted.

Domino was gone—*gone!*—and Lancaster was about to do some serious introspection about how it used the Deep, and there was a general backlash throughout the galaxy against an ideology which embraced things such as mass graves.

There hadn't even been a bomb in over a week!

Tembi giggled in small bursts of joy, and then she started laughing, a purge of emotion as pure as when she stood within the Deep and screamed her frustrations to the Rails. She slid to the floor, still laughing, relishing the sugar-sweet stray thought

K.B. SPANGLER

that she had done her duty and was finally, at long last *finally!* free of Lancaster!

She couldn't stop laughing.

Oh, gods, it felt so *good!*

Ahhhh...!

Tabuu came over and batted at her nose with a paw. She swept him up and placed him on her chest, her laughter stuttering out so he could get comfortable. The cat curled up in a loose ball as she rubbed him behind the ears, wondering if she could feel his fur or if she was just doing a good job to convince herself of it.

New goal, she told herself. *Live my life so I can feel it.*

That was how she fell asleep, drowsy and feeling hopeful for the first time in years. Outside, the Deep's mournful howl died away and the fog lifted.

Hope. A precious, perfect thing, if only for the moment.

Tembi woke when Tabuu decided there should be more food in his bowl, and the resident human must be made aware of this oversight. She topped off his dish, and then stared at the mess around her.

Well! This house wouldn't clean itself!

Invigorated, she started sifting through the clutter in earnest, moving quickly, making piles of dirty laundry, castoffs, trash. The stack of books which Paisano had hurled to the ground were swept up to the counter in a single careless movement, up from the floor and thrust together in a messy pile, a single old volume sliding from the top and crashing back down to the floor—

Tembi froze.

She knelt, pulling the fallen book towards her.

It was one of those given to her by Admiral Wallis, one of the fantastic and forbidden stories of Lancaster's sordid past. She had never bothered to do more than thumb through the first few pages. If she had, she might have found Matindi's note. It was taped to a dog-eared page, its edge poking above the book's cover, as if Matindi had been aware that merely turning down a corner wouldn't be enough to catch Tembi's attention.

She sat, Matindi's note in her lap. It was very short, and sketched in her second mother's light familiar hand.

Tembi, Sweetling,

We're entering uncharted territory. Be brave, and know that while others have come before us, there's never been a promise that others will follow. You might be the last. Make your mark.

Love always, Mom.

At the bottom of the note was an arrow, pointing towards a copy of a very old digital print that had been reproduced in the book. The print was of several smiling faces, with a caption to let the casual reader know that this was the last known visual record of the Witches who were on duty during the Turtle Incident.

Winter was among them.

She stared at the print. It was definitely Winter. Even if the caption beneath the print showed a different name. Even if her face was of an older woman in her seventies instead of a wrinkled creature perpetually on the verge of death.

Tembi looked towards her cat's food bowls, where Tabuu slowly gummed his food. A cat who would never die, even though he was long past his time.

She shut the book. "She was one of your first," she whispered. "So you kept her. Even though she wasn't shiny and new anymore. Even when the memory of her caused you pain. You still kept her."

The Deep had never brought her to Winter, nor had the Deep brought Winter to her, no matter how she had begged, ordered, demanded…

"Deep?" she asked quietly. "Could you please ask Winter if she'd come here and talk to me?"

A long pause, and then the usual *crack!* of displaced air as

Winter, most ancient of ancients, the last of the first Witches, stepped out of the Deep and into Tembi's kitchen. The old woman nodded at Tembi as she went straight to the stasis box and began shoving food around. When she emerged, she had a bowl of hot feijoada in her hands and was balancing a cold glass of beer in the crook of her arm.

Tembi nudged the open book across the counter so she could see it.

The old woman barely glanced at the print, but she read Matindi's note at least twice. "Such a good girl," she whispered.

"Matindi thought you were testing her," Tembi said. "Were you?"

Winter sat and started shoveling food into her mouth with her right hand. "Doesn't work," she said, rapping on her own head with her left. "Dementia. Dementia. Good days and bad. She got me meds, stuck me full of 'bots. Doctors, doctors, doctors." Winter shook her head. Something with legs fell out of her thin hair and into the bowl, but she kept eating, unnoticing. "Said they couldn't help. Permanent damage, they say. Permanent damage. Can't fix what's gone."

She glared at Tembi, eyes wet. "I miss her."

"Me, too."

Winter stared at Tembi's chest and started to laugh. "Stupid, stupid girls," she managed.

"Winter—"

"Then came Galadriel, bright like the sun," Winter continued. "What did she give me? Do you know? Thinking better than I have in…three thousand years?"

"General Carroll?" Tembi blinked. "She said she gave you a cognitive repair agent. Is it helping?"

"I don't like her," Winter mumbled. "There was a woman? Another woman? Long time ago. Said she wanted to help me. She was kind, but I was hers until she died, and then I belonged to her children, and then they died. Their tamed Witch, they called me. I made their fortunes. Gave them *planets!* Then, one day…*BOOM!*" she shouted, as she slammed her beer on the counter. It foamed everywhere, a small volcano, and Tabuu screeched and ran for the bedrooms. "Your girl? All she wanted from me were answers." She began to cry. "Like I have answers."

After a moment, she noticed at the spilled beer. It obligingly lifted from the table and returned to the bottle.

"We don't use the Deep to clean in this house." The phrase lay familiar on Tembi's tongue: it was an automatic response, something Matindi had told other Witches each time they came to visit.

It was the wrong thing to say. Winter swung from sorrow to wrath in the time it took Tembi to finish her sentence. "We are a *child's toys!*" screamed Winter. "Give us a bottle and we wet ourselves. Let it clean up after us! Let it practice and learn! That's what toys are *for!*"

"Toys are objects," Tembi replied, as she nudged a clean suckcloth towards the old woman. "We are people."

"We are *nothing!*" Winter was temper incarnate, hands curled into arthritic claws, spittle flying from her mouth. "Ants in the hill! Microbes! Squirt us with bleach and rinse us away! Nothing!"

And Tembi felt—but did not see, as there was nothing to see—the old woman reach around the Deep as she pulled the two of them through its feathered edges and onto the Rails.

Their world became black and gold and white and silver, all at once. They stood in the center of nothing, a void between matter. Tembi had fallen through the Rails before, a long time ago, when she and Bayle were first learning how to jump. That had been uncontrolled, and all she remembered was the terror of unrelenting movement and sound as the Deep tried to catch them. Now, the Rails were quiet. Winter stood tall and calm, staring towards the dark-bright horizon, one twisted hand on Tembi's shoulder to steady her.

"Don't scream," she ordered Tembi.

"How are you doing this?" Tembi asked, her voice shaking. She could feel the Deep, its familiar grace distant but still present. Everything she knew about the Rails told her that this was wrong. She could not be here without the Deep.

And yet.

"Tried to teach you this before," Winter told her. "Try to learn now. We can open the way. Don't move around. Don't try. We stand in the pillars of creation. We can bear witness, but they are not ours to use." She pointed. "The Rails belong to *them*."

There was no way to judge scale within this setting. When Tembi rode the Deep, the Rails were insignificant, a backdrop to something grand. Without her friend to provide context, the Rails became vast, a sea of dawn and dark without end. Existence itself, pure, wrought infinite.

In the distance, something...*writhed*.

There were two of them. That was all she could comprehend. The Deep was a grand, faceless entity, but it was as of yet unfinished. These two beings were power incarnate, forces beyond the scope of human imagination. They were the Deep writ large, and all the raw potential of the Rails was theirs to command.

As they moved, they created. Specks fell from them, atoms and molecules and particles, called into existence as they passed, the nothingness of dark matter drawn forth and transformed...*becoming*.

Let there be light.

Tembi wanted to drop to her knees and beg for her life. Would it matter if she did? Such beings could unmake her with a thought. Begging wouldn't matter to them—*she* didn't matter to them!

No, said a quiet voice inside her. *You* do *matter, and that's both the blessing and the danger.*

Winter pulled Tembi towards her, her gnarled fingers knit hard within the sleeve of Tembi's robes. "Call upon your conscience, girl," she whispered in Tembi's ear. "The gods are coming for their baby, and they will not approve of what we've done to it."

Acknowledgements

This was a difficult book to write. *Stoneskin* was a short novel I used to explore the concept of the Deep and its Witches, and Tembi's first adventure found its way onto the page in three months. *The Blackwing War* took three years. Hopefully I've used that time to establish a stable foundation for the sequels, and won't need to spend another three years head-down in the Word Mines, punching plotholes into place.

I'd like to thank Ari at Fox Literary for their valuable notes on the first draft, and for Fuzz's comment that "this is the grimmest thing I've ever read" on the second. Get yourself a friend who reminds you that there needs to be light in the darkness. Thanks to my Patreon supporters who allow me to keep the lights on and the water running while I work. Thanks also to beta readers Gary, Tiff, and Sigrid, and to Danny and Shepherd for the copyedits. Sebastian Maza is responsible for the astonishing cover art.

As always, all my love and gratitude to Brown. You're the most wonderful, patient, and supportive husband I could ever want.

And thank you for reading this book! In these days of information churn and content overload, recommendations are the most valuable gifts an author can receive. If you enjoyed *The Blackwing War*, could you please leave a review or tell a friend? Your words move mountains.